THE PRIMUS LABYRINTH

THE PRIMUS LABYRINTH

SCOTT OVERTON

No Walls Publishing
SUDBURY, ONTARIO, CANADA

Copyright © 2019 by **S.G. Overton**

**Scott Overton/No Walls Publishing
Sudbury/Ontario/Canada P0M 3C0
www.scottoverton.ca**

Book Layout © 2017 BookDesignTemplates.com

The Primus Labyrinth/ Scott Overton -- 1st ed.
ISBN 978-1-9993860-5-4

We acknowledge the financial support of the Ontario Arts Council in the creation of this book.

For Terry-Lynne:
You're in my veins, my heart, my every cell.
You infuse me.

Women are born with horror in their very
bloodstream. It is a biological thing.
—BELA LUGOSI

## 1

Curran Hunter looked into the grey water and thought about drowning.

Not here, close to the pier. Too shallow. Out there, where the grey turned to deep-sea blue like the ocean abyss that had so nearly claimed him six months before. Except this time he would go willingly, just let go and sink to the bottom with no struggle. At peace. At peace for the first time in so very long.

The walk on the pier had become a daily habit: a therapeutic slice of mundane sanity, his heels ringing hollow drumbeats on the worn timbers of the pier. It was a comforting sound, like a heartbeat in silence. The tang of salt air always revived him, although the bright morning sun flashing off the water was punishing to his hangovers. The noises of industry were helpfully muted by distance and masked by the soft slap of choppy waves against concrete pilings.

Most often he came here looking for oblivion. This time he needed his capricious brain to come up with some answers. Sea King Drilling had notified him that they were suspending his compensation payments pending yet another legal opinion on his case. It was just the latest move in the game they'd played for six months. He'd spend another day pleading with legal aid, another waiting in a stagnant courtroom waiting for a scant minute or two of judicial wisdom. So far, the judgments had gone his way; but that wouldn't put a badly needed check in his mailbox tomorrow. He'd be spending a few days with an empty belly, and his landlady was quickly losing patience waiting for her rent. He'd already dodged her twice that week. What if the checks never came again?

Could he return to northern Michigan with the jagged rock-cuts and stunted pines that had framed his youth? With both his parents dead and the old house sold to pay debts, there was little point. His dad had sold sports equipment to turn the end of his NFL career into a second livelihood, but those were the days before multi-million-dollar contracts for endorsements. When the old homestead went on the market, Hunter hadn't been able to buy it.

Hunter's underwater work paid well, but it was seasonal and sporadic. It was only the last few years on the big oilrigs that he'd had a steady income. Too much of that had gone to booze and bullshit, but at least he'd been making something of himself. Then, even that had come to an end.

His attention was drawn to a stooped figure near one of the big wharves. It was an older man fiddling with something—a fishing rod, maybe. Yeah, that was a tackle box beside him. Not many fish worth catching this close to the docks, and you wouldn't want to eat them. Or maybe the man had nothing better to do than throw a line into the water, and let his bobber count the passing of days.

"Mostly garbage fish, this close in," Hunter said. "They like the crap from the sugar refinery, I think."

The older man looked up. His face and hair seemed a little too well-tended for his slightly shabby tan jacket and khaki slacks, but the battered Tilley hat had the fit of repeated wearing.

"Oh, I'm after bigger fish," the man replied in a cultured voice. "And I know where to find them." He plucked his tackle box from the ground with practiced ease and fell into step with Hunter. They didn't speak for a moment, then the older man asked, "Do you fish?"

"Not much anymore," Hunter admitted. "I'm a scuba diver, and when you actually see the fish down there, in their own environment, it changes your thinking about them." He'd wanted to be a diver for as long as he could remember; captivated by old Jacques Cousteau TV specials and an early TV adventure show called *Sea Hunt* that his father had loved. He looked up at gulls wheeling above a sailboat and thought about the world that tugged at him from beneath the surface. Then he realized that he'd stopped walking. He gave an embarrassed shrug and held out his hand. "Curran Hunter. My friends don't use my first name. Neither does anybody else."

"Johnson." The grip had the firmness of sincerity. They began to move again. "Scuba diving. For work or for pleasure?"

"Both. Submersibles, too, although . . . I'm out of work at the moment."

"I might just be able to help with that."

Hunter snapped his head around, not sure he'd heard correctly. "You might be able to what?"

"Help you. Find a job." There was a hint of a smile on the man's lips. Then it faded. He'd enjoyed his little surprise, but business was business.

"Who said I wanted one?"

"What would it take?" The inscrutable eyes narrowed slightly, focused on the middle distance.

"You mean for me to get back into submersibles? I don't know—I haven't really thought about it." That was a lie. "I . . . something really challenging, I guess. Interesting. Worth doing." *Safe* was the word that came to mind, but he didn't want to say it. "And a helluva lot of money!" He gave a grin to lighten the exchange. The other man's smile was more genuine.

"I can't promise that. But interesting? Challenging? Oh God, yes."

A flock of gulls had begun to raise a ruckus out to sea, fluttering chaotically around a spot on the surface and occasionally plunging down to pluck at something.

Water was both the lifeblood of the planet, and the depository for the dead.

Hunter suddenly stopped walking again as the conversation triggered a memory. He felt heat rise into his face.

"Wait a minute," he said. "Let me guess. Actually, you know about my background. You know almost everything about me. Right?" The startled look on the other's face made Hunter press on. "You're working for Sea King Drilling, trying to find out if I'm just faking it."

"I don't know what you mean."

"You guys already tried this once before, OK? I'm not claiming anything—it was the company shrinks who said I had a problem, not me."

"So you're saying you're ready to go back to work?"

"I'm . . . " The words stalled. Was that true? He felt a chill down his spine.

Johnson took advantage of the hesitation. "I know who you are, yes. But I have nothing to do with your former employers or anyone else who might have approached you. I need someone with your special skills."

Hunter wanted to escape. And he wanted to hear more.

"Look," the older man said finally. "Here's a number where you can reach me." He gave Hunter a card. "But I can't wait long for your decision."

Hunter looked at the card and gave a slow shake of his head.

"And all of this . . . " A sweep of his hand took in the shabby clothing and fishing gear. "Was just to check me over?"

The man looked bemused. "Not only that. This might be my last chance to go fishing for a very long time."

They'd stopped in front of a medium-sized pier. About halfway along the right side, a boat rose and fell in the light chop. It was small for a yacht, but too large for a cabin cruiser, and it gave off an aura of age.

His companion turned and walked toward it.

Hunter traveled the rest of the wharf with his eyes wide, seeing nothing.

# # #

Back at his apartment, a ragged fan of unpaid bills stared up at Hunter from the top of the battered dresser, their typefaces bold and accusing. Overlooking the pages with expressions of weary patience were the faces of his mother and father in a frame held together with scotch tape. Their smiles now seemed only pixels deep. He must have been a disappointment to them—his grades at school only average; his ambitions lukewarm. For a time he'd appeared to be following in his father's footsteps toward a pro ball career, but a series of ill-considered drunken escapades washed him out of college; and not long after that, his parents were gone, taken in a flash of tortured plastic and steel. They never saw him return to school to train for underwater work and finally find the calling that had eluded him so long. Underwater was the only place he'd ever excelled, the only place that ever felt like home.

Now it was home to his greatest fears.

Maybe if he faced those fears, it would free him from their power. What other choice did he have? He had to eat.

Could his sanity tolerate a return to the cramped quarters of a submersible, a potential tomb at the bottom of the sea? A cold hand clamped onto his guts.

The darkness was all encompassing and stifling. His chest tightened in anticipation of each breath, fearful that the next would be thick with carbon dioxide, and the next after that . . . empty.

He felt sick. Numbed. It was the pressure. The pressure of having to choose—the terrible weight of a mistake. He curled into a ball and tried to hide.

Sensations bled away. He was drifting. Floating.

He was flotsam on the surface of a grey sea, buoyed up but also paralyzed. Helpless to keep scavenging gulls from tearing chunks of his flesh, only to rise and wheel and tear at him again. He tried to cry out, but could not. His head was all he could move; and as he turned it to the side, he saw a nearby fishing boat with two men at the gunwales. One was the man from the pier. He was crying: salt tears splashing into the salt sea. The other man was one of the phonies who had come from Sea King to trick him. His mouth was open like one of the taunting gulls.

Laughing.

Hunter flung out an arm and sent the empty tumbler from the bedside table skittering to the floor in a spray of broken shards. He cursed and sat up. Motes of dust sparkled in a shaft of weak sunlight, daring him to focus on them. He couldn't, not right away. He waved a hand through the air, as if shooing a cloud of fireflies, then rubbed his eyes and slowly lay back down making the bed springs protest. He stared at the ceiling, but the pre-dawn half-light obscured in its shadows more than it revealed.

Lately, the dream had taken on bizarre elements: noises, apparitions, and the sense of an unseen presence. Things that couldn't have been part of the real event. How could he even distinguish between reality and dream anymore after the way the shrinks had torn his psyche apart and shoe-horned it back together? How could anything ever feel normal again after something like that? Ever feel truly real?

Death had nearly taken him. He'd insisted all these months, to himself and everyone else, that he'd done nothing wrong; but the truth was that he just didn't know. The memory of it was as mutable as a kaleidoscope. And what about those final moments? Had he simply lost his nerve and gone batshit crazy, like they said?

He rolled sideways in a practiced motion and pulled open the door of the bar fridge beside the bed, hoping that he'd remembered to refill the ice cube tray. The only bourbon he could afford required lots of ice to be drinkable. Especially for breakfast.

He tipped two shrunken nuggets of ice into a mug that was waiting to be washed, then floated them with the amber liquid and placed the empty tray on top of the fridge. His first gulp was a large one. So were the ones that followed.

Finally, he snapped on the small lamp beside him, picked up the plain-looking business card he'd left leaning against its base, and reached for the phone.

# # #

The man who'd called himself Johnson sat in front of a screen propped up on a kitchen table.

"Well, what do you think now?" He'd made the video link to his headquarters only moments after finishing the call with Hunter, his new recruit. It was still just after dawn. The face looking back at him from the iPad was as rumpled as the bed sheets behind it.

"We've talked about this before," the other man said, his ebony forehead creasing in a frown. "This . . . Hunter definitely has a gift for handling submersibles, but he's also been through hell. His psyche is fragile. What you're about to ask from him could be more than he can handle. It caused a complete mental breakdown in your first pilot."

"Travis Li has recovered."

"That's not true. He's returned to society, but I'm not sure he'll ever recover."

"You're a psychologist, Truman, and you don't deal in absolutes. We've learned a great deal since our failure with Li."

"And yet this whole thing smacks of *déjà vu*—the government is forcing your hand, just like before. Trashing the schedule. Pushing your equipment beyond its tested limits. That ended badly last time, yet here you go again, throwing this man Hunter into the pool at the deep end."

"The file says he's a good swimmer."

"Joke if you like, Devon, but with equipment this exotic and those new techniques you're insisting upon . . . I can't be sure what will happen."

"What would you have me do? It's a matter of life and death."

"Yes. And perhaps for your pilot as much as for your patient. I wonder if you'll tell him that?"

## 2

Thankfully, the plane ride was smooth. At the slightest provocation, Hunter's hangover was turning his temples into tympani, and he'd had serious misgivings about trading a commercial flight for . . . whatever this was. He'd been paged at the airport about a delay with his flight; and rather than wait, he'd called the special phone number given to him by Mr. Johnson. Within forty-five minutes he was on a military transport with Johnson seated beside him, and no-one else in the cabin. It probably cost all of his taxes from the past ten years just to ferry a bird that size around for a day.

He massaged his temples.

"Not a problem with the pressure, surely, Mr. Hunter?" Johnson asked.

"Only the pressure inside my head. From celebrating your offer, I should point out." He didn't feel the need to mention his bungled encounter of the night before. What a waste! Stoked at the prospect of a real income, he'd blown the last of his cash on the best bourbon O'Flanagan's bartender had been able to find. Then the day had surprised him again in the form of a blonde named Shannon, a spectacular looker with cleavage like the hills of Paradise. Way out of his league. Unable to believe his luck, he'd taken her back to his apartment, but just as they were getting around to the main event, he'd passed out cold.

At least the woman had locked the door when she'd left, and there was nothing missing from the apartment. It was probably just as well that he was leaving town for a while.

"Glad to hear about your enthusiasm," Johnson said. "But you'll find that alcohol isn't a good fit with the work you'll be doing."

"That won't be a problem, Mr. . . . . You know, I still don't even know your real name. I'm sure it isn't Johnson."

The older man laughed. "No, Johnson doesn't really fool anyone. It's a conceit in government circles: you use a fictitious name to preserve anonymity, but you want others to know it's not your real name. Tells people your business must be important because it's secret. My secretary gets batches of cards printed up from a list." He gave a slight nod. "My name's Kierkegaard. Devon Kierkegaard. The last name mean anything to you?"

"I don't think so," Hunter replied. "But I don't really keep up on current events."

"Oh, not current. Not this century, anyway." The man smiled. "Søren Kierkegaard was a Danish philosopher from the early eighteen-hundreds. A distant relative of mine. Ever hear of *existentialism*? Well Kierkegaard believed there was no such thing as objective morality, a right and wrong that is valid for everyone. He claimed that every individual had to find his own true calling, and then his personal code of morality would depend on that choice."

"Sounds like a politician."

"From a superficial explanation like that, I suppose it does. Actually, later in his life my ancestor advocated wholehearted submission to the will of God as being the highest mortal virtue. Our politicians only give lip service to that."

"Because they think they are God," Hunter said. When there was no response, he wondered if he'd gone too far.

Then Kierkegaard spoke softly, "Perhaps all of us are guilty of that from time to time."

Hunter's thoughts returned to the day before, when a black car with tinted glass had picked him up and taken him for a ride, blindfolded. It was like something from a spy movie.

"I apologize for the theatrics," Kierkegaard had said, "But it is a secret laboratory. One the public believes is something else."

Hunter asked himself if he really needed the job that badly. The unavoidable answer was yes.

Near the far end of a nondescript white room, a group of four men in smocks were clustered around a chair that looked like it had been filched from a dentist's office and then tricked out for a gamers' convention. A hodgepodge of electronics was organized into several banks of readouts and keypads. He couldn't begin to guess their function. An overlarge helmet in a cradle mounted to the back of the chair was connected to the electronic equipment by a thick umbilical cord.

"I thought you were going to take me to some kind of experimental submersible," he said.

"And I have, after a fashion. This is only a temporary installation, but it will serve the purpose for today."

The others said nothing. Two of them stood next to the equipment, in a proprietary way. One was a six-foot, large-framed man with a square face, severe eyebrows, and slicked-back white hair; the other was a few inches shorter, balding, with a fringe of hair that ringed his head like a monk's tonsure shot with grey. No young hotshots here. Two men standing farther back were middle-aged and unremarkable. Hunter immediately dismissed them as assistants. It was the two in front he should watch. Their body language said they were reluctant to let him touch the product of their labors.

He turned to face the chair, noticing a wraparound visor on the helmet.

"Virtual reality," he said. "Some kind of simulator? That's what all this secrecy is for?"

"That's a good enough description for now."

The white-haired man looked smug. The bald one was amused, but in a more childlike way—the keeper of a secret he longed to reveal.

"So, show me."

They helped him into the chair, and placed the helmet on his head. Hands fussed over him as the room disappeared behind padding and Perspex.

"Are you ready, Mr. Hunter?" Kierkegaard's voice was now muffled and distant.

Was he? Part of him remembered the cold sweat that broke out whenever he rode in small elevators ever since the accident.

The helmet was too heavy for him to nod easily. Instead he cleared his throat and said, "Yes." Then he waited for the visor to light up with a liquid crystal display. Instead a powerful electronic hum began in a low register and quickly swept up the frequencies until it became inaudible. He felt pinpricks along his scalp from front to back.

And the world swam away . . . .

Vertigo.

What the hell? What happened? Where *is* this?

The room is gone. The chair is gone.

Floating . . . floating in empty space.

The voices have receded into a vague wash of sound.

Colors gone, too. Only shades of grey. Like fog. Fog at dusk.

Something darker in front, like lines extending forward.

Manipulator arms. A submersible with arms outstretched.

OK. A familiar concept to hang sanity on. Except for one big difference—the view isn't like being *in* the craft, it's like *being the craft itself.*

No claustrophobia, at least.

It's not fog. *Liquid.* Some kind of specks or bubbles rising and falling within it, jostling around like ping-pong balls in a Bingo machine.

Time to move—get the feel of things.

Left pedal to pivot left. Right hand for forward thrust.

Oops. Turned too far. Correct with the pedal—just a touch. A little more thrust. Definite sensation of movement, even without visual cues. Sluggish at first, though. Extra resistance, like . . . *thick water?*

A zone of darkness ahead now—not wide, but tall, reaching beyond view above and below. Something cylindrical, maybe. Better ease back.

A shot of reverse thrust.

Nope. Spun the nose to the left. Try again, with a little more finesse, damn it.

Holy mother, is that big! Like a giant black tower as high as the eye can see. No features to give perspective—could be ten meters away, could be fifty. Black matte finish. Are those craters? Or pockmarks? Have to move closer to know.

Shit! Sudden stop produced a disturbance in the liquid. Must've hit the sucker.

What was that? A voice?

Very, very slow, and deep. Pissed off.

Bumped their toy.

All right, then, let's see what this rig can do.

Hard right pedal. Nose down. Full forward thrust. Down the wall diagonally. See what's at the bottom, if there is one.

Like the plunge of a roller coaster—stomach left behind.

Dropping down on something that spreads as far as the eye can see. But why is everything so damn blurry? Poor interface? Or just lazy programming?

Looks like a cityscape seen from above, but all of the buildings are the same height, with deep crevasses crisscrossing at right angles like New York intersections.

Into the canyons of the Death Star. Rush of adrenaline. Pulling up hard. Taste of breakfast in the throat.

Perfectly uniform walls on both sides—no protrusions. Damn good thing. Barely enough clearance as it is.

A corner coming up. The nose snaps around like a car on a track in a carnival ride. Nearly fishtailed into the wall, too. Need to be able to bank a little, like an airplane—work with the resistance of the fluid. This bitch could use some dive planes.

Better on the next turn. Right into the middle of the channel. Just need the nose up and a little rudder at the same time. Try a few more corners—got to put on a good show, right?

A sharp left, a long straight stretch, then a hard right. Swoop down toward the deck, then pull up the nose into a steep climb . . . a little more . . . over onto its back. Now crank it over into a barrel roll. Wow, yeah—effortless. Sweet response, once you get the hang of it. Are they watching all this?

A flash of red.

What was that for?

Another one. Whole field of vision flashing red every few seconds.

Did I lose the game?

No, a signal. But for what?

Danger? In a simulator?

Something's happening.

Vertigo.

Light stabbed into his eyes and he felt like retching. Through tears he caught a glimpse of the white-haired man frantically snatching the helmet out of range, while Kierkegaard hastily slid a wastebasket to the side of the chair.

"The nausea passes quickly. Just relax and concentrate on your breathing."

Hunter nodded, then sat back and drew a sleeve across his watery eyes.

"Well? Did you like our little game?"

"I don't know what game you're playing." Hunter's voice felt like it hadn't been used for a while. He cleared his throat. "But that wasn't a game. That was real, not a simulation. I've never seen anything like it."

"What made you come to that conclusion?"

"The craft responds authentically for a vehicle in a fluid medium—a thick fluid, too. That would be a real challenge to simulate. So if it's a game, why go to that trouble, and yet put up with such shitty visuals?"

White-hair bridled at that. "If you had any idea . . . ."

Kierkegaard stopped him with a look. "Go on, Mr. Hunter."

"Because it's not a simulation. It's a real environment somewhere. Although why you'd leave out the instrumentation, the colors, the sounds . . . I can't guess." He caught another flash of annoyance on White hair's face. "How long was I at it anyway?"

"Five minutes and fifteen seconds."

"*Five minutes?* It felt like half-an-hour, at least."

"Yes, we've noticed that."

Hunter waited for more of an explanation, but none came. Instead the other man looked at his watch. "That's enough for now."

Back in the car, Hunter protested, "At least tell me if I made the grade."

"I think it's safe to say that the head of the project will hire you. Pending one final security check."

"How can you be so sure?"

"Because I'm the head of the project."

Hunter was only mildly surprised. He'd already seen the way the others had deferred to this man.

"One last question. Why were the other two guys pissed at me?"

"Oh . . . well, they've already tried out the equipment themselves."

"And . . . ?"

"You made them look like children riding the bumper cars."

# # #

"When are you going to tell me what this is all about?" Hunter asked Kierkegaard over the hiss of the airplane's ventilation system. The older man gave an indulgent smile and leaned forward, though there was no one who could possibly listen in.

"What do you know about nanotechnology?"

"Small. Very small."

"Indeed. And how did you like your submersible ride?"

"Is that why the graphics were limited? A super-small computer?"

"Not exactly. Perhaps I should ask if you enjoyed life in a test-tube?"

Hunter was speechless.

"An amoeba's-eye view, if they had eyes. That submersible you took for a joyride is about the size of a virus. The 'canyon' you explored is an especially-etched silicon wafer—the kind used for computer chips. The tower you saw is a microfiber filament suspended in the fluid."

"You're not serious."

"That's what the appropriations committee said when I told them how much it would cost to develop."

Hunter's mind reeled. Had he really seen the world at the molecular level . . . traveled through a microcosm like a renegade ion? The sheer audacity of it was numbing. Yet all he could ask was, "Why? What possible use could there be for something that size in the ocean?"

"You're thinking in the wrong terms. The universe is full of fluid environments. Including what we think of as the *inner* ocean."

The light dawned. "You mean inside the human body? In the bloodstream?" A memory clicked. "Don't tell me. You tour around the arteries fixing things. Except the heart. It's 'game over' if you go through the heart."

"*Fantastic Voyage* was a memorable movie and the initial inspiration for our project. That movie left a powerful mark on a pair of nano-engineers named Steinberg and Ellis when they were children; and when they met by accident fifteen years ago, it turned into the driving force of their careers—a compulsion to use their skills to create an audacious new medical technology. How much do you remember about the movie?"

Hunter gave a shrug and his grin was a little sheepish. "I loved it—great concept, great special effects. A lot of fun. The idea of shrinking a whole submarine with people in it was pure fantasy, I guess. Although when somebody wrote the novelization, he came up with an explanation, didn't he?"

"Isaac Asimov. Yes. A kind of hyperspace that allowed the shrinking of matter without the excess mass presenting a problem. That's still fantasy. But the story is correct in the fact that there are incredibly complex mechanisms that do patrol the labyrinth of the bloodstream, produced by millions of years of evolution. Incredibly small, but powerful.

"Some scientists have tried chemical means to adapt those organic systems and bring them under human control. Steinberg and Ellis turned to the technology they knew best: mechanical engineering at the nano-scale. Six years ago, I was recruited to head a team that would take their work to a whole new level of sophisticated machinery. Difficult to achieve, but incredibly robust.

"You mentioned the movie characters' fear of going through the heart, but nothing the human heart could do would damage our submersible. It's made of sterner stuff. Buckyballs and buckytubes—the strongest material known to man."

"Bucky___? Now you're pulling my leg."

"*Buckminster fullerenes*, if you prefer. Named after R. Buckminster Fuller."

"The architect?"

"A tremendously influential thinker. The shape of the molecule is similar to those geodesic domes Fuller was so fond of. It's an extremely rare form of carbon, Carbon 60, and with the right amount of heat—something above 3000 degrees Celsius—we can make it form hollow tubes: *nanotubes*, because their preferred size is just over one nanometer in diameter. A billionth of a meter. The tubes are like rolled up chicken wire, all hexagons and pentagons, and incredibly strong: a hundred times the strength of steel at about a sixth of the weight!" He gave a self-satisfied smile. "The merely mortal human heart could hammer away its sixty-beats-per-minute for a lifetime and not put a dent in our machine."

"That sounds like 'famous last words' to me," Hunter mused.

"Fair enough. In fact, the submersible's sensor array isn't nearly so robust and can be damaged. Then the craft would be blinded and out of contact. Still, if the *Titanic* had hit the iceberg and only lost its radio mast, I daresay no-one would have complained all that much."

Kierkegaard stood up to stretch, then sauntered across the cabin to gaze out the window at the vastness of the ocean sparkling far below.

"We think ourselves so superior, sneering at the simple ignorance of Columbus and Magellan, who couldn't be sure they wouldn't sail off the edge of the world. Yet even we supermen of the twenty-first century know little about what's out there, under the oceans." He turned to face Hunter. "Or even," he tapped his chest, "in here."

"Is that what you hired me for? To explore the bloodstream?"

Kierkegaard's face clouded "When I first selected you, that's exactly what it would have been. Now . . . something has happened. A national emergency, in fact. Our mission has suddenly become a matter of life and death." He stared into space, a mixture of anger, disbelief, and regret playing over his face. "Even so, there will be no danger to you. Nothing so devastating as your nearly fatal experience of six months ago, I can assure you."

Hunter's head snapped up, then bowed in resignation. "Of course, you'd know about that. So why did you hire me?"

"Because I didn't care about it. It's not relevant. You'll be in a virtual reality environment that you can leave at any time. However, I don't get my way on everything. My superiors would only let me bring you in on the condition that you talk to a psychologist regularly."

Hunter felt heat rise to his cheeks. "Did you just say I'll have to see a *shrink*?"

"They insisted."

"*Deal's off.*" He sprang to his feet. "You can turn this bird around or just drop me off at the nearest airport."

"Mr. Hunter, really . . . ."

"I don't think you're hearing me, Mr. Kierkegaard. I said that the deal's off! Find another sucker and play around in *his* head—nobody's doing that to me again."

Kierkegaard was stunned. There was a sheen of sweat on Hunter's face and his breathing was rapid. He stalked to the far side of the cabin and stood staring out a window.

"I thought I knew what you'd been through," Kierkegaard said quietly. "Clearly I wasn't fully informed."

"Apparently not. I've had my fill of bastards who try to turn my head inside out, claiming they're trying to cure me. They were just trying to prove I was nuts
before I was hired, so the company could cut me loose without a cent. It was only luck that I got a sympathetic judge."

"I promise you, this will be nothing more than a
formality."

"It'll be nothing at all, because it isn't going to
happen."

The older man sat down in dismay.

"Mr. Hunter . . . I can't tell you everything about our project yet. But I truly think we'll fail without you. If we do, a life will be lost. Perhaps many more." He looked up to catch Hunter's eyes. "Obviously I wasn't aware of how you've been treated, but I do know that Dr.
Truman Bridges is no sadist and no charlatan. He's a lifelong friend of mine, already handpicked for our team. *Please*, just meet with him—I don't care if either of you says a damned word, but my hands are tied on this and we *must* have your help."

There was a long silence.

"How often?" The words barely pierced the white noise of the cabin air system.

"My orders are for two sessions a week. So here's where you insist on no more than every two weeks, and I reluctantly compromise at once a week." He tried a tentative smile. Hunter didn't return it, but at least his color was returning to normal.

"To save a life, you said?"

"A very special life, in my opinion."

"If this shrink goes Freud on me, I swear I'll deck him."

"I'll be sure to warn him."

It had been an absurd standoff, Hunter had to admit. Soon he'd be using his mind to travel through the bloodstream of a living human being, yet he was more afraid of a quack with a clipboard and a pocketful of twenty-dollar words.

But then, as Kierkegaard had said, with a virtual reality remote link there couldn't be any personal danger.

No danger at all.

## 3

Pulsing bass notes beat against shadows in a darkened room: martial music from the movie *Gladiator*. A tall figure flexed thickly-muscled arms sheened with sweat in a well-practiced rhythm, the heavy weights at their ends like mallet heads waiting to strike.

A flashing light called attention to the telephone. The man waved an arm over a sensor to mute the music. His military-green T-shirt was wrinkle-free and the matching shorts were neatly pressed. Beneath them was a body with lightly tanned skin and limbs that moved with economy, never more than necessary.

He waited deliberately until the third ring was complete, as indicated by the lighting of a green LED on the telephone's cradle, then deftly lifted the handset. He did not say "Hello"—he wasn't in the habit of giving anything away until he'd heard the voice on the other end of the line.

This voice was male, medium pitch. After a slight hesitation it said, "Noble patricians, patrons of my right, defend the justice of my cause with arms." It was the opening of Shakespeare's *Titus*

Andronicus, but in all likelihood the caller was unaware of that. It was something he had been given to say.

"I'm listening." The voice of the man in the apartment was deep, but flat, its edges dulled by years of secrets.

"I have a message for you, Mr....?"

"Call me Kellogg."

"Mr. Kellogg. I don't know how much you've been informed about our...plans...."

"You don't need to know."

The telephone voice didn't react. He'd been warned to expect a conversation that would be all business, curt to the point of rudeness. "I've been instructed to tell you that your services will be required after all. How do I send you full details?"

"Initialize a new web server, well isolated." Kellogg gave a web address. "This site will be open for precisely two minutes at midnight on the tenth of the month. You will post your message on it. Then you will dismantle the server and re-format its memory. Is that clear?"

"Perfectly."

"Arrangements for payment will then be given to you, and my services will begin the moment I receive the money. You will have one opportunity to cancel the operation up to three days before execution. Once cancelled, it will not be revived. In any event, my fee is not refundable."

"I understand."

The phone line went dead. There was nothing more to say, and further words only meant further risk.

The speakers returned to life with a thunder of tympani and brass. The man in green grasped the iron weights again and pulled them to his chest, well satisfied.

He would have done this assignment for nothing.

#   #   #

"Why pick an Air Force base?" Hunter asked, increasing his stride across the tarmac to keep up with Kierkegaard. "And why this one? Because the CIA is nearby?"

They entered a plain grey office building, and Kierkegaard didn't answer as they waited for yet another guard to check their identification, although it had already been checked the moment they'd disembarked. That first check gave Hunter the chance to enjoy a few moments of sunshine, shielding his eyes to try to see the water he knew surrounded the three sides of the peninsula. His view to the south was blocked by buildings, but he could see the line of blue toward the east. After they climbed into the car waiting for them on the runway, he'd tried to get his bearings. Judging from the position of the sun they'd driven north and northeast. He was impressed when they passed through what seemed to be a pretty decent golf course along the way.

"You're confusing the Langleys—most people do. This is Langley Air Force Base, but the headquarters of the CIA is nearly two hundred miles from here in a suburb to the northwest of Washington." Kierkegaard set a brisk pace down a linoleum hallway. The scuff of their shoes bounced back sibilantly from the block walls, which reminded Hunter of a school. He followed through a door held open by yet another uniformed guard.

The space they entered was a cross between a classroom and a corporate boardroom—more luxurious than the first; less expensive than the second. The table that ran down the middle was wood finished to look like oak. The chairs were upholstered in a dark burgundy cloth that went well with the cream-colored walls. The chair springs creaked from years of frequent use. Four people were seated around the table.

Hunter was directed to a seat midway down the near side, and noticed a man at the far end watching a projection screen descend from the ceiling. Kierkegaard sat at the opposite end of the table from the screen. Hunter had the feeling it was his regular place.

"Are we having a briefing when the rest of your team arrives?"

"This is our team Mr. Hunter. The briefing is for you."

There were only five other people in the room: three men and two women. He recognized two of the men from the lab the day before: the white-haired man scowled at him from directly across the table and his balding, more genial companion was the one standing beside the screen.

"Yes, you've already met Dr. Skylar Tyson, at the screen, and Dr. Kenneth Gage. Dr. Tyson is our engineering expert, most involved in the construction of our submersible. Dr. Gage specializes in the instrumentation and sensing, as well as the virtual reality setup. On your left is Dr. Lucy Tamiko. She's our circulatory specialist, which in our case also means chief navigator. Beside her is Dr. Truman Bridges, psychologist, but he trained as a physician first so he's also able to advise us on other medical matters. And Dr. Lorelei Mallory is a molecular biologist. You'll meet the support staff as we go."

Hunter reaffirmed his earlier opinion that Gage was rather full of himself—a handsome man with the head of well-tended white hair giving him what he probably considered a distinguished look. Tyson, in contrast, stood slumped and rumpled near the blank screen. His mind was elsewhere. It was hard to picture him in anything but the creased laboratory smock he wore.

Lorelei Mallory—not the siren of German legend that her name suggested, but attractive enough—had reddish brown hair that fell just past her shoulders. She looked at Hunter, but quickly broke the eye contact. Lucy Tamiko, on the other hand, stared back at him boldly and swiveled around to give him a firm handshake, full of confidence that he sensed was a product of her intellect rather than her looks, though she had the face and figure of a model. Her jet black bobbed hair and Asian features reminded him of Filipino women he'd known.

Last of all, he exchanged a quick look with Dr. Bridges, the shrink. He felt his jaw tighten, but he had to admit the man had a pleasant face: square, but not severe, with deep brown skin and short-cropped curly salt-and-pepper hair. Bridges fought a battle with his waistline, and was beginning to lose.

"I've asked Dr. Tyson to begin," Kierkegaard resumed. "Try to keep explanations at the comprehension level of we ordinary mortals, please, Doctor."

The scientist looked like a monk as he gave a little bow in acknowledgement of the warning. Clearly he'd heard it often.

"We call it the *Primus*," he said. "The submersible. Actually I christened it that only about a week ago."

"The *Primus*, Doctor?" Hunter interrupted, with a smile. "Not the *Proteus* like in the movie?"

Tyson looked stunned. "I never noticed the similarity!"

Gage laughed loudly. "Seriously, Skylar? I thought it was your idea of a sly *hommage*. I was proud of you."

"Should we change it?"

"No, Dr. Tyson." Kierkegaard's voice was warm, but firm. "We have more important things to think about. *Primus* is a first. That deserves to be recognized."

Tyson bobbed his head, his Adam's apple copying the motion, and cleared his throat before speaking again. There was a residual touch of color to his face, though.

His modest voice and demeanor gained strength as he warmed to his subject. From his tablet computer, animations of engineering diagrams and artists' renderings of the sub were projected onto the screen.

Apart from its size, the basic design wasn't very different from other remotely guided submersible probes Hunter had worked with. An oblong main hull bore protrusions on either side, front and rear, reminiscent of diving planes, but with a difference. "They're fans instead of diving planes," Tyson explained. "So *Primus* can change its orientation in any direction, whether moving or staying still. During your test run, you quickly intuited how to flip the craft through several directional planes rather fluidly. Well-done. Some of us found that difficult to master." His shy smile was genuine. Without looking, Hunter was sure that Gage would be frowning.

"What could you possibly use for motors at that scale?" the pilot asked. He'd tried to imagine various exotic processes, but the truth was much simpler.

"Electric motors, Mr. Hunter. Almost no different from the ones in a child's toy: a drive shaft surrounded by a magnetic field that makes it rotate by the repulsion of opposite charges. One large motor drives the main propeller at the stern with separate motors for each of the directional fans, or thrusters—a more reliable solution than trying to manufacture a complex system of gears and rods on a molecular scale. All of the motors were spun up soon after the completion of the craft and they will never stop until the sub wears out or is destroyed. Or if it were to be separated from the source of its power, of course."

"Which is...?"

"I'm getting to that. We explored the piezoelectric properties of molybdenum sulfide, but it wasn't a workable material for our purposes. Happily, Carbon 60 conducts electricity to an extraordinary degree, directed according to the way the nanotubes are wound, although at the *nano* scale electrons no longer flow like the current of a river, but express themselves more like a wave. The quantum mechanics of it . . . oh, but Devon is waving me off." He gave a self-conscious grin that Hunter found immediately endearing.

"Let's just say that most of *Primus'* power needs are supplied from the surrounding fluids and tissues themselves. The concept isn't new. Technology to strip blood glucose molecules of electrons has been in use for some time in equipment such as pacemakers. Our craft continually draws enough electricity from nearby cells to power its motors, sensing equipment, and transmitter. It can also store extra power for its weapons."

"*Weapons?*" Hunter sat forward. "What could it possibly need weapons for?" He turned to Kierkegaard with a dark look.

"Not weapons in the traditional sense," their leader replied. "All of that will be explained."

The submersible's hull was hollow, not to house operating gear, but to carry a cargo of chemicals. The cargo bay door just under the stern retracted like a folding oriental fan. The superstructure itself acted as an antenna for an integrated radio transmitter and receiver. Two manipulator arms extended from near the nose. Multi-segmented like worms, they could fold back into a compact V along the bow when not in use. The arm on the port side included an additional double-pronged tip.

"A pretty complex little machine," Hunter said with a smile. "Just how small is it?"

Tyson's pride was obvious. "As small as a medium-sized virus, Mr. Hunter. *Primus* is two hundred and sixty-four nanometers long and half that at its widest. Seventy-seven nanometers high, not counting the sensor array on top. A nanometer is one billionth of a meter, by the way."

Hunter whistled. It was a scale he couldn't truly comprehend.

"It looks like the manipulator arms are about a fifth as long as the ship itself."

"That's correct, and they're very dexterous but strong, since they're made from the same materials as the ship."

The only design feature that was completely unfamiliar to Hunter was the T-shaped device that rose above the sub's hull like a grossly elongated radar dish. Shaped like a tube cut in half along its length but with the bare minimum of a stalk, its head was nearly the width of the craft itself. Tyson called it the sensor array, but let Kenneth Gage take over to explain its function.

"You wouldn't understand the science, Hunter, so I won't go into detail." Gage's voice was flat and dry. He ran his finger over the tablet computer and a red dot slid across the screen. "The problem of creating a sensing device the size of a large molecule, with any meaningful capability, challenged the top minds in this country. What you see is a crude sketch. The real thing is an exquisite lattice of paired atoms . . . more than two dozen different atomic elements that had to be arranged according to their size and their propensity to interact, all contained within a framework that is rigid and steerable. An impossible task, but we did it.

"The array can detect light frequencies from the ultraviolet to the infrared, as well as sound waves, magnetic energy, radioactivity . . . . The crucial part is how to interpret the reactions of these atomic pairings into comprehensible data, and then translate that data into a virtual reality program that offers sight, sound, and haptic feedback—the sense of touch. The computer processing required is staggering." He swept his hand through the air. "And you felt the need to criticize the *shitty visuals*, as I think you called them."

Hunter felt duly contrite. "I apologize, Dr. Gage. I simply had no idea what I was looking at. Just as you said."

The other man's tone was a little softer as he highlighted another part of the image.

"These twin pods at either end of the *Primus* are still experimental. We believe we can stimulate them to send out pulses of high frequency radio energy and eventually isolate those frequencies from the rest of the information."

"Radar," Hunter said in awe.

"Exactly."

"But at that scale, the timing of the returning impulses would be . . . ." He couldn't think of a suitable word. "How could you possibly do it?"

"We can't. Yet." Gage looked back at the screen and said quietly, "But we will. We will."

He changed the slide on the screen. "As you can see, the sensor array is not only capable of rotating through three hundred and sixty degrees—better than we'd hoped—but is mounted on a track running down the back of the hull, chiefly to allow it to tuck behind the tail of the craft, just above the main propeller. Never forget that the sensor array is by far the most *fragile* component of the whole submersible. If you lose it you are blind, deaf, helpless. Mission over. It would likely be impossible to retrieve *Primus* at all. Goodbye to a billion dollars worth of research."

"I get the message." Hunter smiled ruefully. He wasn't surprised at the implied cost, but scared stiff by the responsibility that was suddenly his.

"The loss of the patient would be even more tragic." Kierkegaard sat forward. "Thank you, Dr. Gage. Unless you have questions, Mr. Hunter."

"Dozens. But they all hinge on the mission. What are you asking me to do?"

"Fair enough." The project leader nodded. "Your diving background includes some search and recovery experience, does it not?"

"*Search and recovery?* For what? Did somebody forget a micro-miniature scalpel somewhere?"

"Nothing so mundane, I can assure you. No, Mr. Hunter, for want of a better word, the things we need you to find would be considered *bombs.*

"Our patient's body has been mined."

4

Lucy Tamiko helped him get into the haptic suit: a thin quilted body suit of a stretchy fabric with dozens of pressure pads sewn throughout it—small quickly-inflatable air bladders linked to a complex plug and harness at his left hip. The term "sensory saltation" didn't mean anything to him, but he understood that the suit's tactors were to provide him with a *haptic interface*—a system simulating the sense of touch and giving him body awareness. It was an adaptation of the Air Force pressure suit that was designed to keep fighter pilots from becoming disoriented in the air.

He'd experienced only the demonstration model of the virtual reality control system. The real thing was more intimidating and alien, surrounded by its web of support systems. The chair was mounted on gimbals, with hydraulics like the motion simulation rigs of amusement rides. Together, the chair and suit would help him feel some of the forces *Primus* experienced in turbulence or sudden maneuvers. However, the system was heavily software-dependent. The sensor array would detect changes in direction and momentum as well as fluctuations in electrical charge from contact with other objects, but the interpretation of that data into sensations recognizable by the human mind was an incredibly complex computational problem. The system had produced bizarre results on occasion, and would be disabled if it proved to be more hindrance than help.

"Don't expect too much this first time," Tamiko said. "The schedule called for months of testing with lab animals before ever experimenting within the bloodstream of a human, but this . . . situation came up. One we couldn't refuse." She gave the barest trace of a nervous smile.

"You're saying no-one's ever driven this thing inside a living human being?" Hunter's tongue felt thick.

"No. Only in a white rat. That pilot . . . well, let's just say he's not with the project anymore."

"Jesus."

The situation was bizarre, even reckless. Apparently the importance of the patient justified the risks. Tamiko and Mallory had been given extensive medical records of their subject, with names and other personal references carefully deleted. Only Kierkegaard and Bridges knew the patient's identity.

"Dr. Bridges is standing by to insert *Primus* into a very small vein in the patient's wrist as soon as we give the word. The ship's in neutral, waiting for your commands. Just stay calm and try to get a feel for the environment. It's a good bet you're in for a rough ride."

Nausea. Worse than before.

Jacked in with *Primus* already spinning. Unable to focus.

Getting a little better now. The world is settling down.

But what world? Shades of grey—nothing else.

Still inside the syringe.

Slight sense of motion, or is that just imagination? No visual references. Try to feel the pads of the suit. Nothing from them yet. Bridges should be performing the insertion soon. Take advantage of the wait to get used to the controls.

Give a kick to each of the directional fans—'thrusters' as Tyson calls them. Yeah, slight pressure from the suit pads. A gentle roll of the chair. Movement.

OK . Bring the main engine online—might need it in a hurry. Vibration in the back. Nice touch. Like a motor building up positive thrust.

Manipulator arms: good smooth control, rotate well, easy to handle. Cross the arms—show them some impatient body language!

Was that movement? Still nothing to see. Feels like . . . moving backward!

Fluctuating pressure on stomach and chest. Maybe the computer needs more visual cues to process. Still backward. *Primus* must be aimed the wrong way. Is there enough time to get turned around?

Whoa, yeah! Spins on a dime. Overspun a little. Now forward motion is definitely increasing. Surrounding fluid taking on a slight texture, like suspended particles in a flowing stream.

Is it getting darker ahead?

Acceleration still building. Building. Becoming uncomfortable. How fast will it get? Might be able to use reverse thrust to slow down.

No. Better to know right away what she can handle. Trust the scientists—*Primus* is virtually indestructible.

What about her pilot?

Wrong thinking. Just an observer here—can't be harmed. No danger.

Darkness coming up quickly. Filling most of the view.

Inside the needle? Can't see any walls. Much too far away on this scale.

Currents. Pressure. Sporadic pressure and vibration coming from all sides.

Kick in the pants from the chair. Another one.

Darker ahead. Red, not grey. Must be programmed that way. Or is infrared kicking in?

Sense of sideways motion. No, a spin. Counteract it.

Earth red. Wine red. *Blood* red. Coming fast.

Surge of acceleration! Another one! Major g-forces, squeezing hard. Inner animal screaming to slow down. *Slow down!*

Gone into a roll. Can't correct. Nose dropping. Starting to tumble!

Rolling. Rocking. Bucking.

Flash of black. Flash of brown. Don't be distracted. Don't turn head. Face front. Face . . .

Holy shit!

"The bombs aren't actually explosive devices in the usual sense," Lorelei Mallory had explained in the briefing room.

"Glad to hear it. For a minute I thought either I was going crazy or you people were. I'm not sure which prospect was more frightening."

"No-one involved with this project is insane, Mr. Hunter," Kierkegaard said. "But I can't say the same about the people who planted these things."

"How much do you know about blood?" Mallory asked.

"Not a lot," Hunter replied. "I know there are different blood types. Red cells, white cells, floating in plasma. Platelets, and antibodies . . . ."

"Fair enough. The white cells and the antibodies are part of the body's defense system—they attack foreign invaders, living or dead. These 'bombs', as we call them, use those very defenses against the host body." She moved to the front of the room and brought up a PowerPoint slide that featured simple sketches of blood cells in various shapes.

"Unfortunately we haven't got a sample of the bombs to study. At this point we aren't even able to keep the patient in our clinic for consistent access." She looked annoyed, but Kierkegaard showed no reaction. "So we only have visual observations and some blood test results from the triggering of a single bomb. Even so, we think we've come up with the most likely scenario to describe how the bombs operate. Basically, they're containers full of a chemical called ADP."

"I just know there's going to be a long name attached to that one."

"Adenosine diphosphate. It's a chemical responsible for helping the body repair tears and holes in blood vessels. It draws platelets to the site of an injury and converts a protein in blood plasma called *fibrinogen* into threads of fibrin that form a kind of mesh across the hole to trap blood cells until a clot forms."

"How is that a bad thing?" Hunter asked. "Oh. You said a 'clot.'"

"Right. A bad thing if there's no injury. With the quantities of ADP that we're talking about, especially in a smaller blood vessel, the mass of fibers and blood cells keeps growing until it becomes a *thrombus*—a large blood clot that can block blood flow completely. Then healthy tissues die—what we call *necrosis*. The bombs may contain another chemical inhibiting the body's natural anticoagulants as well. We're not sure. All we really know is that the one bomb detonated so far was in the patient's pinky finger, and caused a very noticeable bruise. Possibly some nerve damage."

"Blood clots." Hunter shook his head. "Potentially fatal, I assume."

"If they were to happen in the brain or lungs, yes." Mallory's professorial demeanor was disturbed by her obvious empathy for the victim. "Or if a clot were to break loose somewhere else and travel to the brain, it would create an embolism, which is a prime cause of fatal strokes. However, the clots could also cause significant damage to some of the body's other major organs—the heart, the liver—possibly with lethal consequences. To make matters worse, we have no way to know how many of these bombs are in the patient's body, where they are, or how they are triggered."

Gage leaned forward. "We believe the bombs are probably a lot larger than white blood cells, but so far they've been impossible for us to distinguish in the bloodstream. We've begun to look for traces of metal and silicon from radio antennae and silicon chips. The bombs have to be programmed in some way to navigate to the desired locations, or at least to stop drifting with the current at a promising spot. Then they must be triggered to burst and release their cargo of ADP by a radio signal. A pre-programmed release wouldn't fit the scenario Devon has described to us."

Tamiko took a turn. "We've managed to get access to a prototype hybrid scanner that combines the highest resolution ultrasound yet developed, as well as positron emission tomography or PET for short, and a form of spectroscopy using x-rays. Scan results from the three technologies are merged by computer, and the result is amazing. Far beyond what's been available to this point. We've also borrowed some cutting edge MRI equipment developed at the Max Planck Institute in Germany. With the best of each technology, compared by computer, it's just possible we might find them."

"In the meantime," Kierkegaard stressed, "we can only use deductive reasoning for the most likely locations of the bombs. We cannot wait for something more precise. We will place *Primus* close to where we think a bomb is likely to be planted, then hope that you can find it on your own. It would be useful for you to spend some time getting a grasp on blood chemistry and its fluid dynamics, as well as human anatomy, especially the bloodstream. Doctors Mallory and Tamiko will help."

"I don't understand." Hunter said quietly. "Why would anyone do something like this?"

Kierkegaard replied in a voice heavy with disgust.

"Leverage."

Primus is a projectile, sling-shot into the bloodstream. Incredible impression of speed, and still accelerating!

Huge planetoids everywhere, the current somehow dancing the ship past them by the narrowest of margins. Over, under . . . . No, bumped that one, the chair shuddering, *Primus* fishtailing toward port. Going into a spin. Pulling heavy lateral g's.

Now tumbling. A tilted cartwheel at breakneck speed. Can't stop it.

Hit something. Tail glanced off . . . what? A blood cell? Dark—a red blood cell.

Got to be a way to get some control. Feather the thrusters: port side half thrust . . . more . . . now fore starboard to full—dampen the spin. That's working. Try all four blades planed flat with downward thrust in front, upward at the rear. There, the tumble dying out. The machine reacts so positively. Real danger of oversteer.

The current swirls wickedly close around a pair of cells. Another fishtail beginning to starboard. Got it corrected in time. *Shit!* It's like taking a carnival bumper car into a demolition derby with supertankers. On glare ice.

Can't keep this up.

What if . . . .

Flip all four thrusters to face outward, away from the hull. Their thrust will cancel each other out. At 90 degrees to the plane of motion, maximum revs, they should act like . . .

Gyroscopes.

Yes! Some stability. A lot straighter through eddies and side currents and whirlpools-in-the-making. Smoother, but steering is badly limited. The thrusters can be slaved together in pairs, fore and aft—a kick to the starboard nose fan triggers a slowdown in the portside fan and the ship turns left. Slow, though. Not quick enough . . . OUCH . . . not quick enough to avoid collisions.

House-sized objects popping up everywhere. Like a minefield. No way to avoid them all. What are they? Antibodies? Are they swarming?

Damn sure hope not. That would mean the alert is out and the heavy artillery is on the way.

No, they seem to be thinning out and falling behind.

What the hell is that?

Dark vortex on the port side.

Primus snatched sideways into it—suddenly pulling three or four g's to starboard. Accelerating again. Huge surge forward. A greater impression of space, too. Walls farther away—blood cells spreading out.

Where is this?

No idea.

How fast?

No idea.

What nasty surprises are hiding in the murk ahead?

No frigging idea.

Still accelerating. Unbelievable speed. Visual resolution is starting to break down—everything blurring. Occasional blood cell jumping into view, keeping pace for a few seconds, then vanishing like a ghost. What's happening? No way to avoid collisions. No possible way to see them coming. Another one! Damn it, if the ship hits the ceiling at this speed . . . .

Shit. Got to move the sensor array behind the tail for protection.

It's sliding aft, but too slow. Too damn slow. Got to stay mid-channel, but can't see a damn thing.

The computer can't handle the speed. Can't stitch the visual references together quickly enough. Must be in a major vein.

That wasn't supposed to happen.

That means being carried through the whole frigging circulatory system. Once a minute, 'round and 'round, maybe hundreds of kilometers a second at this scale. Incredible!

And absurd. How could they ever have expected to control something at this speed?

They didn't. It wasn't supposed to happen. *Primus* was supposed to have stayed in minor veins, or even capillaries. At a sane speed.

Now . . . right off the map. Out of control.

The pilot can eject, but the craft is lost.

End of story. End of *mission.*

5

"We're counting on the bombs giving themselves away once they're ready to be deployed. With their radio antennae."

"I don't follow you," Hunter said.

"Antibodies and white blood cells attack foreign objects because they sense that the invaders don't belong," Gage explained. "A white blood cell bumps against an object and discovers that the shape and outer texture aren't right. It sounds the alarm, and more defenders come to its call: antibodies, and larger killer cells called *macrophages*."

"Wouldn't the bombs feel foreign anyway?"

Mallory fielded the question.

"We believe that whoever created these things was clever enough to have sheathed them with a lipid and protein shell—a shell of the host body's own cellular material—to trick the natural defenses. A disguise. But if the bombs extend an antenna once they're in position, that would be a giveaway."

"Why don't the macrophages just gang up and destroy the bomb before it does any harm."

"We have to assume they're made of tougher stuff than that," Mallory replied. "The disguise is only to let the bomb slip through the defenses until it's in position. Then the bombers would actually want to have white cells crowd around as ready material to start building the blood clot."

"Then I don't see what's important about their antennae giving them away."

"Once a cell identifies an interloper, antibodies, white cells and macrophages are chemically tagged to be a match for the invading organism. Those tagged cells are something we can detect."

Hunter finally put it together.

"A test. You can test the blood for tagged cells."

"Right. Then we might at least get some idea of how many bombs we're up against. If we're really lucky, careful sampling might even tell us where the highest concentrations of tagged cells are—narrow our search a little, anyway. That could mean the difference between success and failure."

"I'll be grateful for any advantage." Hunter frowned. "I keep picturing myself looking for a needle in a haystack thousands of miles long."

"We'll do everything we can to help you," Mallory said earnestly. "We've drawn blood from the site of the clot in the patient's finger, and we should be getting the first batch of test results any time now. By the time your first test run is completed and evaluated, I'm confident we'll be able to give some good advice about where to begin the actual search."

"I hope so." Hunter nodded, wishing he could sound more confident. "But how do we get *Primus* past the body's defenses? We won't accomplish much if our ship is swallowed by the cellular equivalent of Moby Dick."

Tyson smiled. "You're absolutely right, Mr. Hunter. Which is why we've given *Primus* the same disguise as the bombs."

Is it time to pull the plug? Get the hell out? Why haven't they done it already? Their screens and instruments should be showing them the same blurred insanity of uncontrollable speed. The same undeniable signs.

The signs of a failed mission.

No-one wants to admit defeat. A permanent defeat, with *Primus* lost forever in the endless current of the bloodstream, a patient with a death sentence, and who knows what else at stake.

No. Too soon to give up. Too much to lose.

Think, then, damn it. How to get off this mad carousel—slow down enough to regain some kind of control, then find a place where *Primus* can be found and extracted.

Have to try kicking the drive into reverse.

Nothing.

Full reverse thrust.

Still can't see a damn thing.

Should be a slower current flow near the vein walls. Or is it artery walls by now? Try edging over. Bound to be wicked turbulence closer in, though. Oh yeah. Getting rough as hell.

Christ! Must've hit the wall. Again! Damn it—can't navigate by collision! Feel the back swell—find the balance. Like navigating near a rock wall with the tide coming in.

Still not slow enough. No choice but to turn the ship around and use full thrust against the current. Shit, this is going to be tricky.

Off the wall again! Knocked into a spin. A good thing this time—go with it. Now hard lateral thrust! Straighten out. Swing the thrusters vertical again for stability.

Jesus, Mary, and effing Joseph—the angels must've been riding shotgun on that maneuver.

No time to celebrate, though. Bring up the throttle.

Half thrust. Bucking.

Full thrust. Shuddering wickedly. *For shit's sake*—maybe next time they should make the chair motions a little less realistic. Feeling nauseated.

Still can't see. Vibration rattling the eyeballs like dice. The sensor array is tucked behind the tail, looking straight back through the vortex of the propeller—got to be serious prop wash there.

Wait . . . . Some blood cells. An impression of a wall to the right. Ghost images. Flashes. Like the wall of a subway tunnel between stations. Snatches of data that the computer can correlate. Speed must be dropping.

How long can the engine run flat out?

Whoa! A giant backward surge. Another—the engine useless against it. A regular rhythm, almost like a . . .

Beat.

Oh shit.

The heart.

"You've disguised *Primus* like a *bomb?*"

"No," Tyson had replied. "We just used the same disguise: covering the *Primus* with a shell made of lipids and proteins taken from the patient's own cells. We don't know how they got their material—possibly the same way we did. She's a blood donor. The point is, the body's defenses will believe that *Primus* is one of them, and will have no reason to attack it."

It was the first time Hunter had heard the patient was a woman. He didn't point out Tyson's slip. Who was she that a billion-dollar research project would drop everything to come to her aid? One of the rich and privileged, he supposed. The average Jane on the street would have been shit out of luck. But then Jane wouldn't have been a target. He suddenly felt empathy for the woman. She seemed less like a laboratory experiment, more human.

"I have to ask: has the patient agreed to all this? To what we're going to do inside her body?"

No one but Kierkegaard met his eyes. "No, she hasn't. She knows nothing about it."

"*What?* You're going to inject a . . . mechanism into her body, learn every microscopic detail you can, and she *doesn't even know?*" Hunter gave a dazed shake of his head. "Big Brother would have loved you guys."

Kierkegaard leaned forward on the table, his jaw muscles rigid. "We are trying to save her life, Mr. Hunter, and the President has explicitly commanded that she *not* be told what has happened to her."

"It doesn't matter who ordered it. No-one has the right to perform that kind of . . . *invasion* of another human being without their consent. I'm not going . . ."

"You're not going to what? Not going to play ball? Not going to *save a woman's life* because of your *principles?* Or is it because you feel sorry for yourself for the way *you* were mistreated?"

Hunter's face burned. Was that the real reason? He couldn't deny it outright.

"She should be told the truth."

"I can't do that. I won't. I personally believe that keeping it from her is the kindest thing we could do. She could be killed at any moment, without warning, and we have only a completely untested strategy upon which to offer any hope whatsoever. Is that your idea of benevolence, Mr. Hunter? The whole truth, no matter the cost?" Kierkegaard straightened, and spoke more softly. "It doesn't matter anyway—my orders are not negotiable."

Primus in the heart.

Chaos. Anarchy.

No up, no down—

Collision

—tumbling, twirling, twisting, an electron around a nucleus—

Collision

—starbursts flashing, vanishing, strobes of color, fireworks exploding across the mind, ghosts of circles, spectral lightning; the universe tears . . . shreds . . . chasm of black, fountain of red, falling . . . falling—

Collision

—snapping into a frenetic spin, whirling madly, pulled, stretched . . . the projectile on the end of a sling, now rising, geysering, riding the volcano, erupting . . . erupting into . . . .

Sanity.

Coherence.

Stability.

Survival?

Need to do something? What is it?

Breathe, yes. Swallow, yes. Fight down nausea. Open eyes? Not good. Ugly reddish blur—dark and menacing. Brain in a fog. World in a fog. Red fog, dark . . . .

What was that? Hitting something. A wall? Yes. Vein wall. No, artery wall. Outward from the heart—that makes it an artery. Shouldn't be hitting the wall. Should move: move arms and legs, head, hands. Move the ship. *Move the ship!*

Groggy as hell. Arms feel like wood—marionette's arms on strings. Hands have no grip. Got to stop *Primus* spinning and try to slow down again. What's next anyway? The lungs? Nowhere to be extracted there. Better to run in forward orientation and ride it out. Turn around later.

How long has it been? An eternity? Or only half?

Is this real? Or only a dream . . . a nightmare.

Horrible thought: what if that *other* life was the dream, and *this* the only reality?

The thought of performing an experimental medical procedure on a woman without her knowledge was utterly repugnant to Hunter, but the faces of the others in the room made it clear they agreed with their leader. Their course of action was the lesser of two evils.

Hunter couldn't claim to be unbiased. He'd been violated by psychiatrists paid by his former employers, trusting that they were trying to cure him when they were only searching for evidence against him. Thankfully, he'd always had a clean bill of health, and the bastards had come across with the money. But he was still a victim.

And so was she: this woman, their patient. Except she had people busting their asses trying to help.

He sighed and sat up straight, but couldn't look at Kierkegaard.

"How strong is this . . . protein shell you were talking about?" he asked.

Tyson gave a look toward his chief, received a nod, then cleared his throat.

"Strong enough to hold together for most purposes, but nowhere near as strong as the ship itself. It can be damaged. The manipulator arms have to be able to poke through the coating, and then retract within it again. So the shell is able to heal itself to a point. However, hard contact with other objects is quite capable of tearing it, possibly beyond its ability to self-repair. *Primus* would be left with patches of exposed hull."

"And if that happens?"

"If that happens . . . it's only a matter of time. The white cells will attack."

The dull redness seems to be a bit brighter. Is that actual outside light coming in through the patient's lungs, or is it only imagination? Why would there be light? Are they shining a probe, trying to find the ship?

Ridiculous. *Primus* is the size of a virus—they'd never see it, never even try. Must be imagination. Or some kind of chemical reaction.

Chemical reaction in the lungs. Oxygenation? Who knows what it looks like on a molecular scale?

No way to be sure. Still too much speed. No visual resolution. Maybe the computer has packed it in.

No, just going too fast. Is it time to slow down? What's after the lungs . . . the legs . . . arms?

Shit, no. Doesn't work that way. Remember dive school—the classes on the circulatory system. After the lungs the blood needs another boost to carry it around the body, which means . . .

Through the frigging heart again.

Oh God.

There it is again—the drumbeat, the sixty-times-a-minute cataclysm coming closer. Closer. Make it stop. *Make it stop.*

Wrenching, twisting, shearing . . . no escaping it. The chair shaking, kicking . . . teeth-shattering vibrations building, growing . . . the worst torment still to come. Vibrating becoming bucking becoming hammering, jolting, jarring, concussion after concussion . . . mounting, swelling grotesquely like . . . feedback. That must be it: haptic stimulus feeding back on itself, growing terrifyingly out of control. Shaking like a straw in a tornado.

Can't stand it . . . can't . . .

Blackness . . . .

. . . becoming grey. Dim. Dull.

Where is this? What happened? The world has gone dark, blurred . . . tinged with red.

The heart. Where is the heart?

Gone through it. Must have blacked out and passed through the worst of it. Be thankful for small mercies. The haptic feedback was murderous. Kick somebody's ass over that.

How long ago? Seconds? Minutes? Hours?

Assume only minutes.

Why didn't they break the connection and pull him out of here? Aren't they monitoring? No way to know. Can't think about that now. Time to turn the ship around again and slow it down. Could be the only chance to get out of the main trunk of the bloodstream. With ocean currents, a slower object near the edges stands a better chance of being drawn off into a side current or eddy. Here, that would be a lesser artery in an arm, or even a finger—somewhere the *Primus* could be found and possibly removed. Slim chance.

Only chance.

Shit. Hit the wall. Too tired for this. Bounced off a blood cell, then the wall again. Slam the thrusters to full. Stop the spin. Ignore the shuddering.

Can see some definition now. Several huge red blood cells keeping pace, and something bigger. Pale. *A white blood cell?*

It's not going away.

What's that other movement? Something flickering, or flapping. Hard to make out. Something small and close . . . something *peeling away from the ship.*

Oh shit. Big trouble. Very big trouble.

6

Two hundred miles to the north of Langley AFB a man made his way through the lower floors of the White House complex in Washington, DC.

Behind his back, many of the inner circle called Gerard Mannis "The Silent Man" because, although always present at high-level meetings, he never spoke. Most of the people at those meetings didn't know his real name, they only thought they did. The regular White House Staff could never have described him, they saw him so rarely.

Mannis waited for a retinal scan to give him access, then entered a dark room and flicked on the light. It was not a large office, and spartan by some standards, but the few furnishings were good ones. He rarely used anything but the computer desk anyway. He did not have visitors here. The room was in one of the most remote sections of the complex and he liked it that way. It reinforced his sense of security to be surrounded by layers of rock and steel, with no windows that might permit someone to watch him or record his conversations with laser equipment. He was a creature of the hidden places, even when he walked in the light.

He tried to sort through the events of the past few days in his mind while he waited for the computer to boot up. He keyed in a password. The machine accepted it, then asked for a second one. He typed that in. It returned a screen that warned the operator about the punishments for accessing government information without authorization, then it asked for a third password. He made a mistake typing it in, but the computer gave him a second chance. This time he gave the correct response, and the menu screen for his personal files began to appear. This final sequence, error included, was deliberate. If anyone provided the third password correctly on the first attempt, the machine would deny access and begin to erase all of its files.

The subterfuge was typical of the man. His habits were a product of many years of working for some of the world's most prominent men, both public and private, and operating invisibly within the circles of the most powerful. His few friends joked that he would order roast pork at a restaurant just so the waiter wouldn't know he really wanted steak.

When the computer was up and running, he reached into his shirt pocket and pulled out what looked like a straight pin, the kind that manufacturers of dress shirts for men used too enthusiastically when packaging their shirts for sale. The likeness was intentional, but this wasn't a pin he'd missed when unwrapping a fresh shirt. Ordinary pins didn't include thousands of dollars worth of micro-circuitry and the capability of recording sixty minutes of conversation.

Mannis let the pin drop into a small circular tray connected to his computer. There was the mere hint of a hum as data was transferred. He could pluck the devices from the fabric of a chair, a curtain, a jacket sleeve, and within minutes be listening to the most sensitive secrets revealed in startling fidelity.

He'd developed pretty good sleight-of-hand in placing and retrieving the things. This one had come from the office of the White House Chief of Staff and included a meeting Mannis had just attended, about the current crisis. He felt the irony in using such a marvel of micro-miniaturization to record a debate over deadly nanotechnology.

Sometimes the smallest of things could pose the greatest of threats.

The itch in his chest resolved itself into a powerful craving for a cigarette. He had quit ten years earlier, once he'd discovered how much you could learn about a person from their discarded tobacco, but the craving returned often. It had little to do with nicotine—it was simply the tangible form of a stronger inner craving: a craving for answers.

He worked directly for the president of the United States, ostensibly as a secret security advisor, but in reality as a covert operative within the wheels of government. He reported to the president alone. Top staff tolerated his presence, but they didn't like it. He knew that. It gave him no satisfaction, nor did it bother him in the slightest. He had been the only 'unbribable' in a special U.S./Mexican anti-drug unit, the only $500 suit in mega-corporate boardrooms, and the only infidel among multi-billionaire Arabs. He had grown a thick skin.

Now he was beginning to regret how little he knew of the man he worked for. The relationship was only two months old. Before he accepted the position, he had done exhaustive research about his future employer; but facts could not reveal the depths of a man's character, especially not a man in politics. That took time. That took living: day after day, through successes and failures, triumphs and tears, the former often revealing more than the latter. He didn't have that kind of history with the president, and now he needed it.

He peeled off his dark sports jacket, put it on a hanger, hung it on a rack in the far corner of the office, loosened his tie, and sat in front of the screen.

He also knew frustratingly little about the bizarre situation the president now faced. Nothing that told him how to proceed. Earlier events had shaped the current crisis, no doubt, but it officially began when the president received a threatening message via the internet. Threat Day. Call it "T". On T-Minus-One everything had been calm, or as calm as it ever got at 1600 Pennsylvania Avenue. By T-Plus-Three all hell had broken loose.

The threat had arrived through White House servers, but so far had proved completely untraceable. It had come from more than two dozen separate, unconnected sources in seemingly random chunks of data that only pieced themselves into a coherent whole when all of them had been received in a proper time sequence.

FBI computers had cracked nine of the sources so far, only to find more encrypted layers behind them, and every indication of a long such chain, including a half-dozen brilliant samples of misdirection. Eventually they would find the origin. Eventually was too long.

At first the chief executive had dismissed the message—it was too fantastic. Bomb threats, trained snipers, or anthrax-tainted letters he could understand. A battery of deadly devices in an unsuspecting victim's bloodstream was the stuff of science fiction. Not to be taken seriously. The few top-level people brought into the secret all agreed.

Then they saw a woman's little finger suffused with blood in a small, dark bruise. It had not been caught in a car door—she herself had no idea what had caused it, and they hoped she would never be told. It was a signal: a harmless, but undeniable proof that the preposterous scenario was not so preposterous after all.

The bruise had appeared on the same day as the message, but she hadn't told anyone about it right away. No-one made the connection until two days later—a whole forty-eight hours had been lost—and the president went ballistic, though not in her hearing. Then had come the nearly impossible task of mobilizing the resources of a chief executive without ringing alarm bells across a nation.

But what resources? Who was equipped to deal with something so exotic?

For the very first time, the Silent Man broke his silence, in a gathering of the most trusted few. He knew of a top secret project as incredible as the threat itself, and not on the radar of any of the nation's press. The president had apparently heard of it but was still the hardest to convince, perhaps because he had the most at stake. He hadn't even wanted Mannis involved in the case, suddenly acting like the parent of a kidnapped child who refuses to call the police. But the situation argued for itself: there was simply no other choice. Four days after the arrival of the threat the head of the project was briefing his team and hunting for a pilot.

A sharp tone from the computer made him jump. He punched in a coded command. It was a transmission from Langley AFB about the project itself.

The word *Failure* leaped from the screen.

He slammed his hand on the desk and spun away.

The technology was too damned new. It was maddening to have to risk so much on something so wholly untested, but there'd been no other choice. He knew little of science, but he did know about extortion. The government could never capitulate, which meant the only other option was to capture the perpetrators, interrogate them, and break them.

The demands that had come with the threat could not be met until the upcoming G20 summit in just over two weeks. That span of time was a gift they must use to the fullest. But two weeks to find and crack a terrorist bloc no one had ever heard of? The FBI stood a better chance of stopping the drug trade.

The project had to work. It wasn't just the only way to thwart the extortion, it was also the only way to save the victim's life. There was no guarantee the extortionists would destroy their lethal devices even if their demands were met. It was all too likely they didn't even have the technology to do so, which meant this very special woman would continue to bear the seeds of a death that could be awakened at any time.

He turned and looked again at the damning message on the screen.

No, this failure could not be the end. The project team was a collection of geniuses. They would find a way.

If they survived to complete their work.

A sour burn in his gut told him the project was no longer a secret, and attempts would be made to stop it.

A threat such as this could not be carried out without special assistance. *Inside* assistance at the highest level.

With a shake of his head he realized that one of the many directions the evidence pointed was at the president himself. A bizarre idea, like pointing a gun at one's own head and demanding a ransom. Yet, how many others had the means to pull off such a fantastic plan, including the necessary access to the victim herself? And there was the president's reluctance to let Mannis become involved.

Someone within the White House was dirty. All of his instincts said so. He had only days before the poison would take a heavy toll.

#   #   #

"You said the *Primus* has weapons." Hunter's stomach had been queasy at the thought of ravenous blood cells the size of buildings.

"No, no! You can't think in those terms," Tyson had replied. "Remember that the *Primus* was created with medical purposes in mind. It has a very limited capacity for carrying cargo, either for taking samples or for delivering a payload of medication to a precise location. The ship only carries a payload of anticoagulant chemicals and *plasmin* to counteract the ADP deployed by the bombs—a weapon to prevent the formation of a blood clot. But of no use at all against the bombs themselves, nor against the defenses of the body."

"Then how else am I supposed to attack a bomb? Ram it with the sub?" Hunter asked.

"I'm sure you could, and with enough force you might indeed be able to crack open the casing. However, that would allow it to fulfill its mission by spilling its cargo of ADP."

"OK, sorry. I'm still new at this." He felt like an idiot for missing something so obvious. "So what, then? Almost anything we could use to attack the bombs would allow their chemicals to escape."

"You may yet be right," Tyson acknowledged. "However, our team chose a method we believe has the best chance of success. Incineration."

Hunter's reaction was a stunned silence. Tyson had expected nothing else.

"If you'll look closely at this enlargement of the manipulator arms you'll see that the one on the left is equipped with a special tip: twin electrodes a small space apart. The *Primus'* power system includes a device that acts like a microscopic capacitor. It is able to store up a powerful electrical charge that it can release in one quick burst, which will produce a white-hot spark between those electrodes. We hope it will be able to ignite the bomb and incinerate its cargo before it can do any harm."

"And not burn a hole through the patient's blood vessel?" Hunter's eyes were wide.

"We believe the resulting heat would be contained by the surrounding plasma, especially if the bomb has already been swarmed by macrophages. If you have a better idea, Mr. Hunter, please let us know."

"No . . . no, I . . . I'm just having a hard time absorbing all this." Hunter rubbed his face. "Are you sure it will work? Have you tested it?"

"Only on a scale model, larger by several orders of magnitude," Tyson reluctantly admitted. "The results were encouraging. Our real misgiving is not about the effectiveness of the burn or its danger to the patient, but something else I mentioned earlier: the behavior of electricity on a *nano* scale. Since it doesn't flow like a current at that level, it may produce no spark." He gave an embarrassed shake of his head.

"The damn thing might not work at all."

His words silenced everyone in the room.

Hunter finally asked, "If it does work, could I use the . . . torch . . . to fight off a macrophage attack?"

"Torch. That's a good name for it." The balding scientist gave a childlike smile, then frowned again. "No. Unfortunately, drawing its power only from the surrounding blood, the capacitor will take a very long time to build up the level of charge required—possibly hours. Even then you could only attack one cell per charge. Not much use, I'm afraid." He looked concerned.

"Once the white cells know you're around, they'll swarm like sharks."

Sweat beading on the brow. Fear sweat.

The damned white blood cell isn't going away. Shit, it's big. Is that another one just beyond? Too hard to tell—still moving too quickly to see anything at a distance. The computer must be having kittens, trying to keep up.

Options? Not many. Could try using the torch on it. Might draw the rest to the scene of the damage while the ship gets away.

Damn. Moot point anyway—the capacitor hasn't got enough charge for a spark. Haven't been in the body long enough. Hard to believe. Feels like a lifetime.

Second option: tuck tail between legs and run. Turn the ship around and let it go flat out . . . give the white cells a run for their money.

No. Speeding up would risk losing any chance of getting to an extraction point in a smaller artery.

Out of options.

What was that sound? An earthquake?

A voice?

Incredibly slow. What's it saying?

Turn? Turn where? Nothing but tunnel and more tunnel, and hounds nipping at the heels.

Hold on. Darkness up ahead. Dark like a vortex?

Hard starboard thrust. Skim the wall but don't bounce off. Hurtling backward like a damned crayfish. Engine braking already at maximum. Hope it's enough.

Pulling heavy g's around the curve, bucketing from side to side in the clash of currents. Keep it under control. Hug the wall.

Extra turbulence calming a little. The current's slower, isn't it? Seems slower, more manageable.

With luck, a much smaller blood vessel. The feel is different, more confining. A good sign.

Scratch that. A *bad* sign. White cell still tagging along. White *cells*—three . . . maybe four more within visual range. The first one pulling alongside like a Greyhound bus trying to pass.

Bus nothing. More like the frigging Houston Astrodome.

It's moving up, just slightly ahead. Why?

The perfect position for ramming.

Slam the throttle back to kill the braking thrust. Pick up speed!

Too late! Like a giant sledgehammer battering *Primus* into the artery wall. Bouncing off. A glancing blow off something big and rounded attached to the wall. That cost some speed, but velocity is beginning to rise again.

Not enough.

Shit! Like a tennis ball hitting a fruit fly.

Got to get far enough ahead to have maneuvering room. That means flipping the ship around to get the main engine into the game. All right. Let's find out what this bucket has got.

Watch it. Too close to the wall! Just missed another one of those clumps. Throttle flat out. Nearby wall racing by.

Have to risk a look backward. Hairs on the back of the neck demand it.

White cells are farther back, but still pursuing. Half a dozen or more now, blocking nearly all the tunnel behind, and the leader is . . . . gaining? No, it just looks that way because of the way it moves . . . expanding and contracting, or maybe rotating.

Have to turn the sensor array and see what's ahead. Can't afford to miss another turnoff . . . find a way to the patient's skin—the only chance of getting pulled out before the ship ends up as prey.

There! Another blood vessel branching off to starboard ahead.

Got to give up some speed or the ship will overshoot.

Slew through the turn. Steer clear of the far wall—too damn close.

Collision from behind.

There goes the neighborhood.

Picking up speed again on the straightaway. Might buy a few more minutes, but red cells are packed a lot more closely in here. Have to keep steering to avoid them. Will they slow down the pursuers too?

Shit! Guess not. Body slam nearly snapped the old head off.

Oh Christ.

The artery—it's coming to an end. Something's blocking it! Pale,
bloated white cells. And something else—something bigger, dead
ahead.

Macrophage.

Star shells burst. Arms nearly snap off. Like slamming into safety
barrels at a hundred mph. Instant stop. Dead stop. Feel dead. Can't see.
Can't move. Impacts from behind . . . from the side . . . all over. Like sharks
battering a carcass.

A voice. Very faint. Very slow. Screaming, "Get him out of there! Get
him out!"

Blackness.

## 7

"You had us a little worried."

Lucy Tamiko stood over Hunter with her arms crossed. Truman Bridges was just behind her, re-coiling the blood pressure hose. They were in the infirmary, a modest room, but clean, in the requisite clinical white with light grey accents. Hunter lay in a reclining cot that looked like it could double as a dentist's chair. His head throbbed.

As if responding to a signal, Devon Kierkegaard walked into the room and pulled up the only other chair, left vacant for him.

"What an interesting day you've had, Mr. Hunter." He smiled at the responding groan. "I'm glad to hear you making sound. For a half-hour or so you were catatonic. Not completely unconscious, but apparently not aware of us. How do you feel?"

"Like I've been hit by a blood cell the size of Cleveland." The hoarseness of his own voice surprised Hunter. He cleared it a few times before he was satisfied. "What happened?"

"You *were* hit by a blood cell the size of Cleveland." Skylar Tyson stood in the doorway, then came a few steps closer, followed by

Gage and Mallory. "Or you hit it, from the looks of the playback. Then a few suburb-sized cells tackled you for good measure."

"Did you get the *Primus* out? Is she safe?"

"We did, and she is . . . barely," Kierkegaard replied. He looked at Lorelei Mallory.

"Watching the VR monitor," she explained, "we could see that you were into a smaller artery. We were sure it was one of the arteries of the arm—that's the way Lucy tried to steer you. But . . . I nearly chose the wrong one."

Tamiko interrupted. "Easy to do. We were pretty sure that after the second time through the heart *Primus* was carried into the subclavian artery—that seemed the most likely, but not a hundred per cent certain. Our visual monitors are almost no help at all. The nano time effect that makes it possible for you to navigate doesn't extend to our equipment."

Hunter gave her a look as if she'd suddenly spoken in Greek.

"The *time dilation* effect, Mr. Hunter," Tyson said. "You remarked on it before, when you did your first test run in the *Primus* . . . how the test seemed to have lasted a long time for you, but in real time took only a few minutes. How long did this trip seem to last?"

The pilot thought about his answer. So much had happened in that other world.

"Hours," he said. "At least an hour-and-a-half, but it felt like more." He looked at them for confirmation.

"Twelve minutes, thirty-two seconds," Tyson said quietly.

Hunter was speechless.

"So you see our problem," Tamiko said. "Everything happened too fast. We could only get detail by using a kind of slow motion replay every so often. We had to try to guess at your speed and eliminate your possible locations by deduction and mostly by landmarks you didn't come to, like a major organ. Once we were pretty sure you hadn't gone to the lower body, we guessed—correctly—that you'd gone into the axillary artery of the left arm, and then on to the brachial artery toward the elbow. Lorelei saw something in the monitor view that made her believe you'd gone to the right arm instead. She had a fifty-fifty chance of being correct."

"And I thought gambling was one of the few vices I'd managed to avoid," Hunter said. He saw a glass of water on the instrument table to his left, and took a long drink. It felt wonderful: the most basic need filled, a primal link to reality. "So how did you get it out?"

"From the brachial artery the blood vessel splits at the elbow into the ulnar and the radial," Tamiko continued. "The radial is more accessible. We hoped that was the way you would go, and we took a chance. Drained about a quarter-liter of blood at what we calculated would be the optimal time and we were right. Gage and Tyson just got back from the lab. *Primus* is safe and sound."

"Not quite," Tyson disagreed. "It has virtually none of the lipid/protein shell left. Your disguise, Mr. Hunter—you left it behind."

"Not by choice, Dr. Tyson, I can promise you that. It was insane in there. I was drawn into a larger vein almost immediately, and there was just no way of controlling the ship. *Primus* was an acorn in a waterfall."

"Yes, we saw that." Kierkegaard frowned. "Nobody's blaming you for the loss of the lipid shield. It's a setback, but it can be replaced. On the other hand, thank you for an excellent job of protecting the sensor array. The mission is still a go."

"It's a remarkable ship," the pilot replied. "Well-designed, incredibly maneuverable. I'd have to say that was the experience of a lifetime, for good and for bad. But to be honest, I'm not in a hurry to repeat it." With a major effort he hoisted himself into a sitting position, but dizziness made him hang his head for a moment before slowly raising it.

"Not repeat it?" Tyson's voice matched the alarm on his face.

"I just mean that I don't want to repeat what I just went through. We have to tone down the responses of the motion simulator—it nearly tore me to pieces. And that second pass through the heart . . . some kind of a haptic feedback loop happened, I assume. It was brutal. Made me black right out."

The faces that looked back at him showed only confusion.

"What are you talking about, Hunter?" Gage demanded, his face reddening. "There was nothing wrong with the motion simulator."

Hunter looked around the group. "The chair . . . pitching around so violently. It was realistic, I suppose, but my body can't take the punishment. Let's just adjust it, that's all I'm saying." He felt like a whiner. Apparently they expected him to be made of sterner stuff.

"Hunter," Tamiko said softly, "The chair hardly moved at all. It tipped and shifted like it's supposed to, but there wasn't any pitching or bumpiness. Are you sure you're remembering what actually happened?" Her look of concern was real.

"You're kidding, right? Are you saying the chair didn't vibrate like a jackhammer when we were shooting along that main artery? Didn't kick like a bucking bronco when *Primus* went through the heart?"

"Nonsense." Gage snorted. "The system behaved exactly as it's supposed to. It had about the same motion as a flight simulator going through basic maneuvers. There were only a few seconds during the second passage through the heart that the pressure pads of the suit climbed beyond the normal response range. I dampened it very quickly. You have a vivid imagination, Mr. Hunter. Or a very tender hide."

"Enough commentary." Kierkegaard interrupted more loudly than usual, seeing the blood rise in the pilot's cheeks. "It appears that the experience of riding the *Primus* is a very subjective one. We shouldn't be surprised by unexpected results. What we're doing has never been done before, in an environment no one has ever known. I suggest we all be quicker to collect data, and slower to judge." His gaze rested on each of them in turn.

Hunter slowly shook his head. "It couldn't have been my imagination. My whole body aches like I've been hit by the defensive line of the Green Bay Packers. I blacked out. How do you explain that?"

He was far out of his depth, and knew it. He tried to shake it off, like a boxer shakes off a blow, but too many blows and the foundation of his reality would crumble.

"I'd certainly like an explanation." Truman Bridges stepped close and rested the back of his hand on Hunter's forehead. "Your temperature's getting back to normal, but people don't just go unresponsive without a reason." He turned to Kierkegaard. "I couldn't let him go back under the VR without a period of observation first. You said it yourself: this is all new territory. I know the time pressure we're under, but if you lose your pilot there won't be any mission." There was something more to the look he gave his boss, but he didn't explain it.

The head of the project nodded. He stepped to the nearest window and splayed his fingers along the sill.

"It will take some time to replace *Primus'* protective protein shield at any rate," he said finally. "Twenty-four hours, Dr. Tyson?"

"Uh . . . at least that." The scientist was taken aback. "I'll get everyone I have on it. But the first one took several attempts over nearly two weeks. Twenty-four hours . . . !" He began to shake his head absently, as if making and rejecting calculations in his head, and left the room.

"Will that be enough for you, Dr. Bridges" Kierkegaard asked.

"I can't promise you that, Devon." The psychologist stood his ground. "I don't know what we're dealing with. But I will give you a professional opinion at that time. It could be just a one-time glitch. Let's hope so."

"A kill switch." Hunter said. The faces turned to him. "I want a kill switch. For the virtual reality feed." He looked at Kierkegaard. "Something right at my hand that will instantly cut off all of the simulator responses. Not your instrument feeds—you can still monitor everything coming back from *Primus*—but I want . . . ." He sighed, pushing aside his embarrassment. "I want to be able to come back to reality right away, if I have to. Whatever happened in there, I don't intend to be a prisoner to it again." He lay back slowly onto the cot, closing his eyes in obvious pain. Gage took a breath as if about to protest, but Kierkegaard held up a hand to stop him.

"Very well, Mr. Hunter. Although I hope you'll be properly grateful to Dr. Gage for the extra work he and his team are about to undertake." The leader gave a nod of his head and Gage left the room, clearly displeased. "When you've rested, I'd like you to go over your recent experience with Dr. Tamiko in as much detail as you can remember. The more quickly we can learn about the circulatory environment, the better we can plan the rest of our missions. Our success will likely depend on that, now."

He gave another curt nod, and walked from the room, followed by everyone except Hunter and Bridges. Neither moved or spoke for several minutes, then Hunter shifted his eyes. He wasn't about to unload his mind to a shrink again, but this man had stood up for him.

"What do you think, Doctor? Did I have a short circuit, or something?"

Bridges didn't get much clinical practice anymore, but he still knew how to look and sound reassuring when his patient needed it.

"It's too early for me to make promises," he said, "but personally, I doubt there's anything wrong with you at all. I was standing nearby for the whole mission, and it's true, the chair didn't make any unusually violent motions. But I'm not doubting what you went through, either. I was monitoring your pulse, respiration, blood pressure . . . adrenaline levels were through the roof. I'd expected high readings—the strangeness of the experience would account for that all on its own. Your brain has to learn what to make of it all. Until that happens, there's a strong fight-or-flight response, even if you're not consciously aware of it."

"The physical punishment was so real."

Bridges was opening cupboards, removing various pieces of equipment. Then he began to attach them to a device in the corner that was clearly a scanner of some kind. "Very vivid dreams can sometimes produce pretty strong physical results," he replied. "Look at sleepwalkers. Their bodies respond physically to a kind of virtual reality not all that different from what you experienced." He held up some wires with electrode pads at the ends. "I want to run a few tests. For our peace of mind." He smiled reassuringly.

"Tests? Uh-uh, Doctor, I don't think so."

Bridges looked surprised, but then he nodded and tapped his lip with a finger. "Yes, of course. Devon said you were . . . reluctant to have me involved. Bad experiences with other psychologists?"

"Bloodsuckers. Sadistic meddlers with no sense of decency."

"I've met a few like that. Usually the top students in the class, quickly recruited by the government, or the richest corporations. No field of study is immune to that, Mr. Hunter, when money becomes involved."

"Were you top of the class, Doctor?"

"In fact, I was. Do I look like I'm in it for the money?" He gave a bemused smile as he glanced down at his rumpled clothes and scuffed brown oxfords.

"Doesn't matter. You're a shrink—that means you're a busybody. I'll keep the contents of my head to myself, thanks."

Bridges sighed. "I have no intention of psychoanalyzing you Mr. Hunter. I simply want an EEG and some other readings to compare your current brain activity with the way it was while you were piloting the *Primus*. That may be revealing."

"You think I might have dreamed all of the rough stuff?" Hunter's wide eyes showed he was still badly shaken.

Bridges thought hard for a moment, then came to a decision. He spoke in a quieter voice, as if he didn't want to be overheard.

"No. No, I don't think you dreamed it. I think your brain . . . made a *leap* we weren't really prepared for. I can't say much more than that, without more information. But I think the explanation is both simple and profound: I believe that in some way, your brain was able to step beyond virtual reality and link with the environment of the *Primus* much more directly."

"What does that mean?"

"If it's true . . . ." Bridges' face turned serious. "It means that you can't rely on the detached safety of virtual reality. As far as your brain is concerned, *that* existence is as real to you as *this* one—and the brain is all that really counts. For good or for bad, Mr. Hunter, you'll have to accept that from the moment you give yourself over to the world of nano time, that world is your reality."

8

The darkness was like a creature; he could hear it breathing, feel it circling him like a predator around its prey. Glowing eyes . . . . No, glowing readout lights. Except the lights were dying as the power failed

A noise. At first a whisper, then a rustle, and finally the obscene chittering of thousands of crabs clambering over steel. Castanet clicks washed in waves over him . . . louder, penetrating, myriad cries of metal under pressure. Unbelievable pressure.

Downslope lay another two thousand feet into the abyss, dark as a nightmare.

Then something was different. Huge balls, their surfaces undulating like soap bubbles, appearing out of the twilight like specters and charging the sub with soggy impacts that shook his world. He could feel it shift, slide, twist and tip.

And then began the long fall . . . .

His head snapped up and a lance of fire shot through his brain.

Excruciating. The base of his skull throbbed. He gave up any thought of moving and lay still, hoping the waves of pain would subside. Sure, he'd had a lot to drink the night before with some of the young bucks from the support staff—trying to unwind, he'd told himself—but he'd never had pain like this from a hangover: a stabbing pain from his spine. Was it some kind of whiplash from the beating his body had taken the day before? Except his body hadn't really moved much at all. So they said.

His head hurt far too much for thinking. He needed coffee and an aspirin the size of a golf ball. After nearly an hour of suffering, he pushed to his feet and went to find some relief.

Bridges gave him a couple of extra-strength painkillers. He almost seemed to have had them ready. Then the two of them went together to the cafeteria where Gage and Tamiko were midway through their meal. Gage was finishing off ham and hash browns; Tamiko had opted for fruit and yogurt. The white-haired man looked tired. Up late working on the "kill" switch for the VR equipment, the pilot guessed. Good.

Hunter needed protein and carbs. More proof that the pain in his head wasn't from a hangover because his stomach was fine. He went for eggs, ham, and hash browns, toast with honey, and the largest mug of coffee he could find.

Between mouthfuls, Hunter asked, "So what is there to keep a person busy until *Primus* is ready to go again?"

"Now we analyze the data from the first run and decide where to send her next." Tamiko looked concerned.

Hunter stared at her. "Where to send her next? You mean you don't know?"

"We had several options in mind," she replied defensively. "But I think those will be reevaluated, in light of the way things went yesterday."

She was proven right when Kierkegaard gathered them together a half-hour later. He looked as uncertain as Hunter had yet seen him.

"We've got a tough decision to make," Kierkegaard began. "A new course for the *Primus*. I don't believe we should follow the original plan." He looked at Hunter then raised his head to scan the group. "It was overly optimistic, it would seem."

"What was the course?" Hunter asked.

Mallory started to reply, but Kierkegaard held up a hand to forestall her.

"The key question, Mr. Hunter, is where are we most likely to find the bombs? Where would our adversaries place them?"

"In the main organs . . . the brain . . . places where they'd cause the most damage."

"Exactly the conclusion we came to originally. Now I'm not so sure, and it's not certain that we could do anything about it anyway." His words left the occupants of the room in shock. He walked to the front of the briefing room, hands clasped behind his back. Then he turned to face them in a professorial stance, fingertips resting lightly on the polished table in front of him.

"From all of the information I have been given, it is not the death of the patient, but the *threat* of her death that is important to the enemy. They are trying to pressure the government, so if she dies, their leverage is lost. A good thing for us because, judging from yesterday's mission, it is evident that we can't protect the patient's vital organs at all."

Gage thrust forward against the table. "Are you saying the mission is a failure before we even start?"

"No, Kenneth. But a close study of the mission data confirms what all of you saw—we cannot control *Primus* in the main bloodstream." He shook his head slightly and continued. "We can't navigate her with any reliability in a current as powerful as a main vein, let alone an artery, and that's the only way for the *Primus* to travel to any of the major organs or to the brain itself. At least, the only practical way. To try to follow the lesser channels of anastomoses or even capillaries would be like crossing the United States on dirt roads. We simply don't have the time."

"Anasto. . . ?"

"Anastomoses, Mr. Hunter. They're the very smallest of blood vessels. Blood has to be able to reach every cell in the body."

"OK, so there are a lot of them, but there has to be a way."

"I agree." Gage slapped the tabletop with his hand. "It's too early to talk about failure."

"I wasn't saying that we've failed," Kierkegaard protested. "I'm saying we've got a terribly difficult problem to overcome. Let's leave that for the moment and look at the first part of the equation. If instead of the patient's death, the enemy wants to exert pressure on the government, where would they locate the bombs?"

"Damage to the critical organs or the brain is too likely to cause death," Tamiko said. "They wouldn't risk losing their trump card too soon."

Mallory sat forward with her hands clenched tightly together. "They'd choose places they could use for demonstration purposes first. Like the pinky finger. Then places where a blood clot would cause health problems but not immediate death. Maybe the kidneys?"

Gage shook his head. "If they create a blood clot anywhere and it breaks loose and travels to the heart, lungs or brain, it's game over anyway."

"All the more reason to place them in minor veins or arteries near the skin," Tamiko countered. "They're less likely to get loose and do serious damage ahead of schedule. Then you gradually trigger them in more and more dangerous locations to build up the pressure until the government gives in."

Kierkegaard nodded. "I agree. Which means that we may have a little more time before we must venture into the major blood vessels and deeper into the body. Some practice time, at least."

"Wait a minute, Devon." Gage raised his voice. "Don't we want to get to the most serious ones first? To take the patient out of danger as quickly as we possibly can?"

"I agree with you in many ways, Kenneth, but for now we have no choice. We simply aren't capable of going after those prime targets. The test run yesterday proved that. It may be that all we'll be able to do is buy the government some time to solve the problem in another way."

Gage was struck dumb. Clearly it had never occurred to him that their creation could fail to perform as required, or that their leader could ever question it.

Hunter looked around the room, then cleared his throat. "I may have an idea about that," he said. "About *Primus'* performance, I mean. I think you're selling her short."

Kierkegaard was taken aback. "You of all people. What you went through yesterday . . . ."

"Was a bitch, yes. What do you expect from a test run of brand new technology? In a place no one's ever been before? Maybe you folks are used to working with computer models and scale tests in laboratory conditions; but in my world, you never expect a hundred percent out of the starting gate. If you run a shakedown cruise and don't destroy the craft, screw the mission, or hurt anyone, you figure you're ahead of the game. I think we did fine."

Gage gave him a look of gratitude and grudging respect, but the other faces showed only skepticism.

"Are you sure that was only a painkiller you took, Hunter?" Tamiko asked.

"I must admit that I'm confused, too," Kierkegaard said.

The pilot took a deep breath. It was pure arrogance for a sub jockey to give advice to a group with credentials like these.

"Look," he said. "I don't think it's out of the question for *Primus* to navigate within the major arteries. It will require some modifications, that's all. The ship is tough, and it has power. I still have to learn how far I can count on those things, and then I have to learn how to use them to full advantage. That might take some time.

"I admit that the whole bloodstream environment threw me off my game. Way off. But . . . I think I can adapt to it. I've got to." They didn't interrupt. That was a good sign.

"The way I see it, there are two main problems we have to solve: the speed of the current, and the same difficulty all explorers have had to face throughout history. Figuring out where they are on the map."

Tamiko looked annoyed. "I can name any blood vessel you want on an anatomical chart," she said. "Our scans have even produced a three-dimensional model of the patient's bloodstream. The trouble is, we have no way to track *Primus* in real time. It's not powered by a radioactive particle like the movie submarine. That Michaels guy could tell exactly where the sub was at any moment. Tell the pilot every single turn to take. Untie my hands—give me a way to track the ship."

"I don't have any ideas on that—I wish I did—but I'd bet a computer could make estimates that would be a big help. I'm talking about collating a number of factors. The color of the surrounding blood cells could tell us whether we're in an artery or a vein. The size of the blood vessel would narrow the list more. An estimate of travel speed combined with the time spent in transit, could tell the distance traveled from the starting point. The number of possible locations that fit all of that data at any given moment would be limited. Maybe a large number, but not infinite." He hesitated. "I don't know about the capillaries and the . . . what were those others called?"

"Anastomoses. They're like a web between larger blood vessels."

Hunter nodded. "Well I don't know if we could ever map those, but with most larger vessels we'd only be asking the computer to choose from among a limited number of options, weigh the percentages, and give us the most likely location. What's the line the polling companies use? Accurate nineteen times out of twenty?"

His audience didn't seem convinced, but they weren't dismissing the idea out of hand.

"What about the excessive speed?" Kierkegaard asked. "For most of the mission yesterday you were completely helpless."

"That was because I couldn't see anything—the computer couldn't keep up; it didn't seem to be able to stitch the images together quickly enough. If that's true, we either have to speed up the processing . . . " He waved to acknowledge Gage's shaking head. "Or cut back on the resolution of the picture."

"What do you mean by *cut back*?" Gage asked.

"We'll have to decide what elements to sacrifice . . . color, contrast, sharpness . . . likely a combination of all of them. With less to process for each image, maybe the computer will be able to do the job. Your team tried to give us the sharpest picture possible. But the priorities have changed."

"I thought you considered the visuals *shitty* enough already," Gage muttered.

Hunter looked at the ceiling.

"You've performed a miracle to give us any picture at all," Hunter offered. "But if the data overwhelms the best computer we can get our hands on . . . then something's got to go. I think we can live with a drop in resolution. It's all I can suggest." He crossed his arms and sat back.

Kierkegaard looked thoughtful. "A worthwhile suggestion, Mr. Hunter, and a good example of why we need firsthand experience. But what about the rough ride? You were very convincing about that."

The pilot hesitated, forced to face a memory he'd rather forget. "The worst punishment was definitely the transit through the heart, like being stuck at the bottom of Niagara Falls—even astronauts don't train for that kind of battering anymore. But with a VR kill switch I'll be able to cut myself out and wait for calmer waters. In the rest of the blood stream, the ship was pointed backward with the engines at full thrust fighting the current. Naturally, that kicked up a huge amount of turbulence. If we bring the VR processing up to speed, and I don't need to use the engines for braking . . . then I think I can handle the ride."

"Glad to hear it." The Project director smiled with genuine relief. "And the so-called *haptic feedback loop?*"

Hunter caught Gage's scowl out of the corner of his eye. "Whatever that was," he said simply, "it only happened in the worst of the turbulence. That's what the kill switch is for."

Kierkegaard didn't speak right away. Instead he took a hard look into the faces around him. What he saw there must have been satisfactory.

"Very well. Dr. Gage, you and Mr. Hunter get together and decide which parameters of the VR visual feed can be reduced.

"Dr. Tamiko, assemble your team and see if you can produce some software that will estimate the location of *Primus* in the blood stream. I realize that's asking a lot in the time we have; but, if it helps, you can concentrate your data input on the blood vessels of the hand and the face first. Those will be our next destinations.

"We've seen how important it is to know exactly what we're dealing with, so we'll have *Primus* pay a visit to the blood clot in the patient's little finger, to see if there are any remnants left of the bomb that caused it. Then we will search the skin of the face. It's my feeling that the enemy will strike there next, creating a demonstration that will be harder to ignore.

"That is all. Good luck everyone." He walked quickly from the room, as if someone important were expecting an immediate report. That was likely the truth.

Before following Gage to his lab, Hunter fell back a few feet and signaled Truman Bridges to stop in an empty doorway.

"When we were talking yesterday, you said you thought my mind made a closer link to the sub than expected. If you're right, is that something I should encourage or discourage?"

The doctor was surprised by the question. "I think that is up to you. Is it a help or a hindrance to you? I expect it will be both. You'll have to decide whether the benefits outweigh the drawbacks. In that reality—the *Primus* reality—you're pretty much on your own."

"The *Primus* reality. You're right—it is like a whole other world. Like a labyrinth, and I'm the only one there."

"I can imagine."

"So if I wanted to encourage this link, what would I do?"

"I suppose, as with most methods for improving concentration, relax as much as possible and avoid distractions. Try to make yourself receptive. That's the essence of self-hypnosis, too. Have you ever tried that?"

"No." Hunter made a derisive noise.

"Don't sneer at something you don't understand. I should think you'd be learning to have an open mind by now."

"And if I want to fight it, I . . . what? Tense up, and try to think of Tamiko in a bikini?"

This time Bridges snorted. "Now you're just plain dreaming. No, I . . . I'm not sure there is any way to deliberately fight it. Or deny it. How do you deny reality?"

## 9

Hunter had been nervous before his first mission into the bloodstream. This time he was afraid. A part of his soul quailed at the thought of putting his fragile body through the kind of punishment he knew was waiting for him. That voice said what they were doing was an aberration, a violation of universal laws, and there would be a reckoning. He told that voice to go to hell.

It didn't listen to him.

Gage and his team had needed another twenty-four hours to modify the virtual reality program. They'd decided to reduce the display's color range all the way down to 256 colors and cut the number of pixels per centimeter by fifty percent. To compensate, they boosted the contrast.

Gage was convinced the changes would degrade the image too much, so he rigged a simple control dial that gave Hunter three options: the original high resolution feed, the new very low resolution settings, and a middle ground in between. In theory, the three modes would cover everything from high-speed travel, to low-speed surveillance, to slow detail work. Hunter was gratified to see the kill switch he had requested on the right-hand controller, out of the way, but easily reachable by a twist of the thumb.

The modifications to the computer navigation system required new software and a massive amount of new data. The programming team would need a string of eighteen-hour days to pull that together. Tamiko wasn't speaking to him.

Lorelei Mallory helped him into the VR suit.

"*Primus* is obviously too small to carry much of a payload," she said. "But we think it can carry enough plasmin to make a difference. As I said at the first briefing, these bombs release adenosine diphosphate—ADP—into the bloodstream, which draws platelets to the site and also converts a blood protein called fibrinogen into fibrin threads. Those knit together to make a kind of net that traps passing blood cells and platelets, and forms them into a giant mass.

"There might also be another chemical released that suppresses the body's natural anticoagulants to allow the mass to keep growing until it blocks the artery. We're not sure. The blockage is what we call a thrombus—a blood clot. The plasmin that is carried by *Primus* is an enzyme that breaks down the fibrin threads. That makes the clot come apart and the debris is able to disperse in the bloodstream.

"*Primus'* small cargo of plasmin would be better suited to stopping the formation of a thrombus in the early stages—it's probably not enough to disintegrate a full-sized clot like the one in our patient's finger, but we should be able to see something happening."

"Don't be nervous, Doc," Hunter said, correctly interpreting her uncharacteristic verbal outpouring. "It's another test run. It's not life or death yet."

"Everything we do now is life or death," the biologist insisted. "Because, if we can't do what we need to do, the patient will die."

"How do you know? Maybe the government will find these guys and stop them. Or give in to their demands."

"They won't." Her voice was emphatic.

"How can you be so sure? You don't even know what the demands are."

Mallory reached over and thrust the helmet over his head, as if to silence him. Then he heard her muffled voice say, "They won't. They don't do that." She snapped the chin fastenings harder than necessary, then turned away to the control panel. Hunter was sure there was a story behind her remark, but he was also sure Lorelei Mallory wasn't someone to talk about her past.

Vertigo.

Hard to get used to that.

But something else, too. Was that . . . *elation?*

Why? Because of the novelty? An adrenaline rush? A current leak from the VR gear directly into the pleasure centers of the brain? Don't need that. The environment is too hazardous. Got to stay sharp.

Yet isn't this some kind of miracle? Existing inside another's body— within their very flesh. A body inside a body, soul within a soul.

Where was the soul? Could it be seen? Felt? Tasted? Was it only within the brain, or did it inhabit each of these myriad cells in their millions being passed by so casually? There'd been no time to wonder about any of that on the first mission; no time to think at all. Only react. Survive.

Knowing what to expect, insertion was better for him this time. No raging torrent at the entry into the bloodstream. A smaller blood vessel than before. An artery, outward bound for the clot in the patient's finger.

Doctors could have injected plasmin or anticoagulant to break up the clot, but it wasn't a danger. Better to leave something for *Primus* to look at.

Definite difference in the VR feed. Testing out the VLR—very low resolution. A hint of grittiness, but individual pixels not quite visible. More like a photograph processed to look like a pastel sketch. Might be hard to distinguish small details at high speed, but that shouldn't happen on this run. Just check out the new settings for a while and go to high res if needed.

Got to keep an eye out for the junction of the blood vessels—it could be to starboard or port, above or below. Watch for blood cells being pulled toward a tributary.

Current slow enough there's no need to use the fans for stability. Like cruising along a busy multi-lane highway instead of hurtling down a roller coaster track after brake failure. A good opportunity to get a feel for the controls again—do a few deliberate rolls. Maybe try swooping around some of these arena-sized blood cells. Wouldn't want the turnoff to be hiding behind them.

Shit. Nearly missed it. At eleven o'clock, and coming up in a big hurry. Just enough time to make the turn.

Not bad. Slid neatly into the slot, near the middle of the channel. Must be getting the hang of it—need less and less conscious thought to make maneuvers.

Not much turbulence this time either. Nothing like the monster vortexes last trip. Current's a lot slower.

Of course. The clot must be causing a complete blockage of the artery. That should also mean no blood cells following. Good. More maneuvering room.

The clot isn't far from the junction. Could encounter debris anytime. Better switch the VR to high resolution.

Wow! Like using naked eyes underwater, then popping above the surface and seeing through air again. Didn't appreciate the sharpness before. Truly impressive. Able to see the dappled quality of the fluid again. What is it? Individual molecules, nearly visible? Have to ask Mallory. Walls still too far away, though . . . just a sense of texture there, no detail. Try sidling over to starboard. Should be able to get within a few ship lengths of the blood vessel lining. None of those fatty clumps embedded in the wall so far, and no truck-sized platelets to dodge yet. Presumably the ADP is all expended and not drawing them anymore.

First chance to actually see the honeycomb pattern of cells in the artery wall. Fascinating. Extraordinary. The architecture of Life. No computer drafting or robot engineering involved. Just a blueprint of DNA and . . . what? A guiding spirit?

Uncharacteristically deep thought. Better stick to business.

Darker up ahead. A sense of enclosure or obstruction. How can the VR distinguish the difference? Where is the light coming from? Slight ebb and flow happening, too, as if from a backwash. Waves of blood crashing against a cellular breakwater. Better stay ready for minor thrust adjustments. Don't want to tear any more strips off *Primus'* newly-replaced protein shell. Mild-mannered Dr. Tyson would turn into Mr. Hyde.

Mother of God! The clot does fill the entire artery, wall-to-wall. Impressive as hell. Like a shield of dragon scales covering the horizon and stretching up to the sky.

Almost forgot to throttle back. Very hard to judge distance.

Can make out the shapes of blood cells now, mostly white ones. Lots of them. Gage and Mallory were right: T-cells identify the bomb as an intruder and call for reinforcements, making perfect raw material to build a huge blockage once the ADP is released and the fibrin threads go to work.

Can distinguish platelets now. Threads of fibrin, too. Like a primitive wall, with stones of different sizes mortared together and a rampant growth of ivy overtop. Sterile. Still, yet . . . ominous.

Not much current at the face. Blockage must be nearly complete.

Time to release the plasmin. Don't know how long it will take to work. Dump it, then hang around searching for debris samples worth gathering. With so little movement of the fluid, it'll be better to make some headway while releasing the stuff. Spread the enzyme around.

Cruise slowly along a few ship lengths away from the surface of the clot. Punch in the cargo release code. Do a slow loop parallel to the blood vessel walls.

Close up, the clot looks like old wharf pilings seen underwater—hoary old ends of timber with snakelike strands of seaweed swaying slowly in the bow wave from the ship. Like in some good memories of scuba diving in northern lakes, except the reddish tones evoke a more sinister feeling. Or maybe that's from knowing this blockage of vital blood is the enemy of life.

Plasmin release complete. Some time to search around a bit while it does its stuff.

Better look over the perimeter of the clot. Maybe there are gaps that can be widened to restore some of the blood flow. Not part of the mission, but the clot projects an aura of menace. Why? It's just a natural object reacting to chemical processes and molecular attraction.

No, not natural. Engineered. Fabricated. Life's guardians subverted to destroy life.

No gaps visible. Fibrin must seek out the holes and plug them. Would the ADP simply disperse through the bloodstream, or settle onto nearby surfaces? Try positioning the cargo bay as close as possible to the clot, and allow some fluid to be drawn in. No other equipment for gathering liquid samples. It'll have to do.

What's that? Something pale, but with a different sheen than the white cells. A dull finish instead of the faint glisten of cellular material. Is that a jagged edge?

It's embedded between two red cells and wedged in by several smaller discs: platelets. Might be tough to remove. Have to slide the sensor array all the way forward and try to get a partial view of the cargo bay between the manipulator arms, then hope the fragment will fit inside. A little practice would have been nice.

Damn. Tough to get a grip. Surface is slightly curved, and it's dug well into the neighboring cellular material. Try to push the cell structure inward with one arm and peel the object back with the other.

Got the clamp over an edge, but it's not budging. Have to hold tight and use the engine to pull it out. Slowly . . . making a bulge in the wall. Fibrin threads must be incredibly elastic.

A platelet has broken loose. Now the shell fragment, if that's what it is. Bigger than expected. Bitch of a job to maneuver it into the cargo bay.

Fatigue beginning to set in. Easy does it. No need to rush.

How long did that take? Long enough for the plasmin to begin working? Head back to the center of the clot.

Wow. Big change in the neighborhood: building-sized oblong shapes beginning to peel away and fan out. Smaller clumps of platelets and maybe antibodies bobbing free and colliding with monstrous white blobs of T-cells. Can actually see the progress as the rupture spreads, like pastry being broken in half in slow motion. No way to know how thick the clot is on this scale, but hopefully a breach will open up.

Something else at the edge of the tear. Another shell fragment from a bomb? And another nearby. A dull, gritty surface with a grid of lines in it. Maybe some kind of lattice or crystal structure.

Wait. How is that even visible? Maybe the VR system was mistakenly set on medium res before, and switched itself to high somehow. Everything's sharper, better defined. Can actually distinguish the reflective qualities of the different objects.

Can't explain it, but gotta like it.

Time is becoming a factor. Must have been inside for an hour or more, ship's time. *PRT—Primus Reality Time*, as Bridges jokingly calls it. Fatigue growing. Have managed to load three shell pieces into the cargo hold. Even so, it'll be an incredibly small sample to analyze.

A big hole has opened all the way through the clot. The current is growing strong now, especially at the edges of the hole, with bigger and bigger patches tearing loose. Almost had to abandon the last shell piece. Too hard to keep the ship steady and manipulate the arms. Need a co-pilot. Why didn't they plan for that? Cockpit space is a non-issue. Maybe they just didn't have the time. Maybe they could never have foreseen the need.

Got to rest soon. Tempting to just find a sheltered spot at the fringe of the clot and catch a nap. Everything's begun to feel so . . . normal in this little patch of innerspace. Controls responding like second nature—visibility has become excellent. What can hurt the supership *Primus* anyway?

No. Wrong thinking. Time enough to rest after the lab staff have got their hands on the samples. Send the "remove craft" signal. Turn the ship around and use half-thrust from the main engine to get out into the open.

What's keeping them? Are they sleeping out there?

Whoa. Sudden strong reverse current. Must be the hypodermic. Concentrate on avoiding collisions with the other stuff being sucked in. Switch off the VR only when the ship is in the clear.

Time to go home.

Brace for the vertigo.

SCOTT OVERTON

Feeling anxious, reluctant.

Or is it just . . . *regret?*

## 10

"What about the Surgeon General? It could be her."

"Maybe. But is the Surgeon General really important enough to be worth something this sophisticated? Enough to pressure the president into something big?"

"I suppose you're right. This is definitely a high-stakes game, so the victim must be somebody who's right up there in the circles of power. High profile, too. " Hunter stepped back and stretched, then rubbed the back of his neck. He'd been leaning over Tyson's shoulder, getting a lesson in how to operate the VR recording equipment, and had taken the opportunity to draw the scientist into a guessing game about the identity of their patient. Now he changed the subject. "So the same software records all of the sub's telemetry, the patient's vital signs, and both the audio and video feed? Isn't there any backup system? In case the computer hangs or something?"

"There's an automatic backup onto digital media every few minutes, if that's what you mean," Tyson replied. "And a second line feeds into another computer archive offsite, in case this computer crashes. We're pretty well covered. Devon is very thorough. It's been a major headache for him to arrange for the degree of backup and redundancy he wants while dealing with such a high level of secrecy. It's ridiculous, really. I mean, obviously we can't let people know about this extortion scenario. But our work in creating the *Primus* should be published in the scientific journals and shared with the world. Think of the possibilities. The potential benefit to people everywhere." Tyson ran his fingers through the sparse fringe of graying hair that ringed his balding scalp.

Hunter thought Tyson was being incredibly naive. "Have you ever looked at the project from a military point of view? I mean, they've got quite a weapon here."

"*Primus* a weapon? You're joking. It's the size of a virus for heaven's sake."

"In warfare you get the biggest bang by hitting the leaders, and that's what *Primus* could give them. What are we doing right now, but dealing with a nanotech threat to some key political figure? A pretty crude one, too. Think of what could be done with *Primus*? Injected into an enemy leader, you could cause pre-planned health problems at critical moments . . . even death. I'm sure with a little tweaking, it could spy on them in the meantime. Who would ever suspect? As long as we don't let the cat out of the bag here in Langley."

The scientist's face was a mixture of distaste and disbelief.

"That's a horrible idea, Hunter. Which means you're probably right—someone in the Pentagon has thought of all that and more. Damn them." He rose from his chair and began to walk out of the room, then stopped and turned. "Do you think that's why there was all this secrecy from the beginning? I thought they just wanted to show some concrete results before going public. I suppose I've been stupid."

Hunter instantly regretted his words. If Tyson had a sudden attack of conscience and decided to quit the Project, the shit would hit the fan, for sure.

"What about that new head judge of the Supreme Court?" Hunter asked. "Maybe it's her. Maybe organized crime has gone high-tech."

Tyson shook his head, biting his lip. He replied in a dull voice, "Maybe it's the prime minister of Israel. Maybe the warfare has already begun." Then he walked out of the room.

Hunter dropped into the vacated chair and gave a low whistle. *Stupid move*, he thought. The military implications of the *Primus* technology had been so obvious to him that he hadn't even considered others might not see them. Maybe scientists had always been naive idealists. Maybe they had to be.

He turned to the VR playback unit. Along with a regular computer keyboard it had controls similar to a normal video viewer with a few refinements to provide easy bookmarking, more precise single-frame viewing, and pinpoint magnification. Tyson had been replaying part of the most recent mission, reviewing the dispersal of the plasmin and the subsequent breakup of the clot.

The resolution of the recording depended on the setting Hunter had used at the time—"High" at this point in the playback—and the monitor screen was state-of-the-art. Yet the crisp definition that had impressed Hunter during the mission wasn't there. The image looked positively muddy, with no three-dimensional sense of distance, like computer animation from a very old video game. Why such a difference? Surely the screen in his VR headset wasn't that much sharper.

What about Bridges' speculation—the extra link between his mind and the *Primus*? Could this be an example of it?

He tapped a few keys. A smaller window popped up, showing the ship's telemetry at the time. The engines were running at about sixty percent capacity; the ambient temperature was a perfect 37 C; there was even a sensor to show when the cargo bay was empty. Toggling another key he could view the scene in infrared. With a few more commands he could sharpen the picture . . . augment, enhance. It still wasn't the same as being there.

He nearly laughed out loud. *Being there?* That was a bit of a stretch, wasn't it? His own body had sat safe and comfortable in a padded chair in a laboratory half a building away from the body of the patient. Yet . . . he *had* been there, in a way he couldn't explain.

On a whim, he brought up the menu for sound control. Boosting audio volume produced a strange blend of swishing sibilants and deeper muffled notes that reminded him of whale song. He hadn't noticed the noises much during his time in innerspace probably because they were so reminiscent of the ocean sounds he'd heard so often. This time it was the ocean of life itself.

He'd pay more attention next trip, to the sounds and everything else. He'd been given an extraordinary opportunity to witness the processes of life firsthand, at their own level and to witness mysteries that had spurred the curiosity of the race since the earliest glimmer of human consciousness. He wasn't just a sub jockey anymore. He was the first explorer of a new realm.

Man, that was corny.

True, though.

Scientists might go over the data from his missions for years, and gather more knowledge than centuries of study had produced. Yet the real experience was his.

That was a double-edged sword. He was also responsible for the patient's life, and he couldn't afford to miss anything. He'd have to make a conscious effort to notice every little detail.

The remembering would be easy. He closed the software program and the images vanished from the screen. But they remained incredibly vivid in his mind.

#   #   #

Later, at a workstation in a small alcove near the sleeping quarters, Hunter scanned major Internet news sites. He searched, looking for references to the new Israeli prime minister. There was no indication that the woman might be in the United States, even clandestinely. A number of articles from the past two days placed her in various government locations in Tel Aviv. Threats from yet another radical Palestinian faction seemed to be keeping her close to home, unless a double was being used to keep up appearances in Israel while the real leader lay in a clinic bed at Langley AFB.

A pretty far-fetched idea. But then, he'd just spent hours cruising a human bloodstream in a nano-sized submarine. What counted as far-fetched anymore?

He went on to hunt for the most recent whereabouts of the surgeon general, the new chief justice, and even the first lady. There were few references about any of them, except a small number of stories about the first lady's tour of a children's hospital three days earlier. He toyed with the idea of searching for their office phone numbers, and bluffing his way through to a personal secretary or someone like that, but if any of them were the project's star patient, the cover story explaining their absence would be a good one.

He heard a noise and found Truman Bridges standing beside him.

"Are you doing what I think you're doing?" the doctor asked, looking alarmed.

"I just figured it could help if I knew more about what we're dealing with. And who," Hunter answered.

"Well keep that up and you'll be asking for more than just a slap on the wrist. If they wanted you to know, they'd tell you. If they don't tell you, then you'd damned well better not be caught trying to find out." Bridges clearly wasn't joking. "I think I would have preferred not to know."

"Come on, Doctor," the pilot said. "What would they do to me but slap me on the wrist? Who would pilot *Primus* and carry out the mission?"

The psychologist's eyes narrowed. "Don't get cocky. The people we're working for now can offer you connections that will keep you happily employed for the rest of your career. They can also play hardball. No-one better." He cast one more look at the offending computer screen, then walked quickly down the hall.

## 11

Tamiko's face was flush with excitement.

"We're sure that's one of them. One of the bombs. Here . . . in that Y junction where the two arteries are almost capillary-size. If so, then the bombs are too big to travel through the capillaries, and that reduces the number of possible sites by hundreds of thousands, maybe more."

"We were able to analyze those shell samples you brought back," Gage added, "and we were right—they are made of silicon. That's something we can scan for. This second shadow over here is also a strong possibility."

Hunter looked more closely at the piece of glossy paper with its grid-work of faint lines. The scan had been taken from the patient's face.

"How big is this image?" he asked.

"Do you mean, how big an area of skin does it show?" Tamiko straightened and brushed back a lock of black hair. "Only a centimeter square."

"And how deep is this scan?"

"A couple of tenths of a millimeter," she said. "We can produce a better 3D rendering on the computer screen."

"There are dozens . . . hundreds of blood vessels showing. Are you sure you can single out the one that has the bomb in it?"

"Most of those are capillaries. Barely big enough for a red blood cell to pass through. A lot of the rest are lymphatic vessels—kind of a parallel circulatory system that passes excess fluids and proteins from cell breakdown so they can be filtered out and eliminated from the body. Only a dozen or so of what you're seeing are actual blood vessels big enough for the bombs to pass through. Yes, I think by using the computer to rotate the image through several cross-section views, we can find the right one."

"Why not just insert a needle and draw the bomb out, the way we remove the *Primus*?"

Tamiko looked annoyed. "Sure, when the bombs are this accessible from the outside. Anything within the brain or the organs will be completely out of reach. It's far better to refine our procedures with the *Primus* now, in a relatively harmless location like this one, so we'll be ready for the tougher jobs ahead."

"OK, I get you," Hunter said. "Practice makes perfect."

"Perfect, hell," Gage muttered to himself. "I'd be happy with anything short of a disaster."

Back in the saddle again.

It feels good. Still can't figure out why.

Mission Number Three. The *Primus* has been inserted into the patient's face—a tough injection to explain if she still hasn't been told what's going on. That's ludicrous, and disturbing, but there's no point getting worked up about it right now. There's enough to do just to keep from bumping into things. Lots of red cells in the facial arteries—blood flow very reactive. The arteries and veins are much smaller than the previous missions, this close to the surface of the skin, but laid out in an incredibly complex web: a labyrinth with a deadly device at its center.

Trial by fire for Tamiko's navigation system. The "head's up" display is a little larger than before to allow for text messaging. Letters get in the way a bit, but the mind adapts.

Maybe that's why the view has also become sharper, the colors better defined. The mind is adapting.

*** *Turn** **

Simple one-word messages whenever possible, to save time. Time for Tamiko to speak it, the computer to translate it, the pilot to read it. Before the ship has passed by the junction.

Damn. A branching immediately to starboard—another one just visible farther ahead to port. Which one to take?

Decision by default. No time to turn into the starboard one.

Tamiko would allow for the time lag. Wouldn't she? Or could she? Did the new program compensate for the periodic slowing and quickening of the current produced by the heartbeat?

Lining up for the port turn. Like rolling a marble through a maze on the pitching deck of a ship at sea. How could they expect to navigate something like this?

Rumbling sounds. Voices.

Distracting.

*** *Turn!** **

Shit! Almost missed it. Directly above, nearly blocked by a passing white cell.

Can't afford to be distracted. Distraction prevents local awareness, like keeping track of a dozen nearby cars on a busy freeway. Automatic, after years of driving, but prone to failure if the brain is distracted by sipping coffee, or using a cell phone.

Need total concentration. Problem is: how to be *in the zone* for two hours at a stretch? Is that even possible?

** * * Turn * * **

There it is, right below . . . starting to vanish behind the bow. Peel off to port to avoid a red cell charging underneath with a string of platelets behind it. Slam the shift into reverse. Full throttle. *Primus* wallowing in its own propwash. Is the opening still there?

** * * Turn back!* * * * * * Turn back!* * **

Easy for her to say.

"Is your navigation system capable of distinguishing among this many blood vessels and telling me where to go?"

Hunter wasn't making friends. Tamiko said coldly, "My screen will show a tracking icon superimposed on the image of the blood vessels, projecting the estimated location of the *Primus* at a given time. I'll also have a readout of the probability that the location is correct, based on speed, time elapsed, size of the artery and other factors. We can assume that probability percentages will drop as the mission goes on and the estimated distance from the starting point becomes less and less reliable. In the meantime, I'll give you simple directions to keep you on course—they'll appear in text in your visual display. If the percentages drop too low, we wait until we have more data. Or scrub the mission."

Hunter couldn't help shaking his head. "There are dozens of off-branchings—up, down, on every side—what if we make a wrong turn? How can we expect to be right every time?"

Tamiko didn't reply.

After a long moment Gage said simply, "Because we have to be."

Reverse thrust isn't enough. Only managing to stand still against the current. Going to have to make a quick turn of the ship and use forward screws.

Scan the vicinity for obstacles. Flip the thruster fans to oppose each other and push up the power.

This thing spins like a top—that's a big help.

Making some headway now. Slow, but sure. Don't need more than three-quarters power. Keep some in reserve. Is it best to travel past the junction, then turn around and approach with the current again? Or try to drive straight in, first time?

The direct approach. Need to know if the ship can do it.

OK, pure cussedness, too.

Easing slowly over to starboard. Watch for oncoming blood cells. They might be going the same way, into the branch. Not good to be sideswiped against a wall.

Nearly there. A red blood cell and several platelets approaching, probably heading for the turnoff. Ease back to two-thirds throttle to maintain station and wait for them to go first. Caution, not courtesy.

Now it's *Primus'* turn. Hit the throttle and ease inward. Plenty of room to enter the tunnel sideways and then straighten out once the ship is well inside. Easy does it.

Voices again—that low background rumbling. No text command—just chatter? Distracting. Worse than that: *disconnecting.* A noticeable drop in visual and aural acuity, as if the whole scene recedes a little. Got to concentrate. Tune out the noise.

One white blood cell appearing out of the gloom, coming toward the junction. Should have seen it earlier. Better to back off and wait. Not smart to try to outrace a blob of protein the size of an amusement park.

Wait. *It's not turning!* It's coming straight on like a freight train. No way to dodge around it, absolutely no way.

No choice but to run.

Full reverse. Snap spin and slam the throttle forward again. Go like hell!

Neck and back muscles knotting up in anticipation of the collision. Is it going to hit?

No. A major kick in the ass, but probably only the bow wave. *Primus* must have matched speed just in time. Now got to ease to starboard and get out of the monster's path. Not easy when the damn thing takes up most of the tunnel.

** * * Turn back! * * * * * * Off course!* * * * * * Off course!* * **

No shit.

No turning back now. Way too far past the turn—it would take a half-hour or more at full throttle even if the way were completely clear. And it wouldn't be.

Like trying to swim up a logging flume.

No way. Have to find a sheltered spot, maybe on the inside of a curve. Pull over and maintain a holding thrust.

Pull the plug. Rethink the options.

This run is over.

## 12

Kellogg thought about the money newly deposited in his secret account. It was an obscene amount, but he'd need to pay top dollar for the people and hardware he would require.

He was smiling, though none of his pleasure showed in his cold eyes or thin eyebrows. Having a mission to work on always put him in a good mood. The target group of civilians—scientists, mostly— would be easy to intimidate. Their security infrastructure was deliberately low profile. That was something Kellogg could exploit. And the fact that the target complex was on Langley Air Force Base in Virginia, home of the First Fighter Wing, made it an irresistible challenge.

He spread a series of aerial photographs over the table in front of him. He scarcely needed them—he was thoroughly familiar with the area. Yet sometimes seeing everything laid out on paper triggered ideas.

His first glance produced a handful of possibilities right away. The base itself was on a point of land bordered on two sides by the Back River. The target facility was located in the northern part of the base near a residential section, and close to some undeveloped land that lay between the river proper and the mouth of a large creek. It was a perfect setting for a clandestine night landing. The golf course not far from the lab had a lot of open space, but still a substantial amount of cover.

Although there was excellent road access to the base, trying to bluff the way through guarded gates with a dozen men using false documents was too great a risk.

Yes, by water would be the best way. With such a large municipal area surrounding the base, it would be easy enough to marshal his team and their equipment in one of the nearby neighborhoods, or bring them in on the night of the mission in a couple of vans. Pull up on one of the darker streets near the waterfront—who would pay any attention to them, or do anything about it if they did?

He'd draw up a few different scenarios later, when most of his team had arrived.

There was Kowalski—an ingenious planner. Rakov, one of the best night insertion men he knew. The rest had been recruited in the usual way, by careful calls to cell phones, and subtly worded ads.

He'd had some of his best success with the military's own publications and web sites. Ex-military people still tended to keep up with the world they knew, through its press and other media. There were a lot of ex-military types out there, looking for money. Even the former elite of the special services.

It had always been a mystery to Kellogg that the armed forces of nearly every country in the world could be willing to spend so much on training their soldiers, and then so tightfisted when it came to paying their salaries. It made no sense. If you didn't reward good people, you lost them. The corporate world had recognized that for years.

But the military was funded by government, paid for by taxes, watched over by elected watchdogs who based decisions on the way the latest political wind was blowing. Even the highly trained and motivated special forces soldiers like Navy Seals and Delta Force, who would tell you they did it for their country, sometimes lost their enthusiasm when they saw how little their country did for them. Then it just took the right nudge to bring them to Kellogg.

He found ripe pickings from among the discards of the American and Canadian military communities, and several of the mainland European countries. Not so many Brits—their attitude was different, somehow . . . maybe a holdover from their success against long odds in the World Wars.

Of course there was an endless supply of soldiers from former Soviet republics, if you just wanted muscle. None of those countries could afford their war machines anymore, so even with recent Russian recruitment a lot of lifetime soldiers went begging, looking for any kind of work. A bit old, perhaps, but they followed orders and asked no questions.

The timeline was going to be tight; they'd have to be ready within five or six days, for a mission just days after that. Not much time to get them armed, refine the plan, and most of all, practice it until they could perform flawlessly on the darkest of nights. He didn't anticipate much resistance, but he was not a man to take chances. Even with the simplest missions and the best plans, sometimes the difference between success and death was a sudden cruel turn of bad luck.

With a lifetime deliberately spent on the fringes of the establishment, he'd learned that the successful made their own luck. Many years of careful planning, swallowing his pride and pandering to wealthy fools had finally put him in a position to take his rightful place and exact some sweet revenge.

The masquerade would soon be over.

13

"What was all that chatter out here? Were you guys ordering a pizza, or what?" Hunter slammed a palm against the wall, just as Devon Kierkegaard entered the room.

"I was monitoring from my office. What happened?"

"Hunter missed the turn," Tamiko snapped. "The ship is off course . . . too far to go back." She flung herself into a nearby chair and crossed her arms over her chest. Gage just stood still, looking uncomfortable.

"What's this about ordering a pizza?"

"It was nothing like that," Gage replied. "Tamiko and I were discussing the next part of the course. The difficulties that would be coming up, and how the nav system was working. We weren't even talking loudly—we didn't want the voice recognition unit to pick it up."

The project head turned to Hunter and simply looked the question.

"I believe them," the pilot said with a sigh. He turned away, gently shaking his head. "But it was still a distraction. It seems that if

I'm able to concentrate fully—really focus—I get much more from the VR equipment. My brain adjusts to it, or . . . something."

He looked earnestly at his new boss. "If anything competes for my attention, like trying to interpret slowed-down speech, I lose some of the contact. In this case, I might have seen the white blood cell coming in time to avoid it, or steered the *Primus* into the other artery first. I can't say for sure. I do know that we just don't have any margin of error in this damn job." Frustrated, he slumped against the wall and began rolling his head slowly from side to side to ease the knotted muscles in his neck.

Kierkegaard didn't say anything for several seconds. Then he raised his head in a decisive posture they were coming to recognize.

"We're learning everything as we go—there are bound to be surprises. I chose all of you because I believe you can handle them. However . . . ." He turned to Tamiko and Gage. "We will try from now on to make this room as free from distractions as we possibly can. Dr. Tamiko, would it be possible to make it so that Mr. Hunter can navigate for himself? Eliminate the *middle man*—or woman—so to speak?"

The pilot nodded. "Maybe give me the navigation data directly in my heads up display. A flashing warning icon to indicate a turn coming up would probably work as well as a verbal command. Might even be quicker." He looked at Tamiko with an expression of apology, and pleading at the same time, knowing that it was yet another unreasonable demand on her time. Her initial angry reaction evaporated.

"You people need to give me a little more help. Like maybe Microsoft."

The sudden humor was so unexpected it drew a burst of laughter from them all. The tension in the room broke. Then Kierkegaard clapped his hands together.

"In the meantime, what's our next step? Can we get back on course? Or must we try to retrieve the *Primus* and start over again?

"I've been thinking about that," Gage said. "Lucy, pull up the graphics of the area again. A little larger. There, you see? The lymph system. If we could just find . . . .

"There. Two small channels that loop back around toward where the *Primus* went off course. If you follow them along a bit farther, this lower one leads to a small vein, then continues right alongside the artery we were using. Can you zoom in just a bit more?" He leaned into the screen and traced a finger over it. "Yes, you see? I'm sure those are tiny capillary connections with the artery, ahead . . . uh, upstream of the turn that Hunter missed. We could use that, couldn't we?"

Tamiko looked thoughtful.

"It could work," she muttered softly, rubbing a knuckle along her lower lip, "if *Primus* can go against the current."

"The arterial current?" Hunter asked doubtfully.

"No, nothing that strong." She shook her head and looked up. "The lymphatic system collects excess fluids and waste products, along with producing some specialized white cells. It's somewhat like a second circulatory system, but with nowhere near the same velocity. Very small capillaries run from the arteries to the lymphatic vessels—a one-way flow, but not high-pressure."

She traced the faint lines showing on the screen. "As Kenneth said, you'd have to take the *Primus* out of the artery into one of these lymphatic vessels, and double back . . . this way, to the area of the artery before the turnoff that you missed. I don't know which way the lymph current will be flowing, but it shouldn't be very strong. The heavier going would be here, where you'd have to follow a capillary like this one against the current, back out into the artery. That might be tougher." She searched their faces to see if they understood.

"I follow you," Hunter said. "Just how small would these capillaries be?"

"A lot smaller than you've been using up to this point," Tamiko replied, "But still with lots of room for *Primus*. More like . . . "

"A rat running up a sewer tunnel," Gage finished for her. He drew a sour look from the others, and shrugged. "Except running uphill."

The pilot of the craft shook his head. "The question of current doesn't bother me as much as just finding my way. Navigation looks like a nightmare. There aren't any signposts to tell me if I've even turned into the right lymph channel, and from there it's pure guesswork . . . calculations of speed and distance that might all be based on the wrong location. I could get the *Primus* so lost we'll never get her out."

"No fear of that," Kierkegaard interrupted. "We could remove a large-enough section of tissue surgically, without leaving much of a mark. Still, it does seem to involve rather large margins of error at every turn. Is there no other way?"

Gage looked serious. "No other way except to extract the *Primus* with a needle and try to start over again. But . . ." He held up a hand for emphasis. "Once the extraction needle goes in, *the route changes.* Suddenly you've got a gaping hole punched through the artery wall, with fluids leaking out in every direction, probably impossible to navigate through. That's unless we drive the ship well downstream of the bomb's location, first. Of course, in both scenarios, with every minute it travels, its location becomes less and less certain. It's your decision, Devon. Either way will be a bitch."

"Succinctly put, Kenneth." The older man nodded. He folded his fingers together behind his back and stared hard at the screen, as if to persuade it to unlock its secrets. Then he turned away and took several slow steps away from them, toward the door. Before he reached it, he stopped and said, "Take the lymphatic system. Successful or not, it might teach us things that could prove useful in the future." Then he allowed a trace of a smile to show on his face. "If this were going to be easy, they could have got anyone to do it."

#   #   #

Hunter had been right: the navigation was a nightmare.

Still steering by Tamiko's verbal commands, his nerves were on edge within minutes. The capillaries were large in comparison to the *Primus*, but terribly small compared to the artery itself. Like trying to spot a manhole cover on a twelve-lane freeway at sixty miles an hour. Then, with no other references to guide them, they'd had to take the first one they found.

It was a bad choice, leading forty-five degrees away from the direction they'd intended, an unfortunate fact they only determined later. The detour led to a fruitless two hours—ship's time—of nearly aimless circling. The only bright note had been the ease of travel through the lymphatic vessels. There were occasional white cells, lymphocytes, big enough to nearly block the way, and the odd loose string of protein or other matter to avoid. But the current, even when contrary, was manageable.

The visibility reminded Hunter of scuba diving in the Great Lakes after a spring storm: lots of particulate matter suspended in the liquid, creating conditions like a thin fog. It could have felt confining. Instead it was almost comforting in its familiarity.

Good visibility or poor made no difference. In the end, the computer simply could not tell them where *Primus* was. The programming used a starting point in one particular lymphatic vessel, but the ship immediately went astray. Every step from then on was a false one. A roll of the dice would have been as effective.

Finally, soaked with sweat, Hunter stabbed the kill switch, lifted the helmet from his head, and acknowledged defeat. No one said anything. Gage and Tamiko were uncharacteristically contrite. After a moment, she left to ask Kierkegaard to arrange another scan of the patient's face to find the lost ship. It was an admission of failure that felt more like a betrayal of trust.

Hunter felt a surge of sympathy for the unknown woman. Did she submit gracefully to all of these mysterious procedures, with no clue as to the real reason behind them?

Who was she? His desire to know was becoming a powerful need, as if the fact of his traveling through her body created empathy that grew with each contact, each . . . violation. Was that it? Did he want to know who she was so he could apologize? Or was it more like a kind of kinship: he was working in her body, *with* her body, to try to cure it. How could he do that without knowing who she was?

He wasn't simply navigating a thing of struts and circuits through a foreign landscape. His mind was moving through flesh, the very essence of another human being. Could it be an invasion and a symbiosis at the same time?

It was this possibility that made him insist on trying again with the *Primus*.

"Are you out of your mind?" Gage stormed. "We just put the patient through another scan so we could find the *Primus* and remove it. Now you want to just get it lost again? Why in the world do you think this time would be any different?"

Hunter had to lay all of his collateral on the line.

"Look, the patient is still under sedation," he said. "Keep her under for another ten minutes. Give me that long, and if I haven't made any progress, we can take another scan and still get the ship out of there. That's all I'm asking.

"And . . . let me do this on my own. Without advice from out here." He forced the last words out in a rush, and tried to ignore the look of venom from Tamiko. "If I get nowhere, then . . . write me off as a decision maker. Don't trust my judgment anymore."

Gage's face clearly showed that he never had. Yet, somehow, Kierkegaard had been convinced. Or perhaps it was simple desperation.

So, Hunter went back in. He cleared his mind of distractions, trying to invoke a state of near-trance.

And he found the way.

Within four minutes, lab time, he had re-entered an artery. After another six, he'd brought the ship to rest in front of his destination: an almighty mammoth globe of manufactured death.

## 14

Mannis had been at the White House for nearly a day-and-a-half straight. He'd caught four restless hours of sleep sprawled in a thinly padded chair against the side wall of his office. Apart from unavoidable meetings, and an occasional change into a cleaner shirt, he'd spent almost all of his time at the computer or on the phone. He'd even taken his only two actual meals at his desk—submarine sandwiches brought over from the commissary.

The search had been fruitless. Searches, he corrected himself. He'd tried several angles. First, the technology. Who could've developed micro-miniature bombs with the necessary sophistication? An enemy nation? Several had technology industries, but had always focused their efforts on more traditional nuclear and biological technologies. There had been no indications of cutting-edge science like this. It wasn't something many countries could have kept secret—their leaders could never have resisted crowing about it.

There were still a handful of African countries that wavered in their attitude toward America, depending on the warlord-of-the week. None could have sustained sophisticated research. The two or three former Soviet republics with unfriendly dictatorships simply didn't have the money. Cuba . . . well he, himself, had vacationed in Cuba last year, now that sanctions had been lifted. It was hardly ever considered a threat anymore.

That left the freelance terrorists, most of them small and scattered. Even the last remnants of Al-Qaeda had fallen to bickering amongst themselves in the ten years since their last success of any significance. There were cells that still had some rich backers, and they might have been able to buy high-tech weaponry, but such weapons had to exist in the first place.

His contacts within the CIA and the military—and his contacts were the best—said that neither the Russians nor the Chinese had succeeded in developing nanotechnology weapons of any kind. The Russian program had just lost its funding because of its lack of progress.

His second approach had been to "follow the money", a tried and true method of counter-espionage. Nanoscience of this caliber would take big money.

He'd tapped into as many resources as possible to search for shell companies with the required connections: backers of dubious affiliation, shadow-links to prominent western research universities or possibly pharmaceutical companies. There were many. Most were known to the government, and tolerated, but none seemed to fit the profile he was looking for.

The kind of weapons technology involved in this threat screamed of the military. Any private corporation with such abilities would have found a dozen ways of making profits from them that would far outweigh what a terrorist organization could pay.

At least, that's the way he saw it. Most of the president's other advisors disagreed. They favored treating this event as a terrorist threat, in spite of Mannis' objections. He had stopped objecting, and had gone to work on his own.

What he had learned left him with a distasteful conclusion: the technology they were facing was most likely American. The financing behind it, almost certainly American as well.

Which led to his third field of scrutiny: finding the bad apple.

He searched for big money connections to the biggest players in White House circles. The result shamed him. All of them had secret bank accounts. Every one had questionable ties to corporations, lobby groups, rich eccentrics, or all of those. The search had been a challenge because all of the really powerful had learned how to cover their tracks well. His best efforts to pierce the veil any further had failed. He'd have had better luck penetrating the databanks of the former KGB.

The numbers on his screen were blurring, becoming meaningless. It was time to go home. The long walk through the corridors to the parking garage felt like a defeat.

The interior of his dark blue Impala sedan was a piece of home. In truth, he spent more waking time in the car than in his Arlington apartment. It had served him faithfully and faultlessly for eight years.

Which was why he was caught so utterly off-guard when it left his control and became a hurtling projectile.

He was trying to divert his mind from the frustrations of the day by leisurely scanning the view of the National Mall from his driver's window, painted golden by the rays of the setting sun. He particularly enjoyed the view of the Lincoln Memorial at this time of day as he caught fleeting glimpses of it between the trees. He rolled slowly across 23rd Street, gazing south toward the familiar façade, seeing the Doric columns in his mind's eye.

As he was accelerating up the entry ramp onto the Roosevelt Bridge and drawing toward the curve, he eased his foot back on the gas pedal. Instead, the car continued to pick up speed toward a clumped pack of vehicles ahead.

Thinking the linkage was sticking, he gave the pedal a sharp kick to free it, but that only raised the engine revs another thousand rpm. The pedal went down, but did not return.

He stepped hard on the brake and the momentum threw him forward against his seat belt as his foot went straight to the floor. The brakes were gone. A surge of adrenalin shot through his body, and his throat clenched tight.

There was a gap in the left lane. Without thinking, he wheeled over into it, then back right, and left again, dodging the line of moving vehicles, ignoring the blare of horns.

A delivery truck suddenly appeared from behind on his left, merging from the Rock Creek Parkway onramp. He cut the truck off, evoking a squeal of protesting tires. He dodged far right again, up beside the curved guardrail, but there was no reprieve. An old beige Chevy close behind a moving van blocked his lane. There was nowhere else to go.

At the last possible second, a gap opened up, and he took it with a wrench of the wheel. Had he clipped the Chevy? He thought so, but there was no time to dwell on it.

He pulled right again to avoid a black Mercedes, but the guardrail was ending in a clump of overhanging trees, replaced by the two lanes of the onramp from Interstate 66.

Frantically, he tried to downshift. The engine howled in protest, and then he was forced to shift up again to get ahead of oncoming traffic. With relief, he spotted a gap across both lanes that allowed him to quickly cut over to the outside guardrail again. Something in his brain said that it was the slowest lane—the safest place to be. Still, he was gaining on the line of traffic ahead much too quickly.

Did he dare to shut off the engine? Or even throw it into Park? The transmission would be ruined, but that didn't matter. Would it stop him? Or would it make him lose control, maybe cause someone to hit him from the rear before they could react? He didn't know, but he was out of options. He switched off the ignition.

Nothing happened.

He was out over the river now, nearly into the back of a white Buick with at least three cars ahead of it. There was room beside him, in the middle lane. He took it, pissing off the driver of a green Lexus that suddenly appeared in his rearview mirror, blasting its horn as it wove around him on the left. He pulled over on its tail, up next to the center barrier, but it wasn't where he wanted to be.

A trace of a plan had formed in his mind. There was a short gap up ahead in the lane next to him, and possibly another forming to the right of that. He wheeled hard over, waited for a couple of seconds . . . .

The outside lane wasn't opening up. *It wasn't opening up.* A brown SUV had gunned its way forward. It wouldn't be out of the way before his runaway Impala would hit the low-slung red sports car ahead, climbing up onto it and its defenseless driver.

In desperation, he downshifted again. He could only pray it would slow him just enough to provide extra seconds . . . allow the brown vehicle to get out of the way. The sound of the howling engine clawed at his spine. He couldn't see past the bulky SUV in the outside lane. If there was another car behind it, he was out of luck. In front of him, the rear bumper of the sports car began to vanish behind his hood . . . .

He threw the wheel over, somehow missing the tail of the SUV, and forcing a minivan not far behind to slam on its brakes. In a reflex action he hit his own brake pedal again. No response, and his back end nearly fishtailed, but he was next to the outside guardrail again—hopefully in a slower stream of traffic.

Ignoring the protests of the engine, he tried to shift down into first gear. It wouldn't go. Probably there was some kind of guard that prevented it above a certain engine speed. That left only one choice.

Gritting his teeth, he moved the car onto the narrow paved shoulder ribbon, gripped the wheel harder, and steered into the guardrail.

Sparks flew, accompanied by a monstrous noise, and he had sudden visions of plunging through the rail and the wall, far down into the Potomac River.

He'd hit the rail too hard. The car bounced off, and with a surge of panic he felt the back end start to stray to the left. *Damned front-wheel-drive.* Too goddamned hard to correct a skid.

He clutched the wheel fiercely, and fought to get the Impala under control. Thankfully, the impact hadn't triggered the side air bags.

By now the car's computer would probably be calling his roadside assistance company—signaling a problem, getting a satellite fix on his location, even alerting the White House. The swaying stopped. His heart pounded. Did he have the guts to try it again? Risk spinning sideways across three lanes of speeding traffic?

No choice. There was another delivery truck just ahead and he was closing fast. He gulped a breath and slid the car over, but eased it more gently across the last few inches. The hellish grinding began again, and a seam tried to knock him away. He kept the wheel turned hard. It was working . . . he was sure it was working.

He nearly lost his grip on the wheel as the car jolted over a piece of orphaned rubber tread from a truck tire. The shock steeled his determination, and he pushed the car harder against the shredder-like panels of the railing. Through the chaos of noise and sparks he dimly registered other cars veering around him. They were no longer part of his world—his world was the car and the guardrail; the guardrail and the car.

The sedan began to buck as the engine fought for life. Finally, endless seconds later, it gave up the battle, coughed, and died. The assault on his ears faded. He gulped for air. With only a quick glance back, he threw open the door and staggered around the car to the railing, nearly retching into the river below. It wasn't the first time he had faced death, but the aftereffects of adrenaline left him trembling and weak.

It was over.

No, that wasn't true. He had survived, but it was far from over. Not until he had found who was responsible, or they managed to stop him first.

Someone had found out what he was doing . . . had decided to silence the "Silent Man" forever. Had nearly succeeded. The thought sent a tremor of rage through his body.

With a start, he realized that he smelled smoke. The car was on fire.

That didn't make sense. He shouldn't have punctured the gas tank or lines.

Of course. The car was too incriminating. Mustn't leave any telltale evidence.

He had to get to a safe distance. Theodore Roosevelt Island was nearby, but there was no easy way down to it. Grimly he began to trot back toward the east end of the bridge, waving his arms in an attempt to warn traffic away. It finally began to have an effect as the drivers spotted the growing plume of smoke. From somewhere in the distance he heard the sound of sirens.

## 15

A vast, milky globe, motionless and silent. Death in tangible form. Soulless. Remorseless. A testimony to human ingenuity, perverted. Up close it has a gritty texture, the molecular lattice nearly visible.

The bomb.

No, only one bomb of many. An infestation waiting to strike. The scale is overwhelming. Like trying to attack a battleship with a rubber dinghy, knowing that the remainder of the fleet still lies in wait.

The obscenity of it is palpable: recognizing that human skill has willfully brought such death into the very sanctum of life itself. Yet, human skill has also brought a chance for renewed life.

The approach isn't easy, and the whole area is littered with massive blobs of protoplasm—dead and dying antibodies and white blood cells called to do battle, but unequal to the task. The detritus of the fallen. They no longer move of their own volition, but drift with wayward surges of current—most of the artery blocked off by the huge globe of silicon. It's possible to maneuver the *Primus* slowly between the walls of cellular matter, ride the upwelling fluids between cliffs of protein. The remarkable craft is truly in its element, with no raging torrent to combat, like a creature of the deep silently gliding toward a fellow predator.

The controls are light and responsive, barely noticeable as constructs and mechanisms, but more and more like an extension of human muscle and nerve and tissue. No, even more than that. Like an extension of human will.

Never experienced that in other submersibles—not like this.

It is unexpected and intoxicating. Addictive.

No time for that, now. There's a job to do.

The procedure has been established: get close, make contact with the shell, attempt to incinerate it. The "torch" is mounted on an extendable arm that can reach well beyond the lipid and protein coating of the *Primus*. Not a good idea to ignite the bomb casing and fry *Primus'* protective disguise.

The bomb is a behemoth. Close up, its wall is flat, with no perceptible curve. It's not pristine, either. There's a thick, gelatinous coating over most of the surface—the bomb's own protein disguise, plus the entrails of killer T cells that have given their lives in vain battle. Can the covering be penetrated? Probably. Will it catch fire itself? Or put out the flame? A help, or a hindrance?

Better try to find a clear spot.

That takes longer than expected, scanning the vast surface for patches of darker color, detouring around clinging, ragged appendages of milky protoplasm. Dodging drifting clumps of clotted jelly. No knowing what might damage the ship's protective cloak.

There. An octagonal area, shinier and nearly the size of a house wall.

Time to extend the torch arm. It moves smoothly, erupting through the sheath of protein—a skin peeling back like petals. A slight vibration as the probe tip contacts the surface of the bomb. The silicon shell won't burn, though enough heat can fuse it into another form. The success of the mission depends on igniting the chemicals within, destroying them before they can work their evil. The shell must be penetrated, but there's no way to be sure the torch arm won't crumple in an attempt to just force it through. That would be disastrous. Not repairable within the narrow window of time available. So, try to melt a hole through, instead. Heat the silicon into something glasslike and brittle.

If only the damn torch will light.

Its capacitor is inclined to discharge all of its power in one brief instant, but a step-down system is designed to allow it to burn for short bursts of several seconds. With luck, the sudden violent differential in temperature over a small area will make the silicon crack.

A slight forward thrust to keep contact . . . key the switch, close the circuit.

The flare of light is startling, like the painful brilliance of an arc welder.

The immediate reaction is to close the eyes, protect them. Except the danger is non-existent. This is *virtual* reality—the blinding light has no direct route to the retina. Real eyes are safe in a wire-and-plastic helmet somewhere far away. That's not the impression, though. The sun-like radiance burns a ragged bolt of lightning into the mind.

Tyson will be cheering, somewhere. The contraption works! Now shut it off to conserve power.

The sudden darkness afterward is impenetrable. Even with computer help, it takes long seconds to be able to see the bomb's surface again. A surface ravaged by a miniature sun played over its face. A surface . . . unscratched. Undented. Unmarked.

No sign of damage. A failure.

Is the heat being dissipated by the surrounding fluid, or channeled away by the silicon? No, silicon is not indiscriminately conductive. That's why they use it for computer chips. The fluid, too, is an unlikely conductor of the intense heat.

Could there be structural damage not visible to the eye? A hidden weakening of the molecular lattice? Maybe it's worth risking a tap.

A light shot of forward thrust.

Contact.

Nothing.

Try again, just a shade harder.

Nothing.

That's it, then. Don't dare use any more force. If the torch arm breaks the whole mission is over, the patient lost.

Something strange is going on: tiny globes have suddenly appeared nearby, and then edged away, most in the same direction. They scamper and skitter along the surface, like beetles across a tabletop. Are they alive? Are they molecules, broken free of the casing material, their attractive forces disrupted by the supercharged energy of the torch? *What are they?*

Bubbles.

Bubbles of hydrogen and oxygen, probably, containing only a few molecules each. Electrolysis. The fiery spark of the torch has split the surrounding water into its component gases. Common with underwater welding jobs. Not a hazard, because the potentially explosive gases float harmlessly away. They're not floating here, though, only sliding haphazardly over the surface, to join the gelatinous covering farther away. But they're not in the way. Focus on the job at hand.

Problem: the resistance of the shell material versus the charge life of the *Primus'* battery-like capacitor. That charge took the whole day's travel time to build up but will take only moments to expend. The charge gauge is like a bar graph in the corner of the heads-up display. It reads one quarter discharged already. Even if a second or third attempt succeeds in rupturing the shell, at what point will the charge be too low to kindle a spark? The ADP inside the bomb must be ignited before it leaks out.

Not much choice. Have to try again.

Another sunrise in this dark cavern. Another surge of bubbles chasing each other across the silicon shell.

Shut it off. Charge is down three-quarters. No, closer to seven-eighths. Look at the shell.

Nothing. Not a damn thing different.

Not enough charge left for another burn-through attempt.

What then? Brute force? Bump the surface with the side of the ship, while the silicon is still hot, and perhaps vulnerable? No time to waste thinking it over.

A tweak of the fan motors, the ship rotates . . . no hint of danger.

Danger?

An image frozen within a microsecond: the bubbles of gases pooled within and around the nearby cell residue . . . the white hot torch tip sliding over toward them . . . .

Then a blast that rocks the whole world.

16

Hunter lay in bed staring at the ceiling above his cot, and tried to make patterns out of the cracks and blemishes in the paint. His body ached like a wall had fallen on him. He felt weak. But it was all in his mind. Wasn't it?

He was asking that question far too often.

A phone call from Bridges had awakened him from evil dreams: dreams of helplessness. He remembered an image of quicksand or something similar, and then scuba diving, alone—something he never did in reality—and some part of the gear on his back snagged on an unreachable piece of wreckage in the dark night at the bottom of the sea.

Waking up was a relief. Except Bridges had called to say that Hunter's first therapy session was scheduled for right after breakfast.

Damn. He'd hoped everyone had forgotten about that.

Would they have let it remain forgotten if he hadn't lost his cool the night before?

He pictured the last moments of the mission as the errant torch ignited the oxygen and hydrogen bubbles trapped next to the bomb casing. The explosion was tremendous on that scale, tossing the *Primus* like a wood splinter in a tornado, embedding it deeply into the wall of the blood vessel.

And worse, the bomb's shell had cracked, spilling its cargo of ADP.

Stunned by the blast, both physically and mentally, Hunter had somehow kept enough presence of mind to free the ship and then dump its own cargo of plasmin and anticoagulant, spreading it as widely as possible. It had worked—no clot had formed.

More remarkably, the giant blast had peeled back the ship's fragile shielding of lipids and proteins, but not beyond its ability to self-repair. That was the good news.

The bad news was that the pressure wave of the explosion had burst open the artery and several others surrounding it, enough to leave a noticeable mark on the patient's face from the spilled blood. With its plasmin supply gone, there was no choice but to remove the *Primus* from the body so it could be re-stocked, a task that was still far from routine.

Gage was furious. Tyson sulked. Tamiko avoided him, and Mallory simply made herself scarce, as she often did.

Kierkegaard pointed out that the potential for such accidents was the very reason that *Primus* carried a cargo of plasmin in the first place. But his calm acceptance only made it harder for Hunter to accept his own failure.

That night, he made a serious dent in the base canteen's supply of bourbon, then proceeded to smash things. He even tried to pick a fight. None of that was like him, not even when drunk; but then, it hadn't felt like him doing it. It was as if he were an outside observer, detached and curious, watching his body behave outrageously.

He didn't plan to mention any of that to Bridges.

"We need to talk." The older man looked up from the file he was reading, removed a pair of glasses and slid them onto the desk. "Sit down. Be comfortable. I know the suits are expecting me to do some kind of official assessment, or even perform some sort of trauma therapy with you, but I don't want it to be like that. I just want us to talk, all right?"

"You mean I don't have to lie down on the couch?"

"If you can find one, be my guest. They took mine out ages ago. I think they suspected I was taking too many naps on it."

"When I agreed to this, Kierkegaard said it would just be a formality. I wouldn't even have to say a word."

"And I think he meant it. But you screwed up last night."

The sub pilot tried to come up with a sarcastic reply, but all he said was, "Yeah, I know."

"Devon Kierkegaard isn't easily impressed, but he's been impressed with you—especially your coolness under pressure. Now, all of a sudden you go smashing things. Why?"

"I...I don't know. I really don't. Something just snapped."

"Have you given up on the project? Do you want to quit?"

"No."

"Is there a personality problem with someone on the team?"

"No. It's nothing like that. I'm just frustrated, I guess."

"It's a difficult undertaking. It must be frustrating a lot of the time. What made this time different?"

Hunter shook his head. "I have no idea. No, that's not true. I felt like this one was all my fault. I didn't have any technical problem to blame it on. I screwed up. Simple as that." He looked into Bridges' face. "I don't like to screw up."

"I'd say that's obvious." The doctor reached for the folder and put his glasses back on. "You don't like to talk about your accident."

"No. And I don't intend to talk about it now."

"Why not? Did you feel that you screwed up that time, too? Were you to blame?"

Hunter let his annoyance show. "You've obviously read the report. It was inconclusive. The evidence was too confused to draw any final conclusion. I don't think I did anything wrong. I don't remember doing anything wrong."

"Do you think we're pushing you too hard? Expecting too much of you?

The younger man was puzzled by the question. Then his face lit with recognition.

"*Shit.* My father—you're trying to link this to my father. For Christ's sake, Bridges, every shrink I went to after the accident brought that up. Haven't you guys come up with any new theories since Freud?"

Hunter stood up angrily, but didn't leave the room. Instead he walked to a nearby wall and tried to find something to look at. "Yes, my father had high expectations of me. Yes, I disappointed him by washing out of college football. Sometimes I try too hard to prove myself. And by the way, if I continue this bullshit psychoanalysis for you do I get a cut of your pay?"

He turned back to face the desk. "Dammit, Doctor, there's a hell of a lot riding on this project. Can't it just be that I was fried and had too much to drink?"

Bridges looked calmly back. "Are you trying to convince me? Or yourself?"

"Like I've never heard that one before. What happened to the *I'm your friend, not your shrink* approach?"

"I'm trying to be your friend."

"Then cut the psych textbook stuff. I've had my fill for a lifetime."

The room went quiet. Hunter felt like sitting down, but didn't want to put himself back into the role of patient.

"Maybe we should be shooting the breeze over a couple of beers," Bridges said softly.

"Good idea."

"Why do you drink so much?"

The question caught Hunter off guard. He grasped for a pat answer.

"I like it. I learned to like beer in college, and bourbon was even better, when I could afford it."

"Do you drink when you're scuba diving?"

"No, that would be stupid. You can't afford to make mistakes. Even tying one on the night before makes you more susceptible to decompression sickness and nitrogen narcosis. Divers who do that don't live long."

"So you can control it. You can choose not to drink so much."

"Of course I can control it. What are you suggesting, that I'm an alcoholic?"

Bridges didn't back down. "Then it's OK to be drunk or hungover as long as it isn't *your* life at stake."

The shot struck home. Hunter's fingers clenched the foam of the chair back.

"Are you implying that my drinking is impairing my work on this project?"

"I don't know, I'm not there. You tell me."

Hunter was about to snap off a bitter reply, when a sudden thought struck him hard. He sank slowly into the chair, while his mind raced. There had been times when his interface with the VR equipment had come effortlessly, like an extension of his own body, and other times when it had been a painful struggle. Was that the fault of the alcohol? He found that he couldn't rule it out.

Bridges sensed an advantage and pressed on. "Do you take risks when you dive?"

Hunter sat still. His voice was quieter when he answered.

"No, I don't. I did some yahoo stuff when I was young and stupid. Not for long."

"Is that because you had an accident? Got into trouble?"

"It never went that far. I remember one time early on when a buddy of mine talked me into doing a deep dive—beyond what I'd been trained for. One hundred and fifty feet, on ordinary air, not mixed gases. Cold water. Dark. Very risky. You can get seriously *narc*'d that way—nitrogen narcosis—and forget to check your air, or anything." His face was blank as he stared at the wall, reliving the memory. "I went down to about a hundred feet and then called it off. In fact, I faked a problem with my mask."

"You were scared?"

"Sure I was scared. That's not why I called it off."

"Why did you?"

"Because it was stupid. I knew it was stupid going in. It just took me a while to realize that being stupid wasn't something to be proud of."

The doctor leaned back in his chair, then said softly, "Maybe you need to remind yourself of that a little more often."

## 17

The briefing room was still, the atmosphere thick. A draft of air-conditioned air from the wall vents only stirred the tension.

Kierkegaard, both hands planted firmly on the desk, raised his head to survey the room. He spared no breath for trivialities.

"Did anyone anticipate that the oxygen and hydrogen given off by the torch could ignite?"

After a moment, Tyson moved his right hand, as if he'd intended to raise it, but realized there was no need. "Mallory . . . ," he began. "Mallory and I discussed it once. We felt it was very unlikely." His discomfort was evident.

"So unlikely that you felt it unnecessary to mention to any of the rest of us? Why?"

Tyson licked his lips. "Because bubbles created by such processes rise, as all bubbles do. They displace the surrounding fluid, are buoyant, and travel in the direction opposite to the pull of gravity. It must be so. We concluded that any bubbles produced by the action of the torch might collect on the ceiling of the blood vessel, and so be of no concern."

"Except that *ceiling* turned out to be the shell of the bomb. *Primus* was working in a vertical position, and the gases did not conveniently get out of the way, but collected nearby." The Kierkegaard's tones were calm, but cold. His stating of the facts in such simple terms was an implied rebuke to the high caliber minds ranged in front of him. He knew it. He did not wait for an answer, but continued, "And although that state of affairs was clearly visible in the monitor, no one thought to mention the danger?"

"I was not. . . . ," Tyson had begun to say *not in the room*, but realized that it sounded like an excuse. He had been monitoring events from time to time in another lab. He looked over at Mallory. Her head was down. She'd been one of the assigned observers for the mission.

Hunter cleared his throat and spoke. "I should have caught it. I've done underwater welding before—I've even seen the gases collect on the underside of ships' hulls. I just didn't recognize what I was seeing. I should have. It's my fault."

Kierkegaard turned his face toward the submariner, but his expression did not change. "Much as I appreciate your attempt to take the blame upon yourself, Mr. Hunter, the fact is—as I'll remind everyone . . ." He swiveled his head to include them all, "This is a team effort. It does not—it *cannot* rely on one man. Mr. Hunter has enough on his plate just piloting our unique craft under circumstances never encountered before. He must have all the help he can get." He looked at Tyson and Mallory. "I trust that you will share any future insights you may have with the whole group."

He allowed a long moment for his words to sink in. Then he straightened his back and assumed his familiar stance. The lecture was over. There was work to be done.

"Now. What we must solve is the real reason behind what happened: the failure of the torch to cut through the shell of the bomb. Dr. Tyson, any thoughts?"

It was an offer to redeem himself. The scientist took it.

"We had expected that the non-conductive properties of the silicon would act in our favor, and heat would remain concentrated in one small area. That would have allowed the spark to melt a hole in the shell. Unfortunately, it appears there is enough conductivity at this scale, especially with the effect of the surrounding liquid, to dissipate much of the energy."

"Hunter?"

"It's a common problem."

"What's the common solution?"

"What we've got on the *Primus* is like an arc welder. I've never trained as a welder. I've only seen arc welding done, as an assistant. There are special alloy welding tips for specific purposes. They produce different temperatures and different types of results. It's the same with cutting tools. Some rigs also use high pressure gas jets to dry out the weld site while the welding or cutting takes place." He looked at their leader. "I don't see any of that helping us, sir. We can't exactly lay the *Primus* over for a retrofit."

"No, we cannot. Anyone else?"

"It has to do with the micro-distances involved," Tyson said. "As you know, we weren't completely sure that it would work."

"Can we turn up the heat? Make a hotter spark?" Kierkegaard asked.

"In fact, we can," the engineer replied. "But the cost may be one we're not able to pay."

"How do you mean?"

"The device we're using to power the torch is essentially a capacitor. It stores up an electrical charge drawn from the surrounding molecules of the body. Its natural tendency is to discharge that energy all at once. One of our most difficult tasks was to create a system that would release that charge more slowly, to sustain the torch for a few seconds of cutting time. In doing so, we have to sacrifice some heat. If we allow the capacitor to release all of its energy in one quick burst, we will produce a hotter spark."

"But ... ?"

"But there will be no charge left to ignite the contents of the bomb. It would not catch fire the way the hydrogen and oxygen did, from the hot tip of the torch alone. We will have punched a hole through the hard casing, only to allow the ADP to slowly leak out while the *Primus* is building up another charge."

"Which could be as long as six to eight hours, our time?"

"That's right, sir."

"That would also limit us to one or maybe two missions a day," Hunter interjected. "Does our patient have that much time?"

"I'm sure none of us missed the significance, Mr. Hunter. What are the other alternatives, then? Any suggestions? Anyone?" Kierkegaard's hands remained casually clasped behind his back. He was under tremendous pressure, but it was impossible to read in his face or body language. The group needed to believe they could solve this problem. That he was sure they could solve it. That was exactly the confidence he showed to them. Even so, no-one spoke, cowed by the thought of their recent error, or simply out of ideas. Finally Hunter felt compelled to break the silence.

"Ram them," he said simply.

"*Ram them?*" Kierkegaard echoed, as if he hadn't heard properly. All of the heads in the room turned with expressions of disbelief.

"That's right. Run the ship into the shells of the bombs with enough force to open them. If we can."

"And spill the ADP all at once?" Gage's voice was thickly sarcastic. "We've just found a brilliant way to do that. Why search for more?"

"Obviously we'd have to find the smallest amount of force we could get away with." Hunter said. "Crack open a hole large enough for the torch probe to fit through, without spilling too much of the ADP. Once inside, the electrolysis from the torch may even provide fuel for the fire we need. A fire has to have oxygen."

His words were met with silence. "You've told me that, except for the sensor array, the *Primus* is nearly indestructible. I'm not talking about taking chances with the manipulator arms. We'd swing them out of the way and batter the shell with the nose of the sub."

Hunter's body was stretched forward over the desk, to press his point with more intensity. He leaned back slowly and softly concluded, "I don't think we have any other choice."

Their faces were like stone. Kierkegaard waited for someone else to raise an objection, but when none came, he targeted them individually.

"Dr. Mallory, you first. Your thoughts on this idea, please."

The biochemist shifted uncomfortably in her chair. She cleared her throat and couldn't bring herself to look at Hunter. "I think it's a foolish risk, sir. We have only one *Primus*. It is irreplaceable. If it is damaged, the mission . . . the whole project is over." She looked around the room for support. "The patient would die. We would have failed the president, and the country. There must be a better way."

"As soon as you find it, be sure to let me know. Dr. Tamiko?"

She turned her dark eyes to the pilot across from her. "It's understandable that Mr. Hunter would favor a simple, direct approach—brute force, rather than science—but I think we all know that this is a very complicated situation, with engineering, chemical, and biological challenges never encountered before. To suggest that the best solution is to take a nearly miraculous piece of engineering, and . . . use it as a *battering ram* . . . is not worth considering, sir. We simply can't do it."

"And the alternative is . . . ? No, I suspected as much. Gage? Tyson?"

With nothing new to offer, Gage simply reiterated points made by Mallory and Tamiko in an even more condescending manner. Tyson, however, was silent for a moment, then said simply, "I think it could work."

There were startled reactions around the room. Kierkegaard raised an eyebrow.

"A solution doesn't always have to be complicated, sir," Hunter offered. "Sometimes the simple way is the best way."

Kierkegaard nodded, and then turned his back to them for a full minute, staring at a pull-down diagram of the patient's circulatory system, as if asking for her help to make such a difficult decision. At last, he turned back and said, "I agree. Let's get to it."

There was no further discussion. His word was law.

This time Kierkegaard did not leave first, but stood by the door while the others withdrew. Hunter was last of all. Before he could turn down the corridor, Kierkegaard stopped him.

"Forget what I said in there, Mr. Hunter. It was your fault. See that it doesn't happen again." And he walked away.

## 18

Studying the diagrams for the next mission made Hunter feel a little voyeuristic and he was amused to see an outright blush on Tyson's face. The target site was in the skin of the upper chest, along the inner curve of the patient's left breast. The *Primus* had been removed in order to replenish its chemical cargo of countermeasures, but they weren't re-loaded yet. It was decided to use the cargo hold to collect a fluid sample, once the "burn" had been accomplished.

The re-insertion went badly wrong. They miscalculated on the depth. Or the patient's skin twitched at the wrong moment, or the needle simply missed by a fraction of a millimeter. Whatever the reason, the ship was released a hair's breadth from its target. On that scale, it was like entering the basement of a skyscraper and having to navigate to the penthouse, using only the stairwells and the corridors.

Tamiko had mapped the area well, and had refined her navigation system to place simplified two-dimensional maps in the corner of Hunter's heads up display. She no longer gave him verbal directions unless absolutely required. It was an added burden, to read the maps and steer the craft on his own while still dodging the hazards of the bloodstream. But verbal directions had been too much of a distraction, interfering with his use of the VR link.

He'd tried to explain to Truman Bridges about the enhanced sense of *presence* that he'd been experiencing: the unexpected something extra in the way his mind was processing the VR input. The doctor had offered the word *'dasein'*. It was a term coined by a German philosopher of the mid-1900's, Martin Heidegger, to explain the peculiar status of human existence. The word conveyed a sense of being not only physically present within a system, but also being an essential, interactive part of the whole.

Whatever you called it, verbal communications interrupted his sense of *connection* the way a flash of bright light ruined night vision—it took crucial seconds each time before he could fully process all of the sensory input again. For that period of time, his full immersion in the three-dimensional environment was reduced to a two-dimensional representation on a screen, accessible by his vision only. It was a serious impairment. So Tamiko removed herself from the equation, and gave him near-autonomy. A few quick tests showed that the system was efficient and elegant—the lady knew what she was doing, and he'd said so.

Neither suspected it would be wasted effort.

Within minutes of beginning the mission, dismay washed over him. Tamiko's maps were clear and precise, simplified just enough to make them easy to scan, yet providing exactly the information he needed. They were placed in precisely the right spot in his display so as not to block his vision. They were just what he'd asked for.

And they produced exactly the same distracting effect as the verbal commands.

All sense of unity vanished. His *dasein* collapsed. The only difference was that he had to mentally perform the disconnect himself by putting aside his mind's acceptance of the reality it was processing, and forcing it to see the images as a flat screen once again. It was the only way he could see the HUD. It was like changing the focus of his eyes from a video screen across a large room to words on the page of a book only centimeters away. His mind's eye quickly grew fatigued, and his head began to ache.

He didn't dare say anything. Tamiko would think he was trying to discredit her. Hunter hadn't explained about his special connectedness to anyone but Bridges. The others would consider it total bullshit.

What choice did that leave him? If he kept trying to switch back and forth, he could miss something important, or even cause a collision. He would soon have a splitting headache. If he ignored the maps he would get hopelessly lost, and the result of one missed turn on the last mission was only too fresh in his memory. Was there a compromise that would work?

Maybe he could quickly memorize the key details from each map as it came up, then navigate for as long as possible from memory. Tamiko would have no way of knowing how often he accessed the display. He'd just have to be careful not to trust too far to his power of recall.

It worked. Memorizing the maps became easier with practice, and he soon fell into a routine: a quick look to commit the pattern of colored lines to memory, followed by a long period of careful steering, reveling in the deeper feeling of *dasein* . . . of *connection*.

Inevitably, as his comfort increased, his glances at the heads up display grew shorter, the periods between, longer.

There came a time when he just *knew* where he was going. The route took a convoluted series of turns, switchbacks, and extended runs around countless obstacles, through nearly every possible plane of motion. Yet he didn't get lost.

And then, the bomb was there, in front of him, vast and menacing, and it was time to put the second part of the plan into play.

Easy to suggest, terrifying to carry out. His mind filled with the vision of a billion dollars in super-advanced technology crumpling into useless junk. Swallowing hard, he steered straight into the bomb and knew right away that the force of the impact was too small. He backed up and did it again, harder. Each jolt from each progressively stronger collision, made him shudder right along with his craft. He didn't want to know what the other team members were thinking.

The manipulator arms folded neatly back along the body of the ship. As long as he could keep the craft straight, *Primus* herself should not suffer damage. He kept telling himself that.

He was right. With the sixth collision, at a speed he'd carefully noted, he could see a split in the bomb's shell. It was small and narrow, but once the molecular bonds were broken it might grow quickly into a significant leak. Hunter didn't hesitate. He slipped the tip of the torch deftly into the hole, and hit the ignition button.

At first nothing seemed to happen. The spark formed, but with no result. He pictured the bubbles of oxygen and hydrogen boiling furiously away from the electric fire. With any luck, the hydrogen would dissipate, but the stream of oxygen would ignite and . . . .

Whoomp! Hunter saw the thin shell of the bomb light up from within like a flame inside a Chinese paper lantern. A spray of burning material jetted through the hole, past the still-embedded probe. He'd left it there like the Dutch boy's finger in the dike, to prevent a flood of burning chemicals that might ignite the proteins and plasma of the surrounding blood. The probe wouldn't burn.

He watched in awe as the lantern flickered and flared, and eventually died. Once the amount of carbon dioxide and other waste products of combustion grew greater than the combustibles themselves, the fire could burn no longer. Hunter withdrew the torch, rotated the ship, and opened the cargo bay, deliberately left empty for this run. When he was reasonably sure a small sampling of material had been sucked into the bay, he maneuvered *Primus* to its removal location.

# # #

Tests of the sample showed that virtually all of the ADP had been consumed by the fire. They finally had an unqualified success.

Kierkegaard made a special point of praising Hunter and Tamiko.

"Together, your navigation was right on the money. Exactly what we needed. Thank you."

As he left the room with a rare smile on his face, most of the others followed. Hunter turned and caught Tamiko staring at him with a mixture of incredulity and chagrin.

"What is it? Did I do something wrong? We found the bomb, didn't we?"

"Yes, but you took a wrong turn."

"Why didn't you tell me?"

"Devon told me not to. The others didn't see." He could tell that she was angry, but there was something more behind it. Something he couldn't read.

"But I still found the bomb. I must have subconsciously used the map to get back on track right away."

"No," she said, shaking her head slowly in puzzlement. "You went completely off course. I had no maps prepared for that contingency. You found a new route all on your own."

## 19

They couldn't run another mission until mid-morning of the next day, at least. The *Primus* had to be re-loaded with its plasmin cargo. Hunter chafed at the delay. A full-sized submarine could probably be re-armed and re-stocked in a similar amount of time, because they could use as many people as needed for the task. With a vessel the size of a virus, and cargo measured by the molecule, the process could not be hurried.

As he drifted down a hallway, Tamiko came out of a nearby lab room. He nodded and meant to go on his way, but she thrust out an arm to stop him.

"How did you find your way on your own? Find the bomb. Tell me."

He sighed. "Luck, Lucy . . . just luck. How hard could it be?"

She pointed with one arm and pressed against his back with the other. He entered the lab and stood near her as she used a few keystrokes to call up an image on a large monitor. It was a picture of the patient's chest in false colors, possibly infrared, with a sheet placed carefully to conceal her nipples. This time Hunter found himself more aroused than embarrassed. The site of the mission was highlighted by a small red circle. Tamiko tapped some more keys and the view zoomed in, concluding with a computer-generated rendering of a cross-section of tissue. Its diameter had to be extremely small, yet it contained a daunting tangle of blue, red, and grey lines: blood vessels and lymph vessels. He swung his head away from the monitor and found himself looking at Tamiko's cleavage above the square-cut neckline of the knit cotton top she wore. He quickly looked up, but her frown confirmed that she'd caught the motion.

"If you can keep your eyes on the screen," she said thickly, "you'll see the path we had planned for the *Primus* to take . . . ." She punched a key and a jagged pattern of lines glowed brighter red. "And the way you actually went." The second string of vessels glowed yellow.

It was easy to see where it deviated from the first, and carried on for a significant distance before concluding at the same point: the bomb. It reminded Hunter of the mazes in puzzle books that a favorite aunt had occasionally bought him when he was a kid. There weren't supposed to be two solutions.

Tamiko turned to him again, her mouth set tightly. "How hard could it be, you asked? You made at least ten turns after going off course. Ten turns, apparently at random, and yet you still managed to reach the target. The odds against a flipped coin landing on heads ten times in a row are more than a thousand to one. This . . . *this* . . . ." She swept her hand toward the monitor. "I don't know how to calculate it."

"It's not as preposterous as you think," he said. "Most of the time in there I only have one possible turning at a given moment. I can take it or leave it. It is like flipping a coin. That makes it long odds, sure, but not impossible."

"Ridiculous," Tamiko snapped. "Each change of course provided dozens of completely new possibilities. Yet you beat those odds and managed to find the bomb. Luck! Do you actually expect me to believe that? How stupid do you think I am?"

"Well then, what do you think happened?" He didn't really expect an answer. He just didn't know what else to say.

"I've thought about that." She reached over and cleared the display on the screen. "Since Devon told me not to say anything about the course deviation, and then pretended afterward that nothing had happened, it's pretty clear. The two of you cooked up another course somehow, and followed that instead. What I can't figure out is why he'd send me off on a wild goose chase with all the resources that went into the new nav system."

"Oh, for Pete's sake, Lucy. Kierkegaard wouldn't do that to you. Neither would I. There has to be a logical explanation but I honestly don't know what it is. Maybe you and I can figure it out together." He raised his hands in a placatory gesture and said, "Have a drink with me. I could use one. Especially now."

"Why? So I can watch you smash some more glassware?"

He shook his head, embarrassed that her already-poor opinion of him had sunk to a new low. "No, I . . . I don't drink that much anymore." And he wanted to believe it himself. "Just a beer or two. Wherever you want to go. I need a break from this place, and we . . . we need to build some trust. We're on the same side. Honest."

Her face was still dark with anger, but she finally nodded and walked from the room, flicking off the lights as she went. The object of her displeasure followed a few steps behind.

The club was in a part of the base he hadn't seen before. The clientele appeared to include more civilians than the other base watering holes. That would make sense. Lucy Tamiko had a low tolerance for the military type.

She made no pretense of asking his preference, walking straight to a corner booth and saying nothing until after the waitress had taken her order for a martini. Hunter felt the urge to comment on her choice, but decided against it. Right then, she would take everything he said as implied criticism.

While they waited for the drinks to arrive he thought hard to come up with some small talk that might lighten the mood.

"Tamiko . . . it sounds Japanese, but you don't look . . . ."

"My father was Japanese, my mother was Filipino, and I was born in Canada."

"You're Canadian? How did you get in on a secret project like this one?"

"I imagine Devon had to pull a few strings, but it shouldn't have been that hard. Most Americans don't make much of a distinction between Americans and Canadians—they mainly figure we're American-wannabees."

"Is it true?"

"No. Oh there are a few who'd like us to become the fifty-first state. There are also Americans who choose to go north and live in Canada. But mostly we admire the good things you do, shake our heads at the bad things, soak up your culture, and congratulate ourselves that we don't have your race and gun problems."

"Why did you come here, then?"

She sighed. "Like a lot of others—about half of Hollywood, I think—I found there just weren't enough opportunities in my field in my own country. So you go where the work is. America's been good to me. I have no complaints."

He couldn't decide where to go from there, but then the drinks arrived. Once the waitress was gone, his companion wasted no more time.

"So why would you and Devon lead me on . . . keep me out of the loop? Tell the truth—nobody can hear us."

Hunter sighed as he leaned back in the chair, took a long sip of bourbon, and set his glass down firmly. "OK. Forget about me for the moment. Why in the world do you think Devon would do that to you? His job is nearly impossible as it is, without wasting the few resources we have."

"I don't know why," Tamiko hissed. "I only know that what you did isn't explainable by luck, and until you offer me a better explanation . . . ."

"*There isn't an explanation you'll like any better.* That's what I'm trying to tell you. I don't understand it myself. Somehow I just . . . know where to go. I've been feeling that kind of thing more and more each time I go *inside*. I don't know if it's just that my brain is adapting to the VR equipment, or if something else is . . . guiding me." Her face was taut—non-committal, but clearly skeptical. "I know that sounds ridiculous, but I truly can't describe it any other way."

Would she accept that? She took a gulp of her drink and made a face.

"Damn drink has too much vermouth. Well, at least I'm convinced that I'm not going to hear a more believable explanation from you tonight." Her hand tapped the table irritably. "I need a smoke. Except I quit. You smoke?"

"Nah, alcoholism is enough for me."

She didn't smile, but she didn't bite his head off, either. "Are you really an alcoholic?"

"I don't . . . think so," he said. "I may have had a few too many the last while. Doc Bridges would probably tell you it's a reaction to an accident I had a while ago. But in the oil rig business, it was just a given that you downed a few beers after your shift to replace all the sweat you lost. Maybe now it's time to cut down. Not so much manual labor involved in my current job." He smiled to himself, and thought he actually saw a softening in her face. Or had he just imagined it? "You date many alcoholics?" he asked.

Her eyebrows shot up. "Don't go thinking this is a date. I don't date people I work with."

"Why not? A bad experience?"

"That's not a story I need to tell you."

"Just please tell me it didn't involve someone on our team."

She gave a look of disgust. "Who did you think I'd be romancing? Skylar Tyson? Kenneth Gage? Or did you figure Lorelei and I had a little fling?"

He laughed. "So what, then? No, let me guess . . . you were a graduate student, or an intern, and he was a professor. A May/September thing."

She glared at him. "I was a full faculty member, I'll have you know. More than that, you don't need to know. Anyway, it was a good thing. It made me realize that the academic environment wasn't right for me. I needed to be in research. At the cutting edge."

"Well you made it there, in spades. But it seems to me you just admitted that dating a co-worker could be a good thing." He smiled and took another sip of bourbon. She responded with a look of annoyance, then put the ball back in his court.

"So why don't you have a girlfriend waiting off-base to fill your spare time? Or do you?"

"Nope." He shook his head. "Not as of a few months ago, anyway. I figure it's just as well."

"Why? What happened?"

He swallowed the last of his drink and ordered another for each of them.

"Ever hear of a place called Stingray City?" he asked, watching the waitress walk away.

"Stingrays . . . cars or fish? No, wait—I have heard of it. In the Cayman Islands, right?"

"Yeah. It's a shallow sand bar in the middle of a big lagoon on Grand Cayman. The stingrays gather there like pigeons in a park, waiting for people to feed them. Dozens and dozens of them, tame as anything. Charter groups have been going there for years. A guide feeds them scraps of squid while you stand in chest-deep water with mask and fins, watching. Touching. I mean these things swoop around you . . . between your legs, sometimes. One of them even gave me a hickey on my back—I must've rubbed against a bit of squid."

"Doesn't anybody ever get stung?"

"They say nobody ever has. Of course, you're pretty careful about where you step, but they aren't menacing. They're fantastic to watch—some are about a foot-and-a-half across, others are twice that. Or more. It's amazing."

"Except your lady friend didn't like it."

"Hated it." He nodded. "Freaked her right out. I couldn't even get her to go back in the water for the rest of the trip. Then I made the mistake of reminding her about it a few weeks later."

"At a party? No . . . in the bedroom."

"Yeah, stupid move. I pretended I was a stingray, swooping around . . . . She went into hysterics and started throwing things at me." He gave a sheepish laugh at the memory. "I think it was then that we got the idea maybe we weren't the perfect match." He took the second bourbon from the waitress, and took a long sip. The image in his mind was comical, but the memory was still painful.

Tamiko shook her head, but couldn't help smiling. "Of course you weren't a good match. You're a scuba diver, right? And a submersible pilot. Obviously you like to be out there, exploring on the edge. You needed somebody with the same curiosity as you, and a scientific mind."

"Yeah. That's what I've been thinking lately, too." He paused, looking at her eyes, gauging them. Then, "You know there's a place . . . ."

"*Hunter! Tamiko!*"

They looked around for the source of the voice. It was Gage, approaching from a few tables away. He motioned with his arm.

"Devon's pouring champagne in the staff lounge. He sent me to find you. Come on!"

Hunter looked at Tamiko with a twinge of regret, and imagined that he saw the same thing mirrored in her eyes. They quickly finished their drinks and followed their comrade.

The rest of the project team was scattered around the room in comfortable chairs, glasses in hand. Clearly the others had consumed a few rounds before their arrival, and Gage hastened to the nearest bottle to make up for lost time.

"There you are," Kierkegaard welcomed them. "I thought it would do us all some good to have a bit of a celebration, now that we really have something to celebrate." He poured them generous servings of the champagne, and they chose a couple of seats next to each other. Evidently their entrance had interrupted a friendly discussion that quickly resumed.

"It's the...audacity of what we're doing that gets to me," Tyson began. "Sometimes I just can't accept the reality of it all."

"But what is reality?" Gage smiled. "That's the crux, isn't it? Look at Hunter. One minute he's here in front of us, swilling champagne. The next, he's parading around a human body, riding a machine that's so small we can't see it with the naked eye. Or at least his mind is. Isn't that what counts? Which is the real Hunter, the big one, or the little one?" He laughed and gulped half a glass of wine. "What do you think, Hunter? Which is the real you?"

The *Primus* pilot was caught completely off guard. The offhand remark was too close to the question that had begun to dominate his own mind.

Bridges came to his rescue. "It's the *Tao*. Universal oneness. Hunter is real in both places at the same time, because he exists in all places at all times. So does everything else."

Gage snorted. "Oriental mysticism, Truman?" He tossed back the remains of his glass and filled it again.

"Just because they didn't view the cosmos with modern scientific instruments doesn't mean they didn't see," the psychologist replied. "An eighth-century Indian philosopher named Samkara said we're all part of the *One-Self*, and the attributes that make us individuals are only like a jar filled with air. The jar makes it seem as if the air inside it is separate from the air outside, but it's the same air. Only when we fully realize and accept our oneness with the *One-Self* are we eternally reunited with it. Indian mystics spend their lives trying to achieve that." He swallowed some champagne. "Even F.H. Bradley, at Oxford in the late 1800's, believed that everything that exists is part of a seamless whole, and only the whole can be considered ultimately real."

"I don't think I buy that," Tamiko objected. "That's like saying I don't have any individual choice. Determinism. I hate that idea."

"Not quite determinism." Bridges shook his head. "I'm not saying that all of our actions are set in stone. You act according to your nature, but the way you're meant to act as an integral part of the whole."

"I'd forgotten you were such a student of philosophy." Kierkegaard raised a glass to their medical man. "I don't believe we can come to a complete understanding of the things we're doing by purely scientific means. And we have to remember that everything we do can have an effect on many other aspects of our world." His face was solemn.

"I can agree that there are a lot of connections in the universe," Gage said. "Six degrees of separation, and all that. But it's not all one big unit."

"But the closeness of those connections is critical," Bridges insisted. "The philosopher Leibniz believed that each individual object or entity has a certain range of individual action, but affects every other entity so profoundly that we could learn the essential attributes of any one of them by really coming to understand the essence of any other. Even Alfred North Whitehead, at Harvard last century, talked about a *nexus*, meaning the interconnection or inter-relatedness of entities throughout the universe."

"I think you've had too much to drink, Doctor." Tamiko laughed. "You're starting to speak a language all your own."

"Not mine, that's for sure." Bridges smiled. "The words of many wise souls over centuries, as they tried to make sense out of what we experience."

"But we're talking about *virtual* reality." Skylar Tyson sat forward. "A person using Dr. Gage's equipment sees and hears...maybe even feels things detected by the instruments of the ship, then the brain processes it into meaningful sensory information. The perception is *like* reality, but the person isn't really there...in the bloodstream, I mean."

Bridges raised his glass of champagne, peering at the engineer through the bubbles in the amber liquid. "Perhaps the perception is everything," he answered. "Whatever ultimate reality is, our only way of experiencing it at all is through our senses. We perceive things as real, so who's to say they are not?"

Kenneth Gage gave a wicked laugh, and then said loudly, turning to look at Hunter, "It's like the old question: If you're killed in a dream, are you really *dead*?"

## 20

The water was black...black as eternal solitude.

The edge of the abyss, a place where the cocoon that gave him refuge would be crushed like a discarded paper cup.

Amorphous behemoths battered against it in their fury, determined to repulse the intruder. Punish him for his presence: a defilement to be cleansed.

He could feel the shift, the slide.

And then the fall without end.

He threw himself forward over his knees and gasped for air.

His hands clutched at the sheets of the bed, desperately trying to hold onto reality and not slip back into the dream. His eyes stared wildly into blackness until finally he fumbled for the bedside lamp.

The familiar sights of his quarters nearly brought him to tears. His body shook.

He thought, *If you're killed in a dream, are you really dead?*

# # #

He awoke again before dawn, and couldn't get back to sleep. Breakfast wouldn't be available for a couple of hours. Even coffee would be hard to come by, unless someone nearby had been working through the night and had a pot on the go. Probably no one on his team—they'd still be sleeping off the effects of the champagne. It was strange to think that he'd likely had less to drink than any of them. Had he been trying to impress Lucy Tamiko? Or Truman Bridges?

There was a coffee machine at the far end of the building, near the administrative offices. He pulled on the pants he'd worn the day before, and shuffled down the hall.

The coffee was as bad as every other vending machine coffee he'd ever had, but it was hot. He sipped at it as he wandered back through the building. Then something caught his eye in one of the cubicles. It was a computer, left on overnight, with a screen saver of one of the aquariums at Sea World. Ripples of light and shade chased each other through the water, and once in a while a large shape would come into the foreground, speed past, and then disappear again. It was a killer whale, an orca, that teased the viewer by cavorting off in the distance, and then occasionally allowing itself to be seen up close. He'd never dived with one of those, only the occasional shark, and that not by choice.

Now he adventured in an *inner* ocean, among creatures far stranger and more mysterious than orcas and sharks.

His thoughts turned to their patient. The same old questions nagged at him: who was she? Who had done this to her, and why? His need to know grew with every mission. It was more than simple curiosity. His sojourns within her body had become a...

relationship—a connection between them that grew deeper all the time. It was pointless to deny that.

He looked back to the computer. On impulse, he grabbed the mouse and began to search the directory. It wasn't likely that classified information would be left on an unsecured computer, but there might be hints. References in medical records... anything.

The information on the machine appeared to be mostly finance-related. He searched for files that had been modified within the past few days. Nothing looked promising. He typed in the name of the first lady. "No files found." The president. Nothing. He tried to think of other high-profile women in the government, but could only remember the name of the Surgeon General, and wasn't sure he'd spelled her name correctly.

No luck.

He glanced at the clock on the wall. When did the day shift start in this area? Weren't there security guards who made their rounds?

He was pretty sure he would be able to hear someone coming, and there were exits at both ends of the room. He turned back to the screen.

The patient had to be someone prominent. You didn't commandeer a multi-billion-dollar research project for the average Joe on the street. Or Jane. He thought again about the news websites. A government functionary in the spotlight would need to give the press some kind of explanation for her frequent visits to an Air Force Base, or disappearances for a day or two at a time.

As he launched the computer's web browser, it struck him that the project staff might even monitor news stories to make sure reporters weren't getting too close to the truth. He checked the "Favorites" list.

All of the usual default sites were there: CNN, Fox News, ABC News, CBS, several major newspapers, plus a handful that looked like military sites. He couldn't tell if some were accessed more regularly than others. What about the browser history? If someone had been sloppy about clearing it at the end of the day....

Suddenly he heard footsteps on a hard floor coming down the hallway behind him, approaching quickly. He shut down the browser and ran out the other end of the room on the balls of his feet, crouched over to keep his head below the tops of cubicle walls. Once in the clear, he slowed to a walk.

Damn. He'd nearly been caught without finding out anything useful. He wouldn't get many more opportunities like that.

Would it be better after all if he didn't learn her identity? If he could think of her clinically and objectively as a faceless Jane Doe to be treated and forgotten?

Impossible. He didn't merely breach her flesh with cold instruments of steel and plastic, he trespassed within her very life's blood with his mind. A connection so close he was almost afraid to acknowledge it. What if it ran both ways?

He had invaded her body. Had she infected his soul?

Looking up, he was surprised to find himself past the living quarters, near the end of the hallway leading to the clinic. A thought stopped him. Did he dare try the direct approach?

Glancing around a corner, he saw two men in suits stationed midway down the corridor. Secret Service, or guards of some other kind, he assumed. Yet there was a lab running the whole length of the hallway on the left side. One entrance was right beside him. What if the other end of the lab room had a separate connection with the clinic?

He cautiously tried the door. It was unlocked. Inside he saw no one—in fact, the room held little equipment except basic furniture: long tables and wall cabinets. Clearly it wasn't being used. After easing the door shut behind him, he began to walk quietly but directly, hoping to give the impression of someone going about legitimate business. He was three-quarters of the way down the room when he heard a voice behind him.

"Excuse me, sir. You shouldn't be here."

He turned as casually as he could, heart suddenly pounding, a child caught with his hand in the cookie jar. It was a tall, good-looking woman in a well-tailored suit. He didn't see a gun, but the angle of her right arm said there was one within reach. Secret Service, obviously. Was it true they had no sense of humor? He had a feeling he was about to find out.

"Sorry. . . I. . . work on the project. I. . . think I left some notes somewhere around here. Possibly in the clinic." The lie didn't sound convincing, even to him. A slight curl of her lip showed she felt the same.

"If I spot them, I'll be sure to let you know. But you need special clearance to be in this area. What's your name, sir?"

"Uh. . . Hunter. It's Hunter. I meant no harm, Agent. . . ?"

"Purdue." She saw that he expected more. "That's my name."

"Good. . . great, Agent Purdue. Somehow I feel like you're less likely to shoot me if we're on a. . . last name basis. I'd be even more comfortable if there were a first name to go with it."

She offered a wry smile. "Karen. I still have to ask you to leave." She pointed to the way he had come. Her economy of motion and self-assurance spoke of long training, although she only appeared to be about thirty. Hunter was aware of her presence several measured steps behind him as they exited the room. She moved around the corner and raised her voice to her companions. "Give me five minutes. I'll be escorting the civilian back to his quarters."

As they moved up the hallway, she was still behind him to his left. He turned his head. "I know my way. I really do work on the project."

"I know you do," she replied. "I've memorized all of your names and photos." Which meant that she'd wanted to see if she could catch him in a lie. "Why do you think I didn't shoot you?"

The startled look on his face made her laugh. After a moment of uncertainty, Hunter laughed, too. Relief flowed through his body, letting the muscles in his neck and back begin to unknot.

"Agent Karen Purdue," he said, "You have me at a disadvantage. I feel that I've disturbed your work. I'd like to make it up to you. Perhaps with a drink sometime?"

They had reached his door. She stood waiting for him to turn the knob. "I'm afraid not. We've been instructed to show special consideration to the members of your team, but that does not extend to fraternizing." It might have been true—he'd never seen any of her fellow agents in the commissary or bars. Either way, it was a handy excuse for a woman who must be used to such overtures.

Hunter shrugged. "Then. . . thanks for your restraint. Not shooting me."

"Glad to oblige. But Mr. Hunter. . . ." Her face became serious. "*Don't do it again.*"

He nodded and stepped into his room.

It was later, during his lunch break, that two uniformed security officers came to take him away.

# # #

"What can I say?" Kierkegaard stared him down like a schoolmaster with an errant pupil. "That I'm very disappointed in you? I am—in both your persistent disregard for protocol, and your disturbing lack of wits. It didn't occur to you that we'd have security cameras in every part of this facility? That we'd have monitoring software on the computers? That there'd be Secret Service agents watching the clinic?"

Hunter hung his head.

"It was a spur-of-the-moment thing," he said. "I didn't think it through."

"I suggest that you do more thinking in the future, in all of your activities here." The project head was thoroughly angry, and a steel edge showed beneath his professorial veneer. "In your background there was nothing to indicate that you're inclined to break rules or disobey orders. You wouldn't be here if there was. A bit irresponsible but never a rebel. Are you rebelling now?"

"No, sir, I'm not."

"Would you like to tell me why you're so obsessed with learning the identity of our patient that you're willing to violate national security?"

Hunter hesitated, then shook his head. "I just believe I can do my job better if I know more about the person we're working on." He looked up. "I'm working *inside* her. . . poking around in her very veins, for crying out loud. Why shouldn't I know who she is?"

"That's not for me to decide," Kierkegaard said. "I have no leeway on that. The directive comes directly from the White House, and you are not on the list. It's a top security issue, and believe me, they're very serious about it. I don't think you realize whose garden you're playing in." He leaned on his desk for a moment, considering something. Then he looked into the pilot's eyes.

"Can you tell me any valid reason you would be able to perform your task more effectively by knowing the identity of the patient?" It wasn't a rhetorical question this time. He actually wanted to know.

Hunter thought hard and then said, "No." He couldn't explain his reasons because he didn't understand them himself. All his life, he would have said that he had no tolerance for mysticism, or even so-called intuition. Now he was coming to realize that he'd been lying to himself. He did play hunches and he did follow his intuition often, and usually well. He always had. He'd simply never been willing to acknowledge it.

He had used some other sense to find an alternate route to the site of the latest bomb. He'd told Tamiko that he'd felt guided by something, and it was true, except he had no proof, not even an explanation. Could he tell this man that he believed his *empathy* with the patient would increase the more he knew about her and that such knowledge could somehow help him locate and destroy deadly nano-technology weapons? It sounded like utter crap, even to him. No, it wasn't ammunition Kierkegaard could take to his own superiors.

And Hunter didn't want to acknowledge, even to himself, that there might be an emotional reason behind his need to know. It was all right for him to be concerned about the patient's welfare, but any feelings more personal than that were not appropriate.

"No," he repeated, hoping the interview was nearly over. They couldn't very well fire him, could they? Who would pilot *Primus*?

"Then I can't help you," Kierkegaard said flatly. "The security restriction stands. I would advise you not to try a stunt like this again. I know you're thinking that we can't fire you." He didn't seem to notice the younger man's reaction. "But I can have you watched like a hawk, twenty-four hours a day. Don't make me do that."

The words were clearly a dismissal. Hunter lifted himself stiffly out of the chair and turned to leave.

"Hunter." The man's tired voice caught him before he reached the door. "I went way out on a limb when I brought you into this project. Don't make me regret it."

The latest news was bad.

While they'd been trying to neutralize the bombs in her face and upper chest, three more devices had been detonated: one on her ring finger, and one in each of her feet. The latter had both caused blockages in the *dorsalis pedis*, the dorsal artery feeding the big toe. As a result she was suffering some numbness, but it had been decided to use normal surgery to correct that. So far the blockage in her finger had only produced another bruise.

Their team was falling behind.

The bombs in the extremities and the outer skin were warnings—they were immediately visible, but wouldn't do much damage and were treatable by conventional methods. The next round would be different. To crank up the pressure on the President and his cabinet the enemy would use sites with potential for serious damage that wasn't quickly fatal: kidneys, spleen, and probably the liver.

Intensive blood testing and deep scanning of the patient's organs finally produced a handful of likely targets by late afternoon. A priority list and preliminary mapping was completed by eight o'clock, but they had to call it quits for the night, too drained to do anything more. They'd make a fresh start in the morning.

Hunter tried to think of something to do to fill his time. He considered going to find Lucy Tamiko, but decided against that. It was too soon. In the end he simply drifted toward his usual stool at the enlisted men's bar.

The crowd was light and Ed the bartender didn't have much to do by the time Hunter began his second beer.

"You don't look like a happy man," Ed offered.

"I suppose not," Hunter replied. He'd never told Ed anything about himself or his work on the base, and the other didn't seem to expect it. Inquisitive bartenders don't keep jobs on military bases. "I guess you can tell I'm a civilian. I've never worked for the government before. I'm beginning to think I don't fit in."

Ed laughed. "Do you have a brain? Can you think on your own? Then you don't fit in. Unless you're an ambitious bastard who'd stab your mother in the back to get ahead. Then you belong at the top of the class."

"You don't mean that. You must like being in the service."

"Oh, sure, the Air Force is OK." Ed nodded, wiping a barely-noticeable smudge from the counter. "Although they still prefer you just follow orders. Government bureaucracy is worse. The ultimate machine, grinding away with all the speed of a glacier, and if you're a cog, don't even think about doing something on your own. It's not worth it and nobody will thank you for it."

"It's not just that," Hunter said. "But I'm used to having some idea of the bigger picture. Here, the only reason they told me where to find the john is so nobody'd have to clean up the mess."

"Ah, a *secret* project." The bartender smiled. "Don't worry. Nearly everybody around here treats their work as if it's a state secret, even if it's only taking out the officers' trash. Makes them feel important. Don't let it get to you. Most of the secrets aren't worth knowing anyway. Just act like you don't care—that pisses 'em off." He laughed loudly. A few heads lifted over one of the pool tables at the far end of the room, then went back to their game. He leaned closer to the submariner. "Are you thinking of getting out? Quitting?"

"No, it hasn't come to that." Hunter shook his head and then gave a sheepish grin. "I just guess I've stepped on a few toes lately, and my welcome isn't as warm as it was."

"Anything left for you back where you come from?"

"Nope. Not even a job. No woman. . . although there was one prospect that was looking pretty promising." He grinned again at the memory. "This gorgeous blonde. . . a face like a movie star, fantastic figure. We met the night before I was scheduled to come here. That could've led to something worthwhile, maybe."

The bartender gave a snort. "Yeah, I understand those ladies know their stuff."

Hunter's beer hand stopped halfway to his mouth. "What do you mean?"

"It's the oldest play there is. At least it beats sending some goons over to go through all your gear. Or did she do that too?"

His memory went back to that night, and the next morning. Nothing had been missing, but he'd had an odd sensation that things had been moved.

Shit.

He opened his mouth to order another beer, then stopped.

He'd made a promise to himself to cut back on the booze because it interfered with his telepresence interface with the *Primus*? Had he meant it?

What's the difference between a good-time guy who likes his beer and bourbon… and an alcoholic?

An alcoholic can't stop himself.

Time to put that to the test.

"Thanks for the chat," he said, tossed some bills on the bar and made his way out.

Ed raised an eyebrow at the half-full bottle.

#   #   #

The *Primus* is at high speed, traveling along the *renal artery* toward the right kidney. Not too many obstacles—red cells are becoming easier to dodge, and white cells are behaving themselves. So far. But it's been a wasted trip to this point. The artery is large and easy to navigate in midstream, but it's too easy to miss spotting something from there. So the only choice is to pick a wall and stay close to it. The passage is so convoluted that there are lots of curves where a bomb could hide on one side of the blood vessel while a pilot is looking at the other.

It's the second pass along this same route. The first took about twenty minutes, ship's time, but then more than two hours of following smaller veins and lymph vessels to get back into position for a second run over the same stretch. A tough time for Tamiko to keep her advice to herself.

The renal arteries are a good choice to create a blockage, if it can be made big enough. One huge blood clot could cause the kidney to pack it in.

Not likely fatal—most people can get by on one kidney—but one heck of a wake-up call.

The team believes the bad guys will have planted several bombs close to each other at a sharp bend in the artery, just before it branches off into smaller tributaries. That way either one monster clot could block the whole passage, or a whole lot of smaller clots could plug the mouths of smaller branching vessels. It's a good theory.

So far, no evidence to back it up.

The blood vessel wall is dropping away quickly below to a big bend in the passage. Got to drop the ship's nose. . . bank to the left to bring the side thrusters into play.

Hell of a blood flow in such a large artery, rocketing the ship along at terrific speed. Bad news for a scouting mission. High speed means dialing down the VR monitor system to low-resolution, the only way the computer can stitch the rapid flow of images together. A blockage already in place would have been impossible to miss, but there wasn't one. So the second pass is to spot unexploded bombs—huge in comparison to *Primus*, but small in relation to the diameter of the blood vessel. Easy to miss. With a low-res view screen and a high rate of speed? Much too easy to miss.

Gage has tweaked the color balance to make the milky silver-white bomb material stand out from the ruddy tones of the blood cells and the vessel walls themselves. It might help. Anything is worth a try.

Watch out! The wall of the artery suddenly shoots up like the side of a mountain. The layout of tubes is like a demonic roller coaster. Dips, twists, spirals. . . no pattern. How are you supposed to spot anything when steering takes all the concentration you've got?

Pilot fatigue is a big factor on this second run. Maybe something else, too. Go ahead and say it. *Alcohol withdrawal?*

Don't need any extra handicaps.

Really tight bend here. Huge amount of space compared to tiny *Primus*, but the bombs—if they're here—must be tucked up along a wall, maybe partially embedded in it. Got to stay close. Can't let the current fling the ship into the middle of the flow.

Is that. . . ?

No. Only another blob of plaque along the artery's inner sleeve. They're all over the place, every size. The really big ones trick the eye. . . make it see a bomb dug into the tissue. It's damned hard to tell the difference.

The difference between failure and success.

Got to be coming to the end of the line again soon. If there's nothing to see when the branching-off starts, what next? Take one of the offshoots? A successful stoppage of blood flow after that point would require bombs placed in dozens of smaller arteries. How many could they possibly have injected into her?

Which way to go?

Pilot's discretion, they said. Means they don't have a clue either.

A change of light up ahead. Must be the first junction. Lots of others soon after that. Then on to the hilus of the kidney—the notch into which the blood vessels, excretory ducts and nerves connect like an electrical plug into a socket. That's what Tamiko's briefing said. Hard to picture from here on the inside. Probably time to slow down—use some reverse thrust. Don't want to be drawn into a side tunnel before getting a chance to look around.

Here it is. The main artery divides into three, then dozens of much smaller tunnels spring off in every direction. The only feasible route from this position is up to the right. There's the first offshoot, right at the mouth. . . three more just becoming visible ahead, before the next bend.

And is that. . . ?

Yes! Something pale and milky, just beyond the nearest tributary.

Full reverse on the main engine. Kick the port thrusters to full. Ship doesn't like that much. Heavy vibration. Hope the force of the current isn't as strong closer to the wall. Bound to be suction from the tributary, though. Can't get too close.

Target coming up very fast. More vibration. Shaking. Shuddering. Have to bring in the starboard thrusters—the current's trying to pull the ship into that growing hole in the wall nearby. Pounding's getting tough to take. Starting to cross the mouth of the opening.

Maelstrom!

Damn it! Right into the strongest convergence of cross-currents!

Starting to spin. . . now yaw. Bucketing. Wrenching. No way to control it. Engine thrust just adds to it. Throttle adjustment too slow to do any good.

Cut the power. . . ride it out.

That's wishful thinking. Riding a vortex, pounded against rocks. Like the turbulence going through the heart.

Not a good memory. If conflicting motions keep building, how long before. . . ?

Feedback. *Haptic* feedback.

Shit! Here it comes.

The vibration building to a crescendo—earthquake to battering ram to jackhammer. Fingers useless. Vision blurring. Got to bail out.

The job's not done, but no choice. Hit the kill switch. Wait for the nausea. The escape.

Wait.

Wait.

Wait.

It's not coming. *The change is not coming.*

No nausea. *No escape!*

The switch isn't working.

Try again. Punch it. Stab it. *Pound* it.

Wait. Something's changed. What's different?

Still in the bloodstream. . . spinning, tumbling, but. . . bearable. Tolerable. Has the feedback subsided?

What else? What else is different?

No readouts. No heads up display. How can that be?

Has the kill switch cut only part of the feed?

No. It's not only the readouts. The feel is different. The sound is different. The whole damn view is different. What's missing?

All the telltale clues. . . the hard-to-define traces that speak of computer imaging, synthesized sounds, artificial tactility. . . the constant reminder of *processed* reality.

Gone.

Gone, as if. . .

Virtual reality is no more. Only true reality remains.

The computer has fled and left the man behind.

God, no! No escape. No escape.

Get me *out* of here! *Get me out of here!!*

GET ME OUT. . . .

Nausea.

Blackness.

## 22

Gage stood over him. Tamiko cooled his face with a damp cloth.

Hunter cleared his throat again. It took an effort to speak.

Kierkegaard walked quickly into the room. "What happened?"

"Hunter says he had haptic feedback again. And something else," Tamiko answered, taking a step back and holding the cloth behind her, as if reluctant for her boss to see her in the role of nursemaid.

"Something else?" He looked down at the pilot sprawled in the VR chair.

Hunter ran a hand slowly over his face and shivered. Instead of answering, he looked up at Gage.

"How did you set the kill switch to work? What does it actually cut out?

"It does what you asked me to make it do," the scientist replied, annoyed. "It cuts the circuit that feeds all of the VR gear. . . the helmet, the suit. . . ."

"It doesn't cut off the actual input from *Primus*?"

"No. We don't want to lose contact with the sub. We're still getting all the data right now." He waved a hand toward the instruments. "It only terminates the feed from the computer processor to the virtual reality gear that you wear, so you stop getting video and audio. The suit no longer reacts."

"It doesn't just adjust the levels. . . eliminate the overload that's causing the feedback?"

Gage's frown grew even deeper. "According to our instruments there is no overload. We never saw any sign of it. No, it cuts the feed completely. That's what you wanted, isn't it?"

"Yes. It is." The younger man dropped his head and rocked it from side to side.

"Are you saying that's not what happened?" Kierkegaard pressed.

"I. . . . Yes, I guess. It couldn't have cut out completely. I was still getting something. I don't know how to describe it."

Bridges had come into the room and was listening with concern. The head of the project turned to the doctor.

"Is it possible that a haptic feedback loop could produce some kind of resonance in Hunter's brain that would carry on even after the source was cut off?"

The psychologist looked from Hunter to Kierkegaard and shrugged his shoulders. "I don't know. I've never been involved with a virtual reality system as sophisticated as this. I don't think anyone has. If we spend a lot of time experiencing certain kinds of strong motion—amusement park rides are a good example—we sometimes feel like the world is still moving even after the ride has stopped. Sailors have trouble walking on solid ground after a time at sea. I suppose something as violent as Hunter describes could get the central nervous system so revved up that it might take a while to wind down. But. . . " He looked into the pilot's eyes and spoke more softly. "Is that what happened?"

Suddenly, Hunter was reluctant to explain any further.

He dropped his eyes and said simply, "Yeah. It was something like that." Then he looked back at Gage. "When I hit the kill switch, does it interfere with anything you're doing at all? Cause any problems?"

"No. As I said, our instruments still get all of the same input. If we didn't look at the VR indicator light, we wouldn't know or care."

"Why do you ask?" It was Kierkegaard.

"If the kill switch could be modified so that I could cut the feed and turn it back on again, manually. . . well maybe these situations could be prevented. If I felt things beginning to get out of hand, I could just kill the VR for a few seconds or so, then jack back in and carry on." He thought the justification sounded reasonable. Did it matter that it wasn't his real reason?

Kierkegaard looked at Gage, who nodded resignedly.

"Why not? What else would I do with my time? It can wait until after lunch, though, can't it? They have corned beef in the commissary."

The pained look on his face broke the tension in the room as they all laughed.

Hunter caught up with Gage down the hall.

" Kenn. . . er, Dr. Gage, can I ask you something else about the VR gear?"

"You mean something else needs fixing?" The voice was close to a growl.

"No, I don't think so."

"What then?" He made no effort to slow down or look in Hunter's direction.

"The nausea. I feel a little sick each time the VR engages or disengages. What causes that? It can't only be from the head mounted display or the sounds. People have been using HMD's to play VR games and simulations for decades. I never felt nauseated before."

"Yes, we all felt a little of that with this system. It's the electrodes."

"*Electrodes?* I didn't know there were any."

"Sure. Three of them, one at each temple and one near the back of the neck, at the top of the brain stem. That's why the helmet has to fit so tightly. They provide a small electric current, designed to make the brain more receptive to the VR… convince it to accept the processed data as real sensory input."

"To boost the feeling of reality," Hunter prompted.

"That's what I said. So… " He stopped at the entranceway of the commissary, clearly trying to discourage the pilot from following him there. "Your brain experiences a sudden shift of environment that it's never experienced before, and so it reacts with disorientation. It feels like you've lost your balance."

"Dizziness. Nausea."

"Yes. Now don't tell me you want me to change that, too. Because… "

"No, I know. You can't. That's fine." Hunter decided to be conciliatory. "In fact, I think it'll be useful, just the way it is. I just wanted to understand it better. Thanks. Thanks for all your help." That may have been laying it on a bit thick. Gage gave him a skeptical look, then turned and walked toward his too-long-delayed meal. Hunter fervently hoped the commissary hadn't run out of corned beef.

This nausea wasn't going to let up anytime soon.

Jacked right into the thick of it. *Primus* still in the maelstrom, spinning, twisting. . .   certain motion sickness. But no haptic feedback. At least, not yet. Got to get moving before it begins.

Escaping this trap will require lots of finesse. Time it exactly right. . . *there!* No! Too late. Have to anticipate the optimal attitude of the ship before it happens. Guesswork, pure guesswork.

There! Main engine and thrusters to full. . . .

No, damn it! That accentuated the spin. Try again. Throttle back. . . wait for it.

Wait for it. . . .

Full throttle! Full everything. Directly in line with the swirling current.

Primus snapping forward, accelerating instantly with the combination of forces, surging ahead into a tight circle around the vortex. Faster. Faster. No more thrust left to give, but the speed is still building. Like an Olympic hammer throw, gaining more and more velocity, more and more centripetal force, trying to escape the tether that holds it. Still faster, the circle growing larger, the invisible leash stretching, straining until. . . .

Freedom! The grip releases. The ship breaks loose, flung outward in a straight line. Upstream, too, with enough force to defeat the blood vessel's current—for a moment. Just long enough to be able to steer back toward the artery wall.

A second chance to approach to the bomb, even more carefully.

The current regains control. The ship swings slowly around, then gains speed, hurtling downstream toward the bomb.

Collision speed. Ramming speed.

Fear. Images of a ruptured hull, flood of fluid, explosion of lost air. Death by drowning.

Not possible. Not. . . .

IMPACT!

Thrown hard against the restraints. The nose of the ship buried within the shell, but strong fingers of current try to pluck it free. Extend the probe arm. . . trigger ignition. . . .

Fireball. A glorious swell of triumph as cascading billows of flame roil upward, and consume the bomb completely. Success. Unexpected, and sweet.

A rest would be great, but there's no time.

If what he learned about diving in rivers applies here, there ought to be an area right up against the wall of the artery nearly free of current. Have to get the ship there before it's swept too far. Nose pointed upstream, full forward power from the main engine, thrusters struggling to push sideways against the punishing current.

It works! The force lets up suddenly, only apparent meters from the wall, and the engine thrust begins to take effect. Slowly, *Primus* starts to regain lost ground, returning to where he destroyed the bomb. If the deadly device has companions, they'll probably be spaced around the circumference of the artery, at about the same proximity from branching tunnels. The only hope to find them is to sidle painstakingly along the wall, like a crab in search of prey.

Locate a bomb. Travel upstream. Turn and ram. Search again, and repeat the ordeal until it can be certain that none are left.

It will take a very long time. It will be exhausting. But there's no better incentive than success.

After the third bomb, Tamiko re-activated his text display and sent an urgent message: "You must be at your limit. We should stop."

"No. Not yet," he replied in a rasping voice.

She made an appeal to Kierkegaard, who told her not to interfere.

After the fourth bomb, she waited until *Primus* was in the stable zone near the artery wall again, then pulled the plug without consulting anyone. She rushed to his side as he went limp in the chair. He had been in VR for six hours straight. Ship's time, it would have felt like days.

He needed help to clamber to his feet and get to the commissary to force down some food. Tamiko supported him with a shoulder, musing about whether it was a clever ploy to get an arm around her, but when she helped him to his quarters afterward, he collapsed onto the bed and was asleep before he could even think about getting undressed.

Tamiko hesitated, then turned out the light with a sigh.

## 23

Sometime before dawn he awoke and remembered that he hadn't tried his plan with the kill switch. Had he been afraid to? It was terrifying the first time, when he thought he might never escape to his own world, the world of sanity.

Was that what he was afraid for, his sanity? Afraid his mind could no longer process two distinct realities, and might unravel? He shivered at the prospect, and the black night gave him no comfort.

Eventually he fell asleep once more, but his last conscious thought was a memory of a motivational speaker he'd once seen, who insisted that we choose our own reality. It had seemed so trite at the time.

# # #

The circle of faces around Hunter looked uniformly blank.

Kierkegaard stirred first, and asked, "What do you mean, you don't have to go back in?"

"I have to move the ship, sure, but I mean I don't have to search that kidney any more. Because the job's done." Hunter was still exhausted and their lack of comprehension was irritating. "All of the bombs there have been destroyed. There were only four." Surely that was clear enough.

Gage scoffed. "How could you possibly be sure of that? Did you search every square micrometer? You didn't. I know, because I was monitoring."

"I know it. I just. . . *know.*" Suddenly the meaning of Gage's remark struck home. How did he know? It had been such an utter certainty in his mind that he hadn't even questioned it. But where was the proof? Could he remember a key piece of evidence that had so completely convinced him? He could not.

"Why are you so sure, Mr. Hunter?" Kierkegaard asked gently.

The pilot felt his face grow red. "I can't say exactly. I only remember that as I approached the fourth bomb I kept thinking that it was the last one—the last one there. Once it was destroyed I knew the mission was completed and steered the ship to a stable spot to park it there. I just had time to match the engine thrust to the current when you pulled me back out." The others were looking at Tamiko in a strange way, and she wore an expression of discomfort.

"He's right," she affirmed. "I checked at the time, and again this morning. The ship is safely parked in a small backwater or whatever. A stable zone, at any rate. As if he'd planned to leave it there for a while."

"I still don't see how you can be so sure," Tyson said. "We have no way of knowing how many bombs were planted there. The scanner still isn't that precise. It can detect the presence of one bomb or many in a given area, but not distinguish the exact number."

"I know that, Skylar." They were right. He couldn't refute their arguments. Yet the certainty in his gut was still there. "Maybe it was a whole series of indicators that I picked up without consciously realizing it. But it convinced me then, and I'm still convinced." He shrugged slightly and turned in time to see a look pass between Kierkegaard and Bridges. It was clearly a look of significance, but he couldn't read its meaning. "I'll go back in and search again if that's what you want me to do, sir."

"Well of course you'll have to search again . . ." Gage began.

"No. No, I don't think so." Kierkegaard surprised them, holding up a hand to forestall a rush of protests. "There will always come a point when we will have to make the assumption that we have finished clearing an area of bombs. We simply don't have the time for *Primus* to search every square micron of every site. We haven't dealt with that fact until now, but it can't be avoided any longer. At some juncture we'll have to. . . take it on faith that the immediate task has been completed, and move on. We've reached that point now."

Several voices were raised in disagreement, but Kierkegaard's voice carried the quiet authority that always served him well.

"As Dr. Tyson correctly asserted, we have no instrumentation to confirm the number of devices in a particular location. However, another full scan could confirm one of two possibilities: there are none left, or there is at least one left. We would be remiss if we did not try to get that confirmation, and so I ask you, Dr. Bridges, to prepare for that process. . . when we can schedule it. Unfortunately it will have to wait." His last words made them stare in surprise. "I've tried to prevent it, but the patient will be beyond our influence for a few days. Apparently she must take a trip."

There were gasps of breath and then stunned silence.

"But this is life or death!" Lucy Tamiko spoke for all of them.

"I am fully aware of that," their leader responded. "And so are the people who make such decisions. Clearly, it's political and of great importance. Don't forget that we're only part of a very high-stakes negotiation. Indeed, I would call it a game of brinksmanship. I don't envy those who've had to make this call, and I will not second-guess them."

"How long have we got in the meantime?" Tyson asked.

"She will be in range of our VR equipment until midday tomorrow. She will not be available for any other procedures until she returns. In fact, she has already left the clinic."

"Well that answers the question in my mind," Mallory spoke for the first time, slumping onto the edge of a desk, "which is how we're going to get *Primus* to the next target site. I guess we're not."

"We have been dealt a setback, Dr. Mallory, but you would be wrong to assume that we will sit on our hands and do nothing. *Primus* is still capable of moving from one place to another. It will simply have to do so under its own steam." Kierkegaard seemed to enjoy the stir his words created. "In fact, I think that's how we'll operate from now on. Physical removal of *Primus* from a critical blood vessel deep within the body is too intrusive, and too dangerous to the patient. It's nothing short of surgery. We couldn't keep doing that much longer, and now our hand has been forced."

"I'm not sure we can navigate with any accuracy throughout the entire body." Tamiko's voice was uncharacteristically timid, her face pale.

Kierkegaard reached out to grasp her shoulder. "I believe you and Mr. Hunter will surprise yourselves in that department. I am. . .

confident." Again he looked at Bridges. The doctor gave a slight incline of his head.

"I'm sorry to have to ask this of all of you," the leader of the team concluded, "but we can succeed. I know we can. You are the best and the brightest. Now it's time to shine." From anyone else, the words would have been hollow pep talk. From Kierkegaard, they were a true reflection of the soul from which they had come.

The team members moved to their tasks with new urgency, and new determination. They were at the mercy of unfeeling reality, a force they could not break.

But that didn't mean they couldn't do their damnedest to bend it.

Finding bombs is easier than finding routes to bypass the kidney. Can't risk *Primus* being filtered with the blood. A nasty image comes to mind of the ship being passed into a bile duct, and pissed away. The only alternative is to find an anastomosis or capillary network linking the renal artery with the renal vein. A lot harder than just chugging up a lymphatic vessel along the outside of the renal artery itself.

Hours later, ship's time, it's done. Now along the renal vein to the inferior vena cava, back to the heart, a side trip to the lungs, the heart again for a boost of speed, and on to the left kidney. A voyage of many potential pitfalls. Have to make all of the correct turns at high speed without a lot of warning. Otherwise the ship will be headed off to an arm, or the stomach, or the brain. Detours too daunting to consider.

The heart is the biggest problem. The first pass will automatically send the ship toward the lungs, along with a surge of depleted blood in need of oxygen. No steering required for that—there's nowhere else to go. But the second time through . . . lots of offshoots and tributaries on the other side. With that extreme burst of speed on the way out, it'll be easy to miss the right one and end up who knows where?

So much for trying to evade the turbulence within the heart. That was a comforting delusion: just unplug, wait out the worst of it, and go back in. Except it won't work.

The odds of *Primus* shooting out of the heart's left ventricle and hitting on the right course without her pilot are no more than a roll of the dice. Can't afford that. Which means the pilot has to stay onboard for the whole ride after all. The plunging, the spinning, the pounding . . . the maelstrom of all maelstroms. The likelihood of more haptic feedback, making the very molecules of the soul shudder.

Oh, yes, and stay conscious please. There's a good boy.

No problem. Piece of cake.

For now, the ship is riding the current of the renal vein, soon to be sucked into the inferior vena cava. No steering needed for a while.

It's time to experiment.

Time to hit the kill switch.

Nausea. . . . Blackness, but only because the headset view screen was off. There was the muffled sound of hushed voices. He couldn't make out words because Gage and Tamiko were trying to be quiet and not disturb him. But it was the lab all right. The *real* world. Even the feel of the chair and the smell of the air were different.

Try again?

Nausea. Getting shorter each time though. Is the brain adapting?

Look around. Everything just as it was. No, the ship is moving faster. Must be in the inferior vena cava then. A few brief seconds in the *outside* world translates into long minutes *inside*. Still enough time to do some more testing before the going gets tricky.

Try again?

Nausea . . . the eyes covered, the skin warm on the back, the pressure of the foot-rest on the back of the heel. Reality again, with the capital 'R'. Why? What was he doing that was different from earlier in the day? Trapped in the vortex of the renal artery, he had hit the kill switch, but hadn't escaped. Why then and not now? Was the effect dependent on the length of time spent inside? If so, he'd just spent a long time traveling through the network of vessels between the artery and the vein. What else was different? What else could be different? Or had it simply been a quirk in the VR system that nobody had detected? Was his theory completely wrong?

And would that be such a very bad thing?

Nausea. Turbulence! *Primus* has had time to reach the heart—and pass through it. Yes, the buffeting is easing off, carried automatically from the right ventricle of the heart into the pulmonary artery. The artery will split soon, one branch to either lung, but that doesn't matter. It's after the second trip through the heart that the steering will have to be done. Still some time until then. But for what?

The experiment isn't working. Either the theory's wrong or the method. Is it even worth trying again?

Yes, and for two reasons—if it's possible to become trapped in this reality, then it's better to know ahead of time, and figure out how to avoid it. Maybe there is a time limit, beyond which there's no going back. Maybe the first time was just on the borderline—a narrow escape.

Or reason number two:

Maybe this reality is as valid as the other one, and there's no need for fancy technology to travel between them, only the *will* to do so.

It's a thought to blow the mind. Tantalizing and terrifying at the same time.

Hang on.

The will. That's it.

The first time it happened was the first emergency use of the kill switch, deciding to escape from innerspace.

But not really wanting to.

There had been a rational choice to escape the turbulence, but the mission wasn't complete, the patient was still in danger. The reasoning mind had said, *Go.*!

But the unreasonable will had said . . . Stay!

What is reality? And how many realities are there?

Concentrate then. Concentrate on staying, on *wanting* to stay. Concentrate.

And press the switch . . . .

God, oh God, it's like a ripple in the fabric of the World.

## 24

Tamiko turned her head and saw Hunter slumped in the chair.

"Kenneth! Kenneth, look!" she rasped urgently, still trying to obey the edict of silence. "He just suddenly went limp. His hands aren't even on the controls."

Gage stepped to the side of the chair, then bent over with his ear near the visor front. After a moment, and a glance at the instrument panel, he straightened.

"Well, he's still breathing," he said in a stage whisper. "And his vital signs are all OK on the monitors. Blood pressure and heart rate a little high, but then it's probably quite a ride in there. Straight out of the heart at high speed and. . . coming up on the lungs right about now. Everything looks all right. What are you worried about?"

Tamiko shook her head slightly. "I've never seen him go like this before. Relaxed, yes, but always in control. Now he looks like he's just along for the ride."

Gage thought for a moment, then consulted the monitor screens again.

"There's nothing for him to do for now. Not until he's just about to come out of the left ventricle into the aorta. So if he is dozing, or daydreaming or something, the turbulence of the heart will wake him up. If not, we'll do something to get his attention." He smiled at the prospect. "In the meantime, Devon clearly wants us to leave him alone. So we leave him alone."

Tamiko nodded and began to return to her work, but a last glance at the pilot made the hairs rise on the back of her neck. His right arm was rising slowly as if to shield his eyes from something. Something she could not even imagine.

The ripple that began in the center rapidly sweeps outward across the entire field of vision, leaving in its wake . . . .

Clarity. Cohesion. Congruity.

And understanding.

The earlier missions have only hinted at this—have only offered enticing glimpses: sharper edges, more authentic perspectives . . .

But this . . . . This is a whole new sense of being.

The colors. They're magnificent. True and pure. Alive!

Before now, there were only pale, dried-out, powder-painted cutouts.

Look. Dark purple-brown blood cells blooming like a rose in time-lapse photography, the bright volcanic red beginning at the core then spreading quickly over the whole.

Oxygenation. The miracle of life-giving breath, revitalizing the depleted red cells to carry the fuel of existence throughout the body. *Incredible.* Hundreds of them . . . thousands . . . spread across the entire cavernous blood vessel, visible five . . . no, *ten* times farther away than they could have been seen before. Legions of Life's soldiers—no longer threatening, vagabond missiles, but troops orderly marching to the call of a cosmic rhythm.

It has happened. There can be no doubt. The meddlesome computer has departed, and reality remains.

Inner space, unblurred, unaltered, unveiled. It was there all the time. Why has it only become attainable now?

Don't know. Bridges might have an answer.

But perhaps the answer is simply that truth has its own time.

Time. How long has it been? Got to get a grip. The ship is still hurtling along at the speed of the current. There's no more oxygenation happening—the surrounding blood cells are all a cheerful red. So the lungs are being left behind. Onward into the pulmonary vein and back to the left auricle of the heart. Soon, very soon.

The heart. The maelstrom. Can it be faced like this? In the full experience of *nano*-reality? Is it survivable?

Only moments left to decide. Where does the real danger lie? There will be turbulence, certainly, but no haptic feedback. No computer-generated insanity of sensory overload. Perhaps only the powerful acceleration the body's own living cells undergo every minute, every hour, every day.

The alternative is to re-engage processing by the computer—if it's still possible. How do you will away enchantment like this?

Or another choice—abandon the ship. Leave *Primus* without a mind present to command it, to be thrown at random into a vast maze.

No. That's not an option.

Bring it on, then. Let the ultimate test begin.

"Is he awake?" Gage rasped. "*Primus* is about to enter the heart again."

"He's awake. He's gripping the handsets. . . taking control again. Something's different, but I can't tell what. It's too late to do anything about it anyway. I only hope he remembers the right course to steer."

Gage made a noise. "We'll be lucky if he can even stay conscious."

With a worried frown Tamiko turned to concentrate all of her attention on the monitor.

Instant insanity

Endless crosscurrents, up-wellings, backdrafts, undertows. . . the *Primus* tossed chaotically through a froth of liquid mayhem, and yet. . . .

Bearable. *Survivable.*

The G-forces change with the rapidity of thought, yet the vibration isn't brutal after all. The ship doesn't fight the current, but becomes part of it. Spiraling, plunging. . . swooping like a bird diving for prey, then riding thermals into the heavens.

An incredible ride. The sensations are all there to drink in—dizzying, but exhilarating. Not a torment to be endured, but a revelation.

If only the VR monitors could capture the vast expanses of taut muscle, stretched in webbed strands lost in the distance, the spinning disks performing their inspired ballet, the whorls of color transforming the view from moment to moment, making it endlessly new.

But the monitors cannot see it. There is only the mind's eye to behold such perfect anarchy.

No, not anarchy. There is an order, an order driven by chemical interactions, nerve impulses, genetic coding and, ultimately, an underlying machinery beyond comprehension.

No time left for sightseeing. The gaping maw ahead must be the entrance to the aorta, so expansive in comparison to *Primus* that the VR view would not have been able to take in more than a fraction of it. The flanking walls would have been much too far away to see, invisible through the murk of insufficient data. There would have been no navigating here at all. Only blind blundering into the unknown, trusting to chance.

The turbulence dies out quickly in the giant aorta as it funnels oxygen-enriched blood outward to all the needy tissues of the body. It will divide soon, and the ship needs to be in the right alignment to avoid being diverted into the wrong channel.

Passing blades of tissue, colossal and curved, like the petals of a titanic flower—the semi-lunar valves, ready to sweep closed behind the outgoing wave, to prevent blood being sucked back into the powerful heart.

That means the coronary arteries should be visible, right and left. What did Tamiko say? The right should come first, and the left is slightly smaller. There's one directly overhead. Where's the other? Down below, just ahead.

Peeling off into a steep dive, like a fighter jet breaking formation. Got to stay clear of the fierce suction from that gaping chasm above. Then pull up and climb again to escape its counterpart.

With the aorta curving and arching over the lung before leading downward toward the abdomen, the key is to keep from being drawn off anywhere else. Like that yawning tunnel up ahead, with a Latin name too long to remember. The wrong way. That one branches off into the right carotid artery—the left carotid should be coming up soon. Worth remembering what they look like, though. It's a good bet that a trip to the brain will wind up on the itinerary before all is said and done.

Better stick close to the underside curve of the aorta, far away from the left carotid—there it is—and the left subclavian just beyond. Don't want to go that way either. Just around the arch and onward for a nice straight ride down the abdominal aorta. One more turnoff to avoid. . . .

There. The ship's in the clear.

Now there's time. Time to think. Try to understand what just happened.

If it can be understood.

The curtain has risen on a secret no human being was meant to see.

## 25

Kierkegaard looked at Bridges across the desk.

"What do you make of that?" he asked.

The doctor looked again at the monitor screen, as if to reassure himself of what they'd just witnessed.

"I couldn't distinguish any detail at all," he said. "Yet Hunter avoided all the traps and steered the right course like a commuter driving home from work."

"You think he's seeing more than we are?" The answer was a shrug. "Is it possible that, as an experienced submersible pilot, using the haptic interface, he could sense the movement of the currents and navigate that way? By the seat of his pants?"

"I don't know what to tell you, Devon. This is certainly beyond any expectations I had. Don't forget how he found that bomb the other day, after going so far off course."

"I haven't forgotten," Kierkegaard said. "It was the first spark of hope in this whole damned mess." He clenched his hands together and his eyes narrowed. "I just want to know how he's doing it. There's something he isn't telling us."

"Hunter is a bit of a maverick, an unknown quantity—we knew that going into this," Bridges reminded him. "In fact, we counted on it. As I told you then, if we pull the harness too tight we may just drive away that special gift of his."

"You're suggesting we just leave him to his own devices and be grateful for the results we get?"

The dark face smiled. "Remember the story of the Goose and the Golden Egg?"

Now what?

Probably time to link up with the computer again—check the navigational readouts and the status reports.

Is there another world out there?

Or is it just a dream*?*

Where does the return path lie?

Does Alice know the way out of Wonderland?

Time to find out.

How can the mind's eye be refocused?

The new navigation system. It required a shift of focus to be able to see the heads-up display. Like turning away from a movie screen to read the lettering on the popcorn box.

There. Something's happening.

The view stretches, expands and distorts like the inside of an inflating bubble, then explodes into a spray of grainy pixels, coalescing at last into a pastel painting. An approximation of the truth: recognizable, yet far inferior!

The resolution is on the lowest setting, to cope with *Primus'* high speed. The sound. . . so muffled and indistinct. Like plunging into a fog. Worse—a newspaper photograph of a fog.

The digital readings in the heads-up display are reassuring, though, projecting their numbers, bars, and graphs as a testimony to rationality.

OK. That's the first step. Feet are planted on solid bottom to wade up out of the surf.

Picture the control room: the couch, the controls. . . picture Lucy Tamiko. Press the switch. . . .

Blackness. Then a piercing dagger of light as the visor was stripped away.

It was there. It was all there. Dorothy had returned from the Land of Oz. Auntie Em looked like a beautiful Asian woman with a look of worry on her face.

Then anger.

It was the real world, all right.

#   #   #

He collapsed into bed that night, thoroughly drained.

Tamiko had torn a strip off him.

As *Primus* was leaving the arch of the aorta, she'd spotted the VR indicator switched off, and assumed that he'd followed the correct course only by more of his damned unfathomable luck. A reckless gamble, and she wasn't shy about saying so. His only escape from her wrath came when *Primus* approached the left renal artery, and his presence was needed.

By the time Bridges demanded that he take another break, he'd found two bombs and neutralized them, but he had a nagging feeling there were others he'd missed. He'd resisted the powerful temptation to shut off the VR again. So far, Tamiko believed he'd used the kill switch while in the heart to prevent haptic feedback, but now she'd be watching for it, and that was an explanation he just wasn't ready to give.

Had he actually experienced another reality? Virtual Reality, no matter how sophisticated, was still basically only a projection, like watching a movie. Add a realistic representation of three dimensions, surround sound, and the extra wrinkle of a haptic interface, and it became easy to suspend one's disbelief. But it was still only a simulation.

Yet, if not by the testimony of the senses, how is reality measured?

He'd never read the philosophers Bridges had mentioned. To Hunter, the simplest measure involved results. In the real world *we affect our surroundings, and our surroundings affect us.* He was certainly affecting inner space, wasn't he? Destroying the bombs?

No, strictly speaking, it was *Primus* doing that. He was only controlling *Primus* through a remote control hook-up from somewhere else.

What about the other way around? Was inner space affecting him?

There was the turbulence. . . but he had no bruises, or other physical damage. The battering might be only in his mind, but the haptic feedback was unquestionably a product of the virtual reality equipment itself.

So there was no evidence that he, Hunter, was actually present in that other reality—only *Primus* was.

Then what had he experienced?

The electrodes in his VR helmet were designed to make his brain more susceptible to suggestion, more responsive to the simulation—

Gage had told him that. But better responsiveness from his brain could not improve the data from the transmitting end. Unless his brain was suddenly able to interpret a whole spectrum of information it had found indecipherable before.

None of this explained how he got the best result of all, and the first impression of true reality—by turning the VR equipment off.

Bridges had said it days earlier: Hunter's brain was making some kind of leap that was not in the design.

What if the VR system created a new kind of link that, once forged, could eventually sustain itself? Was there a physical process that could explain that? Some kind of residual electrical field? A form of—what did they call it—*quantum entanglement?* He wished he knew more about quantum physics. At that level of matter there were all kinds of phenomena that turned the usual rules of science on their heads.

His neurons were being electrically stimulated by the helmet. Could that somehow create a direct communication link between *Primus* and his own brain on an alternate plane of existence?

A *psychic* link?

He'd never, ever believed in crap like that. He'd once dumped a girl because he caught her phoning the Psychic Network.

But this was something else. Not telepathy—he wasn't communicating with anyone else's mind. His brain was receiving information through some channel, some means, that he'd never been able to access before.

Or had he? Was that what intuition was?

Bridges might have an answer, but Hunter didn't dare ask. His bad memories were still too fresh. He remembered Dr. Tanner, on the oil rig, who'd somehow forgotten their two years of friendship, and set the shrinks onto him. The disbelieving faces of his buddies on the crew. The suddenly frosty attitude of the bosses.

No, he wasn't ready to trust again.

At least he could accept one solid conclusion: the universe inside the bloodstream was the reality of *Primus*, but not Hunter. Surely that was a comforting thought.

Comforting enough that he could finally give in to his body's demand for sleep.

As part of him surrendered to unconsciousness, his subconscious brain continued to gnaw at the puzzle.

After a time it came to its own conclusion, a simple one, given the evidence.

In the world that was inner space, Hunter did not simply pilot *Primus*.

He *was* Primus.

## 26

Gerard Mannis sat in the dark.

He could no longer see the reports on his desk. He didn't need to. He'd gone over them so many times they were burned into his memory. Some were original texts of the first communiqués from the terrorists. Others were decoded reports from the few field operatives he trusted. A handful were updates on the Project at Langley AFB. Those were the hardest to come by—at least, the unofficial ones were. The president received regular reports directly from Devon Kierkegaard, and Mannis had immediate access to those. The others, from his own contact within the Langley complex, arrived by a system of tortuous routes, a system as impenetrable as he could make it. And he trusted those to no one else, not even the president.

It was unthinkable that the president could be behind the plot, but the security net around him was far from foolproof.

The investigation into the sabotage of Mannis's car had gone cold. He now drew on the pool of White House vehicles, picking one randomly, with specially-authorized and cleared technicians checking it first for tampering. Or bombs. They could not all be bulletproof, though. He had to hope that his would-be assassin, whoever it was, was not yet ready for open assault.

The Langley messages were just as frustrating. Kierkegaard was clearly trying to be encouraging while refusing to promise what he could not deliver. Gone was the faint hope that the bombs were a hoax. They were real all right, and performed exactly as advertised; but they were being found and destroyed. Success depended on all of them being eradicated before the enemy could find out it was being done.

Mannis had serious misgivings about that one. Something in his gut told him that the perpetrators of this plan knew as much about the progress at Langley as he did. If so, the attack on their unsuspecting victim was about to escalate in a big way.

And she was leaving the lab! How could the president allow that for the sake of a handful of state functions, no matter how important, when the project at Langley was her only possible source of help?

No, that was unfair. It wasn't as simple as that. She had insisted on attending the state banquet for the pope, and her absence would have been very hard to explain to the press. With an election looming, opposition members in the House were like vultures watching for the slightest hint of blood. The administration was already off balance from a burgeoning scandal over a senate appointment, and the second poor quarterly economic forecast in a row. These things she knew. She refused to let the president down.

The president, in turn, refused to tell her the truth about the threat to her life. He had allowed others to mislead her, even to hint about the possibility of a serious disease, because that was the only way to explain away all the testing she had had to undergo. It hurt him deeply to go that far. He would not tell her more. Would not risk her trying to sacrifice herself for his sake. And, without revealing what he knew, he could not force her to remain at Langley.

In truth, the chief executive had never really believed the project would be her salvation. At best he felt it might buy them some time to solve the crisis another way. He had hundreds of trained operatives scouring the world for anything that could lead them to the perpetrators. Naturally, the man would place his confidence in the tools that had served him well in the past.

In the meantime, Mannis sat brooding. The latest messages from Langley were the most disturbing yet, even while sounding like good news. The team had suddenly achieved some real successes, but couldn't explain how.

Winning was good, but winning without knowing why was not to be trusted.

This pilot, a man Kierkegaard had recruited out of the blue, had happened to be in the right place at the right time. A head case. A borderline alcoholic, maybe. Now he was performing miracles.

Mannis didn't believe in miracles.

His secret contact at Langley AFB didn't either, and was deeply suspicious.

Did this Hunter know how to find the bombs because he had helped the people who'd planted them?

Mannis slammed the desktop with his fist, a shocking explosion of sound that somehow served to clarify his thought.

He gave himself two days—the two days she would be in Washington, away from Langley. Two days to learn everything he could about the project's mysterious pilot. In that time he would either have Hunter replaced or killed. Or he would *trust*.

Of one thing he was quite certain: if he made the wrong choice the game was lost.

## 27

The morning briefing was a shocker.

Kierkegaard stood at the head of the table leaning on his hands long after everyone had settled into their seats. Finally he looked up.

"You are an excellent team," he began. "You've developed creative ways to tackle extraordinary challenges. I doubt if anyone could have done better. It is not your fault that we have fallen short."

Shock rustled through the room.

"I'm not saying that we have failed. I'm saying that we *will* fail unless we can make our efforts much more efficient and effective. We're falling badly behind while the time left to us is growing short."

"What's happened?" Gage asked.

"I don't know the details myself. It makes no difference to our work." A chart came up on the screen behind him. "So far we've been able to do little more than guess how many bombs are in our patient's bloodstream based on the number of likely targets and assuming three or four bombs assigned to each of those. Our rate of success shows we'd require months to remove them all. We have little more than a week."

"But we're getting better," Tamiko protested, then looked embarrassed by the weakness of her words.

"You've made astonishing improvements, Dr. Tamiko. It still won't be enough. We have to make a significant change." His head dipped for a moment, and then he looked each of them in the eyes. "Until now we have evaluated each mission and then planned for the next. From now on our planning process—location of the bombs, mapping, course charting—will be ongoing. The successful destruction of one bomb will begin the mission to the next."

Tamiko collapsed against the back of her chair. Gage's assault on the tabletop probably bruised his hand.

"*Primus* is still a prototype," Tyson sputtered. "There've been few enough chances to check over its systems as it is. With no opportunity to spot potential troubles we could be caught off guard by a catastrophic failure."

"I won't be able to give Hunter any ongoing guidance." Tamiko's face had lost color. "He'll have to navigate entirely on his own."

"He'll have your maps."

"Subjectively thousands of miles of bloodstream, with offshoots every few hundred yards."

"You're forgetting something else, Devon," Bridges said. "While the support team may be able to handle eighteen-hour days, each of those days will feel like weeks to our pilot." He looked at Hunter. "He is not a machine."

"I have forgotten nothing," Kierkegaard replied with a clenched jaw. His hard gaze travelled down the table. "Mr. Hunter?"

Hunter couldn't meet those eyes.

"If this is supposed to be a vote of confidence in me, it's misplaced. You could be trusting in blind luck."

"I put my trust in people, Mr. Hunter, and I have chosen the best. But the hand we've been dealt is as bad as it can be. We either face that and adapt to it, or we give up, and giving up is not an option for me."

There was nothing any of them could say to that. The meeting was over. Hunter, Tamiko, and Gage went to the control room.

There was one advantage to the new plan: without Tamiko monitoring him it would be much easier for Hunter to shut off the VR and explore the new link without setting off alarm bells. Gage would likely be too busy to notice.

There were still bombs to be found in the approaches to the left kidney. Hunter was sure of it, and this time no one questioned him.

He'd left *Primus* parked in a fairly stable zone in the renal vein, just downstream from the organ itself. It was unthinkable to return to the entrance of the kidney through the maze of capillaries and lymphatic vessels surrounding it without Tamiko to guide him. He would have to take the long way around—through the heart and back again.

At least now he knew it could be done, and that he could survive it. He knew the secret.

At the first opportunity, he took a deep breath, focused his mind, and willed his psyche to remain within this pulsing, throbbing, mortal universe.

Then he hit the kill switch.

The transformation took his breath away. True reality coruscated like swelling fireworks across his view, overlapping billows of color and sharp relief, quickly obscuring the smeared, indistinct representation they replaced. It was beautiful beyond words. It was an inner landscape no other had ever seen in this way.

He gasped as he found himself hurtling recklessly through the cavernous ocean of blood, teeming with thousands upon thousands of other travelers, many as small as *Primus*, and previously unseen by him. Others were gargantuan beyond his experience. The blood vessel was much smaller than the giant pulmonary artery in which he'd first witnessed this transformation. The sudden sensation of incredible speed knotted his stomach with vertigo.

He clutched his handgrips fiercely, his heart racing. The human mind was ill equipped to grasp what was beyond the scope of human senses. The scale was too vast, with myriad flickering and darting molecules as numerous as any school of ocean fish, and living behemoths far greater in proportion than blue whales in the sea.

As he calmed down, there was a moment of exultation, that he, of all people, should be a witness to this miracle. The sole audience for the spectacle of all time.

And then the pendulum swung again, and his sense of wonder was instantly tempered by a more sobering thought.

Audience, yes. Witness. Spectator—but also something more.

Guardian. Savior.

Because if he couldn't destroy the bombs, this incredible inner cosmos was doomed. Every wave of blood would cease; every glistening cell would shrivel and die. The teeming tide that swirled around him would be stilled within moments, like the sudden death of a vast city, terrible in its finality and inevitable decay.

It was a devastating thought. The full horror of it had never struck him before, not even when he'd caught glimpses of a living, breathing human being lying ill on a white-sheeted bed.

He had to force the image from his mind before it paralyzed him.

Concentrate on the task at hand. Check the instruments. Steer the ship.

He turned his focus to the heads-up display. Nothing happened.

Of course. The instruments belonged to that other existence— Virtual Reality instead of Truth.

As he toggled the switch to return the computer feed, the panorama before him dissolved into a grainy blur. He shook his head, and his hands instinctively rose to his eyes to rub them. A futile gesture. He let them fall again.

His disappointment was like a fist in the gut, but he needed the information the heads-up display provided. It was unthinkable to try navigating the entire bloodstream and the convoluted passageways of the inner organs by trusting to memory or intuition or pure dumb luck. He needed to know the status of the ship, too.

But after seeing the wonders of this inner world with new eyes, how could he possibly give that up?

He had to find a compromise. Could a person exist in two realities at once?

Maybe the problem wasn't that profound. If the brain is an ultra-sophisticated computer, then what he needed was multi-tasking, like driving a car and having a conversation. Or reading music and performing it at the same time.

He needed to train his brain to distinguish between the elements of the VR feed that were desirable, and those that were only distractions. But then he realized that he'd already been doing that since the very first mission. As his mind gradually forged its new link, it had, on its own, begun to discard the poorer raw material of the computer feed.

It was a hopeful sign. He was eager put the idea to the test, but it would have to wait.

He could hear the approach of the drumming heart.

There was work to do.

## 28

Hunter's first mission on his own was a bust. Though he was certain there were still bombs in the approaches to the left kidney, he'd failed to find them.

He needed Tamiko's maps. They showed the most likely locations of bombs, and the best routes to them. Without them, he was adrift in a liquid labyrinth. Yet he could only see them with the VR switched on, and that was like throwing a veil over his newfound sight. He was certain he had missed seeing the bombs because of the limitations of the VR gear.

Time to take a break and let his subconscious go to work on the problem.

Bridges caught him on the way to the mess.

Another head-shrinking session didn't qualify as a rest, but Hunter couldn't think of a way to get out of it.

The doctor started the game with a curveball.

"Were you healthy as a child?"

Hunter began to cross his arms but caught himself and rested his hands on his legs instead.

"I suppose you've accessed my medical records. So you know I had chickenpox. Nothing more serious than that."

"There are references to one overnight hospital stay, but no explanation. You were...eight. What was that for?"

"I didn't have a mental breakdown, if that's what you're asking. I...had a lousy stomach as a kid. Bad digestion. Cramps. Sudden attacks of diarrhea. A weak bladder sometimes, too. They checked me in for some tests. Didn't find anything. It cleared up on its own as I got older."

Bridges leaned on his hand and tapped a finger against his lips. "Barium enema. Cystoscopy. Local x-rays. All very invasive treatments, especially to a young boy."

"I didn't enjoy it. What are you getting at?"

"Were you abused as a child?"

"Hell no!" Hunter snapped straight. "Now you're sounding like those assholes hired by my former employers. If this is just a fishing expedition, we're done here."

The doctor waved him back into his seat and his voice took an apologetic tone.

"You're badly troubled by the thought that you're operating inside the body of someone who hasn't given their consent."

"Who doesn't even know what's been done to her!"

Bridges gave a nod of acknowledgment. "I just wondered if there was a personal reason it bothered you so much. Sexual abuse is extremely traumatic, but even your hospital experience could explain some of your feelings."

"Nobody abused me. Don't even go there."

"Bullied at school? Made to stick things in your throat, your nose, or...other places?"

Hunter looked away and didn't answer. At least Bridges had the good grace not to take notes.

"All right. Let's look at your hate for psychiatrists. You were badly mistreated by the company doctors. Tricked, bullied, given some very powerful drugs without your full knowledge. But is there more to it than that? What about your family history?"

Hunter realized he was chewing his lip. His arms had crossed, too, but he left them that way.

"Not that it's any of your business, but since it's probably on one of those pages in front of you, my mother spent thousands of dollars on a therapist who made her cry for a half-hour every week over being an unfit mother and wife, and then made sure she spent the rest of the time doped to the gills. A family friend finally introduced her to a support group and within months she was fine. Never suffered depression again."

Bridges leaned back with a look of sudden understanding. He said nothing for nearly a minute, then spoke softly.

"Do you see the connection? It's not surprising that you're repelled by the thought of being an intruder into someone's most personal and private places."

Hunter said nothing, but he could feel the worst of his anger ebb away. Maybe it was true. And maybe it was worthwhile to know such things about his own motivations and hangups. It didn't change what had to be done, but it might make some actions easier to accept.

"Are we finished?" he asked.

"It's up to you. You're really the driver here—I'm just a passenger."

Hunter snorted. It was such a cliché thing to say. Bridges usually did better.

He left for the control room, forgetting about his plan to grab a snack in the mess. His attention was already returning to the dilemma of his split vision when navigating the bloodstream. He needed both his VR instrument readouts and his new *mind-sight*.

Bridges' driving metaphor had triggered one of his own: he needed to be able to read the dashboard of the car while still having a clear view of the road ahead.

Maybe that was a parallel the mind would accept.

The first step was to be able to cut through the interference from the VR feed and tap into the rich flow of sensory data from his mind's new link without physically hitting the kill switch. Long periods of travel in large arteries were a blessing there. He forced himself to relax, and tried to cultivate the elusive sense of *dasein*, of belonging.

For a long time the improvements were barely noticeable—a bit more definition, a touch more color. It was frustrating, because he wanted it so badly... really longed to *be* there, in the flesh.

That was when reality finally bloomed.

It was the *wanting* that counted—the fervent desire for transcendence.

He reveled again in the glory of metamorphosis, becoming a creature of the bloodstream—a weapon in its arsenal in the battle for life.

He drank in the sensations, fixing them in his consciousness. Then gradually he experimented with letting part of his mind picture the VR instruments. He thought of it like looking at his wrist to check his watch. The muscles of the eye could make quick jumps in focus from the far to the near, and perhaps he could train his mind to do the same.

Yes. There were flickers of something.

It was like trying to see an image in one of those 3D pictures you could buy—a hidden shape that would suddenly jump out of a repetitive design, if you got the focus right. Some people never could see them.

There! A series of red numbers and lines, floating in space. Nebulous, but better than nothing. He spent the next half-hour practicing how to make the readouts come and go.

It wasn't perfect, but he could function. Better than he'd had any right to hope.

And he found the rest of the bombs.

# # #

Since their patient had already left the clinic, *Primus* couldn't be removed from her body. She would be gone for two days. They'd never left the ship inside her for anything close to that long. The body was a dynamic environment like few others, and it was too risky to leave *Primus* adrift in the bloodstream.

"Could we hide it inside a cell?" the pilot asked. "A tissue cell. . . one that wouldn't be going anywhere."

"As far as we know," Mallory replied, "the body responds to any direct cellular damage."

"Plenty of time for something to wreck the lipid coating and the sensor array," Gage said.

"What about between a bunch of cells?" Hunter persisted. "There's got to be lots of debris lying around in there that never draws the attention of a cleanup crew."

"How would you keep it from popping loose?" Tamiko asked. "Like a bar of soap from a wet fist."

In the end, he maneuvered *Primus* into a tiny dead-end offshoot of a lymphatic vessel that wouldn't be expected to see much traffic, dug deeply into the wall, and spread the manipulator arms like a grappling hook. Then he set the engine revs and prepared to leave.

He didn't really want to. There was no rush—the patient was due to fly out of Langley AFB within the hour, but that was plenty of time on *Primus'* scale. He could tell the others that he'd wanted to stick around for a while, to see if the plan was going to work.

It would be a good chance to practice his multi-tasking.

He relaxed his mind—willing himself into the transitional state.

Colors in surrounding tissues became increasingly vivid, and for the first time he found he could see through the semi-transparent membrane of the nearest cell, into the mysterious workings inside it. Long, oblong shapes drifted slowly past indistinct strands of grey, and farther away he could see a large, round, shadowy object. The *nucleus?* He wished he could remember more of his high school biology lessons.

Whatever processes were taking place within the cell were happening at a rate too slow to see without time-lapse photography. He decided to close his eyes and test his other senses. Did the ocean of life really sound like the swells and surf of that greater ocean he knew so well? Yes, although it was muffled, perhaps by cellular material pushed up against the sensor array. Even here, even now, if he listened closely, he could discern the beat of the distant heart, as its rhythm rolled in waves through myriad liquid passageways and resonant tissues.

Drum of life, indeed.

Primus had no equipment to reproduce smell or taste. Yet Hunter had a definite body awareness. Now, without distractions, he seemed to feel the delicate wash of the fluid lymph at his back, and the elastic, enveloping touch of the cell membranes around him, perhaps even providing him with some of their warmth (or was that just imagination?) It felt. . . protective. *Womb*-like, perhaps. Comforting.

He was completely relaxed.

Vulnerable.

It began as an ache in his chest. A tightening; a constriction growing so slowly that it formed a dull knot of pain before he noticed it. For a frightening moment he wondered if he was having a heart attack. But this wasn't distress from a physical cause—it was a longing, a yearning. . . . A fierce *need*.

Where in the world had that come from?

A spark of adrenaline ran along his nerves and pricked at his skin. It quickly deepened into a spreading anxiety, potent and chilling, and finally into a pervasive swell of fear.

What was happening? Was the VR malfunctioning? Or the electrodes? Were they scrambling his neurons to the point of *schizophrenia?*

He didn't wait to find out. He snapped the kill switch and left *Primus* and its suddenly threatening domain behind.

There were more than enough disturbing emotions in his own world.

## 29

The submersible was like a tomb. Would soon become *a tomb, as he* raspingly drew the last traces of breathable air into his lungs and used it up. Darkness. Pressure. The pressure of the dark.

The watery night was like a vise that would contract, and ultimately crush as the victim took its final fall.

But then... an unexpected reprieve.

Perhaps the sub had become wedged between boulders. Would it stay there long enough for rescue to come from the world of light far above? From the. . . oil rig, that was it. He remembered people there—a lovely Asian woman, an angry man with white hair, a black man with a face full of sympathy. Would they rescue him? Would they bother?

They'd have to hurry. The Dark had long fingers that dug beneath the craft and tried to pry it loose. To take it for its own. He was the intruder. The invader. He could not escape.

He felt his own rage well up.

It wasn't fair! He'd done nothing wrong.

He raised his hands, ready to wield them like hammers. . . to smash and shatter.

A voice cried to him to stop.

Whose voice?

It was coming from somewhere inside him. He could feel desperation, like a drum, beating against the wall of his chest. He had to let it out.

Choking a last few breaths, he dug fingers deep between his ribs and ripped the offending flesh away. Even in the pitch blackness he saw it shred and tear, until he had laid bare the beating heart itself.

And then, from within the heart the voice began to speak. . . .

He rolled to the edge of the bed retching, his dark green T-shirt soaked with sweat. Breath came in ragged gasps.

Staggering to his feet to flee the bed and its evil dreams, he groped for the support of the wall but slid slowly into a limp sprawl on the floor, fighting an overpowering urge to weep. It was an eternity before his shivering finally stopped. The clock in front of him read 6:45.

He would get dressed. He would find himself a cup of strong coffee.

And he would go to see Kierkegaard.

# # #

"What did you say?"

"I can't do this anymore."

Kierkegaard was stunned. His mouth opened as if to speak, then he looked at Bridges, who was equally dumbfounded.

"Hunter, you can't be serious. *Can't do it anymore?* What is that supposed to mean?" An angry flush reddened the man's face. "Do you think this is a game we're playing?"

"No, sir." Hunter tried to keep eye contact, but couldn't. "I know it's a matter of life or death. That's why someone else has to take over." Before the others could interrupt, he looked up at Bridges. "You were right. All of the doctors were right." There was fear in his eyes.

"I'm *losing* it," Hunter said softly.

Bridges forestalled a hot-tempered reply from Kierkegaard with a quick gesture of his hand. This was serious. The project hung in the balance.

"It's all right, Hunter," he said gently, noticing for the first time the clammy pallor of the other's skin. "Take it slowly. Sit down. We have the time. We just want to understand."

Kierkegaard took the hint and sat in one of the nearby chairs, not behind the desk. It took a major effort for him to keep silent. Hunter slowly sank into the other chair. Bridges perched on the edge of the desk.

"What's happened?" the doctor asked. "Why do you say you're losing it?"

"Wicked dreams, for one thing. I've had bad dreams for a long time—since the accident. But they're worse now. Much worse." He couldn't repress a shudder. "You expect strange stuff from dreams, so I didn't attach any meaning to it, but now..."

"Dreams can be a guide to what's troubling us, but they're not a road map. Impossible to interpret with any certainty, no matter what anyone says." Bridges tried to sound gently reassuring. "Is this only about the dreams?" he prompted.

"No." Hunter sighed. He looked into their faces, willing them to believe him. "I'm feeling things that can't be there. Like another. . . *presence*—I don't know how to describe it."

"All of the time? Most of the time?"

"When I'm hooked up to the VR, at least. And. . . sudden mood changes. Strong feelings, for no reason. I mean, really strong. Doctor. . . ." His voice quavered. "Could the electrodes in the VR helmet be causing some kind of schizophrenia?"

"Schizophrenia?" Bridges couldn't hide his surprise. "You have no history of schizophrenia, and there's none in your family—it would have been red-flagged. Why would you suspect it?"

"Some of the symptoms—hallucinations. . . a feeling of persecution."

"Paranoia. Is that what you're saying?"

"We all have some of that in this business," Kierkegaard interrupted. "Unfortunately, we need to. But Hunter.. . . " He tried to keep the skepticism out of his voice. "I'm curious about why you think this has something to do with the equipment. The VR setup."

"Gage explained to me that the electrodes work to make the brain more susceptible to the illusion. To make the experience more real. Well it damned well works! I'm having trouble knowing what *is* real anymore. Inside, outside. . . which one of them is reality? What if I lose the ability to tell the difference?" The prospect clearly terrified him.

"The electrode system has been thoroughly tested . . . " Kierkegaard began.

"Not on someone who was already *mentally ill*."

He had said it. The thing he feared most. It did not bring relief, as movies portrayed. Only a deep feeling of shame.

Silence fell like a pall. Bridges didn't know how to proceed. He didn't dare say the wrong thing—the stakes were enormous. Kierkegaard was numbed by the turn of events.

Hunter slowly got to his feet.

"I only know that I can't do this. If I continue this way, I'm going to wreck something. Do some damage that we can't fix. Then everything's lost. You've got to replace me."

"With whom?" Kierkegaard asked, so quietly that it seemed as if he were reluctant to let the words escape his mouth.

"Train Gage or Tamiko to do it. They're both incredibly sharp. They know things about the systems that I . . . "

"Tamiko has never even tried to pilot *Primus*. Neither has any experience with submersibles."

"You've got to have a simulator program around here somewhere! Try them out on that. I'll help them any way I can." He shook off a spasm of guilt and continued, "We have two days until the patient returns. Tell them. . . for now, tell them that I'm exhausted—that we need to have a backup for me, in case of emergency. Then we can see which one of them performs the best."

"You can't leave the base," Kierkegaard reminded him.

"I know that." Hunter swallowed. "I'm not fit to be anywhere else, anyway."

He left the room quietly and walked down the hall.

## 30

Kellogg snapped off the TV.

The CNN report was about the pope's visit, and the state dinner the next night.

She would be there.

If killing her had been his assignment, her travels would present a handful of promising opportunities. It wasn't. He didn't know everything about the larger operation—didn't need to and didn't want to—but he knew that it hinged on using her for leverage. If she were to die, that leverage would be gone.

His task was to remove those who might help her to escape her trap. That meant neutralizing the secret facility that was right inside the Air Force Base itself. Even with his own level of access, that provided enough difficulties to satisfy any man's taste for challenge.

He sat down at the desk, pulled the computer keyboard toward him, and called up the map of the base with a few strokes. His assault plans were still not final. He rarely asked for advice—rarely needed it—but insertion would be the most difficult part, by far. First, the approach by water: in boats, or with scuba? He wanted

Hennings' ideas on that, and he was due to arrive tomorrow morning.

The second phase would require meticulous planning to make the best use of minimal ground cover. There were only a few regular patrols in that part of the base, but there could be random traffic and they didn't dare leave anything to chance. Rakov was a wizard at assault strategies.

Once the team made it as far as the main building it should be simple. Security forces around the lab itself were surprisingly light. The president's people were handcuffed by the need to draw no attention and were gambling that no one would be interested in the unremarkable structure.

It was a simple one-story building formed around a square central section with wings to the north and south. There was very little good cover for the few military types stationed there, and the scientists and support staff would be helpless.

Kellogg didn't have to kill them, but he probably would—partly because it was good business but also partly for the pleasure of it. He'd been told that it was the equipment that was important. Without it, the people became irrelevant; but to Kellogg, survivors were loose ends. He hated untidiness.

His team would still need special stealth to take out the last defenders inside the lab complex. They couldn't afford noise that might bring the whole base down on them, and although the building had few windows, the unmistakable flicker of muzzle flashes on a dark night would be a dead giveaway. That meant they'd need heavily suppressed weapons. He favored the Heckler & Koch MP5SD when there was a likelihood of multiple targets, though he knew Kowalski preferred the heavier, and noisier, 10mm version of the gun. More likely they would be using their side weapons most of the time anyway and he had a good supplier of 9mm Berettas.

It bothered him that he didn't know much about the equipment he was expected to destroy. He knew only that it involved a lot of computers and medical gear—diagnostic equipment of some kind. If so, some of those devices were huge. An MRI machine would not be easy to dismantle. He hoped that the destruction of its control systems would be good enough. He'd have to do some research and find out.

The demolition element of the mission would depend heavily on the speed of their escape. Could they use incendiaries, and get far away before the fire broke through to the outside? Or would they have to go big and nasty, then count on being able to slip away in the resulting confusion? The latter would be the riskiest. Yet Kellogg secretly hoped it would come to that.

He liked big explosions best.

\#   \#   \#

Kierkegaard broke a long silence, still shocked. "Is Hunter right? Could he be becoming schizophrenic?"

Bridges gave a deep sigh and moved to sit in the vacated chair, staring at the floor with his lips pinched between a thumb and forefinger. He was badly shaken. Finally he said, "You know I can't guarantee anything. But I'd bet my life savings he isn't."

"I feel like it's happening all over again. Like last year. . . with Travis Li."

Kierkegaard had already looked tired. Now he looked sick. Bridges nodded. He, too, found it impossible to forget what had happened with the very first test pilot of *Primus*, a competition-level video gamer who'd been recruited because of his extraordinary reflexes and intuitive skill with VR interfaces.

Travis Li had been too cocky, but had made good progress in test-tube environments. Then the project's government backers had thrown him to the wolves. Pleading a national emergency, they'd demanded he undertake a mission within a living bloodstream, long before he was ready.

The attempt had been an utter failure, never progressing beyond the arteries of a lab animal. Unknowingly turning an already risky situation into a catastrophe, Li had done some dope to "mellow out" before his ordeal. The combination of hallucinogen and altered reality had thrown his shattered mind into a realm from which it had barely escaped, and only then after many months of treatment.

Kierkegaard stared at his desk. "I told the CIA man back then. That they were asking too much. That they couldn't expect us to produce a miracle dreamed up by Hollywood. Do you know what he told me?" Bridges shook his head. "That if our team hadn't been expected to perform the things people saw in that movie, we would never have been given a billion dollars."

"Almost certainly true." Bridges conceded. "Fortunately, Hunter isn't Travis Li. Because the submersible environment was already so natural to him, he's been able to cope with everything else far better than Li ever could have. Otherwise we would have lost him that first time *Primus* went through the heart."

"What is it, then? What's happening to him?"

The doctor looked his friend in the eye. "I think we both know what's happening. He's managed to adapt to the *Primus* very well and control her in the maelstrom. How does he find his way without using the maps? How does he spot the bombs at all in the midst of so much chaos? We've both watched the monitors. We've even tried on that remote VR set you've got hidden here in the office. I couldn't take two minutes of it."

"I get a headache after five." The older man nodded. "I agree. His performance is phenomenal. Unbelievable."

"Perhaps enough to justify what we've done to him, but the jury's still out on that since we were never entirely sure what side effects might be involved. Hunter might be right. I don't mean schizophrenia, but it might well be that his brain has been through too much stress without fully healing. I warned you there was a risk of that—he very nearly died in that submersible in the Gulf of Mexico. In a horrible way."

"There was no-one else."

"I know, but now we ask him to face another submersible environment—even if he isn't physically present—and add other factors that go beyond normal human understanding. Maybe in that sense he *is* like Travis Li—his brain simply can't assimilate what he's experiencing." He looked up with a grim face. "It may be breaking down."

Kierkegaard sucked in a bitter breath.

"God, I hope you're wrong. We can't possibly do without him, no matter what he says. It's pure fantasy to think that Gage or Tamiko could take over. Without his. . . special abilities, months would not be long enough to get up to speed. We'll be lucky if we have another week."

"And getting Li back is out of the question. Even if he was willing to return," the doctor offered, "my conscience wouldn't let me do that to any man."

"What do we do?" Kierkegaard asked finally, indecisive for the first time Bridges had ever seen. "Try psychotherapy?"

The other shook his head. "We try it his way. We put Tamiko and Gage through the simulator and. . . we hope he comes around on his own." He raised his weary eyes and tried to smile. "We have two days."

## 31

Tamiko's reaction was profane.

It took several attempts for Kierkegaard to convince her she wasn't the victim of a twisted joke.

"Why me?" she persisted. "My brother won't even let me drive his ski boat! And the rest of you were hopeless in the early trials."

Gage gave her a black look. "None of us had Hunter's experience. That doesn't mean we can't learn. We didn't get enough time on the simulator, either, thanks to this emergency. Personally, I'm eager to see what it's like in there for myself."

In spite of his dread, Hunter had to be first on the simulator. As detailed as the simulation was, it fell far short of the true experience of controlling *Primus* in the bloodstream, and only Hunter could set it straight.

Its original form was a mishmash of equipment and wiring, but now its software ran on the main computer and it used the same VR gear Hunter had been using every day. For Hunter, that made the ordeal both more familiar and more frightening.

Fortunately, the program was highly adaptable. Through dozens of short trials over the course of two hours he was able to refine the settings until he felt it gave as good an impression of the real thing as it was capable of doing. The resolution of the video display, the apparent speed of travel, and the way the ship behaved in the thick fluid, were close approximations. But the program couldn't provide the obstacles of the bloodstream such as gargantuan blood cells, sudden cross currents, and other hazards. The simulator had been created before live tests had been done with the intention that such details could be added later when accurate data became available.

When the task was complete, Hunter went to the nearest bathroom and retched. As soon as he was able, he returned to the simulator room to see how Gage and Tamiko were doing, and to give them advice if he could.

It only made him feel worse.

The VR system had been designed by Gage, with his own biases and idiosyncrasies built in, so his body didn't fight the simulation. His spatial skills were also better than Tamiko's, enabling him to judge distances quickly and anticipate course changes to avoid bumping into walls. On the downside, he had a hard time dividing his attention between his surroundings and the instrumentation. In a pre-programmed maze of tunnels, his performance was very poor, and his reaction time slow.

Tamiko was nearly the opposite. She had a gift for assimilating both the instrument and the sensory data at the same time. Her ability to picture a complex pattern of course changes gave her much higher scores on the maze.

But she kept bumping into things.

"Fucking machine!" she spat, tearing the helmet from her head after a long session. "Why couldn't they just have given it a steering wheel and a couple of pedals? Not to mention traction. It's like trying to run on glare ice with leather soles."

"It's a fluid," Hunter explained for the fifth time. "There's traction in the resistance of the fluid, but you have to learn how to use it. Anticipate how the ship will react and then allow a small amount of lag time for each maneuver. *Primus* is incredibly agile. You should see what an average submersible is like."

"I think I'll deny myself that pleasure," she snarled, then tore the rest of the equipment from her body and stalked out of the room. Hunter knew her anger was directed at herself. She wasn't accustomed to failure. He told himself she'd get the hang of it, given enough time, and tried to forget that time was a luxury they didn't have.

Kierkegaard did not forget.

He snapped off the monitor in his office and turned to Bridges.

"So much for that. Our patient returns tomorrow around noon. Every extra moment after that could be critical. Do you think either of our backup pilots is close to being ready?"

The doctor shook his head without hesitation. "Tamiko doesn't want to do it in the first place, but she's giving an honest effort. She just can't adapt to the way a submersible craft responds. She'd learn eventually, but...."

"Much too late to do us any good. I know. And Gage?"

"... is a gifted planner and problem solver in his own element, but he isn't able to react quickly enough to sudden changes in the environment. He can't make the necessary snap judgments, and quick physical responses. He'd be slaughtered in the real bloodstream."

Kierkegaard nodded. Then he held up a hand. "Just for the sake of argument, would it make enough of a difference if either of them could tap into that. . . *extra something* that Hunter seems able to access?"

"You know perfectly well there's no guarantee that either of them could. Even with Hunter it was a long shot, and it took its own time to manifest itself. There might not be one in a million people receptive to it." He began to pace the room, clenching and unclenching his fists. "There's also the very real possibility that it's what has pushed Hunter to the edge. If so, I don't know if I could bring myself to do that to anyone else," he finished quietly.

Kierkegaard stepped forward and took his friend's arm in a firm grip.

"Remember that we're not just talking about one life here. There could be fallout from this crisis that we can't even begin to guess. We've got to get Hunter back in the saddle. We have no other choice."

Bridges shrugged his arm free. "Your bosses might be good at convincing a man to put his life on the line for the sake of some intangible concepts and fine phrases, but can you force a man to put his very *sanity* at risk—and expect to get any worthwhile results from him? Best of luck." He turned and left the room.

Kierkegaard slowly sat on the edge of the desk. He should speak to his superiors. He'd delayed his report in the hope that the situation would change, but it looked as if that gamble had been lost. Now he'd also have to explain why he'd delayed informing them.

How could he tell the president they had failed? How could you give news like that to anyone?

## 32

Hunter found Tamiko at the bar they'd visited a few nights earlier.

She looked up from her drink and said, "I guess you won't be getting a backup any time soon. It's still all up to you."

"It's not your fault that you don't have the background," he offered. It was a little patronizing, but all he could think to say. Even so, she appeared grateful for the effort.

"I know we can still continue as long as you get enough rest," she began. "But I feel like I'm letting that woman down. I've been sitting here trying to imagine what she's feeling. I don't know how much of the truth she knows, but all those tests. . . If it were me, I'd be scared to death."

Hunter felt guilt sweep over him again. Tamiko wasn't letting the patient down, he was. Yet he'd asked to be replaced to avoid greater harm. Would the woman herself see it that way, if she were ever told? What must she be going through even now? With every new test increasing her anxiety and her fear.

Sudden understanding hit him like a tidal wave.

Anxiety. Fear.

Was it possible? Could it be that what he'd felt were...

Her emotions, not *his*!

Of course! There'd been no reason for him to experience such strong feelings and that was what had thrown him so badly. The emotions had struck without warning, completely at odds with his own frame of mind just as he was most deeply linked to her.

His presence in *Primus* had penetrated to the level of her very cells, but his *touch* had gone deeper still.

He was thunderstruck. He didn't know whether to be relieved or terrified.

"What's the matter with you? You look like you've seen a ghost." Tamiko was watching him with real concern.

"I hope not. Oh, I hope not." He struggled to his feet, nearly spilling his drink. "Thanks, Lucy. I have... something I have to do." He could feel her astonished stare as he bolted from the room.

When he checked the internal phone directory, he was surprised to learn that Kierkegaard's sleeping quarters were along the same hallway as his own, only a few doors away. Still far from certain about his conclusions, he stopped outside the project leader's door and slumped against a wall.

He was convinced that he'd somehow tapped into their patient's mind, at least to the point of experiencing her emotions—especially her fear. The thought was staggering. It was an unparalleled invasion—a violation without precedent. Probing the recesses of her body with a miniature submarine was bad enough. But the recesses of her mind? The stronghold of her very essence as a human being?

She couldn't have given permission for that.

Kierkegaard wore no jacket or tie as he answered the door, only an unmistakable weariness that had nothing to do with the lateness of the hour.

"What can I do for you Mr. Hunter?" he asked, stepping back to invite the younger man in. He could have said so much more, Hunter knew, and the pilot was grateful for his restraint.

"I need to talk, sir. About our patient."

The older man's eyes lit up, but he still looked wary. He sat carefully on the edge of the bed and indicated the only chair with his hand. "Why? What has changed?"

"I've realized that there could be another explanation for my. . . symptoms. If so, there are some serious implications."

"Go on."

"You say you can't tell me who our patient is, but I need to understand the president's place in all this. He's ordered us to do what we're doing without her permission—explicitly *without her knowledge*. Does he truly care about this woman, or is it only political? If she knew, would she really trust him with that decision—trust him with her life? Maybe even more than that?"

"I'm not sure what you consider more than *life*; but I can tell you this much, the president would trade places with our patient in a second, if he could. She would refuse, though. Yes, Mr. Hunter, there is that much trust between them. That much love." Kierkegaard's face showed he was revealing more than he wanted to.

Hunter nodded slowly. "In that case, sir. . . I'd like to continue with the mission. I'll pilot the *Primus*."

"That's wonderful news, Mr. Hunter. But you said there were serious implications. What did you mean by that?"

"You'll just have to give *me* some trust on that one for now." There was a glint in the eyes, and Kierkegaard decided not to insist.

"Would you be standing here now if Tamiko or Gage had performed well on the simulator?"

"No, sir. I guess I wouldn't. It's not pleasant to think that you're losing your mind. I'm glad to know something else might be to blame. I also know that I'm the only one who has any chance of doing what has to be done in the time we have left. Even if I don't know who this woman is, I can't condemn her to death."

Kierkegaard nodded thoughtfully. "I have come to know her. She's a special person, Mr. Hunter. Worthy of some sacrifices, I think."

The young man responded with a nod of his own.

"I'm sorry for... for all this," he said. "I'll see you in the morning." He left the room, closing the door behind him. He had made his decision, but it brought him no comfort.

Once again he would immerse himself in the essence of another human being, but now he realized for the first time that his own psyche was also vulnerable. The mind of the mystery woman had shaken his own consciousness to the core.

# # #

Gerard Mannis wasn't sleeping either. His computer alerted him to an incoming message, and as he read it, he wondered how the president would react. To the chief executive it would be shocking, but ultimately good news.

Mannis wasn't so sure.

Had the submersible pilot really been determined to quit the project? Or had it been a risky ploy to prove that he wasn't in league with their enemies? If so, the gamble had paid off. Who would question his actions now? If he was a traitor, who could possibly stop him? They would never know a thing until it was too late.

A long career of dark dealings had made it almost impossible for Mannis to accept anything at face value. Yet part of him wanted desperately to believe that Hunter was exactly what he seemed: a troubled but decent man.

He sat brooding for long minutes. Nothing came to him. After a time he simply sat up straight and began to tap quickly on the keyboard.

He had made his decision. He would trust Hunter.

If he was wrong... then God help them all.

33

The patient came back into range of their equipment moments before her plane touched down on the main runway at Langley. Hunter didn't see her arrive—he was already suited up and waiting. Within minutes he was working to gently nudge *Primus* out of her parking space between cells. Signs of residue testified that some of the body's cellular janitors had prodded at the ship as if it were undesirable trash left lying around by mistake.

Hunter had had a bad night, second-guessing himself in the lonely darkness, when it was far easier to believe he was simply going insane. Tamiko and Mallory noticed the pallor of his skin, but said nothing. Tamiko and Gage had been instructed to continue their practice sessions on the simulator when they could; but for now, Hunter was still the team's only option.

Exhausted or not, their pilot would have to fly.

There had also been news from a tired but jubilant Lorelei Mallory.

She and her assistants had succeeded in identifying white blood cells "tagged" to attack bomb material. From a rough calculation of their total number in the patient's body, she thought it was possible to extrapolate the number of bombs.

"Our best estimates put the number at between fifty and sixty," she announced, looking for approval.

"Sixty bombs!" Gage's shock expressed what the rest were thinking. "And we've found how many so far? Ten?"

Mallory was taken aback. She looked at Kierkegaard. "Well, we can run another test. Maybe our first estimate is high."

"Your numbers are close to what I'd personally expected. It's not your fault that we don't like the facts we face. It only proves that we can't let up. We have to keep going." Kierkegaard looked at Hunter as he said it. They all knew the stamina of the *Primus'* pilot would be put to the test.

In spite of the new urgency, or perhaps partly because of it, the first mission to the patient's liver was a bust. Inferior as the computer-processed feed was, Hunter had no choice but to rely on it. He simply wasn't able to relax enough for his special link to form, so he wasted valuable time navigating from the kidney through the lymphatic vessels into larger veins, and to the inferior vena cava. It was almost a relief to rocket along giant blood vessels after that demanding journey.

The liver was near the top of their risk assessment list, but it was terribly complex. Its tissues were nourished by blood from the hepatic artery, which branched off into the five main lobes of the liver, and then into each lobule, of which there were thousands. A blockage in any one of those places could cause serious tissue damage and shut down critical filtering of the blood supply.

There was also a second potential threat, equally dangerous. The blood to be filtered entered the organ via the portal vein. That blood was cleansed of its bile, which was then channeled off into the bile duct, and the clean blood was returned to the system by the hepatic veins. Blockages in that network might produce a backup of blood and bile that could ultimately be fatal.

Searching the entire organ would be a huge task, requiring dozens of trips through the labyrinth of tiny arteries, doubling back each time through smaller veins, then trying to cross back over to the arterial system through connections between adjacent blood vessels or through lymph channels before *Primus* could be dumped back into the larger venous system. Then the ship would have to make the round trip all the way to the heart and back to start the process over again.

After an hour of effort Hunter had found nothing and had to take a break.

The largest section of the hepatic artery was probably free of bombs anyway—it would be very difficult to block. The smaller blood vessels were full of floating obstacles and false targets, and so before long the endless procession of twisting tunnels began to blur together in his mind. He became afraid that he'd missed something in momentary lapses of concentration. Those seemed to happen more and more often, until he was nearly sure he'd dozed off. That was when he gave in. He had to rest.

He found a pot of coffee that had been sitting long enough to distill into a potent dose of caffeine. There were some day-old honey-glazed donuts sitting nearby, and he grabbed a couple. He couldn't spare any time for a nap. If Mallory's test was even close to being accurate, it could take weeks to eliminate all the bombs.

The enemy wouldn't wait that long.

Somehow he had to put his fears aside and give in to the link. It was essential. With it, he found bombs; without it, he didn't. But just knowing the solution didn't make it happen.

When he went back to work after a half-hour break, the coffee-and-sugar infusion combined with his own anxiety to put his nerves on edge and he couldn't relax. Unable to tap into the connectedness that had served him so well, he found nothing. The endless tunnels of the liver's arteries were hypnotic in their monotony. Trying to find the bombs was like over-flying a petroleum complex to spot one particular round shape among all of the others.

After an hour-and-a-half he was forced to unplug again and eat some lunch. In desperation he lay down and closed his eyes for forty-five minutes, but it only upset his stomach and made him feel groggier than ever. The clock was running. He went back in.

His third attempt of the day was yet another failure.

Kierkegaard was in the room as Hunter wearily pulled off the helmet. The pilot anticipated the obvious question with a tired shake of his head.

"I don't know what's wrong. I don't know if anything is wrong. Maybe they didn't plant any bombs in the liver. Or maybe I'm just not seeing them." He waited a moment to gather his strength, then lifted himself out of the chair and peeled off the haptic suit. It was possible that the enemy had passed over the liver, but none of them really believed that.

He had no choice but to take a longer rest. It was only late afternoon. He couldn't focus on a book, so he sat in his room listening to Mozart. It was surprisingly soothing and re-energizing at the same time.

He took a long time over dinner. Bridges and Mallory sat with him, but no one said much. Once he'd stalled as long as he decently could over after-dinner coffee, he reluctantly stood and made his way to the mission room. He was still exhausted, and he knew it.

Paradoxically, it was his weariness that provided the breakthrough.

Back in *Primus*, still awash with fatigue, subconscious barriers began to break down, but so gradually that he didn't notice it happening. Suddenly he became aware that he could see—really see. It startled him, and for a moment the increased perception threatened to vanish, but then a wave of warmth washed over him. It was the sense of belonging. . . connection. . . *acceptance* that he'd experienced before. A comfortable, secure feeling that was totally at odds with his anxiety.

He took a deep breath, and a ripple of relaxation spread outward through every muscle of his body. He adjusted his posture, renewed his grip on the controls, flipped the kill switch and watched the inner universe unfold its miracles before him.

His fears had been for nothing. His mind suffered no intrusions. Within a half-hour of mission time he hit pay dirt and made a kill.

#   #   #

Kierkegaard was waiting in the control room. His squeeze of Hunter's arm in congratulations turned into a grip of support as the pilot nearly collapsed.

"I have. . . ." Hunter stopped to swallow and lubricate his throat. "I have to go back. Back to where we searched this morning. Search all over again. Redo the missions." The effort to talk left him breathless.

As he paused to gulp some air, he saw the look of consternation on Kierkegaard's face and held up a hand. "Can't explain right now. Explain in the morning."

The older man hesitated, then nodded once, and again more decisively to prevent comment from the others who had begun to gather in the room.

He and Bridges helped Hunter stagger to his quarters and collapse on the bed, where he fell immediately and blissfully asleep.

## 34

The darkness was alive.

The darkness had eyes.

The eyes watched him, unblinking. He had thought they were all gone, but a few remained, waiting until the blackness was complete. Then he became aware of their hungry glow. They were all around him, like wolves at the edge of a fire-lit circle.

No. They were not eyes. Could not be. They were just indicator lights that somehow fed on the last dregs of current from the failed electrical system. LED's. Those didn't need much current. Mechanical, not alive.

But he was not alone.

He could feel it. There was someone there. . . a presence lurking like a ghostly apparition in his peripheral vision that vanished when he turned his head. A change in air pressure, like the nearness of another body.

What did it want with him? Why was it intruding on his death?

The presence was coming closer. He could sense it, somehow. Closer. Yet he could see nothing, hear nothing, feel nothing.

Now. . . right next to him!

He swept his arms through the darkness but they were no defense. The presence pushed... and penetrated. It was inside him!

His mind filled with images, fragments kaleidoscoping across his brain. Faces... places he couldn't recognize. The images assaulted him like the surges of the current against the submersible... pushing, withdrawing, then pushing harder, displacing his own thoughts. Finally there came a moment when he knew that momentum had overcome inertia—and the battle was lost.

The submersible toppled. His mind toppled.

He began the long plunge into chaos.

The glowing readout of the clock said 4:02 AM. He slumped back onto sheets and pillow damp with sweat, his heart pounding.

He lay still for a long time, but eventually sleep claimed him again. This time he did not dream.

He awoke again at seven-thirty, breakfasted quickly, and carried his second cup of coffee to the control room. Kierkegaard was already there and turned to face him with a look of impatience.

"What's this about going over the same territory as yesterday morning? That's what you said last night, before you collapsed."

"We have to search those arteries again. I'm sorry."

"You can't be serious. Why? Do you know how little time we likely have left?" The pressure was beginning to show in the project leader's eyes.

"I wasn't making a good interface with the VR system at first. When I finally did, the bomb I found was well hidden by debris." He looked earnestly into Kierkegaard's eyes. "There are still bombs in those arteries, sir. Bombs that I missed. I don't want to accept the consequences of that."

"A hunch? Is that what you're trying to tell us?" Gage said.

"You know that we have no way of ever being certain all of the bombs have been found," Kierkegaard said.

"I do know that."

Their leader gave a ragged sigh. "All right, Mr. Hunter. Do what you have to do. But if you have any more doubts about your fitness for duty, let's hear about them before we waste hours of precious time." He left the room without acknowledging Hunter's repentant nod.

By the twenty-seven-minute mark Hunter had found another bomb. It's destruction brought a feeling of release as powerful as his anxiety and fear had been a couple of days before. It was almost as if the body around him recognized its liberation from an instrument of death.

As he continued the mission, he reveled in the keenness of his senses. He was aware of every swirl and eddy of the current. He could see everything, missed nothing; he was sure of it. He hadn't even switched off the VR feed. He was able to push it into the background of his consciousness until he needed it. The link was strong and steady. Yet it took another hour of following the twisting tunnels before he spotted the next telltale shape.

Once again, it was surrounded by debris, evidence that the body had begun to detect the intruders on its own, though its defenses were no match for them.

Hunter deftly positioned *Primus* and prepared to ram.

Red. His world was flashing red.

He willed his mind to visualize the heads-up display, and its text screen.

"DO NOT RAM. TORCH NOT CHARGED."

They were right. There hadn't been enough time for a recharge. Not enough juice for a spark. If he'd cracked the shell he would only have spilled the ADP himself.

Now what?

"KEEP PRIMUS THERE. COME REST."

Yes, he should take advantage of the break to get some rest, but the currents were strong and variable. Could he find a calm spot to park the ship? He tried an area just to the lee of the bomb, but it quickly became unstable—the sub began to drift.

Perhaps closer to the wall—a little eddy, from the look of it. Again, he relinquished the controls. The craft began a slow spin, but seemed to stay in place. He waited. No, it was drifting toward the outside of the eddy.

No good. He didn't dare leave the bomb—he couldn't be sure of finding it again. There was nothing to do but wait on station. How was he going to stay awake?

He concentrated on his vocal cords and willed them to say the words: "Can't leave the ship." Then he settled in for a long stay.

His vision was crystal clear, and myriad particles of every shape and size constantly drifted past. He enjoyed their varied patterns and colors, but he could identify almost none of them. *Mallory is the one who should be here*, he thought. A laboratory beyond her wildest dreams. A lifetime of research available with a few hours of observation. But to his untrained eye it was like watching leaves and twigs on the surface of a stream after a summer rain. Peaceful at least.

The spinning was annoying. Maybe he could tuck in between the bomb and the blood vessel wall? He carefully nudged *Primus* into position. The flow of fluid over the smooth surface of the bomb's silicon shell tried to pluck the sub away, but a slow, steady thrust from the main engine could keep the nose wedged in with only the occasional lateral correction every few minutes. The drawback was the lack of a view, only the featureless shell to the left and the artery wall on the right.

Or maybe it wasn't so bad after all. As before, he found that he could see into the nearest cell. The shapes within were blurred by the intervening protoplasm, or maybe their edges were never sharp, fuzzy with molecules that weren't quite distinguishable at that scale. Tiny engines of life, quietly performing their appointed tasks before his gaze.

His eyes were drawn to the large, dark shape so dominant near the center of the cell. The nucleus—home of DNA and RNA, the body's blueprints and its ancestral archives. Code to the past, present, and future.

Those genetic chains were among the largest of all molecules. Was it possible to see them? He stared at the nucleus, and his concentrated attention seemed to draw it closer, as if with a zoom lens. He focused his full attention on its dark depths, and in it he saw. . . .

[A lake. . . surrounded by trees. Sunshine on water. Dappled green shadows. Birds flying overhead.]

What the...?

A memory of northern woodlands? But the view wasn't one he recognized. His uncle's place in Northern Vermont had similar trees, but more buildings, and docks along the water's edge. This must be some other lake he'd seen. Why remember it now?

A ripple of fear went through him.

What brought that on?

He checked the status of the sub again. There was nothing wrong.

Focus on the cell—the nucleus of the cell. Yes, that was calming. A place of safety. . . .

[A small room—an attic room with a narrow window. Slanted rays of summer sunshine. A golden rectangle on printed wallpaper. Old. Faded, but warm. Familiar shapes: Winnie the Pooh, Tigger. . . the original illustrations, not the Disney versions. A single bed. Worn coverlet, with flowers.]

Damn it! That made no sense. That wasn't a room he remembered. He must have dozed off. Why hadn't he awakened in the control room?

At least the sub hadn't drifted. There was still a little time left before the recharge was complete. He needed to stay awake. Stay sharp.

He looked at the cell again. The nucleus, floating motionless. . . .

[Faces. Children's faces. Unfamiliar, but friendly. Happy. Laughing. *Dancing.* An impression of space. Echoes. Wood

. . . the smell of wood, and wax. Very large windows along one wall behind thin, white drapes. Small hands grabbing, clasping. A babble of voices. An urge to call out to them. To dance with them. . . .]

Red. Flashing red.

The alert. The charge was complete. He struggled to gather his wits. It was time to destroy the bomb and get out of there.

# # #

"You were right, Mr. Hunter." Kierkegaard greeted him as the helmet came off. "There were two bombs that you—and Dr. Gage—missed yesterday."

"It's not something that gives me any satisfaction, sir. I would much rather have found them the first time." He stretched his stiff limbs.

Just then Bridges and Mallory entered the room with worry showing on their faces.

"Is something wrong?" Kierkegaard asked.

Bridges went first. "I was doing some scans and noticed some extraordinary activity in the patient's thalamus—which is an area of the brain," he said for Hunter's benefit.

"If memory serves, it's more or less the gateway to the cerebral cortex," Kierkegaard said. "Virtually all of the brain's sensory information comes to it through the thalamus. Why would you be concerned to see activity there?"

"I said extraordinary activity," Bridges reiterated. "There should have been less than usual—the patient was resting, with very little sensory input."

"Do you think a bomb has gone off there?"

"No, nothing like that," the doctor replied. "Extra electrical activity—it was doing a lot of extra work."

"What would cause that?"

"I. . . No, I'd rather not speculate on that right now." Bridges gave a puzzling glance at Hunter. "I'm just concerned about anything out of the ordinary."

"Ordinary isn't a word I'd use for any of this." Kierkegaard raised an eyebrow. "And what's bothering you, Dr. Mallory?"

"It's the test, sir. The new blood test. I performed another analysis and, well. . . our earlier estimates of the bombs weren't too high." She hesitated. "I've checked my work twice."

"And. . . ?"

"The actual numbers are even higher." She swallowed hard.

"There are more than twice as many bombs as we thought."

"What was all that about the thalamus? I didn't get what you were hinting at."

Kierkegaard and Bridges were alone in the director's office. He settled heavily into his chair, while the doctor continued to pace the floor.

"That's the problem," Bridges answered. "It is only a hint. A sign of strong sensory activity when there should have been very little. Very little *physical* sensory information, at least." He looked up to see if his friend had caught his meaning.

"You're saying it could be due to other senses? *Extra* senses?"

"You know the evidence as well as I do," Bridges said. "It's why we decided to do what we did to Hunter. One of the main reasons we recruited him in the first place."

"The studies were very convincing regarding the role of the thalamus in extra-sensory activity. We hoped that such an ability would enhance the VR interface."

"Which certainly seems to be the case."

"With Hunter, yes. But what does she have to do with it?" Kierkegaard leaned forward. "Activity in his thalamus was expected, but why hers?"

Bridges raised his hands off the desk. "We don't know enough about psychic phenomena—their nature or the rules that govern them. Do they answer to the laws of physics? There are many who believe that quantum properties are involved, but we really have no idea. It's difficult enough to even accept that these things exist, let alone try to quantify or measure them in any way. We simply don't have the tools."

"What are you getting at?"

"I'm saying that we did some tinkering to create an artificially enhanced psychic environment. The goal was to improve Hunter's interface with *Primus*, but how do we know that's all it did? Maybe instead of turning on a flashlight beam we turned on a bare bulb that lit up a whole room." His voice softened as he looked into the other's eyes.

"I'm saying we may have awakened far more than we bargained for."

# # #

Hunter destroyed two more bombs in new areas of the liver. He didn't experience any more strange images, but his mood became unpredictable. His normal equanimity could suddenly evaporate, leaving him pessimistic and anxious. He tried to counteract it with deliberate happy thoughts—but only once. The resulting swing the other way turned him giddy, and made him fear once again for his sanity.

As he wearily took off the helmet and began to unfasten the suit, he was aware of a strange longing. A need he couldn't identify until Lucy Tamiko walked into the room, bringing more 3D maps of the route he would follow next.

It was the need for female company.

She looked up at him and frowned. "Are you OK?" she asked.

"Better for seeing you," he replied. Gage gave a snort and left the room.

"Lame, Hunter. You can do better than that."

"It wasn't a pickup line. I meant it."

"Sure, because I'm Suzy Sunshine spreading cheerfulness wherever I go with my naturally bubbly personality." She stepped around him to get to the main computer station. He gently took her arm.

"Lucy, why is it so hard to believe that I might be glad to see you? I could use a little company, as a matter of fact." He smiled. "At least in *Fantastic Voyage*, they had a team. You could be my Raquel Welch."

"In your dreams."

"Seriously, though. To everybody else these missions only last an hour or two. To me, it's like spending all day by myself."

"You spend all day inside a *woman*. Isn't that a guy's idea of paradise?"

He released her arm, glad to see her smile. He waited while she finished loading the data, then they headed for the door to get some dinner. Before they reached it, Kierkegaard stood in their path.

"I'm glad you're both here. There's a little. . . wrinkle." He made a face. "We'll be having a visitor tomorrow. Not for long, I hope. We'll need you about eleven, Mr. Hunter. Then there'll be a tour of sorts closer to noon."

The pilot exhaled heavily. "Don't tell me some Defense brass just has to come for a little sightseeing. With something this important going on?"

"Someone a little higher up than that." Kierkegaard turned to leave.

"The president."

# # #

Tyson joined Hunter and Tamiko at dinner. He looked drawn and tired, but refused to reveal what he'd been working on.

"It's mostly out of my hands, now," he said. "Kenneth will finish it off. Hopefully by sometime tomorrow."

"Oh, good." Tamiko smirked. "Maybe you can both show it to the president."

Tyson's fork tipped and spilled his beef noodle casserole back onto the plate. "The. . . the *president?*" he asked. "He's coming here? Good Lord, why? I can't show it to him. It may not work!"

"Relax, Skylar." Hunter laughed. "I'm sure that's not the reason that he's coming."

"He's coming to watch part of a military exercise they hold here from time to time." Truman Bridges slipped his plate onto the table and slid into a chair. "And to take the opportunity to award some medals to a number of officers from the 1st Fighter Wing who distinguished themselves during the last Gulf conflict."

"Lucky them, getting their medals from the president himself," Tamiko said. She reached over and snatched a carrot from Hunter's plate.

"Well that's the official reason. You don't expect him to come here without a good cover story, do you? That would not be wise." Bridges took a long drink of iced tea. Tyson was looking from one face to another.

"Why come here at all?" Tyson asked. "What does he hope to accomplish? He probably won't understand our work. How could he?" He pushed the rest of his plate away. "Perhaps I should see if Dr. Gage needs my help." He began to rise, but Hunter waved him back down.

"Skylar, seriously. He's not coming to see your new gadget. I have a feeling he has a... personal stake in all of this. Beyond politics. Am I right, Doctor?"

Bridges scowled. "You know I can't answer that, Hunter. But just politics would be reason enough. Anyway, you shouldn't be speculating about such things here. It's not secure."

"We're in a closed facility in the middle of a United States Air Force base. How much more secure do we need to be?"

"Truman is right," Tyson said. "You should be more careful, Hunter."

"OK, OK." The pilot threw up his hands. "If a person can't gossip a little, how's he supposed to have any fun around here? I'll just shut up and go drive a submarine for a while." He left his dessert untouched and stood to leave. Tamiko stood too.

"I'll go with you," she said. "It's my turn to do the monitoring." She fell into step beside him, and they headed for the main lab.

"Skylar's right," Hunter said. "The president shouldn't be coming here. There's nothing more we can do that we're not already doing." He shrugged. "Hell, he probably won't want to talk to any of us anyhow."

Tamiko reached out to rest a hand on his shoulder. "Don't let it get to you," she said. "But if there's anyone he's going to want to talk to, it's you."

#　#　#

He pushed himself and did two one-hour missions that evening, with an hour of recuperation in between. He found no bombs. He had a strong feeling that the liver was now clear, but he was more loath than ever to risk missing anything.

At Hunter's request, Tyson tried to shorten the duration of the electrical charge sent to the torch tip, to extend the time between recharges. It hadn't worked—the torch wouldn't light.

"Even so, the recharge times are already much better than I had expected. I've kept track of the charge data from the beginning of our missions." Tyson brought up the results on the computer monitor and pointed a finger. "You see? The recharge time has actually improved considerably from the first few missions, with a rather dramatic improvement in just the last three. I have no explanation for that. According to physics, it should vary very little." He shrugged and gave a weak smile. "Just lucky, I guess," he said, then excused himself and left to check on Gage.

"I'll take any luck I can get," Hunter said quietly. Tamiko pulled herself wearily out of the chair, and they walked slowly out of the room.

"Feel like a nightcap?" she asked. "I could use a little something just to shut my brain down and let me sleep."

The pilot shook his head. "Nah, I need to stay sharp. I'm pretty sure that alcohol really affects my... uh, interface with the VR unit. I should probably be at my best tomorrow, don't you think?"

She gave him a look of disbelief. "One drink? That'd be out of your system by morning."

"Ah, but for me it's way too easy for one drink to become two, or more. I'm trying to be a good boy."

"Well I guess there's a first time for everything," she teased. They had arrived at her door. "I think I still have a few swigs in a bottle somewhere in here. I suppose that will have to do." She pushed the door open and took a step in.

"Of course, there are other things that can help you sleep better," he offered, his cheek dimpling as he tried not to smile.

"Nice try," she laughed, turning back to face him.

"I was thinking of buttermilk."

"Of course you were," she nodded, then leaned closer. "You're a strange one, Hunter." Slowly she brought her face to his and kissed him lightly on the lips. Hers were full and warm, and he willed himself to take in every trace of the sensation while it lasted. She drew back, and brought her mouth close to his ear. "I'm not going to sleep with you," she said softly. Then, as she began to withdraw into the room, she smiled and said, "But don't stop trying just yet." And the door quietly closed.

## 36

Kierkegaard joined them in the mission control room the next morning.

"Mr. Hunter," he asked, "Are there any more bombs to be found in the patient's liver?"

"I can't say for certain, sir. There's still quite a stretch of artery within the organ that we haven't covered yet, as well as some of the other vessels that service it. . . "

"Mr. Hunter." The project leader held up a hand. "Do you believe there are any more bombs to be found there?"

The question took the other by surprise. "No, sir. I don't think there are."

"Then we won't waste any more time there. Prepare the ship to move on." He either didn't notice or simply ignored the shocked faces around the room. Tamiko's reaction was disbelief, since she'd worked for hours to map and plan the remaining routes through the organ, but she said nothing. "Where next?" their chief asked. "The spleen? Is that still your next choice?"

"We should check it." Gage was the first to recover. "At this point there are many choices that would be about equal, wouldn't you say?" He looked to Tamiko and then Bridges. "The pancreas is another possibility. Even the gall bladder, or some of the important glands—if they were disabled the patient could suffer a number of serious but non-fatal results. Or do we want to start looking at some of the more critical systems now, like the lungs?"

"The spleen." Hunter said abruptly. "You, uh... you said that was pretty delicate, didn't you? And likely to cause a bad bleed if damaged? I...." He faced Kierkegaard. "I think we should go there."

The other man gave him a long look. "Very well. Let's get started."

As Kierkegaard left the room, Tamiko muttered, "Terrific. Like I needed an extra navigational challenge. The splenic artery is full of twists and bends, and a lot of branches that shoot off toward the stomach. You're going to have to be sharp to avoid taking a wrong turn." She sighed and rolled her chair over to a nearby computer station. "Give me a few minutes."

She hadn't been exaggerating. The approach to the spleen took all morning. The sudden appearance of a cluster of white blood cells at just the wrong moment blocked him from taking a turnoff he needed, and he had to continue along the aortic artery and around the whole main trunk of the bloodstream to take another shot at it. The current was very strong and allowed no margin for error.

The second time, he knew the best position to place the sub as he approached the junction, and made the turn successfully, but the forceful blood flow carried him too close to the far wall of the splenic artery and *Primus* was immediately swept into one of the offshoots toward the stomach. Tamiko had to scramble to find a likely-looking series of anastomoses that would enable him to double back. Once back on course, the circuitous route taken by the artery meant that Hunter had to use reverse thrust from the engine to slow the sub down and let him stay as close as possible to the middle of the channel. Then, just as he was nearly to the hilus of the spleen, the entry point for the arterial blood, another offshoot swept the craft away again. It took three tries before he could return to the main artery.

When he finally made it into the spleen itself and the blood flow had slowed, he found a place to park *Primus* and jacked out.

"Not a good start to the day." He slumped, with a long exhalation of breath. "I'm hitting the shower before the president gets here."

He was on the tarmac when Marine One touched down. The big Sikorsky VH-60N Blackhawk swept dust into the air with its huge rotors. Hunter and Kierkegaard waited for the rotors to slow considerably before walking toward the craft. Before they got close, the big side door opened and two marines in blue dress uniforms disembarked. They quickly stood at attention on either side of the hatchway and saluted as their commander in chief appeared and stepped down to the ground. He was followed by a pair of dark-suited men in sunglasses who immediately began to scan the surroundings.

Hunter stopped walking, struck by an overpowering sense of the surreal: this scene he had witnessed so often on television screens,

Hunter was waiting for Kierkegaard to make another move forward when motion at the corner of his eye caught his attention. A long, black limousine rolled across the runway toward the landing zone. The limo stopped just short of the aircraft's tail and a Secret

Service agent quickly got out of the passenger side, made his way to the back of the car, and opened the rear door.

Out of the limo came two women. The first was well-coiffed, in her early fifties, conservatively dressed in a grey-green skirt suit. The other was a slim, younger woman, in her mid-twenties, with a pale blue pantsuit and a posture very similar to her companion. Hunter recognized the first lady. That meant the second woman must be their daughter… what was her name? *Emily?* No, *Emma.* He was pretty sure it was Emma.

From where he stood he could see that she was pretty, with fine features and the same mocha skin and curly jet-black hair as her mother, except the first lady wore her hair in a short, professional cut. Emma let hers hang loosely to her shoulders. She gave a broad smile into the morning sun, then embraced her father as he joined them. She was wearing some kind of pager or cell phone on her hip. Was she a doctor? A real estate agent?

The head of the project patiently waited for the small group to exchange words and hugs. Then one of the Secret Service men waved him over. Hunter had been unexpectedly nervous about the meeting—he wasn't normally star-struck by VIPs of any kind. Now he felt a bead of sweat on his brow and hoped it didn't show. He noticed that the president's handshake with Devon Kierkegaard was the kind reserved for a longtime acquaintance.

"And this is Mr. Hunter," Kierkegaard said. "He's a submersible pilot," he added for the sake of the women—an explanation that wasn't an explanation, but they made no comment.

"Mr. Hunter." The president's voice was rich and deep, at once familiar from so many speeches and TV sound bites, and the handshake was even firmer than expected. "I'd like to talk to you.

But first . . . ." He swept a hand through the air. "I'm sure you recognize my wife, Dyandra. And this is my daughter, Emma."

Emma was closest, and her hand was warm and soft. He felt a blush coming on, so he gave a quick nod and a tight smile, then reached for the first lady's hand.

[Children laughing. . . dancing. A room with large spaces and bright with sunlight.]

The image that had suddenly flashed into his mind made his hand and face go slack. He looked up and found the first lady giving him a puzzled look. He quickly took her hand and gave it a slight squeeze, badly flustered. The president was saying something. Hunter turned his head and caught Devon Kierkegaard watching him.

". . . glad to have a little breeze off the river," the chief executive finished. "Maybe you two ladies should go on ahead. I'll catch up in a minute." Then he spread his arms slightly to include the two project members, and walked a few yards to the side. The Secret Service men followed at a discreet distance. The two marines had begun to give their craft a visual inspection. The women returned to the limousine.

"Mr. Hunter," the president began, "I've been getting reports on your progress. I don't pretend to understand how the process works, nor all of the difficulties involved, but it's too slow. Too damn slow. Is there anything you can do to speed things up?"

Hunter was caught off guard and struggled to think of an answer. His boss came to his rescue.

"We're doing all we can, sir. We truly are. Mr. Hunter most of all. He's been putting himself through the wringer, believe me." He hesitated, then asked, "Has something changed, sir? Something we should know about?"

The president hesitated as well, looking thoughtfully at Hunter, then turned toward the older man.

"Yes, Doctor Kierkegaard. My enemies have upped the ante." His face was grim as he stared at the pavement. "They claim there are... other bombs. Bombs we didn't know about, scattered throughout her body." He looked into the grey eyes. "Bombs that specifically attack the immune system, acting like the HIV virus. They say they will begin detonating those *tomorrow*."

The two project men stood in shock.

Kierkegaard finally composed himself enough to ask, "Do they offer any proof of this? I promise you, sir, we have found no sign of any other agents at work in her bloodstream. Of course if they're lying dormant, and are as well disguised as the others..." He looked at Hunter.

The pilot gave his head a dazed shake. "I don't... I just can't say, sir. I haven't seen anything else that looks like the bombs; but frankly, Mr. President, there's just so much activity in the bloodstream, I'm afraid I can't rule anything out." He swallowed. "I'm very sorry, sir."

"Sorry won't help me, mister." The president's face was tight. He turned to Kierkegaard again. "If you need more people, more money ...."

Kierkegaard shook his head. "At this stage more people would only be a hindrance since we don't have the time to train them. That's what we really need. More time. We're finding the bombs, and destroying them, but...."

"Time is the one thing I can't give you," the country's most powerful man admitted soberly. "It is not mine to command. You can't imagine what I'd give if only it could be." He looked at the pilot. "Mr. Hunter, if you can find something within you that will help you pull off this miracle, you will have the eternal gratitude of a president of the United States." His eyes burned darkly. "But if you don't give everything you have to save her... then *God help you.*"

## 37

There's a new level of tension to the mission knowing that *Primus* has a VIP audience this time.

The news from the president is a hard pill to swallow. More bombs? Like the virus that produces AIDS? If true, what chance does the woman really have?

Too many bombs already, and only one pilot.

The tour is just a cover to watch *Primus* in action, with the president no doubt eager to see his greatest fear and greatest hope unfolding in real time.

Terrific. The leader of the country watching over your shoulder.

Three-quarters reverse thrust. Get the ship back in the hunt.

The first lady. It has to be her. That flash of. . . *memory*, just before the touch of skin on skin—children laughing and dancing—the same image from yesterday, while waiting for the torch to recharge. It has to be one of her memories—what other interpretation could there be? Children. Wasn't the president's wife once a schoolteacher?

How can a memory be seen by someone else?

Telepathy? Never believed in that.

Must be hard on the president, helplessly peering into his wife's bloodstream, with no chance to personally confront this enemy. Having to trust an unstable sub pilot with the life of his most precious friend. Poor bastard.

If there are HIV bombs, the spleen is a prime target.

These blood vessels have a different look. A dozen shades of red, ranging into purple, blue, even a deep, purplish green. Arteries shoot off everywhere, many of them too small for bombs. The organ is honeycombed like a sponge, the walls often hidden by huge masses of cells, like nests of enormous eggs. *Lymphocytes*—the body's invader-detection system. If they discover an intruder, they activate a matching defender cell, which quickly reproduces more of its kind and goes on the attack. The spleen is full of them, the arterial walls like fences lined with sentries. Creepy. Dangerous.

Primus has gone undetected so far, thanks to its lipid shield. What about the bombs? Could any slip through this gauntlet? If so, they're going to be damned hard to find. So many side-tunnels. So many choices.

What's that ahead? The blood vessel seems to come to a. . .

Dead end.

What the hell?

Lucy's map shows a continuous run—no blockage. The end wall must be very thin. Thin enough for *Primus* to punch through?

Not worth the risk to the sensor array. Better to turn around and try a different way. Ditch Lucy's plan again. She'll be thrilled.

Shit! Another dead end. They must be deliberate traps for invaders: where bacteria go to die. They can enter, but they never come out.

Got to be bloody careful. A collision with one of these floating behemoths could tear the lipid shield and give the game away.

Another dead end.

And another.

Damn it! This could take forever. She doesn't have forever.

No sign of bombs, either. Of any kind.

Fatigue is becoming a problem.

For Christ's sake! Another blockage! And a shitload of obstacles. Dozens and dozens of huge B-lymphocytes converging on a spot nearby. Have they found a bomb? Got to risk getting closer for a look.

No. Something long and dark, ruddy brown. A small patch of it isn't covered yet. Bumpy, with protrusions slowly waving. Nothing like the other bombs. The terrorists would use a similar casing, wouldn't they? Simplest way to go.

No way to be sure, but gut instinct says this isn't one. That'll have to do.

Back out to a larger vessel. Very tired now. Might miss something vital. Time to unplug? Can't afford mistakes, but the president won't be impressed.

Wait. What's that ahead? A big space—the tunnel opening out into a cavern. A major confluence of several arteries coming together. Lots of traffic and turbulence. . . blood flow coming from a half-dozen different directions. Tricky.

Hang on. Something off to one side. Large and shiny. Looks like the real deal. Oh, yes, it's a son-of-a-bitch bomb all right.

No. . . *Shit!* Two bombs! Side by side. Two giant tankers of poison. Smack dab in a key intersection ready to plug it up tight. Perfect spot, too—a couple of loads of ADP, and every defender cell in the whole area will come running, creating a blockage that might never get cleared.

What to do now? So groggy it's hard to keep focus. Could probably manage to scratch one bomb, but then what? Stay on station and wait for the torch to recharge? In this current? Haven't got the strength left for that.

Time for a miracle.

Or something too stupid to consider until now.

Two for the price of one, winner takes all?

If one bomb burns but the other doesn't, all hell will break loose.

No. Her life is on the line. Have to do the sensible thing—the cautious thing. Take out one bomb, get some rest, and then. . . hope to find the second one again in this labyrinth.

Damn! The current is shifting all over the place. Nearly impossible to make a straight run at the far side of the outer bomb. Glanced right off without making a dent. Have to circle around and try again.

A miss! A complete miss! Sudden current shear at just the wrong moment. Couldn't react quickly enough. Too tired for this shit.

Only option left is to ride the current straight into the notch between the two bombs and divert into the one on the left at the last second.

Hands starting to shake with fatigue.

Shit. Caromed right off one bombshell and crashed into the other.

Hang on. Hold position. . . bring the sensor array around.

Is that a crack?

No doubt about it. What about the other one?

Damn it all. A crack there, too. Either bomb could start leaking at any time and bring on the cavalry faster than a bugle call.

So much for caution. Got to take them both out now. *Primus* better be is as tough a bitch as they say she is.

The lineup has to be perfect, shoulders up like a blocker clearing a path for the quarterback, and go like a sonuvabitch . . .

Jesus! Felt that impact.

There! Two ragged holes. Need to move like lightning. Unfold the torch arm—spear it into the opening on the right. Fire it up. Then back the ship out and gamble that the flame knows where to go.

A forked tongue, then a spray of orange, spitting toward the other bomb. The leaked ADP suddenly flickering, flaring

. . . *It's working!* The second flame swirling and then darting into the fractured shell. . . .

God in Heaven, what a sight. What a sweet, sweet sight. The second bomb glowing brilliant orange from within. Scratch two. The good guys win.

Still a halo of flame near the two holes. A flicker of pale light playing over the shells like St. Elmo's fire.

[*Billows of flame. Snarling, crackling, snapping. A tree. . . a tree on fire. . . going up like a Roman candle. Voices shouting. A child screaming. Now sirens. Something in the branches. Boards. . . planks. A tree-house.*

Sparks spraying into a night sky. Acrid smoke swirling in a strong wind. Coughing. Crying. Tongues of flame stretching across the blackness, touching, tasting shingles and wood. A porch. Large veranda attached to a house.

NO! Please, no!

Now water. Arcs of silver on flame. Black snakes of hoses, writhing over inky grass. Running shapes. . . bumping, spinning. Feet, legs everywhere. Hands grabbing. Swinging into the air. Looking back. Clouds of steam against the orange glow.

The house is safe. People. . . safe.

Looking up, full of fear. Black legs. Tall man shape. Back of head, black hair glinting with the reflected flame.

It was him. *He* did it. *He* did it. *Don't trust him. Don't ever trust him again. . . .]*

Flame orange.

Dull silver.

Blood red.

Jesus.

What in *hell* was that?

Whatever it was, the show's over, and doesn't seem to have taken any time—an aurora is still frolicking over the burned-out silicon shells. The surrounding cell material didn't catch—the pyre is dying out.

They must be having fits in the control room, watching that performance. And those other. . . images? Memories again? Did they see those, too?

No. Figments of the mind, not of the sensors.

It's time to pull the plug on this nightmare place.

Before the brain loses its way for good.

## 38

Kellogg had sent a terse report to his contact, the one he knew as the Money Man. It said simply, "Team in place. Awaiting a 'go'. Remember the termination deadline." All of his team members were now at the training site, practicing for the mission, running scenarios.

He didn't know the Money Man's identity—that wasn't important—but he knew much more than the other suspected. His own father had taught him the methods such "financiers" used to raise funds for clandestine operations while keeping their sources utterly secret. The way the money was channeled through vague invoices for services never rendered, spread out over five years and more, collected by perhaps twenty different shell companies registered in a half-dozen countries from Panama to the Cayman Islands to Lichtenstein.

Such banking was all handled offshore. Most of the first layer was in the Bahamas, where it looked respectable and harmless, but everyone knew that bank secrecy could be pierced there if a friendly police force had a good enough criminal case. So, from there, most of the money went to Switzerland—but that was yet another feint. The end of the line was the Cayman Islands. A huge amount of money spread among a half-dozen different banks, none with any connection to any other. The whole fabric of these financial threads was virtually impenetrable.

Kellogg also knew that his mission was only one project of a growing list, all designed to acquire influence. As if those involved needed more. Each was already a world leader—without the titles, perhaps, but the ones who really held the power. They pulled the strings and made politicians dance.

He knew that some of them in the Arab world thirsted for the blood of an American president. Fools. A dead president was of no use. He would be replaced by another, perhaps a worse one. No, the best president was one you could control.

Every man had his price. Kellogg had been bought and paid for many years before. If his soul had been stained in the process, well, maybe God could be bought off, too.

If there was anyone with the balls for that it would be the man Kellogg really worked for—the leader of the global cabal, the man they called *Patruus*. . . "Uncle". That was a man reaping a harvest of power such as could only be had by a lifetime of cultivation. Brutally ruthless or disarmingly genial as the occasion demanded, you didn't dare turn your back to him, as evidenced by his consummate betrayal underway even now.

It was amusing that Money Man thought Kellogg was simply hired muscle—that even the cabal's financial wizard had not been told about Kellogg's longtime connection to the power at the top.

He looked again at the translated reply on his Blackberry. He'd already received the same message from *Patruus* himself half-an-hour earlier.

A single word.

The word was, "Go."

# # #

The president hadn't witnessed the destruction of the two bombs—he'd been called away to the medal presentation ceremony—but the mission video would be made available to him. Would he be fascinated, or outraged? Relieved, or more disturbed than ever?

Hunter had been right that the memory images, if that's what they were, had not been recorded.

His teammates weren't speaking to him. They considered it the height of arrogance for him to have risked so much, trying to destroy two bombs at the same time. The lipid shield could have been shredded. The second bomb could have failed to ignite, creating the disastrous arterial blockage that they were all fighting to prevent.

If they didn't think the end justified the means, at least he knew damned well that his decision hadn't been motivated by arrogance. It had been more like desperation.

And that had been before Mallory's latest news.

"We've just completed the most thorough blood analysis yet," she said. "We've also re-processed the data from our earlier samples, cross-checked all of it, and tabulated everything we've gathered to date." She fidgeted with her papers. "If these so-called HIV-type bombs do exist, they either have to be of a completely different composition than the others and much better disguised, or look exactly the same as the first, so we can't distinguish between the two.

"But the new tests did show something." Her voice dropped to nearly a sob.

"More bombs. Many more bombs. The number has clearly increased in the past two days."

"How... how can that be?" Tamiko stammered.

"She was out of our hands." Gage slammed his fist on a desk. "They got to her."

"Impossible," Kierkegaard said. "Or maybe inconceivable is what I mean. Someone got to her once, before the threat was known, but no one can get to her now. She is surrounded at all times by a security wall of the absolute highest level. The president himself isn't better protected."

"Then the only alternative," Bridges said quietly, "is that there has been a device within her all along that is still *planting* bombs."

Kierkegaard gave his head a worried shake. "I don't know how that's possible, but you're right—it seems like the only explanation. We'll have to step up our body scans immediately until we find the damned thing."

Hunter felt compelled to speak. "There is another possibility." The faces turned toward him. "The possibility that there's someone against us on the *inside*. Someone with access. Someone in her security detail, or... within the project itself."

Their leader gave him a piercing look.

"A traitor? A *mole*? Is that what you're suggesting, Mr. Hunter?"

The discomfort on the pilot's face showed he had nothing more to say. Neither did anyone else.

# # #

Hunter pushed himself hard for the rest of the day. In three missions he covered nearly eighty per cent of the spleen. It was phenomenal, considering how many dead-end channels he encountered. He found only one more bomb, and destroyed it without incident. Then he gave in to the need for a longer break. His head was reeling, and his body reacted as if he had the flu. Getting some food into his stomach helped with the weakness and the shakes, but he finally had to escape from the confining walls and get some fresh air.

The night had an uncharacteristic chill. He looked up into the dark sky and realized the stars were no match for the bright lights of the air force base. Slowly, he wandered toward the north side of the building, where the worst of the excess light was blocked by walls. His neck quickly grew stiff as he sat on the cold pavement with his back against rough bricks, gazing up at twinkling pinpoints of white. Lately, he spent so much of his time obsessed with the world of the incomprehensibly small that he felt a powerful need to contemplate the infinite grandeur of the universe for a while.

His heart nearly leapt from his chest when a man's voice came from the shadows.

"I hoped I could find you alone."

## 39

Hunter scrambled to his feet.

"There's no need for that. You have nothing to fear from me." The voice was deep and measured—not the voice of anyone he knew. There was no obvious attempt to disguise it, yet its pitch and volume spoke of a desire for confidentiality.

Hunter could see no more than an outline near the corner of the building. All he could tell was that the man was of medium height and build.

"Who are you, and what do you want from me?"

"The classic question, straight from a movie script." There was a low chuckle. "I can't tell you who I am. I don't think that is a good idea yet. But I work for the president."

"You expect me to take your word for that? Why didn't you come to see me in the open? Why this cloak and dagger routine in the middle of the night?"

"It's not that late. By the middle of the night I hope to be in my bed, back in Washington. Although catching a few hours of shuteye at my desk is more likely." He stepped closer. "I arrived with the president on Marine One this morning, but it's not my habit to be seen with him. I prefer to work out of the spotlight."

"And out of any other light, it seems. I don't have anything to say to you. I think maybe the military police would like to know you're here." Hunter made to step around the man, who stopped him with an upraised palm. Then the other hand followed it into the air.

"I'm not armed. I'm not a threat to you. Or anyone else working on the project." There was a small movement of his head, as if to make sure they were alone. "Yes, I know about it. I know that you are the pilot of a *nano*-sized submarine that prowls around inside a very important person. I know your name, Mr. Hunter, and your background, as well as the backgrounds of everyone working in this complex, plus everything you have done on the project to this point. In fact I am the one who recommended it to the president as the only way to solve his… unique problem."

Darkness hid the astonishment on Hunter's face and he made an effort to hide it in his voice.

"I have no reason to believe anything you're saying. And you still haven't said what you want with me."

"Just trying to establish my credentials, Mr. Hunter. If you're having trouble trusting me because I don't want to be seen by the others, consider that maybe it's because I don't know whom I can trust among them."

The man leaned against the wall with hands in pockets, a deliberately casual stance designed to set his companion at ease. "You can go if you must, Mr. Hunter. I won't stop you. But I would ask you to stay for a few minutes. Let me have my say. You can't give away any secrets just by listening, can you?"

"What if I don't know any secrets and don't want to?"

"Everyone has secrets. And everyone wants to know more than they do."

They stood for a moment without speaking, but Hunter didn't leave. Gerard Mannis took that as a cue to proceed.

"You can keep to yourself both what you know, and anything else you suspect. Just let me say that I'm convinced our enemies know as much about what's going on as you do." He turned toward the submariner. There was enough spilled light to show the outline of a strong face, clean-shaven with a full head of hair. A soft sheen as he moved suggested a conservative tie matched to a decent suit. "I can't tell you my reasons for believing that secrecy has been compromised. Besides, you don't want to know." A slight smirk could be heard in his voice.

"Needless to say, anybody who is willing and able to plant micro-miniature bombs into the body of a human being isn't going to spare any effort or expense to ensure that their plan is not thwarted. Or to keep their own identities from being discovered.

"There has already been one attempt on my life for trying to learn who we're dealing with." He turned toward Hunter again. "Hundreds of our country's best intelligence people are working on this case in one way or another, but the enemy tried to kill *me*. That could only be because I got close, and someone knew it. There is no way they should have been able to know that, Mr. Hunter."

The pilot kept his voice flat. "Whatever story you tell, I still don't see what it has to do with me."

"Let me draw you a picture," the other replied dryly. "I'm a discreet man. A very discreet man. There is no way anyone should know what I am doing unless they are very well placed indeed. Inside the administration." He rested his head back on the cold brick and looked up at the night sky. "Your patient is one of the best-guarded people in the entire country right now, yet someone got to her sometime in the past two days."

Hunter couldn't suppress a sharp intake of breath, then mentally kicked himself for it. The man in the shadows did not fail to notice.

"Yes, I know about that. More bombs have been planted, and I'm damned if I know how, but I'm going to find out. I'm hoping you'll keep your eyes and ears open, too. I think you're in a better position than anyone to figure out how that could have been done. I also think you'll be the first to know if there's any more. . . interference, for want of a better word."

Hunter's mind reeled. He was totally out of his element, unused to subterfuge of any kind. He struggled to find words that wouldn't give anything away.

"You tell quite a tale. If any scrap of it were true, I figure I'd be the last person anyone would tell it to. Why are you talking to me?"

The other gave a chuckle. "Very well phrased. You have a talent for this—I'm glad to see it." He shifted his position and took a breath. "The fact is, almost everyone else I know who is working on this problem considers you the least trustworthy of the team, the greatest unknown. You can't be surprised at that, with your history. They can't see past that.

"I've looked deeper, yet with all of my digging I can't turn up a single personal, business, or political connection of yours that might have any possible bearing on what's happening. They say no man is an island, but you're as close to it as I've seen, Mr. Hunter. Even your drinking buddies don't really know you. You've shut everyone out of your life in the past year, and there weren't all that many in it to begin with. You remind me of *me*." He shook his head. "Don't be insulted. I'm one of the good guys, and I'm taking a big gamble trusting you. It could cost me my career, if I'm wrong."

A sudden glow in the dark showed that he was consulting his watch.

"I can't take much more time. You'll be missed soon. First, let me remind you again where we are. It should be obvious that not just anyone could walk in here and talk to you. We're being observed right now—though not recorded. I took care of that. I've told you a lot of things no one outside the project should know. You'll have to judge for yourself what that's worth. All I want from you is for you to be extremely careful and extremely vigilant.

"I'm convinced that someone very highly placed in our government is out to stop me, and they sure as hell will want to stop you. Watch for anything suspicious whatsoever. If it's something you can deal with on your own, do the best you can. If not, be very, very careful whom you trust. Pick the wrong person, and the game is over.

"If you decide you can trust me, you can reach me with this." He passed across a small white object. It felt like an ordinary business card. "It's not some kind of James Bond gadget. Just a phone number for a travel agency. The answering service will say that the number is no longer connected, but I'll know you called and I'll find a way to contact you. And," he added, "be more careful of your own safety from now on. No more wandering outside by yourself at night. I'm convinced that steps are being taken—have already been taken—to stop what your team is doing, so you are all in danger."

"Why should I believe that?" Hunter asked.

The other man didn't answer right away. When he spoke again it was in a softer voice.

"Do you remember a couple of technicians here named Stanton and Brown? Low-level security clearance—little more than repairmen. Stanton was allowed to go to visit his family last weekend, about a two-hour drive from here. He didn't make it. A car crash. Then Brown was called away because of a family emergency. The emergency was real—his father'd had a stroke. But now Brown is missing."

"You're saying this isn't a coincidence?"

"Coincidence? Hardly. And they were only very minor players. Fortunately others were available to take over their work. The key members of your team—and especially you—are *not* replaceable." His voice took on a harder edge. "There has already been one attempt to deprive us of your services."

"Me? What are you talking about?"

"You were supposed to travel here by commercial flight to Norfolk. It was delayed, if you remember, so Devon Kierkegaard brought you by military jet instead. Your original flight did not make it to Norfolk, Virginia. It seems someone made a serious miscalculation about the amount of fuel on board."

A chill ran through Hunter's body. "Do you mean it crashed?"

The other man pushed away from the wall. "As a matter of fact, it didn't. The pilot was a genius and managed to glide it onto a runway in Philadelphia with a dead stick. A one-in-a-thousand shot. I don't think that was what others had in mind." He raised an arm to point at the card in Hunter's hand. "Call me if you need to."

Then he walked softly into the night.

## 40

Hunter made straight for the control room. Halfway there, he turned a corner and walked a dozen steps toward Devon Kierkegaard's office. Then he stopped, leaned against a wall and tried desperately to think. After a long moment he pushed away and ambled in the direction of his own quarters. His mind raced, but got nowhere. His body ended up face down on his bed.

No flash of insight came to him, so he got up and removed all of his clothes, carefully going through every pocket and over every seam, paying special attention to his shoes. He found nothing. It felt like the worst kind of spy-movie-induced paranoia, but he couldn't ignore the risk that some kind of monitoring device had been planted on him, even though he was sure the man he had met had never come close enough.

Naked, he decided he might as well take a shower. Maybe it would wash him clean of the taint of conspiracy. Yet, as the hot water massaged the back of his neck, he realized that he believed the stranger's story. There was absolutely no proof that the visitor wasn't a supremely skilled infiltrator himself, but Hunter had a powerful feeling that the man was on the level. Which meant that someone within the project was working against them.

Hunter had made the same suggestion himself, only hours earlier, but he didn't want to accept it. He found it easier to believe that someone much higher up the chain had gone bad. Politics at high levels was a breeding ground for corruption, as he saw it: a game of sleazy self-interest and lust for power.

Either alternative was an unnerving prospect.

When he returned to the control room he couldn't look anyone in the eye.

The world of the *Primus* was a welcome escape. The strange colors and bizarre shapes had actually become soothing.

It was only much later that he noticed an itch at the back of his brain, a nagging feeling that he was being watched. Maybe someone was looking over his shoulder in the control room. Except he'd had an audience all along, hadn't he?

Paranoia. He forced himself to ignore it.

Except he couldn't.

The feeling grew. He swept his view around and behind *Primus* every few seconds, nervously, like a man with a full wallet taking a shortcut down a dark alley. He tried to push the anxiety from his mind, but it wouldn't go. He found himself no longer looking for bombs, but rather for creeping shadows, unexplained movements, clashing colors.

He couldn't go on. He pulled the plug and sullenly strode to his room to sleep.

It was the sea. The sea knew he was there.
And hated him for it.

The dark, the pressure. . . it was all a part of the sea. He had penetrated her against her will, and she would have her revenge: blinding him, squeezing him, smothering him. He tried to hide, cowering in the dark in his metal shell, but she knew he was there. He had come this far on his own, an invader. She would take him the rest of the way, a prisoner.

He needed to escape. Where were the others? The others knew he was here. They were safe in that other world, above the waves—safe while he did their will. They watched their screens, their clocks, their gauges. They must know he was in trouble. Where were they? Had they abandoned him? Did they, too, fear the sea, knowing she was all-powerful and unforgiving?

The creak and groan of metal, the low hiss of air, the scrape of sand on steel. No, it was voices. . . words. One voice, the voice of his captor accused and threatened in words he could not quite comprehend. It rocked his fragile refuge. . . toying with him. Taunting. Teasing. Squeezing.

Please! he begged. Let me go!

Instead the darkness swirled suddenly like a noose around his throat, a cold breath froze his muscles, and his tiny world turned upside-down, ready to begin the final fall.

The voice said, You have been betrayed.

Hunter's next mission was a complete failure. The paranoia returned in full force, shredding his tenuous extra-sensory bond with the inner world. He was forced to fall back on the inferior senses of the computer alone, until he could relax a little, only to feel the unknown scrutiny begin again, compounded by a seemingly endless succession of dead-end passages. He simply couldn't find his way.

He stuck it out for the better part of an hour, then gave up in utter frustration.

The rest of the team could sense that he was on the edge, ready to explode. They kept their distance. Kierkegaard called a meeting, but cancelled it when Hunter couldn't be found. The sun was shining, and the pilot had gone for a walk in the scrubland bordering the creek to the north of the complex, heedless of his nighttime visitor's counsel not to be alone. He needed space... air... sun on his face, and the trickle of running water. No one made any comment upon his return. Bridges had warned them.

Hunter's link was still wildly erratic. He found no bombs, although it didn't mean there were none to be found. He'd gone so far off the planned route, Tamiko left the control room in disgust.

As he reached yet another blocked passage, his mind surrendered to blind fury. It screamed and raged at the grotesque world that entrapped him—an explosion of mental energy that seemed to send shock waves rippling through the surrounding fluid. He could swear he felt *Primus* vibrate with its force, then jitter as the waves bounced back from the nearby tissues, like a boat bobbing on a wake.

The vibrations died out, leaving a stillness more profound than ever before. It lasted only seconds, and then he became aware of a growing swell of pent-up energy, like a powerful musical note, spreading, growing, spinning harmonic resonances that fed upon each other. It penetrated his craft, his mind, his soul. . . .

WHO ARE YOU? it asked.

He fled in utter terror.

## 41

"He's suffered some kind of mental trauma, but I have no idea what caused it, or what to do about it."

Truman Bridges ran a hand through his graying hair and resumed pacing the floor of Kierkegaard's office.

"The man is transferring his psyche into a microscopic particle that travels around inside the body of a human being," he continued. "How are we supposed to know what that's like? How can we even guess? Now something has given him a terrible shock, and he's not saying what it was."

Kierkegaard sat back wearily in his chair. "Like when *Primus* was attacked by the macrophage? He was practically catatonic for a while, then."

"No. This time there was no attack on *Primus*. It must have been some kind of purely mental shock. Nothing showed on the ship's instruments or recorders at all. Hunter's blood pressure was already very high, probably from frustration—he'd encountered a long series of dead-end passages. Then there was a spike in vital signs that was almost off the scale. A major traumatic event."

"Like a sudden fright?"

"Yes, I suppose. A sudden fear for his life might produce a result like that. In fact, I'm not sure what else could."

"That still doesn't explain anything. What could frighten him so badly in there? He knows he's not physically involved. His life cannot actually be in danger."

Bridges raised an eyebrow. "Perhaps that distinction isn't so easy to remember *in there.*"

The director leaned forward. "I have a feeling we'll only learn the cause when he decides to tell us. In the meantime, is he lucid. . . aware of what's happening around him?"

"He's not catatonic. Anything he knows about what shocked him so badly, he's keeping to himself."

#   #   #

Hunter lay in his bed, his eyes rigidly open but not focused on anything. All of his focus was inward.

Flashes from the past weeks burst randomly in his mind. He couldn't stop them, couldn't control them in any way. A grotesque slide show run amok, it had a dreamlike quality that suggested the subconscious rather than the conscious mind—his brain trying to make sense of what he'd experienced.

Incongruously interwoven through the macabre montage was the image of a *hummingbird.* Sometimes darting like an arrow from fragment to fragment, sometimes sewing the scraps together with golden filigree wire, sometimes frozen in flight as if pulled by pungent nectars in opposing directions.

That one was easy to interpret: it was his mind's attempt to express time dilation within the world of *Primus*. From one perspective it was an accelerated movie, like time-lapse photography; from another it was more like a slow-motion performance with each frame distinct.

He couldn't bring order to the other images, but he began to sense certain themes—bombs amid a chaos of bloodstream clutter, abrupt swings of emotion, *Primus* off-course yet finding its way, and the sudden sharp fragments of unfamiliar memories.

A conclusion solidified in his mind.

He had been watched not by his companions or their machines, and not by any stranger or mole. He had been watched by the *patient herself*. Her body had been aware of him all the time.

He couldn't know whether or not her conscious mind was involved. That seemed unlikely. Would she have allowed such a bizarre. . . *infestation* of her body? Wouldn't she have confronted Kierkegaard and the others?

The confusing memories he had somehow tapped into must be hers. The emotions, too. He had unwittingly penetrated not only her body, but her mind; and that realization shocked him deeply. He felt dirty. A *voyeur*.

The shame of it was made even worse because a bond had formed between them. There was no denying it. He truly cared for her. When he thought ahead to missions, he didn't just picture arteries and organs and parades of cells, but a living, breathing woman. His heart hurt to know of her pain.

How much did she know? Was she aware only of *Primus* making its way through her bloodstream or did she sense his presence, too, as his mind foraged through her hidden places—the most invasive violation of all.

Surely she would have refused to continue, or at least demanded to know this interloper, prying into the secret corners of her psyche.

So she must not know, not consciously. It must be only her unconscious mind tracking her microscopic defender and its improbable puppeteer. Perhaps even aiding them. Did that signify approval?

The answer to that question went to the core of his own pain, and the personal rules of conduct forged from it. With a scarred psyche of his own, how could he willingly breach the mental sanctuary of another without her permission?

That was the key.

He had no means to contact her conscious brain. He would have to take her assistance as implied consent.

Wearily he rolled to the side of the bed and sat up.

He would go on. He had to. And he would do it with her help.

## 42

"It's a phenomenal achievement." Kierkegaard was sincere in his praise.

"If it works," Gage replied.

Tyson looked pleased and slightly pink.

Hunter returned his eyes to the diagram on the projection screen. The shape of *Primus* was totally familiar, yet he'd forgotten about the special radar pods at either end of the craft. They hadn't been active. Now they would be.

"How confident can you be that the sensors won't read radar reflections off objects outside her body?" Tamiko wanted to know.

"The timing of the responses is key," Tyson answered. We believe we've finally got enough computer power available that we'll be able to distinguish the nanosecond differences between a signal bounced off a leg bone and, say, the metal rail of her bed."

"Nanosecond?" Hunter smiled.

Tyson nodded. "Yes. Possibly even *yactosecond*, to get any meaningful results while navigating within an organ, for instance."

"Yactosecond." The pilot shook his head. "If it was anybody but you, Skylar, I'd swear you were pulling my leg. How will this help me? Will the radar identify the silicon of the bomb casings?"

"That's the goal, but there's no guarantee of that right away. We think we've isolated the radar signature of the silicon but there are other elements that might give us false readings." The scientist's smile had faded.

"It's not perfect yet, but what do you want?" Gage bristled. "This is cutting edge stuff. Way ahead of anybody else in the field."

"Of course it is," Kierkegaard agreed. "And it would be wonderful to be able to pause and celebrate such an achievement. But now that we have the tool to do the job, there is a task that has become an even higher priority than locating the bombs themselves. Locating *where they're coming from*." He looked into their faces. "There must be some kind of device that is still releasing bombs into her bloodstream. We must find it, and we must find it soon."

There was no consensus about where to search. Bridges, Mallory, and Tamiko believed any device that released bombs would most likely be some kind of a shunt inserted into a blood vessel of a hand or foot, allowing the blood to flow through a bomb-lined tube. The extremities of the body would allow easy implantation without the risk that a failure would create a fatal blockage or hemorrhage. The others argued that a placement near the skin would make such a device too easy to find, and that it might even be revealed by accident.

Kierkegaard ordered *Primus* into the lower abdomen. Hunter agreed with the decision, though he couldn't say why.

They tried out the new radar right away, to confirm that the spleen was clear of bombs.

"You'll notice interference with the visual display," Tyson told Hunter. "We've designed the receptors to cut out for the instant the radio pulse is sent, to protect them from overload. We'll send pulses manually. By tomorrow, I think I'll be able to give you control over the pulses, but it will take longer to integrate the readout into your visual display. For now, we'll have to steer you using text messages in your heads-up display and a tone in your ears—a *hot* or *cold* signal, if you will, to tell if the bow of *Primus* is aimed at the target.

"As you know, most radar dishes rotate, but we couldn't arrange that. So the only way our radar can paint three dimensions is with the infinitesimal difference between the time a return signal is picked up at the bow and at the stern."

Tyson reminded Hunter of a father letting one of his kids take the family car out for the first time.

On the first attempt, Hunter's visual display went completely white, fading quickly back into a view of the surroundings; but as he concentrated his mind and opened his thoughts, the pulses became less and less intrusive.

The radar showed a spleen clear of bombs. As *Primus* made its way back into the main bloodstream, several test pulses produced distant returns from what appeared to be silicon, but there was still a lot of refining to do. The radius of the radar envelope was unstable. Tyson tried more pulses every few minutes and relayed terse messages to Hunter at first, then elected to remain silent unless a signal return appeared very close to the ship.

Never comfortable that he travelled within an unsuspecting woman's body, the route along the interior iliac artery to the uterine artery bothered him even more. He tried to compare himself to a doctor performing a medical procedure, but that didn't wash. He felt more like a doctor who abused a patient while she was sleeping.

He was startled out of his reverie by a text from Tyson. "IUD," the message said. *Intra-uterine Device?* Why would Hunter want to know about that? Oh. Of course—it could help orient him with the surrounding organs. A very large blood vessel branched off downward and to the left. Most likely the uterine artery. He took it.

He heard the locator tone of the radar begin. A message from Tamiko confirmed that it was the IUD they were painting for him. No bomb signatures were anywhere close—there were no vital organs in that part of the body. Yet Kierkegaard believed it was a likely site for a bomb launcher. He hadn't given his reasons.

The artery was swarming with blood cells, including a much higher-than-usual concentration of white cells in all their variants. Antibodies seemed to increase by the minute, too. If the trend continued, he was going to have a bitch of a time navigating through them all without making contact. Contact was risky.

As he dodged and pirouetted, still navigating the twisting tunnels effortlessly, he understood that he was not alone. The other presence was with him. He knew the best place to turn away from the main branch of the uterine artery into the smaller channels without giving it any thought, and as he came upon each bend and fork, it was as if he'd been expecting them. Then, as he'd climbed close to the lining of the blood vessel and watched the pattern of cells racing past overhead, he had a vivid flash of memory: a long traffic tunnel in a major city, with two lanes of traffic in each direction and caged fluorescent lights in the concrete above.

It was one of her memories, not his, and it was followed by others: a whirlwind of leaves stirred by an autumn wind, a school of darting trout seen through the shiny surface of a stream, even bursting blooms of fireworks in a summer sky. Clearly some part of her mind was seeing what he was seeing, and making associations.

The fireworks coalesced into a burning intensity.

WHO ARE YOU?

This time he didn't run away—he'd tried to prepare himself. He wanted to give her an answer—for her to come to know him, but he had no idea what answer to give. His own name would mean nothing to her. Instead, he tried to picture the lab with its hospital-style layout and people wearing smocks. He hoped she would accept him as someone on the medical staff treating her. It seemed to work. At least the strong sense of curiosity was tempered by relief and. . . was that *trust?*

Again, he felt shame.

What if she learned that he wasn't a doctor? Could he hope to continue such a masquerade while communicating on the level of *mind-to-mind?* Surely what mattered was that he was trying to help her. To save her.

There was a huge white blood cell directly ahead. He prepared to maneuver around it.

Suddenly his mind filled with a vision of a shining silver globe covered with triangular dimples. EPCOT at Walt Disney World. . . the GeoSphere of Spaceship Earth. It gleamed so brightly that he couldn't clear the image from his mind. He couldn't see anything else. *He couldn't see!*

"*Get it out of my mind,*" he pleaded.

But it was already too late.

Primus plowed headlong into the white cell, careened off and was hammered from behind.

## 43

The blinding vision of the GeoSphere vanished, but Hunter's restored sight was little use as *Primus* was battered and spun, carried by the colliding particles of cellular life into a maelstrom of swirling obstacles. Something scraped ominously overhead, dragging the full length of the craft's superstructure.

He was in a swarm of blood material and he had to get clear. Miraculously, the ship still responded to his wishes nearly at the speed of thought. There had to be an opening somewhere. *There.* A gap just ahead and below. But another grey oblong was spinning in from the right. He dived and rolled, slamming the throttle to full, racing between giant planetoids and hurtling meteors. He nearly made it. At the last instant a pseudopod seemed to reach out from the globe on his left, and he couldn't avoid it. The impact sent *Primus* tumbling.

He snapped the nose up and around, pointing for the longest stretch of empty space he could see, then risked a glance backward. His rear view was nearly full of objects, and within seconds he could tell that some were separating from the pack and coming toward him. Chasing him! Why?

A flickering movement caught his eye: something filmy and thin, flapping along the ship's upper surface. He'd seen that before.

The *lipid shield*.

It was torn, almost completely exposing the sensor array, *Primus'* most recognizable feature—a dead giveaway that she didn't belong.

A text message lit his view, a single word.

"RUN!"

His pursuers were gaining. Their abilities within their home environment were almost magical. He spotted a group of half a dozen large blood cells above and ahead, and darted between them, hoping to throw off some of the hounds. The greatest danger to the ship was the giant killer white cells, and any interference from other obstacles would be to his advantage.

The nearest of the T-cells was forced to detour and others piled up behind it. He knew that wouldn't last long, but it would help as long as the cells ahead of him weren't alerted to his presence.

Even as he had that thought, a dark cylindrical shape raced past. An antibody? Some other messenger? He didn't know, but he had no doubt that the arterial throughway was about to become a very inhospitable place.

The ship shuddered, and slewed to the side as two oblong attackers rammed her, like missiles homing in on their prey. He dodged and swerved haphazardly, but they were quick and maneuverable. How did they move faster than the flow of blood? Some kind of attraction at the molecular level?

He darted *Primus* into a small side tunnel. His attackers followed, but the way was much narrower, and the T-cells wouldn't make it through side-by-side. The drawback was that he had much less room for evasive maneuvers, and any alerted white cells in his path would be very hard to avoid.

He felt the pulse of the radar. Then his heads up display lit again: "HEAD FOR THE IUD."

The tone resumed in his headset, and he was amazed to discover he was almost exactly on track. Maybe it was no accident. The IUD would be a reference point for the team to find the ship and extract it. Could the patient's unconscious mind have come to the same conclusion? He couldn't rule it out. He had to trust his rescuers, outside *and* in.

At least half a dozen objects crowded him now, keeping pace seemingly without effort, trying to slow the ship. A pale white behemoth had been steadily gaining from behind, filling the tunnel completely, and there was absolutely nothing he could do about it.

"IUD AHEAD. THROUGH ARTERY WALL."

His mind had already focused on the thin cellular wall ahead—a sharp bend in the capillary—somehow knowing that beyond it lay safety. *Escape.*

He wasn't going to reach it. The antibodies had formed a virtual wall at the bow of the ship, creating massive drag, defeating the straining engine. If he couldn't free the craft of their grip within the next few seconds, he would never free her at all.

A desperate idea burst into his mind, a childhood memory from a Disney movie. As he sent the vulnerable sensor array sliding rearward toward its stowed position for ramming, he extended the manipulator arms and clasped them together into a sharp point. Then he twisted the forked tip of the torch into contact with the other arm and hit the ignition switch.

The sudden electrical charge through the hull made the attacking cells writhe and break contact. *Primus* catapulted ahead, drilling straight into the cellular wall at top speed. The membrane peeled pack in puckered folds as the submersible charged through it, across the wash of cellular fluid, ruptured a second cell, and a third and a fourth, and finally stopped, embedded halfway in a last thick layer of protein with nothing on the other side.

He was through. The white cells could not follow.

His body began to shake as chemicals flooded his own veins. He was safe. *Primus* was safe. Her lipid shield would need repairs, but all was not lost. He breathed deeply, savoring the moment.

The IUD should be near. Would he be able to see it? He looked around.

It wasn't to his right. He looked left, and then swept his view upward.

There. Far enough away for him to take in its outline, and vast enough to dwarf him utterly.

No. Wait. The view was poor, with almost no light, but he could tell the shape was wrong. This thing was round: a nearly perfect ball, and it gave off a dull gleam in the dark. Just like the bombs, except much, much larger.

The bomb launcher.

#   #   #

"She must have been having an affair."

"Nonsense! You don't know that." Bridges responded hotly to the suggestion from Hunter. The whole team was in the meeting room.

"Well it can't have been her husband," the pilot persisted, unreasonably disturbed by the placement of the launcher. "And it was someone she's been with in the past few days."

Kierkegaard gave him a piercing look. "I don't believe you know what you're talking about Mr. Hunter, so perhaps it's better if you don't speculate."

"Besides," Bridges argued, "that launching device could have been implanted a long time ago, perhaps by a doctor. It seems likely to me that it's the source of all of the bombs."

"That should be easy to figure out." Tamiko said. "You ran a full series of x-rays and MRI's when she first arrived. Check them again and compare them to the scans done when she got back yesterday. If the launcher was there all along, we should be able to spot it, now that we know what to look for."

With a nod from Kierkegaard, Bridges went to a nearby computer terminal. After a few moments he stood back.

"There it is," Mallory jumped to her feet and used the mouse pointer to show the others.

"Right next to her IUD, as we found it," Bridges added. "But not in the first scan we did."

"There you go," Tamiko said. "We still don't know how the original bombs were implanted, but that bomb launcher was placed sometime during those two days she was away from us."

"Wait," Gage interrupted. "There's another possibility. Doctor, how about calling up all of the scans of that area?"

They soon saw what he was getting at. Arranged chronologically, the scans showed that the launcher had actually appeared several days after her arrival at the clinic, long before her recent two-day absence. It was placed so close to the IUD that it could easily have been taken for a part of it unless the view was magnified. That area of the body had received much lighter scrutiny than elsewhere.

"Damn! I shouldn't have missed that," Bridges said. "If we had only known. . . ."

"As Dr. Tamiko said, it makes all the difference when you know what to look for," Kierkegaard replied. "None of us suspected a launching device that was still within the patient, and certainly not there. In hindsight, it was a brilliant move."

"Not so brilliant," Hunter said. "With these scans we can place it almost to the day that the thing was implanted. Surely you can find out who had that kind of. . . access to her during that time. Maybe if you interview the patient?" He looked at Kierkegaard.

"I will not," the other replied forcefully. "I am not going to tell her the truth about what's been done to her, nor anything that might start her guessing. She believes she has a rare condition, but a curable one."

"No she doesn't," Hunter blurted without thinking, then felt the startled looks of the others. "I mean. . . how could she still believe that? Coming to a secret laboratory and clinic hidden in the middle of an air force base instead of Johns Hopkins, or the Mayo Clinic? She can't be that oblivious."

Kierkegaard gave him a strange look, but said only, "Checking the dates is a good idea. I'll get someone on that."

Something in his voice told them the meeting was over, and they slowly dispersed.

Bridges followed Kierkegaard into his office and closed the door.

"Are you seriously thinking her husband could have been involved in planting that launcher?"

"I don't know what to think," Kierkegaard answered testily. "But she hasn't even been to a doctor other than our own in two months, and that was for an ear infection. The launcher was put in place within the past two weeks. You tell me who did it."

Bridges sucked a breath. "That puts a hell of a twist on things."

Kierkegaard slumped back in his chair. "It does indeed."

## 44

Hunter had a chance to recharge while the lipid shield of the *Primus* was being repaired, but he knew he wouldn't be able to sleep in the middle of the afternoon. Instead, he found a portable cot and took it outside for a badly needed dose of sunshine. Life aboard research vessels and oilrigs had suited him well, but spending weeks in an enclosed laboratory was a recipe for depression.

Tamiko finally found him near a back corner of the building where he had a good view of the main runway.

"Not much of a socializer, are you?" she asked, standing over him. "Are you trying to avoid us? Would you rather I left you alone?"

He shielded his eyes. "No, No and... definitely No," he answered, then swung his legs over the side of the cot and sat up. "I didn't feel like hanging around, just waiting to go again. But don't leave. It's nice to have you here. Or were you sent to fetch me?"

She shook her head, and sat beside him on the cot as he made room. "There's not much you can do at the moment. Kenneth and Lorelei are working with their assistants to analyze the bomb launcher, but it's slow work. They don't want to break it open yet because they don't want to risk destroying the mechanism inside. Or any remaining bombs it might be carrying. There's so much we need to learn from it, including who built the damn thing." A flush of anger shaded her cheeks. "I've never been a big fan of the human race, but the monsters who did this…"

"I know," Hunter agreed. "It gives me the creeps just being near the bombs."

"Near them? I guess it must feel that way for you sometimes." She brushed her face with a hand. "They're a perversion… a perversion of science—of the best hope that humanity has. Have you seen Skylar lately? It's hit him hard, as if his God turned out to be a two-bit huckster at a carnival sideshow."

"I think I'm partly to blame for that. I mentioned that the *Primus* project probably got its development funding because the ship could be used as a weapon. I don't think it had occurred to him before that."

Tamiko looked into his eyes. "That's something all of us have tried not to think about. But of course you're right. Maybe future generations will think of us the way some think of Oppenheimer and the rest on the Manhattan Project, wondering how their consciences could allow them to create a threat like the atomic bomb." She stared into the distance. On an impulse he took her hand.

"Maybe if we succeed with our mission, the *Primus* technology will be seen as a new miracle of modern medicine. Before they can make a weapon out of it."

She gave a wan smile. "That's what I like about you Hunter. Smart, but almost as naïve as Skylar. You still think they'll let us tell anyone about what we've done." She stood, but kept hold of his hand and pulled him up beside her.

"Come on. Let's get something to eat."

When he walked her back to her room later in the evening, and she invited him in, he was caught off guard.

"I feel so useless," she chafed. "Skylar's still working on the lipid shield. I wouldn't be any help with the bomb launcher. What is there for a plain old blood specialist to do?" She dropped onto the edge of the bed. "I can't even plan any more mission routes until we know more about the capabilities of that damn launcher, and whether we need to go back over old ground again."

He managed a smile. "If you're looking for sympathy, you're looking in the wrong direction. I always feel like a fifth wheel. Class dunce among geniuses."

Her face softened. "I think I can overlook that." She pulled an unopened bottle of Glenfiddich and a couple of glasses from the bedside stand. Seeing the look on his face, she said, "You don't get very far in R & D if you don't learn how to drink with the boys, and it's not convenient to have to mix a martini every time. There's no ice—good stuff should be drunk neat anyway."

Hunter sat beside her on the bed and took the glass she held out. "I'd almost think you had this planned."

"Don't think. Just drink." The single malt was good and tasted like another. That would be his limit, he told himself. There would be critical work to do in the morning. He couldn't mess up his head.

As it turned out, he hadn't finished his second glass before they were locked in a long, lingering kiss.

She was very good at it, her full lips nibbling one moment and then boldly pressing the next. She tasted sweet and smelled wonderful. He felt firm, taut muscles as he ran his hands down her back.

A vision of children came into his head, laughing and dancing. Startled, he drew back.

"What's wrong?" she asked. "Did I bite you?"

"No. No, nothing. I just had a memory… of a mission." It was a bad explanation, and he knew it.

"I kiss you and you think about work? That's not very flattering."

"You're a great kisser. I guess I've just been working too hard."

"Maybe I'll have to try a little harder," she purred, and slid her hand along his thigh. They kissed again fiercely and fell back onto the bed.

For a long time there was nothing else in the world but lips and tongues and teeth, hot breath and frantic hands. Hunter pulled back for some air and let his eyes roam over her. Languorously, she began to unbutton her blouse, enjoying his attention. A twist of fingers released her bra, freeing her breasts for his approval. He did approve. They were fuller than he'd expected, and perfectly shaped. He hurriedly pulled his shirt over his head, pressed himself against her, and found her lips again.

Children and music. A placid lake through trees. A young girl's bedroom, soft and tranquil and welcoming.

His fists clenched. Could they be Tamiko's memories he was seeing somehow? Had he become a mind reader? No, the memories belonged to the patient—the first lady—he remembered seeing them before, while in *Primus*. Why were they coming to him now?

He sat up, dismayed at his own thoughts and the look of chagrin on Tamiko's face. She waited expectantly.

He couldn't tell her the truth. She'd think he'd gone off the deep end.

"Lucy." He cleared his throat. "You're gorgeous, and smart. Desirable. I... I'm just not sure what I'm doing here. I don't see how this can work."

"How what can work? Are you having a problem?" She ran her hand up his leg again.

"No, not like that. I mean... how can this work between us? We have nothing in common. We could never stay together for long."

She surprised him with a laugh that came from deep inside.

"Of course we couldn't. We'd drive each other crazy. Do you think that's what this is about?" She shook her head. "I like you, Hunter—I don't know why. I think we can be friends." She smiled and looked down over her uncovered breasts. "But right now we have this *sex* thing getting in the way of that. You're wondering what I'm like and I'm wondering what you're like, and we're not going to get past it until we find out." She searched his eyes. "So what do you say we just let ourselves go for now, and then... we can get back to being friends again." Her sly smile was irresistible.

They made love. Then they did it again. When morning came, they awoke in each other's arms and were glad.

## 45

Hunter was on a streak. He was doing everything right, filled with fresh confidence and new understanding. His biggest obstacle all along had been his own reluctance to recognize the truth: the patient was guiding the doctor. He couldn't explain it, and there was no point trying, for now. All that really mattered was to accept and make good use of it.

A search of the patient's lungs was overdue. Blood clots there would cause serious damage, quickly interfering with breathing and putting a crippling strain on the heart. It was also possible that a thrombus formed in one of her arms or legs could have broken loose and lodged somewhere in the pulmonary arterial system.

Immersing himself fully in this inner-body world was a liberating experience. He could navigate effortlessly, without hesitation, as he improvised the course: bend after bend, twist after turn. He would call up an image from the latest scan, or paint the area ahead of him with radar. Then the shared abilities of patient and healer would find the targets without exception. Equally helpful, the patient's inquisitiveness was kept at bay and the fragile blossoms of memory every few minutes remained as background instead of dangerous distraction.

They were both learning.

That was a great relief. From being an invader, he'd come to be accepted as a partner in her healing, which both explained and validated the closeness he'd begun to feel toward her—a strange friendship, perhaps even more than that.

It was unsettling to know that when he was about to make love to Lucy Tamiko, his thoughts had strayed to someone else. He wasn't even sure that his own mind was to blame for that, which not only raised the question of how the patient viewed her relationship with her healer, but also how much her mind had infiltrated his.

Their connection hadn't become any less confusing, but it was definitely more productive. By late afternoon, he'd destroyed his thirteenth bomb in ten hours. Damn near as many as all of the previous missions combined. The arteries of the lungs were heavily infested with the hideous things, and he had torched them as quickly as the ship could recharge, but his fatigue finally became too great to ignore.

He self-consciously framed the thought "Goodbye" and pulled the plug. A pang of regret took him by surprise.

As he entered the conference room, Mallory waved a bottle of white wine at him expectantly. He shook his head and spotted a case of Heineken beer—Kierkegaard's private stock, he suspected. As he strode toward it, Skylar Tyson took his hand and shook it.

"Fantastic work, Hunter. Just fantastic. It makes me feel as if we've finally seen some light at the end of the tunnel." The scientist grinned like a kid and took another bite of his pizza.

Hunter turned back to the beer, only to find that Lucy Tamiko was already holding an opened bottle out to him.

"I think you deserve this," she said. "You had a good day."

He smiled and took a long drink. Leaning wearily against the nearest wall, he said, "I hope it's not premature to celebrate. But maybe luck has finally turned our way."

Later, as he found himself in a corner of the room with Truman Bridges, Hunter was forced to admit that in his sessions with Bridges the man had been nothing but sincere and honest. He'd earned some trust that Hunter badly needed to give.

"I was on a roll today," Hunter said. "Angels were on my side."

"Angels? I don't see you as a religious man, Mr. Hunter."

"Well, *one* angel, at least. Our patient. She's helping me, Doctor. I don't know how."

Bridges surprised him by replying, "I believe you. Are you expecting me to explain it?" He laughed, and then took a long swallow of red wine. "I've always been fascinated by the role of patients in their own cure. My medical colleagues have all seen it— an ability that allows some people to help to heal themselves. We attribute it to a positive attitude, the power of prayer, biofeedback... but the simple truth is, we can't explain it. We only know it exists because we've seen the evidence."

"Are you saying everyone has the potential to heal their own body?"

Bridges' dark face wrinkled in a frown. "I wish I knew. I'd love to believe that if I ever get cancer I have the capacity within myself to cure it, but the evidence is far from conclusive. From time to time we see miracles happen that we can't explain scientifically. What stymies us is their inconsistency. When a phenomenon is completely unpredictable, we can't draw any meaningful conclusions from it. My own feeling is that, given the right opportunity and a strong will, the human body will find any way it can to defend itself. To survive." He gave a sly smile. "In which case, perhaps our patient found you, Mr. Hunter."

#   #   #

"You're a very considerate lover. Has anybody ever told you that?

Tamiko lay propped on one elbow, slowly stroking Hunter's chest with a finger.

"Not that I can remember."

"You pay attention... take the time to figure out what I like. You actually seem to care about your partner's pleasure. Are you sure you're a guy?"

"That's hitting below the belt. Literally." He raised himself in the bed to get a better look at her. "Accusing a man of being sensitive and considerate is bad enough without questioning his manhood."

She smiled. "You have a knack. I just might let you stick around."

"My last girlfriend didn't see things that way. As for other women... " He frowned. "None of them complained."

Tamiko laughed. "Is that the best you can come up with?" She pushed herself into a sitting position, not bothering to pull the sheet up over her breasts.

"To tell you the truth, I hardly ever made love to a woman when I wasn't half-crocked. The last one did complain about that, but I didn't listen. As far as I was concerned, three or four beers didn't mean I was drunk. No big deal."

He looked at his hands. "I guess I spent a lot of time that way, the past couple of years."

"Well, you should have tried it sober a few more times. Maybe that's the difference." She leaned over and brushed his cheek with her lips, then rested her head on his shoulder with her eyes closed. "Or maybe you've just changed. Maybe you're starting to grow up." She chuckled as he gave her a mock shove.

"Funny lady." He looked at her peaceful face and smooth skin, and said softly, "Maybe this is... something different. Something special."

"Love?" She looked into his eyes, and pulled back a little. "No, it's not. You're not in love with me, Hunter—don't try to convince yourself that you are. It's OK. That's not what we're here for. I'm amazed we've even come to like each other. Don't spoil it by pretending it's something it isn't."

"How do you know?"

"That's not something I can explain. I just know. You like me— you want to please me. I'm content with that. Sometimes being good friends is better than being in love." Her voice grew softer. "A lot easier on the heart, too."

It didn't take a professional to sense the pain in that remark, but Hunter let it go. They were having a good time together. Better to leave well enough alone.

They slid apart and made themselves comfortable for sleep. Just before it grew too quiet to interrupt, she turned her head back to him.

"You know what I think it is?"

"What is?"

"Your new-found ability to please women. I think it's because of the time you're spending inside the body of a woman. Something has to rub off with the territory. You're going *where no man has gone before*." She laughed.

"Go to sleep," he said. "That's ridiculous."

But he knew it wasn't.

## 46

Time was his enemy. With the sea, and the dark.

The dark and the sea were one, and time was their weapon. It would steal his breath, his life. He had no defense.

The submersible rocked, teetering on a last stable place—a shelf that had caught it unexpectedly, and could just as readily let it go, passing the craft to the deadly drop that would crush it. By then he might be past caring. Time was inexorably robbing him of air.

The fragile shell rocked back and forth. Its rocking became the rhythm of breath: rasping in, then reluctantly escaping. There weren't many breaths left, and a shroud of sadness began to surround him.

The mission was going to fail. There was no escape for him, and that meant there was no escape for her, either. There were too many enemies, and he could not defeat them all.

The darkness was crystallizing, brittle and transparent. Through it he could see marauding blood cells swooping down on Primus... hunting it, seeking to dislodge the craft from its mooring, and sweep it away to be lost among the endless channels of the bloodstream. Even now he felt the jarring impact and sensed Primus shift.

No! No, it could not be allowed to move. Tucked between a pair of straggly polyps there was shelter, a partial protection against assault. Cut loose into the bloodstream, Primus would be at the mercy of ravenous cells, bent on its destruction.

He rasped another breath... two.

There was another impact—and this time the sub broke free.

Desperately, he willed his mind into the rigid shell around him, and fought for control of it. There was resistance like pushing through a wall of toffee... pushing... stretching....

Finally breaking through.

He became Primus, tumbling and spinning along the current, focusing every effort into regaining stability and control. The sea called to him, urging him toward a strange outcropping of cells just ahead. He sought it, circled it, merged with it.

And knew he was safe. For now.

Darkness returned to hide him. The sea smiled, and cast a cloak of calm over him.

It was time. Time to...

"Wake up. It's time to wake up, Hunter. Kierkegaard just called." Tamiko swept the covers from him and gave him a playful shove. "He'll be checking your room next and wondering where you are. I'd just as soon keep that between us, for now."

The air was cold on his naked skin. Yet the remnants of the dream left him with a curious warmth. That was a first. He couldn't remember that dream ever ending pleasantly.

Tamiko jarred him from his reverie with a toss of his shirt that caught him in the face.

Time to get back to work.

#   #   #

Tyson was in the control room when he entered. "The log showed a blip of activity from *Primus* a little while back, but I think it was just an anomaly. All systems check out fine. Maybe a spike in electrical potential around the ship or something like that. Anyhow, it's all ready for you. Good luck."

Hunter suited up and plugged in. He relaxed his body, focused his mind and slid into another world.

It was at once familiar, and suddenly strange. Something was different. Something was wrong.

He took a long look around, trying to fit the details he saw into the picture his mind still held from the previous mission. Smooth, liquid shapes and ruddy-colored tones had become as normal to him as a landscape of grass and trees; but the pattern around him was not the same as when he had left the ship the evening before.

Primus had moved.

Impossible. The submersible couldn't navigate on its own. Had one of the other team members taken it for some kind of joyride?

He couldn't believe that. Unless...

He remembered the unknown stranger's warning about a mole within the project. Could one of them have been hiding an ability to pilot the sub? If so, why use it now? What had they tried to do while he slept?

He took another look around, hoping to spot something familiar, then checked the map display. The ship had moved, but it was still in the same small artery in the lining of the left lung. He had moored her between a couple of protruding polyps for the night, planning to wait until the next day when he was fresh to re-enter a larger vessel nearby and make the transit to the right lung. The distance traveled was negligible, but the implications were enormous.

If someone had truly hijacked *Primus*, the project was in terrible danger, and he'd have to report it to Kierkegaard immediately.

He was preparing to unplug, when another thought occurred to him. Could the ship have broken loose on its own? The current wasn't as powerful as elsewhere, but it was persistent.

That would mean the craft had found another safe mooring purely by accident—had not only encountered a suitable outcropping of cells, but had also managed to jam itself securely among them. What were the odds of that?

Astronomical.

Then someone had guided it. The mole was real. A nightmare was real.

Wait. A *nightmare*.

The truth hit him like a punch in the gut.

There *was* a nightmare. His nightmare... the dream he'd had just before Tamiko had awakened him. *Primus* had broken free from her moorings, and he had brought her under control and steered her safely to shelter. Right into another outcropping.

Right here.

He pulled his hands slowly back from the controls and shivered.

How could that be? How could he unconsciously control *Primus* with no connection whatsoever to the VR equipment—and from a room a couple of hundred feet away from both control room and clinic?

Was there any other plausible explanation? He sorted through the fragments of the dream that he could remember. The details seemed completely authentic—just the way it would have to have taken place.

He had come to accept that his mind had forged a link with *Primus* that went far beyond the VR system itself. He'd seen too much evidence to deny that. But if the link could develop without mechanical assistance at all, even in a dream...

The implications were terrifying.

What if his dreaming mind wrecked the ship? What if *Primus* caused irreparable injury to a vital organ while careering through the bloodstream without conscious control?

He could commit murder in his sleep.

## 47

"That's not Kevlar. Shit, Kellogg, What is that?"

Chavez had been carefully cleaning his HK MP5 submachine gun when their group's leader came around the corner of the building. Beside Chavez, Rakov snapped his head up, sucked a last lungful from his cigarette, and ground the butt into the dirt. Chavez welcomed a diversion to break up the boredom after being up most of the night, practicing maneuvers. His eyes were still irritated by the sunlight as he swept them up and down the figure in front of him.

Kellogg was dressed from neck to boots in a fabric suit with a matte black finish. The torso had a bulky stiffness that could mean a Kevlar vest incorporated into it, but the arms and legs looked to be about the thickness of a hunting jacket. Chavez was already rolling the fabric between finger and thumb.

He looked up at Kellogg and said, "It feels soft and liquid... pliable. A gel of some kind? What good would that be? Insulation?"

Kellogg smiled, though it never touched his eyes. "It can make you warm or cool. Water-repellant too. Not quite a gel—a little more complicated than that. More useful. Here..." He pulled his Heckler and Koch .40 caliber pistol from a pouch at his side and handed it to Chavez butt first.

"Shoot me. Shoot me in the arm." He turned and walked away about ten large paces, then turned to face his second-in-command, waiting.

Chavez had more experience in close-quarter combat and the use of small arms than almost anyone in the professional services. He'd been trained and used by the best. He knew what it was like to be shot. It hurt like hell. What was their leader up to? Even a Kevlar vest at that distance was a risk—a few layers of fabric in a sleeve were no protection at all.

"Go ahead. Whichever arm you want." Kellogg's voice was icy calm. He stood with his arms slightly out from his sides, a little stiffer than before. The stunt was unnecessary—these men were all professionals, seasoned in various special ops units before going freelance—but they were also men who lived on the edge. A touch of *machismo* was good for morale.

"Damn, Kellogg. You're a crazy bastard." Rakov showed bad teeth and stepped to the side, to get a better view.

Chavez shrugged, raised the pistol, took a split-second aim, and cracked off a shot. As Kellogg twisted from the impact of the bullet, he squeezed off a round at the other arm. The effect was as he'd intended. Kellogg toppled onto his backside in the dirt. His face was hard to read, but he didn't appear to be in any pain as he pushed himself stiffly to his feet and made his way back to them.

"Couldn't pick just one arm?" he muttered. "Not a good leadership quality."

"Insurance," Chavez replied with a cocky smile. "Let me look at that." Kellogg's jacket sleeves were stiff and hard. There were only the slightest scuffmarks where the two bullets had hit. "What is this stuff? It was soft and flexible before. Now it's like hard plastic."

"It's called dynamic armor. You've never seen anything like it before. And you haven't seen it now." The narrowing of his eyes emphasized the words.

Chavez raised an eyebrow. Rakov took a closer look.

"Technology that people like us aren't supposed to have," the Russian said, nodding. "An embarrassment to our backers if we were to be caught with it. Is it permitted to ask how it works?"

Kellogg shrugged. "The fabric is filled with micro-miniature tubing containing incredibly small particles that align in a certain configuration when controlled by a magnetic field. I don't know how they do it. We will not be captured with these. It is a measure of the importance of our mission that we have been given them to use. Our employers are determined that we not only fulfill our objective, but also that none of us falls into... unfriendly hands."

Chavez smiled grimly. "They don't want to risk any of us talking and having it lead back to them. That I understand. But to do that they give us technology that could be even more of a giveaway? That doesn't make sense to me."

"I'm sure a theft has already been staged, should such cover be necessary," Kellogg replied. "Frankly, my own assessment of our mission included high odds that we would suffer casualties, possibly even losses. Our opposition is necessarily small, but they're well trained and motivated. Our employers decided it was worth a certain level of risk to improve the odds."

"Remind me to write them a thank you note." Rakov grinned. "Does this material react automatically to impact?"

"No, it's triggered by pressure switches in the gloves." Kellogg flexed his fingers. "Your mobility is seriously restricted when it's active, so you won't be doing any hand-to-hand combat that way. You'll have to decide whether your greatest immediate threat is from weapons fire or close quarters attack. It's not any heavier than Kevlar, and perfectly flexible until activated. You'll all try it out tonight."

Chavez leaned against the wall. "Impressive, but I don't think I'll volunteer as a live-fire target just yet."

Their leader gave another cold smile. "Oh ye of little faith. Nanotechnology is the way of the future. You can ask some experts about that when we meet them at their laboratory—just before you take their future away."

## 48

Hunter was shaken, but determined not to let himself be paralyzed by fear.

Bad enough to know that their patient's life depended on his success, but now he could unwittingly kill her in his sleep! How did he ever get into such a mess? A borderline-alcoholic submarine jockey handed the power of life and death. It was absurd, but it was also real. So he'd just have to deal with it.

He threw himself full-bore into the next mission and tried to clear his mind of everything else. The result was extraordinary. Maneuvering *Primus* had become second nature to him. Now, his mind automatically seemed to assimilate the data from the navigation system and the radar pulses, and he found bombs almost effortlessly.

Twenty-one of them this time. Eight more than in the tissues of the left lung. It was hard to believe there could be so many. The bombs he'd found in other organs must have been from an earlier insertion, far fewer in number. Now he was encountering the cargo of the bomb launcher: unknown dozens of bombs likely released after he had cleared the kidneys and the liver. It was disheartening to think that he'd have to search those organs again.

The high concentration of bombs in the lungs seemed to show that the launcher had loosed the remainder of its stored arsenal all at once, and that would only have been done as a last resort if someone knew the launcher was about to be discovered. More strong evidence of a traitor in their midst.

He swept the thought from his mind as a text message flashed in his heads-up display:

"TIME OUT. PRIMUS NEEDS RECHARGE."

He hadn't even noticed. He'd destroyed bombs as quickly as he could find them, and the ship used less charge each time and recharged more efficiently than ever. Both pilot and craft had to be getting some kind of assistance.

He checked the mission time: forty-five minutes longer than he'd ever done before! He should be too exhausted to function.

He wedged the nose of the ship into a secure position among a group of cells and prepared to unplug. He didn't want to—some rest right where he was with few distractions and pervasive quiet was more appealing than trying to catch some shuteye in his quarters. He shifted his body to get more comfortable, and closed his eyes.

Closing physical eyelids makes no difference because the mind still sees. The mind's view is pure and sharp, with no interference from electrical relays or software programs. What it sees is what is there. And more.

Slowly, slowly, the reddish dome of celled flesh becomes a dome of sunset sky. Floating blood cells are now drifting clouds. Shining membrane gives way to soft grass, wet from a recent shower.

Well-tended lawn stretches to a nearby field of grain that extends nearly to the swollen disk of the lowering sun. Manicured shrubbery sits against a backdrop of randomly waving stalks, scattered clumps of stunted trees and far-off purpling outlines of mountains.

There is a quiet peace, but muted sounds begin to impinge. The view sweeps sideways to include people: large people. Noisy people. People only in silhouette from behind, standing in static groups, their gesturing hands seeming to create gabbling sounds.

They are not many steps away, but the distance appears great. Their height makes it seem as if their heads are in another place. Unreachable.

Someone is leaving. Someone special. It hurts.

Father?

The red-tinged silhouettes move gaily, their voices making nonsense sounds of delight and encouragement, but the trees droop disconsolately. The walls of the house lean weakly. Birds do not fly.

A cold wind rushes from behind, and ripples the blades of grass suffused with green, and the yellow of pale sunlight.

Now hundreds of shoes tread the grass—black shoes beneath black pant legs beneath black robes beneath faces—faces without identity that wrinkle with excitement. The sun shines on these faces, and pride reflects from them. Mortarboard hats fly into the air with overpowering and unwelcome noise. Painful. Sound swirls, around and around, like the chaos of a carnival. At the center of it all is a small circle of shadow, a zone of stillness, where light has been taken away.

The crowd parts for a moment. Beyond it, a car door closes with a sharp sound, then a long, black vehicle pulls away and disappears quickly behind the nameless revelers.

He was here again. A brief appearance for an important event. Then gone.

Black shapes mill around aimlessly on the grass, now dull and trampled, blades, twisted and flattened... and it becomes a carpet of thick woolen threads, heavy and somber on a hardwood floor darkened with age. Stark walls rise high to a dimly seen ceiling. There is no light from it. There is no light from anywhere but straight ahead.

From a doorway with a figure standing in it.

The shape is tall and strong. The face is unseen—but oh, so familiar. So dear. So special. *Will he stay after all? Please, make him stay.* But in a moment, the shape is gone, the doorway empty, and its bright light blurs through welling tears.

The world is too big without him. A world of hard floors, steep stairs, sharp edges, and pain. Too big. Too hard. Too lonely.

He can keep the pain away. Could have.

Pain from things, pain from... people.

He could have protected me.

A flash of a huge, menacing face. A smile that betrays. A room spinning. Running... running. No escape.

Pain. Pain and *shame*, burning hot and choking. Betrayal—keen and acrid like smoke.

Tears... so many. And whimpering. Where is the whimpering coming from?

Please stop. *Please please please please STOP!*

Hide. Close my eyes and hide. Hide deep, deep inside, where no one can find me.

Why weren't you there to protect me, Father? And who have you sent to protect me now? Protect me from within my own body....

WHO ARE YOU?

Hunter's eyes snapped open to an image that was blurred and off-color. He realized that he was seeing the view inside the VR headset: a computer-generated simulation of inner space, flat and grainy. The psychic link had burst like a soap bubble at the force of the direct question.

Who are you?

Again she had asked, more urgently than before. Her mind detected his presence, and demanded an explanation, but was it her conscious mind this time? If so, surely she could ask her attendants— even Truman Bridges. Would they lie to her if she asked a direct question? He couldn't know. There were far too many secrets in all of this.

Whatever part of her brain was responsible, she would continue to ask the question. How should he answer? Would she accept him, or would her psyche recoil with rejection and angrily choke off the connection?

That thought was surprisingly painful. His mental bond with her was something unique. Something special.

How do you introduce yourself to a disembodied mind?

Spelling out his name would mean nothing. What she needed was reassurance... proof that she could trust him. She had every right to ask. He'd just witnessed what must be some of her most private memories: images of loss, of abandonment. Even treachery and... *violation?* Was that what he'd just seen?

He'd unwittingly tapped the deepest essence of her identity, far more personal than a mere name.

No, that wasn't accurate. She had *allowed* him to see it, perhaps had deliberately shown it to him.

Is that what she wanted from him in return?

Could he trust that far?

What image could he use to reveal himself? Where did his truest self lie?

He licked nervous sweat from his lip, unclenched his hands, and tried to relax. He closed his eyes again.

Darkness.

Darkness, like the deep blue-black of the sea. The sea at depth: dense and cool, motion slowed into smooth sweeps and lazy swirls. Slowing time itself.

The sea is a private kingdom, where myriad performers parade in bright array between columns of watery sunlight, and powerful denizens of deep shadows honor a truce between natural rivals.

Slipping calmly beneath the waves, the body is at once free of gravity; the mind free of the cares of that other world. Its sounds are left behind... its distractions, its demands. Hot sunlight mutes to cool turquoise and aquamarine. The impersonal vastness of airy space gives way to a womb-like connection within the fluid world, comfortably bounded by the limits of vision.

Rolling over frees billows of silver-blue bubbles that wriggle toward the glassy surface. Flashes of bright yellow sun prism dancing wave-tops into darting, dazzling spotlights that illuminate weightless motes of plankton floating like pollen on a summer breeze.

Another roll over and a lean forward begins an effortless glide: a free-fall dive in slow motion, with care to feed bursts of pressurized air into the vest-like Buoyancy Control Device to brake descent, reassuring with its light squeeze on the chest. A brief pinching of nostrils and a puff of air equalizes the pressure in eardrums and sinuses. Second nature. Regular breathing—no more labor than a gentle walk.

Hover head down, and survey the world spread beneath. It stretches beyond sight, far, far below where the body alone cannot go. For that you need...

....a submersible with its solid steel shell of a reassuring heaviness revealed in round, ringing tones as metal strikes metal. Dozens of gauges are like friendly faces surrounded by party lights. There is comforting protection in forged steel and the added satisfaction of a technological safety net.

The motion of such a craft is smooth, nearly imperceptible; but its passage through the water is revealed to other senses: *inner* senses sharply aware of increasing depth and mounting pressure. Still, there is only excitement, not concern, not fear. It is the calm of familiarity. Routine. A confidence born of thorough acquaintance.

The oceanaut and the deep blue sea.

This is life. This is home.

This is who I am.

An idea! In this memory there is a flat glass computer screen in the submersible. At the right angle it could become a mirror.

Overhead light spills onto the surface revealing a reflection of a face: dark hair, strong jaw, high cheekbones... a hint of blue in the eyes. A somber face.

My face.

The reflection is not entirely still, as small features and patches of skin waver in and out of focus. Then suddenly the outline changes. The hair is darker, its profile rounder with a suggestion of curls. The skin is darker too, even in the dim reflection. Female. *Her face.*

The face is blank. It has no features. Instead there is a nothingness, like the "blind spot" produced by a trick of the human eye with only a tantalizing suspicion of details that cannot be seen. The blank circle becomes the mouth of a tunnel, drawing the eye inward into shadowed, gloomy darkness, and something more.

A menacing presence is there too.

Him. Him again. The bringer of pain and shame. Hiding within... waiting always to be revealed anew, and to rekindle the hurt.

No. NO. Not again.

The tunnel recedes, and the reflection ripples, shatters and fades. The encircling steel shell reappears, with its winking lights and frenetic needles on passionless faces.

But it is no longer comforting, no longer safe.

The submersible is still. Inert. Not only unmoving, but unable to move. No longer a sheltering cocoon, but a chilled prison. Darkness invades it. Cold pervades it.

No... this is not a place to go. Not a good place to be.

NO!

There was a way out before. There must be a way out now.

"HUNTER!"

What? How could she know...?

"HUNTER!"

"HUNTER! PRIMUS IS RECHARGED."

It was like being slapped awake from a dream. He gasped and felt his body jerk. His impulse was to tear off helmet and visor to get a solid dose of reality, but that would provoke questions he certainly didn't want to answer... didn't know how to answer Better that the others assume he'd simply dozed off.

Maybe he had.

No. It was tempting to dismiss the experience as a dream, but he knew it was not.

In *Primus* he traversed a labyrinth with each new level more enigmatic than the last. He had not only opened Pandora's box, he had fallen in.

The interaction with the woman's mind had been pleasant at first—why would it take such a turn for the worse? Was identity so inextricably entwined with our pain and fear? He was almost sure that she had deliberately shown those things to him, but he couldn't understand why. Was it a display of trust, or a plea for help? And what did it say about her feelings for him, an invader of both her body and mind?

Hunter's own mind refused to open itself again so soon to the link and its emotional peril. Instead, he would have to do his job the hard way, by computer-fed VR alone.

As he worked, he tried to imagine himself as an unfeeling machine, coldly carrying out its assigned tasks. He found eight more bombs. The right lung was clear and the task was done. He stripped off the gear, bolted for his room and collapsed on the bed.

His last thought before unconsciousness was, *Will I dream?*

And will I hurt *her if I do?*

## 49

It was late afternoon when he awoke, but with the blinds drawn it took him a few moments to decide if it was day or night.

He couldn't have been asleep for long, but traces of a pleasurable dream lingered in his mind—a rare thing. He tried to recall details but they were elusive. There was a woman—he remembered that much, and the recollection gave him a warm feeling.

Not Lucy, though.

A woman with mocha skin.

Damn. It wasn't hard to see where that had come from. And it was definitely not a good line of thought to pursue.

He stumbled to the commissary and swallowed some food, not tasting it, then made his way to the control room. Tamiko was already there.

"How's the ship, Lucy? It hasn't... moved, has it?"

"No. Why would it?" she asked. "Didn't you dock it properly?"

"Sure, I think so... but I was tired, that's all." He settled into the pilot's chair. "Are you here to check up on me?"

She responded with a mildly wounded look.

"I think it's pretty clear that you don't need me," she said.

He was taken aback. "I... think my unconscious mind just picks up on a lot of clues and makes predictions about bomb locations from them. But without your maps, I still wouldn't know where I was."

She gave a snort of derision. "I don't mean with *Primus*. I already knew you weren't using the maps to find the bombs—I've accepted that. I mean *in the bedroom*."

"What are you talking about?"

"Come and have a look, lover boy." She sat in front of one of the monitors and began a flurry of keystrokes. "Look at what we recorded while you were taking your nap." The screen showed a series of bar readouts.

"What am I looking at?" He knew she was having fun at his expense, but he had no idea where it was leading.

"Our patient's vital signs." She drew a finger across several of the bars. "Heart rate, respiration, perspiration... and down here are hormone levels, even muscular contractions. Watch this." She tapped a final key and the playback began at the chosen point. Hunter could see all of the levels begin to rise, though at slightly varying rates, then they clearly reached a strong peak, and danced for a time before gradually tapering off to something close to the original readings.

"What was that all about?" he asked, as Gage walked in and broke into a smile. Tamiko swiveled the chair to face him, with an expression that was hard to read.

"An orgasm," she answered. "Your lady friend climaxed. Not long after you'd spent so much time with her. *In* her. I think the connection's obvious." She looked up at Gage, sharing the joke. "I guess it's true what they say. Size really doesn't matter."

"It's not how big it is. It's what you do with it," Gage contributed, then broke into a loud laugh.

Hunter angrily slapped at the keyboard and cleared the screen.

"For Christ's sake. I thought we were above voyeurism here."

The others paused, and looked at each other. "No, not necessarily," Gage deadpanned, and then laughed again. Tamiko's control dissolved and she joined in helplessly. Stung, Hunter swept up the helmet and put it on, as much to hide his expression as for any other reason.

Could they be right? Tamiko had said it happened just after the mission, probably just after he'd fallen asleep.

What if his mind had somehow linked with hers, the way he'd unconsciously piloted *Primus*?

Shit! He was playing around in the psyche of another human being where even the best-trained experts would fear to tread. What gave him the right to do such a thing?

He pulled the helmet off his head. Tamiko was sitting nearby, watching him. Gage was no longer in the room.

"Sorry about that. No offence intended," she said. When he didn't reply she continued, "Frankly, if I were in as bad a situation as that woman is, and still had enough desire left to masturbate... I'd be pretty pleased with myself. Honestly, I think it's a tribute to human nature." She smiled softly. "We were only pulling your leg. How could you have had anything to do with that? You're linked to a micro-miniature submarine in her bloodstream, for Pete's sake."

How indeed? Hunter thought. That was the billion-dollar question.

#   #   #

The next twelve hours was a blur of missions and all-too-short snatches of sleep. He returned to both kidneys and her liver and found them riddled with bombs. They had to be new, released by the bomb launcher after his previous sweep.

With the last of his energy, he purged the spleen of a dozen bombs. He'd learned how to produce the absolute minimum spark from the torch that would trigger a burn, and *Primus* was recharging ever more quickly; but even so, he found the necessary downtime a frustrating impediment. As usual, he failed to recognize his own need for a recharge, until Kierkegaard firmly commanded him to unplug and get some rest.

"You'll need it," he insisted. "We've decided that we can't afford to ignore the pancreas, so that's next. After that...," he sighed. "I feel we no longer have a choice: I've asked Doctor Tamiko to map the brain."

The darkness surrounded him. It permeated him. He was the darkness and the darkness was him.

Air was running short now. Hungry silence circled its prey like a vulture. The dimly glowing eyes that had kept him company here and there around the compartment were starting to wink out. Saying goodbye.

Goodbye. *To sunlight, to surf, to sand... to smiles and sweethearts and songs.*

No one was coming. The indifferent sea would claim him, as it had claimed so many others, never caring to know the names of those it took, nor of those who would miss them.

He blinked. Then again.

There was someone there. Except he couldn't see them. Her. It was her, he knew it. He experienced her, like the darkness enveloping him. Except... cradling, not smothering. Comforting, not tormenting. How had she found him?

How had she come? Why?

To show the way.

With a gentle sense of rebuke, she lifted his head from the darkness, and made him look up into the light. Without words, she told him that he was neither the submersible, nor the silence. She told him that he was the waves above, the smell of salt air, the raucous cries of birds, and the warm kiss of the sun.

And suddenly... he was.

This is not how it happened, *came a whisper from a rebellious corner of his mind.*

No matter. It's better this way.

Fierce sunlight sucked the wetness from his skin and seared away his last remnants of fear like the scattered shreds of morning mist leaving him free and alive. A prisoner given an eleventh-hour reprieve.

Saved.

In gratitude, he turned his head to see her face, aware of its outline in his peripheral vision. Then....

She was gone. He was alone. Lying on his bed listening to the faint sound of air through the heating ducts, and some barely discernible noises of movement in the corridor outside.

There was a loud knock at the door.

"Mr. Hunter? Sir? You're wanted at a staff meeting right away. In the lecture room." It was the voice of one of the military support people. "Mr. Hunter? Did you hear me, sir?

"On my way," Hunter managed, his voice raspy.

He sat up, the dream still fresh in his mind.

It bore no relation to the actual event, but it was a whole lot better.

How had she come to be in it? Was that his choice? Or hers?

## 50

The team was already hotly discussing something when he came into the room. Kierkegaard waved at a chair, then continued with what he'd been saying.

"It would be reckless to assume that they have not planted bombs in her brain."

"But why would they take that risk?" Tamiko asked. "A detonation anywhere in the brain could cause irreversible trauma—permanent brain damage, or even death. A hostage who's become a—I hate to say it, a 'vegetable'—wouldn't be much of a bargaining chip anymore. More likely to seal the president's resolve, if anything. They couldn't be sure a bomb wouldn't plant itself in a key vessel and cause cell death extensive enough to be fatal."

"Unless they got the information from us," Gage muttered darkly.

The project leader shot a glare at the white-haired scientist. "There is no indication of a leak anywhere within this project, Dr. Gage, and I think such suggestions are counter-productive. Please keep them to yourself." He lifted his head to take in the whole group.

"Is there anyone else who believes we could be doing more harm than good by searching the brain?"

Hunter hesitated, then raised his hand. "I think it would take too much time, sir. If we're getting down to the last strokes, the time could be better used elsewhere."

"Where might that be, Mr. Hunter?" The voice carried a film of frost.

"I don't think there are any bombs planted in her brain."

"No doubt you'll share your evidence for this?" Colder still.

Hunter sighed, eyes fixed on the tabletop. "I have no evidence. It's natural to think the bombs would drift into the arteries of the brain as readily as anywhere else, but I have a strong... sense that there are no bombs there, at least not yet. It's the same sense I get after we've cleared one of the organs." He looked up. "You've taken my word on that up to now."

Kierkegaard was not mollified. "It may be that I was in error. Especially since all of those sites have subsequently been found to be riddled with bombs."

Hunter took a sharp breath. It had never occurred to him that Kierkegaard might doubt his explanation for the new infestations.

Tamiko snapped her head toward her boss. "That's unfair and unreasonable," she said. "I was the last one who wanted to accept Hunter's assessments of bomb placements without hard proof. But we've all seen the evidence. He's got some ability to sense the presence of the bombs. It's uncanny, but it's also undeniable, and we've all come to accept it." She waved toward the projector screen. "Don't forget that scans backed him up afterward. Those organs *were* clear. Then they weren't. So unless you're going to start calling into question the abilities of the technicians who performed and analyzed the scans..."

"You've made your point, Dr. Tamiko," Kierkegaard interrupted heavily. "Mr. Hunter, I owe you an apology. I should not have implied..." He gave a slight shake of his head, then stood up straight and addressed the far wall. "I think we've heard all the arguments. I will make my decision shortly. That is all."

No-one else moved until Kirkegaard had stiffly left the room. Gage let out a long whistling breath. Tyson wiped his brow with a handkerchief.

As the others filed out, Bridges rose from his chair and stepped toward Hunter.

"Don't judge him too harshly," he said. "You wouldn't believe the pressure he's under. Most other men would have cracked."

Hunter nodded, still in a daze. "I don't blame him," he said. "Why should he accept my hunches at face value? Half the time I don't believe them myself." He suddenly slammed a fist on the table. "Why does it have to be me anyway? I'd be perfectly content just to put my brain in neutral and steer the sub. That's my job. That's what I was supposed to do. All I was supposed to do."

Bridges gave the wry smile of a philosopher. "None of us really knows what we are supposed to do with our lives. Until it's been done."

# # #

Hunter destroyed three bombs close together within the pancreas, and then was compelled to wait until *Primus* could be recharged. The organ wasn't yet bomb-free; he hadn't sensed the "all clear". Why was it he could recognize the *absence* of bombs, but not their *presence*? Perhaps he'd never really tried. Perhaps he simply hadn't learned how.

Well, he had some time now to start.

He tried to define what the "all clear" felt like. Mostly, it was a sensation of relief like the lifting of a weight or a lightening of darkness. If so, he should be able to sense that darkness, as a man with eyes closed can detect the direction of sun and shadow.

He deliberately slowed his breathing, relaxed his muscles, and tried to picture his mind pushing outward. Sending pulses of thought... ripples that would echo back like sonar from a hard object.

Nothing.

He kept it up for several minutes, but without result.

It must be the wrong approach. Too technical. Instead, he tried to picture his thought as a welling spring of water, overflowing its bounds and spreading slowly through the surrounding space. Not flooding, not forcing, only winding sinuously around, and between, and behind, and through. Then it was ivy, growing in ultra-fast-motion, spreading pervasively, seeking the light, and encountering....

Non light. *Non* heat. A *void*, where warm tissue belonged.

A bomb.

He'd done it! He'd located one.

Were there more?

Another. Close behind the first.

Search again. A trickling, seeping pool of curiosity. Thought invading flesh, imbuing blood, becoming flesh and blood. Surrounding and permeating. Finding... nothing. There were no more to be found.

Only two more bombs were left within the pancreas. He knew it. He was sure.

He pictured them as two stark sentinels waiting in the dark, cold and lifeless. Enemies of life. The more his thought defined their alien-ness, the more clearly he sensed their presence.

Two black objects blocking the light. No... *soaking* up the light. *Draining* the light like colors bleeding from a watercolor picture left in the rain.

Two tall shapes silhouetted against bright light.

Two people, framed in an open doorway, their backs turned. They are leaving.

Abandoning?

It feels like that.

Mommy. Daddy. Don't leave. Don't go. Please don't go. Please don't leave me with him.

But the doorway is empty.

The room is not empty. There is another. Oh, yes. Waiting, just beyond view. In the dim light—light that makes all shapes seem the same. No way to tell good from bad.

He seemed good. *How could she know?* But then... evil. Betrayal. Pain. No way to escape. No way to ask for help.

He is there. He is coming. He touches....

The view recedes. There is the shape of a small girl, head bowed in the fading light, and the shape of a man, tall only in relation to the child but dominant as he leans forward, menacing in the implacability of his movement. They blur together, and a cry of anguish reverberates as the light winks out.

Another time, the girl is taller, but no match for him. The result is the same. The shame and hurt burn like a black flame that consumes the figures, and blots out the scene like inky smoke.

Again....

No! It must be stopped.

...the girl and the faceless man. She tries to resist, but there is no resisting. The only source of rescue has left long before through the open door. Leaving *him* as her protector—her guardian. The irony is bitter as gall. He presses closer...

No! I can stop him. Block him. Stand in the way....

He does not stop, inexorable as the darkness. Hunter himself has no solidity, is only a wisp of mist, easily walked through. The nightmare repeats. How many times?

The girl is a young woman now. Taller, shapely, yet as vulnerable as ever. Abandoned still.

Her protector/tormentor approaches again.

NO.

Suddenly the observer understands. It is darkness that is the accomplice. It is darkness that enables this evil. There must be light. Light to wash darkness away.

There. A window, blocked by thick curtains. Pull them back! Pull them down.

Another, closed by shutters. Throw them open!

Another, obscured by blinds. Pull them up! No more blindness. Let the room be filled with light. Revealing, cleansing, burning *light.*

And so it is.

The man recoils, retreats... staggers backward. He raises an arm to block the stabbing brightness, but it can't be blocked, not entirely. A ray of golden white catches his shielded face and unmasks it!

Old skin. Strong cheekbones. Square chin. Balding head, grey-fringed. Eyes of soulless black.

Then he is gone, plunging into the retreating shadows. Fleeing.

As daylight pours in one door, blackness drains out the other, and the blackness has a name.

Uncle!

And another name:

Frank.

Perfidy unveiled. Identified. Named. And thereby *defeated?*

For now, the dark is banished. Color begins to return, one rich, gleaming dewdrop at a time. A trickle, then a rain of color, flooding the view with joy, and suddenly...

He is back in *Primus*. The warning screen is strobing its impatience, demanding attention with red letters that flare across his view.

He is back. He is Pilot. He is Hunter.

Yet he is not the same. He never can be.

## 51

Tyson pushed his food slowly around his plate without enthusiasm. "I still can't understand who could do such a thing. A cowardly act against a defenseless woman."

Tamiko gave a bitter smile. "There are all kinds of societies around the world where individual life has almost no worth at all. Especially a woman's."

"I don't think it's a foreign country at all," Gage offered, as he lifted a piece of Salisbury steak to his mouth.

"You mean independent terrorists?" asked Tyson.

"Nope." The other shook his head, chewing the meat. "I think our enemies are from among the very rich and very powerful right here at home." He appreciated the shocked looks. "Consider the facts. How many countries could manage to produce this level of technology? Skylar, you should have an idea."

The balding scientist shrugged. "A handful. Less than half a dozen, I should think."

Gage nodded. "And five of the six would be friends of ours. Sure, technology can go missing from labs and be purchased on the open market, but why use this particular method? Taking an embassy full of hostages or shooting down a civilian airliner would be cheaper and easier."

He didn't wait for a reply. "Because there's a *message* in the medium. Whoever it is wants to tell the president they have the power and the money to play this game with impunity, and that they can get to *anyone*." He leaned back, looking satisfied with himself. "We're talking about the power elite, here. The Establishment. Not terrorists."

Hunter gave an uneasy laugh. "You sure you haven't been spending too much time with the Conspiracy Channel?"

"Laugh if you want to. I'll bet if we could read the fine print on those bombs it would say 'Made in the USA.'"

Lorelei Mallory gasped softly. Her face was pale. Noticing their attention, she breathed, "I hope you're wrong, Kenneth. You must be." Then she got up, leaving most of her food uneaten.

"Sorry, Lorelei," Gage said, looking apologetic. "I'm just reading the evidence."

The biologist looked as if she had more to say, but she turned and left the room.

The others exchanged looks. Tyson was the first to speak.

"I hope you're wrong too. The idea is unthinkable, but unfortunately, I'm afraid you may be all too right." He stood slowly, a sour look on his face. "I once had such hopes...." He turned to leave.

"Skylar, wait." Hunter reached out to touch the man's arm. "There have always been people who turn new discoveries to the wrong purpose. All through history. The human race survives and flourishes because most people want what's good for all of us. Don't forget that."

The older man nodded, and then left. Tamiko pushed her empty plate away.

"Well, it's been a lot of fun, boys, but I have work to do."

As he watched her go, Gage muttered, "Who knew that would be such a conversation-killer?"

"It's not your fault for being right," Hunter said. "We'd just rather believe we're fighting a foreign threat, instead of being caught up in a homegrown power struggle."

Gage looked at him over his coffee cup. "You're more perceptive than I ever gave you credit for, Hunter." He took a long swallow. "Look. I know you don't like me much. You think I'm... what? Pompous? OK, I can be pompous sometimes, I guess. Maybe I'm just compensating because I didn't have a star quarterback father to put me through school."

Hunter bristled. "You don't know what you're talking about."

Gage held up a hand. "Truce. That was only supposed to be a good-natured jab—I'm just not very good at it. But I do know what I'm talking about."

He sat back and clasped his fingers together on the table in front of him. "I was a big fan of your dad. I followed every game, every statistic. To me, he was the perfect quarterback: smart and gutsy. Willing to buck the coach's orders if he saw a better way.

"I see now that he might have been too cocky, too sure of himself, but I didn't see it then. I even tried to copy his moves in college ball, except I didn't have the talent he had. Even so," he said, looking into Hunter's eyes, "I can certainly see that it would have been a bitch to try to follow in his footsteps."

The pilot only shrugged a little defensively, wondering where the conversation was going.

"Believe it or not," Gage resumed, a brooding look on his face, "I know what that's like. My father was a star, too, but a physicist—one of the most respected minds in the country. His opinion was in demand everywhere. Just his name could open any door I wanted—educational institution, research job, you name it. Except I would have been expected to measure up to him. How could I hope to do that? He was a giant—I was bound to disappoint. So I did: others, him, and most of all, myself."

He forced a smile and hid behind his coffee cup. "Oh, I'm not looking for a shoulder to cry on. It forced me to seek out my own path, and work my ass off, which means it was probably a good thing in the end. Except I never got over being defensive about it. So instead, I come across as a cocksure prick sometimes." He looked up. "What about you?"

"I just come across as a regular, average prick." Hunter laughed. "And a drunk, and a mental case. I suppose you've heard about my accident, too?"

Seeing Gage shake his head, he hesitated, then continued, "I got trapped in a malfunctioning submersible on the bottom of the Gulf of Mexico. I nearly died. By the time the surface crew realized something was wrong they couldn't find me.

"Anyway, somehow the sub did surface—just in time—but it was all smashed up inside. They figured my mind had snapped. The company tried to get out of paying me compensation by trying to dig up proof of pre-existing mental illness. They failed, but it could have been the end of my career. Still might be. Kierkegaard took a big chance hiring me."

"Devon is a smart man," Gage said softly. "He made a good choice." Then, as if deciding he'd said too much, he cleared his throat and stood, gathering his dishes into a pile. "See you back in the control room."

As he watched the scientist walk away, Hunter sat in quiet thought, amazed to learn that Kenneth Gage had a human side.

#   #   #

The two remaining bombs in the pancreas were destroyed easily and quickly, but Kierkegaard had still not announced his decision about whether to search the brain or to trust Hunter's intuition that doing so wasn't necessary. If they opted to leave the brain alone, and they were wrong, there would be no hope of a last-minute deliverance. If they wasted their remaining time searching for bombs where there were none to find, any devices left undiscovered elsewhere in her body would be free to sow destruction.

It was a decision to test the wisdom of Solomon, no doubt about that.

In the meantime, Hunter snatched whatever rest he could, but he couldn't fall asleep. The mysteries of the past twenty-four hours saturated his brain like caffeine.

Had he really been witness to the woman's appalling memories or were they fictional scenarios that she projected?

No, creating such fictions would be a sign of an unbalanced mind.

And so, what he'd seen was truth: the woman had been abused repeatedly by someone her parents had trusted enough to leave him as guardian of their daughter. An uncle? "Uncle Frank?"

He shuddered with disgust. To him, people who preyed on children were no longer fit to be called human beings. This monster had been a friend or relative. The very worst kind of betrayal.

Why had she shown all this to Hunter, who himself was an invader in her body? The irony was grotesque. The kind of torments she had faced were the darkest secrets of a lifetime, surely not even revealed to a professional counselor without long hours of trust-building. Or perhaps to a lover. What would make her give such trust to him? That seemed to prove once again that he was interacting with her subconscious mind alone, and from that mind's depths had come a heartsick plea for help. Yet he was still faced with the same dilemma: even if he could do something to help, did he have the *right* to do so?

He longed to ask Bridges or Kierkegaard for advice, but how? He'd become convinced that the mental connection he experienced was no thing of mysticism or the occult—it simply involved energies and a mechanism not yet understood. But that which is not understood is often not believed.

Maybe his greater fear was that, once they knew, they would stop him. After all, he could tap into the patient's most private store of thoughts and memories and, worst of all, control *Primus* without any supervision of his conscious will. Sublime potential, yes, but also horrific danger.

Wait a minute. Why did such control have to be unconscious?

He lay flat on the bed, and relaxed his muscles and his brain. Then he pictured *Primus* and tried to imagine her surroundings as he had last seen them: a small passageway just off the main artery leading from the pancreas. Vein wall nearby. Translucent cell membranes nearly touching the hull on the port side. Darker color of venous blood.

A mammoth white cell drifts by. It doesn't notice the ship.

A red cell gently nudges from behind, then slides past. The current isn't strong here. Nothing is damaged.

It's working. At least in one direction. Reception is loud and clear.

What about the rest? Is there control?

The engines are idling with the fans neutral. Try giving them thrust... there. A gentle push against the small outcropping anchoring the bow, weak but discernible. Test the directional controls. *Carefully.* Mustn't get loose in the bloodstream and then find out the connection isn't reliable.

There is some response. A light surge to starboard. Now back to port. Throttle back.

Try reverse? Is it worth the risk? What if someone notices? Would they believe that the ship has simply broken loose on her own? What then?

They'd come to fetch her pilot.

What the hell. It's worth a try.

Ease her back... gently... gently. If the link starts to falter, find a sheltered spot quickly.

The mouth of the tiny backwater vein is still visible astern. Easiest to turn around and fight the weak current that distance.

In the clear. A feeling of being slammed back by the sudden forward lunge as the full current takes hold.

A junction, out into a larger vein. It's easy to dodge blood cells and other assorted traffic. Still only a moderate current, compared to the main trunk veins.

"Hunter?"

Damn. Too soon.

"Hunter!"

"HUNTER, OPEN YOUR DOOR."

Shit. They've come already. Better find a place to pull off, before *Primus* joins the express lane to the heart. A small opening, a maintenance tunnel to a cluster of cells is best. Close in to the vein wall.

There's one, and in she goes, the current providing a last-minute push in the right direction. Final burst of thrust to jam the prow up tight. Good... very good. Perhaps a touch less precise than with the mechanical controls, but....

Why were his hands in the air?

Oh. Holding imaginary joysticks.

He hurried to the door.

It was Truman Bridges.

"Hello, Hunter," the doctor said as he stepped into the room and closed the door behind him. His face had all the smugness of a mark who's caught the con man.

"Nice trick." He smiled.

## 52

Detective stories and investigative TV shows all said, "follow the money." Mannis knew it was true only to a point. In the real world, those with money—real money—knew how to hide it. It was their top priority to hide it from being taken in exorbitant taxes by profligate bureaucracies. Hide it from meddlesome law enforcement agencies with a naive morality regarding "lawful gain."

His own search had become *follow the blanks*. The blanks were where the money trail—or any other line of investigation—came to an abrupt end.

The end of a trail was always suspicious. In Mannis's experience, where a simple query could no longer solicit an answer, there lay a cover-up. He never questioned that anymore, and he did not believe in coincidences.

The tough part was learning the reasons for the subterfuge. Often such reasons were trivial: sexual indiscretion, a minor business double-cross, simple tax evasion. Some high-rollers simply covered up everything they could because they liked to. Perhaps it gave them an inflated sense of power and control. He didn't care. Let them all play emperor if they wanted to. What mattered was knowing which walls were put in place to stop *him*.

That knowledge came from skill born only of long experience. Fortunately, his tenure in the shadow world had enabled him to recognize most of the petty ploys and ignore them before they cost precious time. Even better, and only after many years, he had come to recognize the styles and trademark techniques of the professional cover-up artist. Small telltales revealed that there was an identity behind them, although too often that identity remained undiscoverable.

True masters of concealment, the real geniuses of the clandestine culture, he had come to identify for his own purposes by letters of the Greek alphabet: alpha, beta, and so on. The best he had ever encountered, he called *Omega*. That one truly reached everywhere with abilities that spoke of the highest level of power and influence. Mannis, the Silent Man, whose connections gave him access to the finest investigative resources in the world, had never learned Omega's identity or whereabouts. He had never even come close, so he rarely tried anymore.

Until now.

After the near-deadly sabotage to his car, Mannis had also survived both a hit-and-run attempt and a fire that had badly damaged his well-guarded apartment. Since then, he slept in his office, or sometimes in an obscure hotel under a false identity created just hours before. His pursuit of the perpetrators behind the president's current crisis had become even more obsessive. All of his resources had been focused on this one labor, yet he'd encountered brick wall after brick wall. The work of a master.

Omega.

The futility of pursuit in itself was an answer. It confirmed his immediate suspicions that the ones he was looking for were no idealistic international terrorists, but denizens of the highest realms of power in the western world.

Could they be stopped? It was hard to imagine how. Even Mannis, with all the powers of the presidency behind him, might be outmatched.

He had exhausted nearly all leads. One of his remaining few involved a faint rumor pieced together from scraps of intercepted conversation on cellular phone frequencies. It suggested that several international mercenaries and some right-wing ex-military types had gathered together on American soil for an unknown mission. Their whereabouts were also unknown, but clues hinted at a half-dozen possibilities: two in Virginia, one each in Maryland and Delaware, and the others in Wyoming and Nebraska. The western sites didn't concern him—they were unlikely staging areas for an attack on the project at Langley AFB. The intelligence was shaky—it might cause him to waste time none of them could afford, but what else could he do? Wait around in Washington until they got to him first?

No, he would go into the field... track down those potential sites himself, keep his lines of communication open with Langley AFB and pray for some good news.

#   #   #

"They have guards posted at each corner of the building, plus double guards at the entranceways here, here, and here."

Kowalski leaned over the diagram, tapped it hard with a forefinger, took a drag from his cigarette and moved his hand in a circular motion.

"Then there are eight more guards patrolling this area about fifty yards out. There are a half-dozen other observer outposts at any given time, but those are unpredictable because they're changed every day so the regular base personnel won't suspect anything. The observers are small groups of soldiers dressed to look like road construction, sewer maintenance, or landscaping crews. Even telephone repairmen. They aren't hard to spot.

"At night they are replaced with camouflaged teams of two, very skilled at blending into the surroundings." He nodded with grudging respect as he drew in another lungful of smoke. "Signs have been posted indicating that it is a restricted area, but the whole thing is low-key, meant to be unobtrusive. The laboratory security people must know there's talk on the base, but they still want to call as little attention to the facility as possible."

"That's why there's no heavy armament?" Rakov asked.

"Exactly. The guards have side arms and standard issue rifles only. Anything more would be a giveaway that something high-level is going on there." Kowalski smiled with half his mouth, the other end of the upper lip paralyzed by a knife wound that had left a pale scar. "Only the base commander and his second-in-command know the real story. Now you."

"What about this vacant zone between the outer ring of guards and the building itself?" Chavez pointed. "Are they using some kind of passive alarm system there?"

"They tried," Kowalski replied. "But birds kept tripping it. That's what it looked like to me." He laughed. "Each time it happened, it showed me a little more of their defenses as everyone scrambled to respond. So they recently removed the sensors, and haven't replaced them."

Chavez shook his head. "Are you absolutely sure this is the right facility? I can't believe the defenses would be so feeble for a target like this."

Kellogg responded. "I'm sure there was a big argument over that, but the president absolutely cannot risk a leak... to the press, or to enemy interests who might take advantage of the situation. Obviously he got his way, but now it will cost him."

"Still," Hennings spoke for the first time, "these are only the defenses that can be seen. They must have taken other precautions to monitor the air space. Or the shoreline?" As their underwater expert, Hennings was bound to ask about that.

"Absolutely," Kowalski confirmed. "The base has underwater defenses active at all times, but they're really meant to detect submarines, and they are fairly old. New, passive listening devices have been placed here and here," and he touched the map, "but they're portables and there are gaps in their coverage. The route I plan for us to take through here," drawing a fingernail along the paper, "will take us through the biggest gap—as long as our navigation is perfect." He looked up at Hennings. "Which is why you're with us." The other acknowledged the compliment with a quiet nod.

"Back to the guards for a minute." Romero, their communications specialist had his hand raised slightly, a holdover from his academy days only seven years earlier. "They must be in communication with each other. Regular check-in times and all of that? If we're going to take them out one-by-one with suppressed weapons—I assume that's the plan—then how do we get through three layers of them without anyone missing a check-in and giving the game away?"

"No-one will miss a check-in," Kellogg answered. "Because we will be in possession of the necessary code words." His matter-of-fact statement silenced the room.

"Jesus," the ex-commando called Branson muttered under his breath. "This one is deep."

"As for the rest," Kellogg added with a cold smile. "Remember that we're talking about a building in the middle of a United States Air Force base. Within five minutes of an alarm being raised, fifty marines on standby will be charging across that tarmac from only a quarter-mile away. Within ten minutes, half the population of the base will be at their disposal."

"In other words, getting in will be child's play for us." He gazed out the window at the clear blue Carolina sky. "But if there is the slightest mistake, getting out will take a pact with the devil himself."

## 53

"Don't worry, I was the only one in the control room." Bridges flashed white teeth. "Your secret is safe with me. For now."

"What secret?" Hunter tried, not expecting much from the gambit.

"Only the fact that you can control *Primus* without being anywhere near the VR equipment." The doctor sat down casually on the bed, doing his best to make the other man feel comfortable. "That's quite a bit more than we expected."

"Than you...? What do you mean, *expected*?"

Bridges' face creased into the Cheshire cat grin of a man with a secret that he is finally able to reveal. "You must have wondered why we picked you for this mission when many others have the basic qualifications and less... baggage?" He watched Hunter give a hesitant nod. "Do you remember participating in some psychology experiments while you were in college? Your first semester, I believe. A rather lengthy series of interviews, but you volunteered for them."

"One of the psych students' assignments. We didn't exactly volunteer, though, the coach volunteered us. What does that...?"

"Well, they weren't really psychology tests. Perhaps *parapsychology* would be closer to the truth. I don't think the students themselves knew that. Their professor was an old colleague of mine, Daniel Lesker. His real passion was psychic ability—everything from so-called ESP, to precognition, to the simple intuition that most of us possess to some degree."

"I fit into this because...?" Hunter asked.

"You can guess what I'm about to say. Perhaps you've known it all along, subconsciously. You had the highest score for psychic aptitude, Hunter. By far. One of the highest scores Lewis had seen in five years of testing. Your name went into a private database, available only to a select number of researchers in the field, but no-one had any reason to make use of that information, until this little... project came along."

He shifted slightly to watch Hunter's face.

"You must have recognized that you have much stronger intuition than most. Powerful dreams, frequent *deja vu*? I don't mean reading people's minds, or moving objects with your thoughts. The ability rarely manifests itself that way." Bridges tugged at an eyebrow. "In any case, that wasn't what we were looking for."

"*We?*" The word had broken through the younger man's daze.

"Devon was involved in the choice, of course. How could he not be? We knew that we had a fantastically sophisticated submersible with tremendous potential, but when most people tried to pilot it, the interface proved to be too demanding. Not only did we feel that an experienced submariner would have an advantage, but we suspected that something more than mere virtual reality might be required. Given the incredibly small scale we were dealing with, we knew we might need a whole new approach to the communication involved." He rubbed his chin. "That part we kept to ourselves. Our funders would have had a stroke. Yet we were right! Here you are, and look at the amazing things you can do!"

"You—and Devon Kierkegaard—believe that I do what I do because of psychic ability?" Hunter asked, feeling his way slowly.

"Are you going to tell me differently?"

The younger man hesitated, then said, "No. I don't know what else to call it." He dropped limply onto the bed beside the doctor. "At first, I thought I was going off the deep end. And then... well it still feels like voodoo or something."

"There is a scientific explanation," Bridges continued. "Skylar Tyson would tell you that your connection to *Primus* taps into something called *wave interference patterns* in the *zero-point field*. It's a concept that many scientists forcefully ridicule, and others claim can explain nearly all psychic phenomena."

"I've never heard of it."

"Not surprising. A significant theory in quantum physics postulates that at the very deepest level of the universe there is a field of primal energy out of which comes a froth of sub-atomic particles—some call them *virtual* particles, because they exist for immeasurably short instances of time, yet they are the blocks upon which everything else is built and kept stable." The doctor smiled. "My understanding of it is very basic, but I am told the concept has gained wide acceptance. What is not so widely accepted is that this so-called zero-point field is an underlying repository of all of the information that makes the universe function."

"Are you serious?"

"Skylar is. Though he's embarrassed to have it connected to the supernatural."

"Connected how?"

"Those who believe in such things propose that human minds attuned to the zero-point field can somehow make use of its information. Communicate across vast distances. Or across time. See the future. Maybe even change it."

"You're not telling me you believe *that*." Hunter didn't know whether to laugh or grab a stiff drink.

"I don't know what to believe," Bridges replied. "All I will say is that the evidence is intriguing. What really matters is that when the results of certain experiments pointed to a connection between the *Primus* interface and the zero-point field, Devon made an intuitive leap. Reasoning that it just might provide a critical advantage, he decided to look for someone who showed signs of being attuned to the field. He found you."

Hunter struggled with his voice. "Why didn't you tell me? Save me so much grief. Let me know what to expect?"

"That's a big part of why we didn't. If you had pre-formed expectations, it might not have worked at all. Abilities such as these almost always develop as part of the mind's own intuitive processes, because it *needs* them. How can you contrive something like that? Besides," he smiled, "would you have believed us? Or would you have thought we were the crazy ones?"

Hunter grudgingly admitted the truth of that. If there'd been any suggestion of the paranormal about the project, he would have turned them down flat.

The doctor stood with knee joints protesting, and began to pace, as much as the tiny room would allow.

"There's so much I want to ask you, like how well it works, what it feels like. Are there any side effects?" He arched an eyebrow. "But first there's something else I need to tell you... and you may never trust me again once I do." He stopped pacing and took a deep breath. "We implanted a *device* in your body. In your neck."

"*What!*" Hunter jumped to his feet.

"Please hear me out before you do anything violent."

"What kind of *device?*"

"Something very small, I promise you. These people are the experts in nanotechnology, remember. Implanting it only required a kind of large hypodermic needle, like putting a radio frequency ID chip in your dog."

"You're dodging the question, Doctor," Hunter growled. "What does it do?"

"Part of it is simply a monitor that measures certain of your body's vital signs and brain activity, and then transmits the information to receiving equipment in the laboratory."

"And the other part?

"Yes, well, the other part is . . . experimental, but it has produced encouraging results in others. Without any harm," he added quickly. "It's implanted in your neck so as to be next to a part of the brain stem called the thalamus. Have you heard of it?"

Hunter nodded. "Sure. I remember you talking about the patient's thalamus once. Kierkegaard said it was where sensory information passes through to the brain."

"Very good. It is also the part of the brain with the greatest body of evidence linking it to what we consider psychic phenomena. Scans show that psychic functions are often associated with increased activity within the thalamus. We wanted to... stimulate that."

Hunter's face was as blank as a mannequin's as he struggled to comprehend.

"Why. Why would you even consider something like that?"

Bridges looked as if he needed to sit down. Instead, he swallowed hard and continued.

"You weren't the first pilot of the *Primus*. There was a young man named Travis Li—a gamer, with lightning-fast reflexes and other skills we were sure would be enough for the job. Except they weren't. His brain apparently couldn't handle the overload. It needed help. We came to believe that a certain amount of psychic ability would provide just enough of an edge, and we knew of an experimental means to give that ability a boost."

Hunter suddenly remembered the morning he had awakened with unexpected pain in his neck. "You implanted hardware into my neck to artificially stimulate my brain? *Who the hell gave you the right to do that?*"

"No one. You have every right to be angry. At first I was dead set against the idea myself. But... well, it began to look like it might be the only way. As I said, in testing done by others, the device had provided significant results and caused no discernible harm."

"No harm! Do you know what I've been going through?" Hunter nearly screamed, stepping close to the smaller man.

"I'm so terribly sorry," Bridges abjectly shook his head. "So much was at stake. Even so, we were wrong to keep it from you. It was... criminal—I know that. If you want to break my nose or knock out some of my teeth, I won't blame you." He stood there defenseless, ready to accept his punishment.

Hunter slowly unclenched his fists, and turned away.

Finally, he asked, "Are you going to tell Kierkegaard? About how I control *Primus?*"

The psychologist's shoulders slumped in relief. "No. No, I'm not. He suspects, I know, but he has no real evidence. If he did, I'm not sure he could keep it from his superiors, as bizarre as it would sound to them, and..." His face was forlorn as he looked into the younger man's eyes. "If the government learns what you can do with your mind *they will never let you go.*"

That hadn't even occurred to Hunter. The prospect was as frightening as anything he had so far imagined.

"What do we do now?" he asked in a subdued voice.

"Now," Bridges rubbed his hands together and sat back on the bed. "Tell me everything. *Tell me what it's like?*"

#   #   #

He didn't tell Bridges about his forays into their patient's psyche. When he was alone again, he went to the nearest available computer.

It was a wasted effort. The first lady didn't have an uncle named Frank. No uncles, no great-uncles... only a distant cousin named Francis a few years younger than her, who'd always lived on the West Coast. He couldn't even find any record of friends of the family named Frank. Maybe it was a dead end. Maybe he was wrong about the name.

The woman needed help, but it wasn't something he could do on his own.

How much farther could Bridges be trusted? Was there anything the doctor could do?

He sat frozen with indecision, then finally pushed away from the desk and turned toward the medical office.

## 54

"She has a fever."

Bridges dropped into the chair behind his desk, his face creased with concern. "It's mild, but it's getting worse. I've asked that she be confined to the clinic for now, so we can be ready at a moment's notice if something needs to be done." He leaned forward onto the desk, wringing his hands.

"What would have caused it?" Hunter slowly sat in the office's other chair.

"I have no idea." The dark face had a sheen of sweat. "Do you, Mr. Hunter? Is there any chance that it could be from something you have done with *Primus*... or left undone?"

"Doc, if you think I have an answer to that one, you're giving me way too much credit. Of course it could. I'd never know the difference. I'm like the neighborhood bricklayer performing heart surgery while getting instructions over the phone."

"Of course. I'm not looking to place any blame," Bridges said. "I suppose what's really worrying us is the threat the president mentioned of a new kind of bomb—a biological agent that would attack her immune system. What do you think are the chances of such a device existing, without our having found one by now?"

Hunter lifted his hands in a gesture of helplessness. "On that scale, the human body is a huge territory to cover. There'd be no need to plant that kind of device in a stationary position like the others. They could just roam around the bloodstream at the speed of the flow and our scanners would never pin them down. I couldn't begin to guess the odds of *Primus* running across one by chance in a blood vessel the size of the Hudson River."

"I know, I know. An impossible task we've set for ourselves." Bridges' lips trembled.

"Doctor," Hunter said, "if it's any consolation, I don't think the HIV scenario is what we're seeing here. I can't promise there aren't any devices like that, but I don't believe anything has been detonated. Yet."

"How would you know?"

"You should be able to answer that one for yourself. You put that damned *psychic amplifier* in my neck. I've learned to sense the presence of bombs, as well as their absence. I don't sense any other kind of attack, and I think I would. Could a bomb we missed have damaged something vital?"

"There are no signs of that," the doctor answered with a shrug. "No disruption of blood flow or other indications of trauma."

"Maybe the cumulative effect of everything that's been happening in her body has finally triggered a reaction."

Bridges nodded. "That occurred to me too. In which case I haven't the faintest idea what treatment to try. Any remedy could just as easily make things worse. So all we can do for now is keep her cool and well hydrated. A witch doctor could do as much!" He glared at the wall that held his medical certificates in their frames as if they mocked him. Then he noticed that the submarine pilot was making no move to leave.

"Something else on your mind, Mr. Hunter?"

"Nothing to suggest...," Hunter's reply stalled. He didn't know how to begin. It was one thing to reveal his secret—what right did he have to reveal hers? But he knew no other way to get help for her, and not doing whatever he could for her was out of the question.

"Doctor," he tried again. "I need you to tell me who she is. Our patient. It's the first lady, isn't it? Please tell me."

Bridges' eyes widened. "Why do you say that? And why the urgency? What's going on?"

"I trusted you."

"Only because I caught you with your hand in the cookie jar. What haven't you told me?"

Hunter took a deep breath. There was nothing left but to take the plunge.

"I think she's been sexually abused."

"*What?*" The doctor nearly leapt from his chair. "Why in the world would you think a thing like that? Do you have any idea what you're saying?"

"Yes, I do." Hunter leaned forward. "I'm saying that this woman needs help in even more ways than we thought. I know that because...." He clenched his teeth and forced himself to say the words. "Because my mind isn't only linking with *Primus*—it's linking with *her*... with her unconscious brain, damn it! *I can see into her mind!*"

There was shocked silence. Bridges slumped back in utter bewilderment.

"You're not… you're not serious," he finally managed.

"I am so goddamned serious you wouldn't believe it. And it's probably thanks to you and that fucking implant you put in my head. Do you know what it's like to read someone else's pain? Their most secret thoughts?" He realized he was nearly yelling.

He took a breath and tried to calm down, to give the other man a chance to catch up. "I can actually see her memories… see them as if I'm there, as if I'm a witness to everything."

Bridges looked sick.

"And you… you saw that she had been abused?" he rasped.

"Yes. But I'm not suggesting the president was involved," he added quickly. "He wasn't. It was during her childhood. Her parents sometimes left her with a man—a relative, I think—named Frank. Uncle Frank is the name that comes to me, but I've searched the internet. She doesn't have any close relatives or family friends with that name." He waited for a response, but Bridges couldn't trust himself to speak. "She needs help," Hunter pleaded. "Professional help. That's why I came to you."

"Of course. Of course." The psychologist gave a dazed nod as he struggled to pull himself together. "I… I believe you, Hunter. I wish I didn't. You can't imagine what the consequences of this might be." He swallowed hard. "You said the name of the man was Frank?"

"Uncle Frank is the way she thinks of him, but it's not affectionate, as you can imagine. Why? Do you think you know who he is?"

The doctor did not reply right away, his eyes cast toward the floor. When he lifted his face, he looked years older.

"I might," he answered simply. "But I pray that I am wrong." He drew a hand over his face. "F. Arthur Black. Does that name mean anything to you?"

The younger man shook his head. "It sounds familiar for some reason. Who is he?"

"The 'F' stands for Frank. He hasn't used it for years—none of his professional life, as far as I know." His eyes were wet. "He's the president's chief of staff. A lifelong friend."

It was Hunter's turn to have his world rocked. The confirmation of his fears was like a sudden explosion in his chest. He could hardly breathe. Then his mind saw the flaw in the revelation.

"No," he blurted. "That doesn't make sense. The man I've seen is older than she is. Much older."

Bridges nodded, then deliberately stepped behind the desk, pulled the keyboard toward him, and began to tap the keys.

"I want you to see something," he said. "And may God and Devon Kierkegaard forgive me."

A view screen mounted in the corner came to life, and quickly changed to a scene that was instantly recognizable as a medical setting. An array of equipment, a hanging intravenous bag, and pulled-back curtains framed a bed with a prone figure in it. The view closed in on the face. The features became clear.

Hunter gasped.

It was not the first lady.

It was *Emma*, their daughter.

## 55

"Captain?"

Kellogg looked up from the map he was studying for the hundredth time. Chavez stood in the doorway, waiting for permission to enter. His leader nodded. When the door closed, he said, "Diego, you know I don't want you using my rank. To those men I am simply Kellogg. I want it to remain that way. What are the others doing? And what is it you want?"

"Sorry Cap... sir. They're going over their re-breather gear with Hennings. They've all done scuba, but most haven't used re-circulating equipment before." He paused to gather himself. "I was hoping you had a minute to fill me in on a few things."

"Things that haven't been covered in the briefings? I thought I'd been excruciatingly thorough."

"I don't mean about the mission. About the men, sir." Chavez was clearly uncertain of the reception to expect. His superior's habitually expressionless face gave no clues. "I was hoping you'd tell me something about their backgrounds. I've never worked with any of them before—even that's unusual. The only one I've ever heard of is

Hennings, and that's only because of his decorations from the British military. I didn't even know he'd come over to... our side."

"To the dark side, is that what you're saying?" Kellogg's laugh was as cold as his stare. "Why do you need to know? And why should I tell you?"

This was a point on which Chavez felt on solid ground. He took his command responsibilities seriously—and he knew Kellogg appreciated that fact.

"Sir, I'm your second-in-command. You'd expect me to lead when you're not present... ensure that the men follow your orders, and place the mission above all else. I need to know where their loyalties lie, and how far those loyalties can be trusted. How far they can be pushed before they crack. Otherwise, I could be going into combat with a serious handicap, sir."

"Do you suspect some of them are not loyal to the mission?"

"Who is loyal to a mission? We're loyal to money. Some fools are loyal to some cause or another, but unless I know their true motivation, how can I control them in a crisis?" Chavez paced across the room. "Usually, by now, the stiffs are working off their pre-combat jitters by talking about what they'll do with their money. These men? None of that." He turned to face his leader. "What hold do you have over them? How strong is it?"

Kellogg kept his face blank, and then seemed to come to a decision. He gave a perfunctory nod and waved Chavez to a seat.

"All right, Diego. I see your point." He sat down hard on an office chair nearby. "You're right, it's not about money with these men. Not for personal use anyway. Rakov and Romero want money to support their causes: Rakov is Chechen, Romero is FARC."

"FARC? Colombian revolutionaries?"

"Yes. After blowing their chance politically a few decades back, the Revolutionary Armed Forces of Colombia have used up lots of explosives lately and would like to have access to more high-tech goods that are available only with American dollars. Besides, who do you think is bankrolling Colombian efforts to defeat FARC? The American government, naturally. As for the rest, Kowalski, Branson... they're National Alliance...."

"McVeigh's group?" Chavez interrupted.

"Old news, my friend. Bombing's not enough anymore. They've got their fingers in some very big political pies now." Kellogg smiled, but there was no warmth in it. "Evers and Jackson are Aryan Nations—I think Evers calls his branch 'The Order.' Wahlberg is Black Bloc."

"Black Bloc? They're protestors. They don't have a military wing."

"You tell him that. I suggest you have your gun ready when you do," the other said with a sneer. "MacLeish...? MacLeish is a Christian Patriot, I think. One of those groups—it doesn't really matter. Hennings *is* in it for the money. He just doesn't get pre-combat jitters."

Chavez shook his head slowly, trying to assimilate the information.

"OK, all those neo-Nazi groups... a black president, I get that. But there has to be more to it. The Black Bloc is anti-globalization. What's Wahlberg's interest in this?"

Kellogg appeared to be scrutinizing his fingernails. "They've all been told we're going to destroy a new research project that would destabilize the global economy, and what little balance of power is left in the world. The neo-Nazis have been told it's something that would benefit non-White minorities. The others... various other fictions." He looked pleased with himself. Chavez sucked in a deep breath.

"None of them has any idea who's really backing this mission?" he asked in a near whisper. "What if one of them was to figure out the truth?"

"Then..." Kellogg raised an eyebrow. "They would have to be *retired* from the field." His features showed no emotion whatsoever.

#　#　#

Hunter was in Kierkegaard's office. The silence was thick. They were waiting for the phone to ring.

The head of the project was furious, but he couldn't decide what had angered him the most: that Bridges had revealed their patient's identity, that Hunter had concealed a critical element of his interface with *Primus*, or that the pilot had a powerful contact in Washington and both had kept Kierkegaard out of the loop.

He'd met the President's special operative, Mannis, and it was this so-called Silent Man who had brought the *Primus* project to the attention of the president in the first place. But Mannis wasn't part of the official reporting structure and Kierkegaard didn't have a direct line to him. The scene they were now playing out smacked of a spy novel.

Hunter had called the phone number of a supposed travel agency, which had led to a convoluted series of follow-up calls. Kierkegaard and Hunter had been waiting for nearly half an hour for the mysterious man to contact them.

The harsh ring of the phone made them jump.

"This is Devon Kierkegaard. Yes. Yes, he's also here. The room is as secure as we can make it. Very well." He put the call on the speakerphone. Hunter quickly recognized the carefully controlled voice.

"Mr. Hunter. I was hoping I wouldn't get a call from you, because I'm sure it's not good news. I hope it's important. I also assume you have a good reason for bringing Dr. Kierkegaard into our confidence. No offense, Doctor." The director of the facility merely frowned more deeply.

"I didn't feel I had much choice," the pilot answered. "And I needed a scrambled phone line. I guessed that Dr. Kierkegaard would have one."

"An easy guess. I have no choice but to bow to your judgment for the rest. What have you got?"

Hunter explained. Doing so for the third time made him better at keeping to the salient points, but it didn't come any easier. When he was finished, the room was quiet.

"That's a lot to swallow at one meal," Mannis said finally. *"Dr. Kierkegaard, how much credit do you give this information?"*

The project leader cleared his throat.

"Regarding the psychic element... Mr. Hunter has had an extraordinary edge when it came both to piloting *Primus* and to locating the bombs, neither attributable to experience and practice alone."

He gave a sigh of reluctance at what he was about to reveal. "What you may not have been told, sir, is that Mr. Hunter was recruited in part because of a strong, latent, psychic ability and was given a special electrical implant for precisely this purpose.

Although he chose not to tell us about its additional effects until now!" He darted an angry look at the younger man.

"You clever bastards. You clever, sneaky bastards."

"They didn't tell me about the implant," Hunter said.

"Are you expecting me to be surprised? These are deep waters, Hunter. You should know about deep water." He paused, then, *"What about the rest? What about the... abuse? How credible is that?"*

"It's not something we ever considered... that he might actually be able to make contact with her thoughts," Kierkegaard admitted with a shake of his head. He looked wearily at his submarine's pilot. "However, for all that he's kept some serious secrets from us, I have no idea why Mr. Hunter would fabricate such a story, nor any reason to think he would."

"I wouldn't," Hunter said. "Believe me, this isn't anything I would ever want. Far from it! I also want to stress that the speculation about Mr. Black as 'Uncle Frank' is just that. Guesswork. Although the name she associates with the abuse is 'Uncle Frank', I have no other evidence to prove who he is. We could be completely wrong."

"I heard you, Hunter, and you are wrong. You must be wrong. But my duty is to the president of the United States, and I can't afford to ignore anything." The voice lost some of its official tone, and Hunter recognized the sincerity that had convinced him once before. *"I can't promise to get back to you on this—I'm up to my ass in alligators. But I will check it out—that's a promise—and if there's any substance to it, I'll deal with it. In the meantime don't do anything about this on your own, and tell no one else. Is that absolutely clear?"*

"We're in complete agreement on that," Kierkegaard replied dryly.

"Oh, and Hunter...." The pilot looked up. *"Try to restrain yourself while you're in the head of the president's daughter, would you?"*

The phone went dead.

## 56

Kierkegaard's expression was hard to read. After a long moment he waved at a chair, and took one himself.

"I suppose since you're in this deep, you might as well hear what this is all about," he said. He steepled his hands on the desk and paused a moment, as if examining the grain of the wood, then lifted his chin.

"Now that you know our patient is the president's daughter Emma, I'm sure you can guess that this whole travesty is about bringing great pressure on the president. The White House received a *communiqué*, apparently from a terrorist group, describing what had been done to Emma and threatening to kill her if their demands were not met. I'm still not at liberty to reveal those demands, but they involve action only the president has the authority to take, and something to which he is utterly opposed.

"Publicly, it's government policy not to negotiate with terrorists, but of course it has to be done when there is no other workable course of action. It's a measure of the president's abhorrence of these demands that he went ahead with enlisting our team." He sat forward for emphasis. "It's also a measure of his trust. I do not want to betray that trust, Hunter."

"Believe me, sir, even before I knew it was Emma, I took this project very seriously. It was never my intention to... invade her mind."

"I do believe you," Kierkegaard nodded. "You've never struck me as the *voyeur* type, and I must accept the blame for implanting our psi amplifier in your neck and not telling you about it. In hindsight that was clearly a mistake—just more of this damned secrecy and paranoia."

He slapped a palm lightly on the desktop, his strongest concession to emotion. "Now that I know how far your enhanced capabilities extend, I can't agree with our Washington friend about your contact with Emma's mind. I've always believed that some part of us has a far greater awareness of the body's state of health than our conscious minds ever recognize. Bodies sometimes heal themselves in miraculous ways." He shook his head with a bemused smile. "It could be that, all this time, her unconscious mind has been your greatest ally."

"I can't quite believe I'm hearing you say that," Hunter said with a look of surprise. "I came to the same conclusion some time ago, but I couldn't rationally accept it. Even now, with all that's happened, I can almost convince myself that it's a dream."

"You can believe in a submarine the size of a virus, run by remote control and virtual reality, and yet you can't accept that the human body is aware when it's sick, and why? That's a measure of our modern hubris." Kierkegaard sighed. "Whatever we believe or don't believe, the evidence is there. You've become incredibly adept at locating and destroying those bombs. Perhaps some part of her thinks you can solve her emotional wounds as well."

The idea was utterly fantastic, and cruelly daunting. Hunter had never felt so inadequate in his life.

Before he had a chance to say anything, Kierkegaard leaned over the desk and spoke again.

"I'm going to get the team together in twenty minutes to announce our next step. I need you to go back in, Hunter," he said softly. "All the way in. As close a rapport with her mind as you can achieve. She's come down with a serious fever, and we have no idea at all whether it's because of an HIV-type bomb, or *Primus*, or some damned flu germ... or even whether the cause is physical or psychological. We just don't know—but maybe she knows, deep down. That's where you'll have to reach her."

His eyes narrowed. "What we do know is that time is running out. The deadline is forty-eight hours from now, at noon. After that we're on borrowed time—she's on borrowed time."

Hunter gave the barest of nods and got to his feet. Before he reached the door, he turned.

"What if the enemy finds out where we are and what we're up to? Shouldn't we have more protection for Emma?"

"More protection than we have now can't easily be hidden," Kierkegaard said. "I have a strong feeling that our opponents do know what we're up to, and have known for a long time; but as long as there's any hope that they don't know where we are, we can't risk blowing our cover with conspicuously heavy security."

Hunter was alarmed to see the fatigue in Kierkegaard's troubled face.

"At some point we have to trust to luck," the director said. "We must be due for some by now."

\# \# \#

Hunter lay on his bed and stared at the ceiling. His head reeled, still trying to accept that the patient was Emma, not the first lady. Now he could see clues that he'd missed. When they'd met, he'd thought Emma was a doctor or real estate agent because of the device hanging at her hip. It was probably both a bio-monitor and the virtual reality relay itself, the conduit that linked *Primus* with its control center. For the two days she was out of contact, she must've been too far for its signal to reach. Did that mean the rest of the time she stayed on the base? That alone would have ruled out the president's wife.

Then there'd been the flash of a vision as he was about to touch the first lady's hand, just *after* touching Emma's. Children laughing and dancing. He'd thought it was a memory of Dyandra's days as a school teacher, but now he remembered that Emma was a professional dancer, or had been. It was one of the few things he knew about her. She probably taught dance classes.

It was all clear enough in hindsight. What wasn't?

Other things were far from clear. Could he carry on as if nothing had changed?

He needed to probe deliberately into Emma's mind, as invasively as *Primus* delved into the cells of her physical body. That had been distasteful enough when he'd thought he had the implied permission of her husband, and with a nation's security at stake. It was much worse now.

Because there was one more element that changed everything.

He realized that he was falling in love with her.

## 57

"We're not sending *Primus* to the brain."

Kierkegaard's words drew a mixed reaction in the room. Most were relieved, but Tyson and Mallory looked puzzled.

"I'm convinced that an attack on the brain would be an act of revenge only, not persuasion," he continued. "We can't say with certainty that they have not sent bombs to her brain, but we have to assume they will not trigger any until they know they have lost. We don't have enough resources to cover all potential threats, so we will have to focus our efforts where we can still sway the course of events." He stepped to the side to reveal the view screen. It showed a diagram of the lower abdominal area.

"What has us very concerned right now is our patient's fever. We don't know what's causing it; however, the scans we performed while trying to find the bomb launcher have revealed something new, as you can see. There's a dark spot at the edge of her right ovary where it joins the fallopian tube. So far, we haven't been able to determine the composition of the dark area. It's not metal. There's even the possibility it is some kind of ovarian cyst. But I don't believe that."

"You think it's another bomb launcher? Or one of those HIV bombs?" Gage asked.

"Those wouldn't have to be stationary," Hunter interrupted. "In fact they'd be more effective if they weren't."

Tyson nodded. "Unless they were too large to be mobile. In which case they'd need to be disguised."

"*Hormones.*" Lucy Tamiko sat forward quickly. "What if it is to release something that looks like estrogen or progesterone?"

"I don't follow you, Doctor," Kierkegaard said.

"Ovarian hormones can have a powerful effect on neurotransmitters, particularly serotonin. What if that thing on her ovary is releasing something chemically similar, or even forcing production of natural estrogen to abnormally high levels? Our blood monitoring doesn't check for that. It might have been overlooked on a general blood work-up too, because the IUD she's using is the type that releases a synthetic form of progesterone."

"Serotonin is a neurotransmitter chemical that regulates dozens of body functions," Mallory added. "Particularly brain functions. Neurotransmitters trigger nerve synapses so that signals can proceed along the neural pathways. Without them, the message stops. Serotonin itself acts on more than a dozen different synaptic receptors, and high or low levels can affect everything from pain sensitivity, to mood, to appetite, to quality of sleep. It can constrict or dilate blood vessels, stimulate or depress the heart rate—its presence or absence affects the pH of the brain itself."

"Would it affect the immune system?" Tyson asked.

"Absolutely," Mallory replied. "It could affect nearly every body system, over a period of time."

"All right," Kierkegaard said. "But why would they go that route? What would be the advantage?

"It's a means to wreak real havoc in the patient's body," Tamiko answered. "A serious imbalance of serotonin could give her hallucinations, make her suicidal, produce agonizing migraine headaches, or even put her into a sleep so deep it would be almost like a coma. All of it would be reversible—without the permanence of an infection from something like HIV. As you said before: leverage, not just revenge."

"And it might easily look like an auto-immune disease at first," Bridges added, "and fool us into thinking they've detonated HIV bombs. Perhaps that's what's causing her fever."

"Poor woman," Tamiko muttered. "It could be making her want to slit her own throat one minute, and the next, make her randy as a racehorse." She gave a meaningful look at Hunter, who looked away in discomfort.

"Dr. Tamiko, a little sensitivity, please." Kierkegaard moved to the end of the table again. "All right, then. That is *Primus'* next target. You know what to do by now. Dr. Bridges, please see to it that our patient's blood is tested for elevated levels of estrogen or progesterone, or anything similar that we can find. That's all."

As they filed from the room Hunter fell in beside the psychologist.

"It would seem," Bridges said in a low whisper, "that our dear Emma's husband has some serious explaining to do. But Devon has already had their quarters checked—the man's not there."

Husband!

Hunter nearly stopped in his tracks. Instead he faked a cough and asked, "Their quarters?"

"Married quarters here on the base. He's a military man, stationed here. All we could find out is that he's on assignment somewhere. It would seem he managed to get some leave time at home in the past few weeks. Damn him."

Not trusting himself to say anything more, Hunter followed the doctor down the hall until their paths separated. Then he closed the door of his room and stood leaning weakly against the wall.

She was married. Why hadn't he known that? Had he heard but forgotten? After all, he'd believed all along that the patient was the first lady—he hadn't given any thought to the daughter. Even so, shouldn't he have picked that up from his contact with her mind?

Was Tamiko right about Emma? Was she suffering from a hormonal imbalance so severe that his interaction with her subconscious mind was enough to give her orgasms? His own mind had apparently interpreted her reaction as something more meaningful—had imagined a relationship that wasn't there. Now he felt dirty, haunted again by the thought of violating a married woman.

Yet Kierkegaard was ordering him to go even further.

What choice was there? Her life was still in the balance. Surgery could remove the device on her ovary, but Bridges would be very reluctant to operate, given her condition. Was it the cause of her fever? In the time remaining to them, there might be only one way to learn the answer quickly enough.

Primus.

Damn it. He was no miracle worker. None of this was ever part of the deal. His feelings for her, least of all. Yet he could no more abandon her to her fate than he could deliberately harm her.

He'd just become a hoary cliché from romance literature—he could never have her, but he had to save her.

## 58

A body racked with pain. A soul filled with fear.

Both call out for attention. They are different, but they are one.

How can both desperate pleas be answered?

On one level, *Primus* plies the waters of the bloodstream, closing in on the new site; on the other, her tendrils of consciousness advance with trepidation, like cautious fingers gently seeking a hand to clasp, seeking salvation from the terrifying fate that beckons.

On the scale of *Primus*, the new device is gargantuan, the size of a city. Its smooth, dark surface has accessed dozens of small blood vessels, each fed by a narrow rimmed slot. Outlet vents—possibly hundreds of them—spew a clear fluid not visible on its own that gently ripples through seams of protoplasm like a current over kelp. A current of insidious purpose, masking itself as one of the body's own.

Yet the outpouring that is the device's weapon is also its weakness. It has created an open space of clear liquid between the surface and the surrounding tissue, just large enough for *Primus* to pass. To have traveled through each of the affected blood vessels individually—advancing, backtracking, seeking new routes—would have been the task of days. Instead, the monstrous manufactory has provided a path.

It is far too large for the *Primus* to destroy. Even if it were flammable, such a conflagration would do too much damage to the surrounding tissue . . . but what about the vents? Can they be closed, or blocked? The ridges running the length of the slots, top and bottom... are they rigid? Could they be squeezed together?

One way to find out.

Primus's manipulator arms respond nimbly and smoothly like extensions of one's own hand. The claws extend and spread just widely enough. Like the tips of finger and thumb, they press gently against the flat rims, then squeeze.

It works! The slot pinches together like stiff dough, sticking shut where the lips meet. The flow is blocked.

With a slight nudge sideways, it is the work of only a few moments to seal the other half of the slit. Then it is finished. One outlet is out of commission. Only one vent of hundreds, perhaps, but if a sufficient number can be closed, perhaps the symptoms will ease enough to permit surgery.

YOU'RE BACK.

Yes.

There is an image of a darkened room, walls striped from dimming light leaking through closing shutters. Then it is nearly black. Void. Empty, although not for long. Someone waits outside....

HE WILL FIND OUT. HE WILL KNOW. HE WILL RETURN!

No. He is not a threat to you anymore. He will be caught and punished.

NO. HE IS HERE.

The room pulses with hurt, like ripples of dark flame washing along its walls. It is the grip of the fever. Lancing shards of glassy pain pierce through like knife blades. A dark figure is in the doorway.

NO! PLEASE, NO!

Light. There must be light. Open the blinds—tear them down. He must not be allowed to hide in the dark.

Fingers grip, muscles contract, wood splinters.

[The claws of *Primus* contract—another vent is sealed.]

Curtains now, rod bending, snapping, fabric tearing.

[Another vent closed.]

Shutters. Twist their latches, fling them open.

[Another vent, and another.]

Light beams slice through the shadow, scattering and reflecting a complex geometry of luminance, cool where it touches. The pain recedes a little.

The dark figure is indistinct, braced against the rush of radiance as against a powerful wind, but weakening... retreating.

Tear down the walls! Batter out bricks. Smash the prison.

[*Primus* moves like an automaton, pinching, squeezing. The flow begins to falter. The current is weak now in many places. So weak that the tissue walls close in, but the craft slips through.]

Light. Cleansing, purifying light! The room is suddenly vast and bright. The dark presence has fled, to hide once more. Not defeated, but at least repulsed.

The pain is not gone—it is too great. But there is comfort. There is hope. There is healing.

THANK YOU.

I don't deserve thanks. I've violated you, too. I've invaded your being without permission. I had no right. Maybe I'm no better than he is.

NO! THAT'S NOT TRUE. YOU CAME TO HEAL.

YOU HAVE MY PERMISSION, WITH ALL MY HEART.

COME TO ME.

There is a meadow, the tawny grasses rippling in a warm breeze, hazy blue sky beyond. A gentle scent of wildflowers, and the occasional hot tang of cinnamon.

Someone is coming.

It is she, parting the grass with slow strides as she glides up the gentle slope, her hips swaying seductively.

Her hair catches bright glints of sun in its black curls. Golden rays fall on naked skin the color of mocha. [*HOW COULD I HIDE FROM YOU?*]

She circles, slowly, shyly revealing herself. Warm, dark eyes. Full lips. Full, round breasts, nipples brown and large. Her shape is the form of fertile womanhood, natural and vital.

She faces him as she circles. Then, slowly, she steps forward.

Her touch is like fire and ice at once. Skin sparks with the contact. Lips moist, radiate their fever heat.

The world dissolves into raw sensation. Two become one.

Time is exiled. Love remains.

There is the smell of...

    sun on skin.

          tang of sweat   *Sound of...*

  jasmine   *vanilla*   *shallow breath*

    mango   *pounding heart*

      wood smoke   *nails over skin*

        rustle of hair   *rustle of leaves*

Light of...   *salmon sunrise*   *soft trill of flute*

  burnt ebony   *aged ivory*   *gliss of bells*

    polished coal   *swelling rhythm*

fired clay   sea blue   Touch of...

latté   mocha   chocolate   warmth   softness

amber sunset   moist breath   firm muscle

flowing hair   pliant lips

Taste of...

Toffee   salt   peppermint

honey

Fire, panting, sweet, musk, glistening, slick, drumming, squeezing, coruscating   color,   driving   pressure,   brilliant,   hot, roar...reaching...reaching...

Oblivion.

Eons later, the world coalesces into meadow again. She lies stretched out on the grass, face down and relaxed, smooth skin glistening with a sheen of sweat. A long, lovely expanse of coffee and cream.

No. There is something else. Patches of another color. Red. Blotches of angry crimson either side of her spine, and another larger one closer to the center. Farther up her back, a darker shade beginning to spread.

Something is very wrong.

She's hurt. *Injured.* And she knew all along, but hid her back. Until after....

Oh no. What can we do? *What can we do?*

In the control center, Tamiko looked up at the sudden spike in the bio readings. She'd seen them like that once before.

"You've got to hand it to Hunter," she muttered with a twinge of jealousy. "He does know how to tickle a lady's fancy."

The sudden trill of multiple alarms snapped her head toward another pair of monitors.

"What is it?" Gage stepped quickly to her side.

"It's her blood and fluids analysis. Look. Blood in the urine... high protein level, too. Albumens, I'd bet. Bilirubin count starting to climb. This is not good."

"Kidney failure?"

"More than just that. Look here. I'd say that almost certainly means her liver is shutting down, too. We've got to get a full body scan on this woman *right now!*"

## 59

"Blood clots in her kidneys, liver and lungs. If there's any more damage, she'll die within days... maybe hours."

Bridges was visibly shaken as he delivered the news.

"What is the most serious injury? What do we attack first?" Kierkegaard asked.

"Right now, I would say her kidneys are the most immediate problem," the doctor answered. "But it's the combination of all of the injuries that will kill her. The treatment for some symptoms will worsen others. I have a terrible feeling that we haven't seen the last of the damage." He couldn't help looking at Hunter. "How could so many bombs hide from us?"

Tamiko responded instead. "A number of them must have been programmed to keep circulating in the bloodstream until commanded to embed themselves in an organ and detonate. Odds would be in the billions against Hunter encountering one by accident. I'll bet our scans have been showing us shadows of moving bombs, but we just didn't know what we were looking at." She turned to face Kierkegaard. "Someone knew of our progress, sir, and knew it was time to detonate these secondary bombs... maybe even knew our strategy from the beginning, and how to beat it with free-floating devices."

Kierkegaard merely nodded, his face a mask of stone. Then he gave a curt nod at Bridges, signaling the man to continue.

"The damage to the kidneys is significant, but manageable so far," the doctor said. "However, as more kidney cells fail, the pressure increases on the ones that remain. They're like tiny dams holding back a flood. Once a few more start to go, they can begin to topple like dominos—and very quickly you've got a catastrophic failure."

"What about dialysis?" asked Tyson.

"Of course, and the equipment is being put in place right now. We already had it on hand, just in case. Still, the combination of injuries is the problem. The best treatment for the blood clots in her lungs is an aggressive dosage of a clot-dissolving thrombolytic such as one called 't-PA', then a drip of heparin to thin the blood to improve the flow around the clot and help break it up. This also calls for high fluid intake by the patient. Unfortunately, dialysis doesn't remove much fluid, so we could easily end up with dangerous swelling of tissues. Maybe even around the heart and lungs, which are already under a strain."

"And her liver?" Mallory asked.

"The damage appears to be very localized there," Bridges replied. "The clot hasn't blocked a major artery, but a smaller vessel deeper inside the organ. Even so, the trouble will spread, and there isn't any quick remedy. We can only monitor her blood protein levels, and the concentrations of certain chemicals, while her body weakens. The liver dysfunction puts even more strain on the kidneys."

He looked at Kierkegaard. "In my opinion, other dangers are more immediate, but the liver damage is the most serious long-term threat to her life. The success of liver transplants is not encouraging. If we can't save her liver, we could still be sentencing her to a long, slow death."

"You're not narrowing this down for us," Kierkegaard observed. "What do you recommend?"

"I'm sorry." The doctor wiped a hand over his face. "It's like doing triage in an emergency room, except more injuries could still occur. It's not easy to prioritize." He cleared his throat and sat up straight. "First, I think we need to use plasmin to break up the clots in the kidneys and the liver."

"*Primus* only carries enough for one clot at a time," Hunter interrupted. "You'd have to remove the sub and re-load her. Twice."

"I know that," Bridges answered. "I suggest we send *Primus* to the liver. That clot is deep inside—we can't get at it any other way. The blockages affecting the kidneys are both in branch arteries just before the organs themselves. So they should be accessible by needle with the HPIS... the robot High Precision Injection System that we've used to position *Primus*."

"And the lung clots?" asked Kierkegaard. "No plasmin for them?"

"As a last resort, perhaps, but I think we'll have good success with the t-PA and heparin, as I mentioned. It will be a good preventative measure to have those chemicals in her system anyway, in case more bombs detonate. The damage hasn't affected her breathing yet, because the damaged areas are still fairly small and isolated.

"But there's another step I'd like to take...." He waited for a nod to continue. "It's risky in her weakened state, but I'd like to implant a

Greenfield filter. It's a sort of conical filter that's placed in the inferior vena cava—if a blood clot breaks loose and starts to travel through the bloodstream, the filter will trap it before it can get through the heart and into the pulmonary arteries. I've called in our backup surgeon, Anthony Vitale—he's an expert in this surgery, and also with thrombolytic treatment."

"Why didn't we use one of these filters in the first place?" Hunter's face clouded with anger. Had they missed a chance to protect her because of some careless oversight?

"Because the bombs themselves are too small for a Greenfield filter to catch. However, if we're really seeing evidence of drifting bombs, I think there's now a significant risk that a clot created elsewhere could travel to the lungs. A large blockage in the wrong artery and we could lose her within minutes."

The room fell silent. Their confidence was badly shaken. Hunter was devastated.

"What are we waiting for?" he blurted. Surprised faces turned to him.

"Mr. Hunter is right," Kierkegaard said. "We've seen our best options. Let's get to it, people." He swiftly left the room. His superiors would be waiting for his report, and they wouldn't be waiting patiently. He looked up at the clock on his way out.

11:25 pm. It was going to be a long night.

# # #

Mannis loved helicopters. He always had. In his military days he'd even begun pilot training on them before he'd been promoted and moved into the intelligence community.

Now, as he sped through the night in the belly of the huge MH-53J Pave Low he was too distracted to enjoy it, consumed by his thoughts. The thirty heavily-equipped soldiers with him left him alone. He was dressed in clothing similar to theirs, but they knew he wasn't one of them. They didn't know where he fit in, so they minded their own business.

That business was close at hand. He'd paid a heavy price to learn the location they were heading for: two suspected traitors released from life-sentences in prison. In return for their freedom, they had separately and independently revealed a secret training facility in this part of the North Carolina countryside, used by right-wing hardliners. Quick work by the FBI had narrowed the search down to an isolated farm. No one in the sheriff's office of the nearest town had seen or heard any unusual activity. In fact, they knew almost nothing about the property.

Mannis had recognized the signs from long experience.

Now he was aboard the Pave Low transport helicopter full of special ops troops, only minutes away from finding out if he'd been right. Slightly behind them and to the left flew a smaller MH-60G Pave Hawk, also fully manned. The giant rotorcraft and their specialized passengers were testimony to the seriousness of the threat. If the mercenary squad he was looking for was here, they would be heavily armed and exceptionally skilled—and he had no idea of their numbers.

He'd already briefed the pilots. There was to be no fly-by to assess the environment. They couldn't risk alerting their targets, so they would have to go straight in.

They were flying only a few hundred feet above the trees. He felt the sudden drop of the aircraft as it began its dive. Within moments, its descent flattened out, and seconds later came a springy jolt as wheels touched the ground. The rear door was already opening, and the men began to spill out in well-drilled order, without words.

As the last soldier hit the dirt, the helicopters lifted off again since no one knew what kind of weapons the enemy might have and there was no sense in risking forty million dollars worth of aircraft close to the ground. They'd been needed for infiltration and delivery, but now all they could do was to stay out of harm's way and listen to the fight.

Mannis chafed at the need to remain in the Pave Low. He was a man of action, but he knew that he was too old for these games. Instead, he took advantage of his official status and leaned over one of the flight engineers to see out the windows.

The night was overcast and very dark. The most he could see was occasional quick sparks of light from flashbangs—flash grenades that made tremendous noise and a blinding light, but did little damage. The troops would be using them to temporarily incapacitate anyone inside a structure before they risked entering it. Short bursts of words over the radio sounded routine and unhelpful. There was no gunfire that he could see.

It was all over within six minutes.

The farm was empty. Abandoned.

Dammit! Were they already gone? Or had they never been there? He had to know.

He ordered the pilots to land, and in another five minutes he had his answer. At his instruction, the special ops boys had brought metal detectors. They found shell casings—a lot of them—scattered in the grass. Large caliber, probably from automatic assault weapons.

Quick inspection showed they'd been fired recently. Someone had been there—now they were gone.

But where?

One of his other inquiries had implicated a private property in a Poquoson subdivision just to the north of Langley AFB. The information was graded only medium reliability, but a ground assault on the *Primus* project might require a staging area close by.

He transferred to the Pave Hawk and ordered its troops back aboard. The others would stay behind to try to find more clues. If the bad guys were now in a residential subdivision, he couldn't go in with planeloads of heavily armed commandos. A different approach would be needed. He'd have to think that through.

As four giant blades dug hard into the night air and heaved the helicopter from the ground, Mannis used the radio to update the commander of the project's security contingent who, in turn, would notify the base commander.

He hoped to hell that the enemy hadn't jumped the gun and already put their assault plan into play. If so, he'd be better off going straight to the base.

But the deadline was still a day-and-a-half away. If they wanted the president to drop his plans for the G20 summit without raising suspicions they wouldn't risk everything in a headline-grabbing bloodbath. Would they?

No, he decided. He would go to Poquoson first.

## 60

Kellogg's goggles were held firmly in place by his headgear, but the slight pitching of the rubber dinghy made it difficult to find the two tiny pinpoints of light he was looking for. If he hadn't imagined the lights, it meant that the north-facing shoreline of the small inlet was protected by passive detection systems. Maybe if he tried thermal imaging. He flicked a dial.

There they were. Four... possibly as many as six.

His high-level information had said that the mouth of the creek was unguarded, but that was wrong. It looked like there was a series of infrared sensors just above the waterline. He had been correct not to depend on the intelligence, and risk going ashore by boat since they would have been spotted hundreds of yards out. Instead, they had a long swim ahead of them. Hennings would have to be dead accurate with his underwater navigation, but they stood an excellent chance of passing undetected up the inlet, under the bridge, right to the verge of the Eaglewood golf course that bordered Langley Air Force Base to the north. That would place them just northwest of their target, with marshland and undergrowth to give them cover.

He'd never seen the base from this direction before, but he could pick out certain features of its shadowy silhouette and fill in the gaps from imagination and memory. The runways were well south of where they were going. The wind was moderate from east-northeast, so the control tower would be directing even small traffic onto the long runway from the west.

"This is as far as we go," he said in a low voice to Chavez, who passed word along. He thought he heard a small groan from the stern. Probably Rakov, realizing how far they would have to swim. He was their weakest swimmer—maybe there weren't a lot of good beaches in Chechnya—but he was their night insertion specialist. If anyone could keep them unseen, it would be Rakov. "Can't go any closer," Kellogg explained. "There are infrareds on the shore." Chavez nodded silently. He, too, had expected as much.

They were already suited up, with weapons in weighted waterproof cases beside them. Two took turns gently rowing against the wind to keep the dinghy on station, while the others made final checks of their gear. When all were ready, they slipped over the side. The small sounds of tethered equipment knocking against rubberized re-breather tanks did not carry over the light slap of the low waves.

Branson, Evers, and Jackson slit open the cells of the rubber raft with dive knives, ensuring that the weights they'd left behind would carry it to the bottom. Evers and Wahlberg both carried lightweight inflatable rafts in their backpacks for the team's return after the attack.

Hennings and Romero gave the high sign. They had their compass headings.

After slowly pivoting in the water to ensure they were all together and ready, Kellogg took one more look at the well-lit military base in the distance, then held his fist out, thumb pointing downward, and slipped beneath the dark surface of the Back River.

# # #

Emma's liver was only centimeters away from *Primus'* position near her ovary, but it required a journey through most of her body to get there. Truman Bridges and Anthony Vitale would wait until the sub was in position at the target before attempting to implant the Greenfield filter in the inferior vena cava. The filter would be inserted at the end of a long wire through an incision in her neck, fed slowly through the venous system, then opened and wedged into place. No one knew if the process would pose a hazard to their billion-dollar submarine, but it was better not to take the chance.

To Hunter the trip seem endless. Too much time to think.

He had made love to a married woman in her mind. Did that make him an adulterer? In a hideously vulnerable mental state, had she merely grasped at the nearest lifeline out of desperation? If so, he had violated her innocent trust no less than the man who had violated her in the flesh.

I WANTED YOU. I STILL WANT YOU.

The sudden thought, blazing across his mind, startled him so badly that his body jerked in the chair.

No. I will close my mind. The job comes first.

A huge dark mass loomed ahead. *Primus* had arrived at the clot.

It was bigger by a third than the one he had encountered in her finger so very long before, but this one was fresh, only hours old—not so tightly bound together. He felt his confidence rise. He could do this. With the right spread, *Primus'* cargo of plasmin would be enough.

As he worked, he had the uncanny feeling of someone watching over his shoulder.

#   #   #

Kellogg floated motionless in the water, about ten feet below the surface. It was tempting to go all the way up and take a look around, but it wasn't necessary, and would only increase the risk of detection. Hennings and Romero had to break surface to check their bearings. The presence of underwater electrical cables, even a nearby metal shipwreck buried under the silt could be enough to affect a compass and throw them off course. The two navigators knew what they were doing. They had no wish to find a welcoming party waiting for them onshore.

Kellogg could see flashes of light that winked every few seconds, spread in a rough circle through the dark water around him. They were a necessary evil, too: small strobe lights attached to the first stages of the breathing apparatus, behind the diver's neck. It was the only way to be sure no one would accidentally lose the others in this inky water. The lights were only activated while submerged. The odds were hundreds to one against anyone above the surface seeing them, let alone knowing them for what they were.

A slight pressure in his ears told Kellogg he had sunk a foot or two. His index finger squeezed the trigger on his inflator hose, bleeding a little air into his buoyancy control vest. Long experience told him precisely how much was enough to stop his slow descent without making him positively buoyant. He hoped the others were being equally attentive to their depth. In the dark, it was much harder to tell if you were rising, unless you watched your depth gauge. Once begun, the ascent would accelerate with the dwindling pressure until you popped above the surface like a cork. Disastrous in their present situation. They were easily within range of the infrared detectors, and the motion sensors that almost certainly accompanied them.

He held the lens of his flashlight over the face of his dive computer and gave it a quick flicker of light. The resulting glow lasted long enough for him to check the time. Not quite on schedule, but not far behind. He would have preferred a buffer, in case any unexpected obstacles delayed them, but a minute or two wasn't critical. He was still completely confident. He had more than surprise on his side. Much more.

And when the crucial moment came, could he still do what he had to do?

Yes he could. Very definitely. He almost smiled at the thought.

A disturbance in the water caught his attention. Hennings and Romero were on their way back down. When they had reached him and pointed the way, he shined his flashlight on himself, drew a circle in the water with his forearm, then held it out in their direction of travel, letting himself tip into a horizontal position as he did.

With regular kicks of their fins, the predators continued into the gloom.

## 61

There were tears in Hunter's eyes as he saw the clot begin to break apart. The matted clump broke into small knots of cells that quickly dispersed in the growing current, and relief swept through him like a wave. He could only pray that the rest of his team had been as successful.

Now what? Leave *Primus* in the liver until needed? No, better to be circulating in the open bloodstream. That might save precious time if he had to reach another target in a hurry. He steered into the current, chasing the flotsam from his recent victory. Just as he reached the main channel of the central hepatic vein he sensed the pulsing red light of the alert indicator in *Primus*. The ship would be safe for a while. He disconnected.

"What is it?" he gasped, as he pulled the headgear off.

Tamiko pointed to her monitors. "From these readings it looks as if more bombs have detonated." She stabbed the screen and he looked over her shoulder. "Her lungs... at least one there. A kidney. I'd say her spleen, too. Of course the damage is well established before we see the difference in her blood chemistry, so there could be many more." Her face was pale, and Hunter could see fear in her eyes for the first time.

"What do we do?" he asked. "*Primus* is out of plasmin. Without a reload it's only useful against one of the bombs themselves. The torch is no match for something the size of a blood clot."

"Could *Primus* do any good by ramming a clot?"

Hunter shook his head. "It'd be like a fly hitting an elephant, and the elasticity of the cellular material would probably absorb most of the force."

"You'd better get back to *Primus*," Gage said as he walked into the room. "Find some backwater to hole up in. Bridges and Vitale haven't inserted the Greenfield filter yet. They're just about to go in now."

"*What!* What took them so long?"

"They haven't been dawdling, I promise you. It takes time to prep a patient for that kind of procedure. You've had time dilation on your side."

"But...." Suddenly pain stabbed through Hunter's head, leaving a haze of surprise in its wake. It was like the impression of a sound, echoing through his mind. A cry...

A cry for help.

He collapsed into the chair and flung his head forward onto his knees, wrapping his arms around it to block out distractions.

It was a terrified mental scream from Emma. Because of the surgery? The pain of the emplacement? No, that made no sense. The doctors would have used anesthetic. How was she communicating at all?

COME TO ME. COME TO ME QUICKLY!

His mind filled with an image: a dark, amorphous shape... massive, relentless. It rippled slowly as it passed through a dark fluid.

Oh God. A blood clot—a huge one, traveling through a major vein.

Traveling toward the heart.

They would never get the filter placed in time.

He snapped his head up. "The heart. They've got to *stop her heart!*"

"Are you insane?" Tamiko stared in shock. "Do you want to kill her? She's already shot full of anti-clotting chemicals and surgical anesthetic, and her body is critically weakened. Half of her vital systems are beginning to pack it in..."

"What are you talking about, Mr. Hunter?" Kierkegaard had just entered the room, his face full of thunder. "Why in God's name should they stop her heart? Quickly, man."

Hunter felt a flood of relief that the one who could make the life or death decision stood before him.

"It's a blood clot, sir. A huge one, headed for her heart. There's no way Bridges and Vitale can get the filter in place in time. This is the only way. Stop her heart. Stop the flow of blood so *Primus* can catch up to the clot before it gets through and into her lungs."

"And what then? What can the *Primus* do without a load of plasmin?"

"I... I can't be sure, but there must be something. We've got to try. I'm certain this is a major clot—a *killer* clot, if it gets to her lungs."

"How can you know...," Gage tried to interrupt.

"*Do it!*" Kierkegaard barked. "Don't argue, just do it." He stepped to the main console and his fingers flew over the keyboard, entering the code that would make the previously forbidden video connection directly to the clinic. Instantly they could see the operating bed and the gowned and masked medical team hovering over the patient. Her face was obscured by the breathing mask.

The project leader turned his head. "Don't just stand there, Hunter. Get back to *Primus*! And you'd better be right." He knew that his next order could cause the death of the daughter of the president of the United States. If he didn't act, his failure to do so could be equally fatal.

"Bridges, Vitale...," he snapped. "Forget the Greenfield filter." He took a deep breath.

"*Stop her heart.*"

## 62

Kellogg gratefully pulled the dry-suit hood from his head and laid it on a patch of matted reeds. He piled the whole suit together in careful order, ready for his return. A screen of reeds hid them from the actual shore a few feet away. His team would rely on GPS and a very weak radio beacon to find the spot again in a few hours.

The dive gear was covered in mud and bits of weed from the last ten minutes of half-floating half-crawling through shallow water to get into the protective reed bed close to shore. This tiny baylet didn't appear to be guarded in any way. Clearly, the sensing equipment closer to the mouth of the creek was considered to be adequate.

His regulation fatigues were wrinkled from the scuba suit, but it was unlikely that anyone would notice that in time. He replaced his night vision headgear and looked around. Each member of the team was carefully checking over his own gear, ensuring that none of the waterproof coverings had leaked. He barely heard a sound. These men were good at their work—the best. He felt his confidence rise again.

With a softly whistled note he caught the attention of Rakov and Jackson. They quickly took helmets from the bag that Wahlberg had towed, and stealthily began to step through the reeds, ten feet apart. Two more soft whistles signaled 'all clear', and the team began to move out.

# # #

Hunter had three minutes.

The medical team hadn't been able to cool her body temperature or slow her metabolism in any other way—there hadn't been time. Longer than three minutes and Emma's brain cells would begin to die.

How could that possibly be enough?

He felt a wash of turbulence lift *Primus* and spin her off kilter, as the huge river that was the bloodstream slowly came to a stop. The pressure wave rippled forward, and bounced back and forth off the walls. He could see it by the way it tossed and shook blood cells around him.

Now it would be harder going. The submersible was already at full throttle, and it was the only thing moving. Instead of gradually overtaking obstacles, he now had to dodge them like a skier daring a heavily treed slope. The blood cells themselves were giants—detouring around them stole precious time, and they often hid others.

Even as he focused on the controls, a part of his brain was still in disbelief.

Emma had reached him with her mind, and her mind alone. Somehow she had known her danger, and her panicked need had provided the impetus to break through to him. The implications were staggering.

However that link worked, he needed it now. He needed it badly.

No sooner had he framed that thought, than an image of the clot appeared in his mind. Dark and menacing, it floated within some large space. There was a suggestion of a vast latticed structure in the background, but he couldn't quite make it out. At least the killer was held motionless. Part of him had endowed the monstrosity with a will of its own, and a means to propel itself. It had no such powers, but where was it? *Primus* had traversed most of the inferior vena cava. Could he have missed it? Passed it by without realizing?

No. This clot made even mammoth white blood cells look tiny. They were only the building blocks of its bloated body. Kierkegaard was right. What could he possibly hope to do against such a giant?

He had to come up with a plan soon. He must be nearing the heart.

Suddenly he remembered the latticed structure that he had only ever seen in flashes before, as *Primus* was tossed through the maelstrom. It was the inner webbing of the heart itself. The bomb was already there.

The chambers of the heart were enormous. How could he hope to find anything in such a vast space? Radar wouldn't be able to distinguish the clot from the surrounding tissues.

How much time was left? What did three minutes of *outside* time become when stretched across the *nano*-world? *Damn!* He had to find out.

He tore off the VR headgear. *"Time."* he snapped at the startled faces of Tamiko and Kierkegaard.

"Two minutes, seventeen seconds remaining," she called out, and he had the helmet back on before the last words were out of her mouth.

Space around the submersible had already increased tenfold. He must be in the right atrium of the heart, the first of the gigantic pump's four chambers. On every previous venture there, he'd had no choice but to go with the pull of the current. Now, for the first time, he had to decide for himself where to look for the entrance to the next chamber: the right ventricle. On the *Primus'* scale a wrong guess would send him blundering across the equivalent of one of the Great Lakes.

He forced himself to relax and tune into his senses. Then he spun the ship to starboard, pointed the bow downward, and prayed.

With no points of reference, the journey was an endless time suspended in watery limbo and unfeeling darkness. His body shivered with the memory of another such wasteland. Then, suddenly, shapes materialized from the gloom and he gave an involuntary cry. He eased back on the throttle, his surprise turning to despair.

The way was blocked.

His navigation had been on the money, the *tricuspid valve* was exactly where he'd hoped it would be. But the heart had been stopped at just the wrong moment and the mammoth gate was closed.

## 63

Hunter felt a howl of rage well up in his chest, but he had no time to waste on it. The tricuspid valve of the heart was closed. Was there another way? A back way? It would require penetrating the cells of the cardiac lining and finding a path through the tiny vessels that supplied the heart tissues with blood. Maybe with Tamiko's help and an hour or two on the *nano* scale....

Hang on.

Scale. Maybe it was only a question of scale!

He rammed the throttle forward and raced toward the giant valve. Sure enough, it was much farther away and much bigger than his mind had been willing to accept. He aimed the ship at the exact center, where the massive folds of tissue pressed against each other. The valve flaps themselves were huge. They could never seal tightly enough to keep out something as small as *Primus*.

As the bases of the three vast cusps faded into the distance on either side, he saw what he needed: a roughly triangular crack where the flaps failed to meet perfectly. It would be enough. Seconds later, he broke through into the enormous chamber that was the right ventricle.

He'd desperately hoped the blood clot would be waiting for him on the other side, but it wasn't. There was nothing but a vast cosmos of blood cells, floating like planets in a night sky against a background of chordae anchoring the valve cusps, and dimly-seen papillary muscles farther beyond.

Where to now?

The ventricle was perhaps twice as large as the atrium, like a colossal vase with two branching openings at the top. The far opening was capped by a half-moon shaped valve leading to the pulmonary arteries and ultimately the lungs. In relative terms, that exit wasn't too far away; but if the clot lurked somewhere in the main chamber of the ventricle, he would run out of time long before he could search it all. In desperation he sent a pulse of the radar; but, as he feared, the return was inconclusive. The clot's tissues didn't provide solid reflection.

In desperation he focused his mind.

Emma... you'll have to guide me. I don't know the way. Guide me!

Her heart was stopped. Even before that she might have been in deep anaesthetized sleep. Could any part of her mind be left to respond?

A sense of calm swept over him, and his scattered thoughts congealed. He became *Primus*—accepted its powerful machinery as his own body, its strange and wonderful devices as his own hands and fingers. The hybrid creation knew the way to go. The sub sprang forward in a deep curve, a concave course that would take it to the pulmonic valve. There lay its destiny, its ultimate battle.

Now all he needed was a miracle.

It was a David and Goliath scenario of daunting proportion. *Primus*, out of ammunition, versus an opponent larger than itself by orders of magnitude. Some of the world's finest minds were at his disposal, only an arm's reach away, but he couldn't consult them. He would lose the sole advantage he had left: the time dilation effect of this *nano*-world, that stretched a scant three minutes into the slimmest chance for victory.

He couldn't ram through the immense bulk of the clot. He had no plasmin left to attack the bonds that held the mountain of debris together. Was there something else that could produce a similar effect? He desperately tried to remember his high school chemistry.

Heat?

No, the torch could never produce enough to affect such a huge mass, and most of its energy would dissipate through the surrounding fluid.

The cells and other material that made up the monstrous thrombus were held together by powerful chemical attractions at the molecular scale, ions created from displaced electrons....

He gasped at a sudden idea.

Would it work?

He returned his mind to the control of the ship, and looked ahead.

There it was. An indistinct dark mass of latent death.

He slid the sensor array behind *Primus*' fuselage as the mottled behemoth drew closer with agonizing slowness. Then he could distinguish individual blood cells and other detritus of the bloodstream that had been gathered along the way.

Even if his plan was to work, its range of effect was a complete unknown. The clot dwarfed him, and nowhere could he see any sign of vulnerability. He had no choice but to aim for the densest part. Dead center.

In the last few moments the monster seemed to charge to meet him. Then he was into it—plowing among the clumped cells with all of *Primus'* power. The drive lasted only seconds before the ship came to a lurching halt, lodged deep within a mass the size of Coney Island. *Primus* could never escape the way it had come. The plan had to work.

He thumbed the stud that extended the torch tip on the right manipulator arm, and bent the arm at its elbow.

The trick had worked once before. When *Primus* had been swarmed by defender cells just before discovering the bomb launcher, an electrical charge through the hull had disrupted the cells' grip, long enough for the craft to get away. This time, a single electrical discharge would not be enough. He had to disrupt the very molecular bonds that held the giant mass together, ionic bonds formed of atoms whose natural shell of electrons had been destabilized. So, he would send out waves of free electrons, depleting *Primus'* entire power supply in one sudden burst.

He triggered the spark.

A blinding flare of blue light rippled through the surrounding cell matter. He switched the ship to *recharge*. The electrical system had been built with a governor to ensure that what passed for a capacitor in the nanotube could handle the inflow of current. Hunter bent his every thought to that circuit—he was *Primus* and *Primus* was him. The governor circuit was a part of him and he could feel it, he could control it, he could disable it.

A violet wave like heat washed over him, and the submersible hummed with energy.

Switch again. *Discharge.* And again. *Recharge.*

Discharge. Recharge.

Five times. Ten times. He could sense the capacitor beginning to warp under the strain.

Discharge. Recharge.

Within a quickly spreading radius electrons were being ripped from their orbits, then sprayed haphazardly to strike and deflect and rebound in extravagant disarray. Molecules were forcibly transformed into ions that suddenly repelled their neighbors.

Twenty times. Thirty times. *Primus* could not take much more.

And then suddenly he could see it happen. *He could see it!*

Tangled blobs of protoplasm raggedly lit by an aurora of rippling colors began to tear away, chemical bonds ravaged beyond repair.

Primus came free, and Hunter reacted swiftly, putting the submarine into a flat spin, pushing the fluid into waves to force the rabble of broken blood cells farther and farther apart. The ship spun with the fury of a fiery pinwheel, hurling its energy at the scattering mob. Gaps grew larger—he could see the clot dissolving into a loose cloud of colossal debris—and he knew that he had won.

He snapped out of the spin, exulting in the might of his tiny craft.

The disruptive electrical field still clung to it, batting obstacles aside. He made a quick run up and down the debris field, just to make sure the clot wouldn't re-form.

It was as he returned to the upper end of the shattered thrombus that the final large clump of cells broke apart. What they revealed tore the breath from his lungs.

Floating in the dark fluid... round, dully-sheened, menacing....

A bomb. The largest one of all.

## 64

The project compound wasn't surrounded by a large zone of clear ground. That would have been much better for security reasons, but would also have given away the high-security nature of the building to everyone else on the base. As a compromise, a few small stands of scrubby trees had been left, creating a narrow zone of ingress where the line of sight from other guard stations was partially obstructed. Kellogg's team planned to exploit that weakness.

The first perimeter guard was standing in the shadow of two low trees. That alone indicated that the security detail was on higher alert, possibly expecting trouble. The guard was also equipped with night vision equipment and Kevlar protection, but that had been anticipated. The mercenary squad's own dynamic armor would pass for Kevlar at a glance.

It took long seconds for Evers to get into position. He needed a clear shot with his suppressed Heckler and Koch, but he wanted to make sure there was no chance of another guard position spotting any trace of muzzle flash. Once he had the shot, he took it. The sound of the guard's outstretched body hitting the ground made more noise than the gun. Branson ran to the spot and pulled the corpse back in under the shrubbery, then quickly stood up in the guard's place. Anyone who looked would think they saw the usual guard doing his job. Branson would stay there throughout the mission, ready to give covering fire or create a distraction if either was needed during egress.

Other guards were positioned like spokes in a wheel and could not be taken out the same way. Each was too visible to others; the chance was too great that one of them would see his comrade fall and raise an alarm.

After another few moments of observation, Kellogg and Chavez moved toward the distant building and into the blind zone. Chavez stopped within a shadow and huddled low, while Kellogg stepped out into an area of brighter light and approached a guard. To the soldier, it would appear that his nearest compatriot was coming to talk to him. Unorthodox, but not immediately threatening. Especially once Kellogg used a tiny penlight to send two quick flashes, then a longer one, and another short flash—Morse code for the letter 'F', meaning friendly. Unexpectedly, the other flashed back a 'query'. Was there more to the protocol? That would pose a problem.

Kellogg stuck to the information he'd been given. He continued his approach and repeated his letter 'F', then added the code 'XP'. For that day, it should indicate someone of command rank. The soldier would be wondering why a superior would be approaching from the outer guard position, but he would not fire right away.

So Kellogg did.

His silenced .45 caliber Mark 23 was loaded with armor-piercing bullets. They penetrated the Kevlar easily from the twenty-foot distance, and the man was likely dead as he hit the ground, but the mercenary leader took no chances and swiftly drew his knife across the soldier's neck.

He looked toward the building—there was no reaction from the guard nearest the wall. The man could barely be seen past a chest-high bush, and the view from that direction would be just as bad.

Kellogg waited for Chavez to reach him, then stepped forward again to repeat his performance with another unsuspecting victim. According to plan, Kowalski and Jackson would soon meet up with Chavez, then go left and right, circling to approach the next mid-field guards using the same ruse as their leader. By the time those two did their killing, Kellogg and Chavez would be placed to eliminate the next two inner guards before they could act. The rest of the team would move up quickly after that.

They needed to. A well-lit entranceway remained their biggest obstacle. The staggered shift changes of the guards would not include those already eliminated—they weren't due to be relieved for another two hours at the earliest. But the replacements for the door guards would be on their way within moments. Wahlberg and Romero had to be in place to make sure that those soldiers never reached their assigned post.

So far no routine checkup calls had come for any of the guards. That was good. The team had been issued the radio codes for the day, but it was better not to have to use them. The voice of a stranger, instead of the expected barracks-mate could raise the alarm even more quickly than a botched code.

Kellogg permitted himself a slight smile. Adrenaline always made him feel good, and he couldn't help but anticipate the moment that he would come face to face with his prey.

## 65

The bomb floated in front of him. Menacingly silent.

Hunter pushed the throttle forward and brought the ship to ramming speed. This one was far bigger, so its casing could be much stronger. No matter—he knew *Primus* would be up to the challenge. She felt indestructible to him now, even as he sensed the last remnants of her shredded lipid shield being torn away by her passage through the fluid. There was no point worrying about running afoul of the body's defenses. The heart was stopped, the great current of life stilled. *Primus* charged forward.

Then, at the last moment, he veered off. Something was wrong. This bomb didn't look like the others—its shell seemed strange. Both color and reflectivity were off. Could its casing be a different material? Why?

All too conscious of the ticking clock, he backed off far enough to send a radar pulse. He was right. The returning signature was not the same as that of other bombs.

His mind raced. What could it mean? Why would there be one bomb made of different stuff? The mysterious HIV bomb they'd assumed was a ruse? He looked back at it, straining to spot any possible clue to its purpose. Was there a significance to the fact that he'd found it within the heart itself, placed very close to the pulmonic valve?

There was no time left. He should ram it and get the job done, but he couldn't bring himself to do it. Something was not right. He had to get help.

Wrenching his mind away from the inner world brought a brutal flood of nausea as he tore the helmet from his head a second time.

"There's a bomb in the heart!" he gasped. "A different kind. If you were intending to do direct damage to the heart in a big hurry, what would you use?"

Tamiko and Gage were startled, but quickly grasped his need.

"I... I can't think of anything," the circulatory specialist spoke frantically. "But you've only got thirty seconds left!"

Gage's forehead furrowed in concentration. Then his head snapped up. "A highly reactive metal—pure potassium or sodium. Burns instantly on contact with water. *Very* hot."

"So if I'd cracked open the casing ...." Hunter's legs felt suddenly weak.

"*Twenty-five* seconds!"

The pilot raised the headgear and shouted, "Tell Bridges... use the HPIS—plunge a hypodermic into the heart as close as he can get to the top of the right ventricle, and suck out as much fluid as he can. I'll try to get the bomb to it. Hurry!"

As the helmet slipped over his head he caught faint traces of Kierkegaard's voice speaking to the clinic, and Tamiko saying, "Twenty seconds...."

He was sure Gage was right. The sodium bomb hung there, mocking him with his nearly disastrous mistake. How could he possibly move such a thing? *Primus'* engines, for all their power, would be too slow, the fan blades too small.

Sodium was a metal? Could he pull it with an electric field? But what if the casing was non-conductive? He had no time to experiment.

It was taking forever for Bridges to insert the needle. Hunter had to wait for the intake of fluid to begin, before he could know which way to move the bomb. Wait for the whirlpool....

An image leapt into his mind. *Could he create a whirlpool himself?*

As if on cue, he felt the jolt of a mammoth shock wave. He scanned the gloom desperately for the needle tip. It would have taken Bridges at least the remaining twenty seconds to get the thing into place. They were on borrowed time now. Brain cells would soon begin to die.

There it was—enormous, but heartbreakingly far away. So much for his slim hope that the suction would reach them on its own.

Frantically he moved the ship in front of the bomb and pivoted the drive fans. Giving them full thrust, the sub began to spin, faster and faster. He adjusted their angle of attack, and could feel cavitation begin to build. A whirlpool was what he needed. A maelstrom to draw the deadly device to its doom. He swiveled the fans a fraction more, and as the funnel deepened, the ship began to move.

With fierce concentration, he split his mind into two—one part needed to control *Primus;* the other needed to be able to see without being at the mercy of its violent spin. He stared at the bomb, desperately willing it to move. He looked the other way. The titanic needle had begun to draw. How long would it take to fill? He had to reach it before then.

Was the bomb following? *Yes!* He could see details of the heart valve beyond, disappearing slowly behind the edges of the grey globe. He poured the force of his mind into the straining *nano* engines, goading them to produce extra thrust...110%... 115%.... How far could he push them? The engines themselves might be nearly indestructible, but if the damaged power cell gave out....

Suddenly he felt the change—the engines began to race, their load lightened, captured by the pull of the needle! He backed off the thrust just enough to stop the overload and hung on for the ride.

The ship jolted, as if reluctant. Another sudden lurch... and then a powerful surge as the submersible was yanked sideways and catapulted to incredible speed within fractions of a second, faster than the mighty bloodstream itself.

Somehow, Hunter knew when they passed out of the body.

They had won! Bridges and Vitale would restart her heart. Emma was young and strong; she would recover. He was sure of it.

Shaking with relief, he killed the thrusters and leaned back into the couch.

He had come so close to losing her, had nearly killed her himself by unwittingly triggering the fearsome new weapon. Had that been part of the design? Had the enemy known that their bombs were being destroyed and planted an even deadlier one designed to be set off by Hunter's own actions? Or was it equipped with a remote detonator, to be activated by someone nearby, as a cruel final blow in the event of impending defeat?

Through a fog of fatigue he heard a ripping chord of thunder, rumbling metallically for long seconds. It was followed by another, just as long and frightening. Like distant cannon fire, but stretched and distorted. *What could it be?* Was he hearing it through *Primus*? Or with his own ears in the lab? Could it be the bomb?

He looked at the monstrous orb, startlingly close in the murky liquid, just in time to watch a mammoth crack open in its side.

There was a blinding flash that consumed the world.

## 66

The Pave Hawk helicopter dipped low over the subdivision. Mannis trusted its pilot to stay well clear of the taller structures, especially a nearby cell tower with its winking red beacons. The pattern of streetlamps below reminded him of a crossword puzzle.

"We're coming up on the target now, sir," the flight engineer said. They would make a slow pass, aiming the nose camera at the suspect house. He was willing to risk the noise this time—residents of a neighborhood so close to Langley base had to be used to the sound of aircraft coming and going, even in the middle of the night. He shifted forward to get a better view of the pilots' displays.

The co-pilot was adjusting the intensity controls. "We've got decent thermal imaging, sir," he reported. "It's a good night for it. Heat sources will show red and yellow. That's the house at the top of the screen right now, sir."

Only a trained eye would have been able to extrapolate the shape and design of the house from what they were seeing, but he knew it to be an average-looking two-story home with a small yard and a single garage. They had the layout on file, in case the nine troops with him needed to go in. There was a better-than-average chance that this was a safe house used by right-wing militia groups, and possibly others, but there was no guarantee that it included the people he was looking for. The latest reports from the North Carolina farm made him certain he'd been close, yet it was possible his quarry had caught wind of his pursuit, and gone to ground somewhere else.

"No human presence there, sir," the co-pilot said referring to the heat-imaging sensor. "It's been long enough since sundown—people would stand out."

"Is there any way they could be concealed in a better-shielded part of the house? The basement, maybe?"

"Negative, sir. This here...." He pointed at a small red-orange ball. "That would be the water heater in the basement. There are some high-tech materials that might be able to hide them, but they'd have to know we were coming, and what we're using."

They were past the house now. The pilot began to circle around to line up for another pass, per previous orders.

"What was that other heat source we saw?"

The co-pilot brought a still picture of the structure up on the screen. There was a small yellow smudge near an outside wall.

"Based on experience," the soldier replied, "That would be the oven. It's in about the right place for a kitchen. It could easily be putting out that much heat if someone cooked a meal in it a few hours ago."

Cooked a meal.... Well, if you didn't want anyone to see what you looked like, you wouldn't be ordering in pizza. Had they left the place according to a schedule? Or had they been tipped off that the Pave Hawk was on its way?

And where were they now?

"We're lined up for another pass, sir," the pilot told him. "You want it at the same speed?"

"Thank you Lieutenant. No. How about giving me a pass over the whole row of houses instead? The same side of the street."

"Yes, sir." The rotorcraft swung well over for a few moments, straightened, then heeled over again. "Coming up, sir. We're about five houses away right now."

If the squad he was looking for had been alerted, there was just a chance they might choose to hide by breaking into one of the neighboring houses, occupied or not. So if there was a grouping of more than a dozen people, especially if most of them were clustered in one room....

He hoped that nobody on the street had picked this night for a party.

They passed over the suspected safe house and a further six houses, then he called off the run. He'd also been watching a monitor view of the street below, but there were no suspicious utility vehicles or unmarked vans. There was a pattern of two cars per driveway. There were none at the safe house.

If his targets had been there at all, he had no way to know where they'd gone. The base was nearby—the house could have been a staging area—but for what kind of operation? There was no way to tell unless they landed and conducted a thorough search, hoping to turn up some kind of clue.

As if reading his mind, the pilot asked, "Do you want to land, sir?"

"No, Lieutenant. For now, maybe you should just make arrangements to refuel. I'll let you know if my plans change." He felt like slamming a fist into the seat frame, but he didn't want to show his frustration to the commandos watching. Was he on the right track at all? Even in the right ballpark? He'd rarely felt his confidence so low.

If an op was underway, there was no time to lose. But if he raised the alarm at the base... at the least he would blow the project's cover. It might even bring about the very thing he was trying to prevent: pre-emptive action by the terrorists. He could end up causing Emma's death.

Or maybe there was a compromise that would work.

"Lieutenant," he ordered. "Get the clearance you need and swing over the northeast end of Langley Air Force Base. Then pass me a radio mic, please. I need to make a call."

# # #

The blackness was puzzling. Was it night? Had he somehow gone blind? Hunter could feel the wetness of tears in his eyes, but he could see nothing from them. Yet he could hear a sound like radio static.

The headgear. He still had the helmet on.

As he yanked the equipment off, the bright overhead lights stabbed his eyes and made them tear up again. That had never happened before. There'd always been light in the visor—now it had gone dark. What was wrong? His head felt strange, too—numbed, boxed in.

The room was empty, but lights still flashed on control panels. Computer screens still showed their displays. Where had everyone gone? Why would they leave him alone?

Suddenly he knew what else was missing:

He couldn't feel *Primus*.

For the first time in days there was no sensation of it in his mind. It had become part of his mental landscape. Now it was gone. Did that mean the ship itself was gone? Destroyed? He couldn't believe it.

Then he remembered the blinding flash. The sodium bomb. It must have detonated in the hypodermic, with the submersible right next to it. Much too close. A searing fireball of white heat—a cataclysmic blast on that scale.

So that was it then.

Primus was gone. Inconceivably small, yet to him she had become a mighty weapon. And companion. But there *had* been a means to destroy her after all.

Worse, she had also been his link to someone else....

Emma.

The warm, sweet radiance that had been her presence within his mind was gone now, too. There was only cold emptiness when he reached for her.

Emma, no... she couldn't be dead. He had saved her! He had ripped the deadly bomb from her body in time. The link had been lost, that's all. The connection had been broken, but she would still be there, waiting for him. In the clinic.

He wasted no more time. A desperate need propelled him through the doorway and down the hall at a dead run.

## 67

Chavez smiled. He liked the look of this Asian woman. It had been a long time since he'd had a woman like her. Too bad there would be no time for that. Maybe another day. Instead he enjoyed prodding her hard in the solar plexus with the muzzle of his gun.

"Get back," he barked. "Down that way. The way you came. I have a feeling you were all busy at something. I wonder what that was?"

He pointed sharply at Evers, Hennings, and MacLeish, then made a chopping motion indicating the far end of the hall. They jogged quietly away to continue the sweep of the complex. They knew that security forces within the building were few and scattered. MacLeish would plant explosive charges along the way in case they needed diversions or barriers for a sudden retreat.

Tamiko, Kierkegaard and Gage had their hands raised. They'd foolishly come running at the sound of the two gunshots fired by the guard who now lay at their feet. Mallory was staring, stricken, at the spreading pool of the soldier's blood. She had come out of the small testing lab nearby at just the wrong moment. Now she looked up at Chavez and Rakov with an expression of disbelief. She winced at the sound of another gunshot somewhere else in the building.

"You, too," Chavez snarled. "Move!"

She lifted her arms and shuffled quickly behind the others down the hall and into the control room. The mercenary's eyes lit as he saw the rows of sophisticated equipment.

"Good. Wonderful. Now all of you stand over there together. Perhaps one of you will be good enough... *smart* enough to tell me which part of this impressive equipment includes the radio. The radio to your protectors out there." He jabbed a thumb toward the outside of the building. None of them answered. Mallory looked desperately at each of her companions. They wouldn't talk, she was sure. She stepped forward.

"There isn't a radio," she said. "This is the control room for the project. They monitor the submers—"

"Shut up!" Chavez barked, and took a menacing step toward her. Then he looked at the others and caught the look of dawning horror on Kierkegaard's face. Too late. He turned back to Mallory. "You stupid woman. Was that worth giving yourself away?"

The biologist looked at her companions and read the truth. There was no point trying to hide anymore. Instead she turned back to their attackers.

"Don't do this," she said. "You think you're doing it for a cause, but you're wrong." She looked from Chavez to Rakov. "What you've been told is a lie. The men who are backing you are rich Americans. They don't want to weaken the government; they only want more power and wealth for themselves." Her eyes filled with tears. "Please, stop. You're being used." She reached a hand toward Chavez. "You've got to believe me."

His face filled with alarm. "*Patruus* sends you a present," he said, and fired two quick shots into her chest. Her eyes barely had time to register surprise as the bullets flung her body back over a desk full of charts and diagrams, staining them with red.

Tamiko gasped in shock. Kierkegaard clenched his fists. "Mallory...," he blurted in a strangled voice.

"Ah, you are the leader, aren't you?" Chavez smiled. "Not such a good one. A true leader must choose his followers more carefully." He swept his silenced weapon in a slow arc. "Now, I ask you again. What do you use to communicate with the outside? And don't tell me the telephone—I am not that stupid." When no-one answered, he shifted forward and brought the tip of his gun barrel to rest against Lucy Tamiko's left breast and pushed it from side to side. "Perhaps you haven't been properly... *stimulated* into answering me."

"Leave her alone!" Gage shouted, and pushed in front of the woman.

Chavez' face twisted, and the gun chuffed. Gage crumpled, and Tamiko was knocked backward. Her left arm had gone numb. As she reached across with her right hand and felt a patch of wetness, she stumbled and fell against an office chair, which skidded out from under her and across the room.

Rakov had taken two quick steps back, the better to cover the room. Chavez regained his composure and turned glittering dark eyes to the head of the project.

"Now there is only one of you left," he hissed. "The only question is, are you as stupid as they were?"

"I am beginning to wonder who is the stupid one here, Chavez."

Chavez turned slowly to discover Rakov's weapon aimed unwaveringly at his chest.

"Don't be a fool," he snarled. "The woman lied. She wouldn't know anything. She was only a pawn, an informant. Carry out the mission."

The other man shook his head, his dark eyes glinting with growing anger. "No," he said coldly. "I am no fool. Did you think I wouldn't notice things? The money Kellogg throws around... our exotic armor.... And now that I see our target, I begin to think the woman was telling the truth." He gestured with his chin, but the barrel of his weapon never moved.

It was a standoff, the attention of each man riveted on the other.

Kierkegaard caught a sudden movement in the doorway. As his mind registered what it saw, he dived for the floor.

The guard unleashed a withering stream of automatic fire that flung both mercenaries backward, a pair of computer monitors exploding behind them with a spray of glass and smoke.

Kierkegaard's reaction had given Chavez the fraction-of-a-second warning he needed to press a fingertip hard into the palm of his left hand. The bullets sprayed off the dynamic armor beneath his clothing. Even as he hit the floor he snapped off a shot toward the door. The guard jerked. Another bullet, and another—but the last was simply insurance.

Rakov had been a moment slower activating his armor, and was favoring his right arm, obviously injured. But the man was tough, and could shoot nearly as well with his left hand as his right. They'd been lucky the guard hadn't gone for a headshot. Chavez decided not to make the same mistake. With cold precision he took aim at his former ally. Rakov's body jerked in a last spasm, then crumpled to the floor. Chavez looked at it for a moment with regret, then turned back toward his captive. His eyes widened in surprise.

Kierkegaard had taken advantage of the fleeting seconds to get to his feet. With his fingers locked together he smashed at the main instrument panel with all his might. Gauges shattered—sparks snapped. He swung again. There was no radio, but the critical VR and monitoring system was tied into a special circuit in the central computer's mainframe. With its sudden failure, silent alarms would go off inside and outside the building.

Chavez roared with rage and chopped at the back of the old man's head with the butt of his gun.

Kierkegaard's view exploded into stars.

## 68

As Hunter raced toward the clinic, he should have registered that there was no one who tried to stop him. Instead, he was shocked to see that a dark shape spread out in front of the clinic door was a human being. The Secret Service agent. What was her name? Carrie...? No, Karen.

He saw the blood.

"Karen. *Karen*. Who did this to you?"

There was no response. She was gone.

Hard steel pushed against the bone behind his right ear.

"Shame to waste a body like that." The voice was flat and cold. Hunter felt his whole being tense with rage. "Go ahead. Try for it." The words had no more expression than an accountant reading a spreadsheet. The gun barrel tapped against Hunter's skull with a metallic thud. He clenched his teeth and willed his shoulders to go limp, as he slowly straightened to his feet.

From flat on his knee his arm snapped back hard, his torso spinning to complete the arc. There was a grunt and the chuff of the gun, incredibly close, but the bullet missed the back of his head. He came nearly face-to-face with his assailant—saw the gun swinging back toward him. With another fierce twist, he pummeled the gun hand past its mark to collide with the corner of the wall. He felt a moment of elation as he heard the weapon clatter onto the tile floor.

A knee hammered into his groin, driving the breath from his lungs. He folded in half, retching. Then a hand like iron slammed into the back of his neck and knocked him to the floor. Before he could draw air, the knee ground into his back and he felt a vice-like grip on his throat.

"Try it again, science boy, and you join your friend in hell." The voice had lost its calm, but Hunter got little satisfaction from that, nor from the fact that the fingers at his throat were from a left hand. Had he broken the gun hand? What possible difference could it make now?

"Get inside," Kellogg snapped. "Now!" He allowed the pilot to stand, then gave him a hard shove toward the door. Karen's body had kept it from shutting properly, and Hunter fell through.

It was the first time he'd ever seen the clinic room. Emma's room. His mind grasped at odd details in that first flash: the strange shape of the HPIS on the far side of the bed, its hypodermic lying underneath it on the table. Hanging cameras and monitors. An intravenous bag, tube curving toward the bed, but a breathing mask and hose set aside out of the way. Unused? Hadn't they administered anesthetic after all? He noticed that loose wires dangled from the overhead cameras—they'd been disabled. No one would see his danger and come to the rescue.

Two sets of legs protruded at ugly angles from behind the bed. *Bridges and Natale*, he assumed. He felt a stab of anguish. This killer, whoever he was, had a lot to pay for. But there was no use fooling himself. The dead would soon include Emma, and he had no way to stop it. His heart ached for the helpless form that lay still on the bed.

"Why are you doing this?" he gasped, as Kellogg followed him through the door. The mercenary gave a sharp laugh.

"I don't have to tell you anything," he sneered. "There's absolutely no need for you to know before you die." He slid his foot backward to push the outflung arm of the Secret Service agent out of the way, then closed and locked the door. His right hand hurt like a bastard, but wasn't incapacitated. He slowly raised the gun.

"Oh my God! *Curtis!*" The voice was weak, but intensified by outrage.

Emma struggled to raise herself in the bed, her face a mask of bewilderment. Kellogg clenched his teeth.

"No-one ever calls me that except you, *my love,*" he said icily.

Hunter's mind reeled. "What?" he stammered. "I don't..."

"Curtis Heller." Tears welled up in her wide eyes. "My *husband.*"

#   #   #

Tamiko moaned. The shock of her wound had nearly made her faint, but now a searing wave of agony brought her fully awake.

"As I thought." Chavez smiled, refraining from a second kick. "The good-looking one is still with us." He bent over and fiercely clutched a handful of her hair. "Tell me, my lovely, why would your boss go to the trouble of breaking his own equipment?" He wrenched her head to the side. She could see the bizarre tableau, but she had no idea what it meant. She tried to say so, but no words would come. Instead she gave an incoherent wail as Chavez poked the gun barrel into her wound. Then she fainted dead away.

Angrily, the mercenary turned back to the array of smashed electronics. It had to be rigged to an alarm system. The old man couldn't have been trying to protect secrets since the data was probably stored somewhere else on a central server. Smashing these things would accomplish nothing, unless their disruption sent out an alert.

He needed to call Romero and tell the rest to expect company.

He reached for his radio, and never felt the bullet that killed him.

Gerard Mannis stood in the doorway, lowering his gun and grimly surveying the carnage while his commandos spread through the hallway behind. "*Jesus Christ.* I need this whole complex secured. On the double!" he shouted. "But use extra caution. We have no idea how many more there are, and..." He took a deep breath. "The daughter of the president is somewhere in this building."

## 69

Hunter heard Emma's words, but couldn't make sense of them. *Her husband?* The shock made him stumble back onto the top of a low shelf unit. He barely caught himself, his whole body gone numb. He looked into Emma's eyes and saw the recognition in them, and the dismay. She knew who he was, and knew also that their meeting had come too late.

The mercenary gave a heavy sigh and leaned casually against the wall, keeping his silenced .45 pointed steadily at Hunter. "I go by a different name now, my sweet. It means *slaughterer*. I like it. But then you've never really known that side of me, have you?"

Kellogg slowly shook his head. "Pampered princess. As a matter of fact, my parents named me Kurt, not Curtis. Except a proudly Aryan husband wouldn't be quite proper for the daughter of a black president, would it? Or did daddy find out somehow after all? Was that why *my* father wasn't good enough to be Vice-President?" He spat out the last words like venom.

"Curtis, I swear I had no..."

"Oh don't trouble yourself, princess. My family will soon have its place in the corridors of power. We still have many influential friends. Even the man who introduced me to you." His smile was a thing of poison.

"Uncle Frank," she breathed weakly.

His blue eyes flashed. Even now her obvious suffering brought him more pleasure than her death would. Killing her wasn't the goal. It was her father's capitulation they wanted, but he'd been too fucking stubborn—had put too much faith in his team of geniuses. Now Emma had to die. Maybe they'd have better luck with the black bastard's wife.

"Sorry, sweetheart. Love to chat, but if this pathetic nobody happened to stumble in here, others might too. Time for you to go."

His gun hand started toward her but a movement from Hunter brought the barrel back into line with the pilot's chest. "You're right, science boy, I'd better do you first."

"I'm so sorry," Emma sobbed as she looked at Hunter. "I don't even know your name."

"It's Hunter," he said, regret like an anvil in his chest.

Kellogg's lips pulled back from his teeth.

"*Hunter?* You mean you're the wonder boy who's come to know my wife's body better than I did? The one who's been such a *fucking pain in the ass?*" He took a slow step forward, and then another. "This is too good. I can't use a bullet on you. I wouldn't dream of making it so easy."

Almost faster than the eye could register, his foot shot out and caught Hunter in the upper thigh. The pilot gasped as his leg collapsed, sending him sprawling onto the floor. Kellogg casually holstered his weapon. The foot shot out again and shattered a rib.

"Not so fast, submarine man. First I have to teach you when to quit."

Hunter clambered to his feet and tried to throw a punch but Kellogg's fingers struck like a knife blade under his collar bone. The flailing arm exploded with pain, and went limp, completely useless. Emma was nearly hysterical, but Kellogg ignored her.

"Did she get to you, too, wonder boy? Did she touch your *heart?*" At the word he drove his extended knuckles into Hunter's rib cage. The younger man gasped from the agony, and then vomited helplessly. He was on the verge of blacking out. In a last act of desperation he used his one good leg to launch himself at his attacker, rocking them back against the bed, and then wrapped his left arm around Kellogg in a hold as tight as all of his remaining strength could make it. He had no plan. He only hoped to stop the killing blows.

Kellogg bucked and writhed, but Hunter was fighting for his life. The weight of his limp body could keep the other pinned and impotent for a moment, but no more than that. The unequal struggle could have only one conclusion.

Suddenly Kellogg clapped his hand to his neck as if stung. He gave a gut-deep moan of pain. Emma was right next to him with something in her hand. *A hypodermic needle!* With a burst of rage he flung Hunter from him, and turned to the woman in the bed.

"*Bitch!*" he screamed, and smashed her face with the back of his hand in a blow that seemed sure to break her jaw. Then he knelt beside Hunter and locked an elbow around the pilot's neck. "Now," he hissed, "You're going to die."

Hunter felt agony flow in waves over him. He couldn't breathe, couldn't think, the very light of his consciousness beginning to ebb.

His mind didn't want to die alone. It reached out... reached out and found...

Primus!

There was no mistaking it!

Crimson liquid, shining protoplasm, a current flowing; it was in a human body—had to be. Not the hypodermic needle. *How was that possible?* But the more critical question was: *whose body?* What did it mean? Had he been given a chance for life?

He should be dead by now. Maybe his body already was. Maybe the time dilation was giving him a few more moments of precious sentience, even as his brain began to give out.

Brain. That was it. *Primus* was surrounded by brain cells.

His killer's brain. He was sure of it! He'd dimly seen Emma stab the man in the neck with something. It had to have been the hypodermic needle.

Maybe the ship's communication relay had been burned away, and he could only make contact from a very short distance. That didn't matter. *Primus* was there when he needed her, and he only had seconds left to exploit that.

With a powerful effort of will, he sent a low current to the torch. The fluid around its tip began to bubble furiously. Would it be fast enough? He could do no more. He could only wait for the gases to build up. Pray that the universe would grant him a few more critical seconds.

The light was growing dim. The colors were fading.

He was dying.

With no more time left, he sparked the torch.

A giant fireball billowed through the tunnel shredding its walls, the compression wave powerful enough to shatter its way through a dozen blood vessels in every direction. *Primus* was tossed savagely, and then sucked out with a tremendous flood of fluid that burst its bounds and rampaged through the stacked cells that held the mind of a man. A mind that was instantly stilled, a catastrophic brain hemorrhage snuffing out its life in a heartbeat.

Hunter tried to imagine the look of surprise on his enemy's face, frozen in place as life left him.

Even as the thought came, he sensed his own life returning; frothing blood blooming with fresh oxygen. He could feel it, hear it, a fountain of energy, grand and glorious.

Then Emma was there. Emma was with him in his mind.

But she was in pain. Terrible pain and fear.

His consciousness filled with the images of bombs.

No. *No!* There were still five within her. Ready to go off! Her body would never survive that—there was too much damage already. What could he do?

COME WITH ME. I KNOW WHERE THEY ARE. I HAVE ALWAYS KNOWN.

He saw her standing with him in a formless place, her slim body radiant with light. He reached out to take her hand. The world *moved....*

In an instant they were with the first bomb. The surroundings looked like lung tissue, porous and stretched. Blood cells and fluids swirled by, instantly familiar, yet different, the whole area suffused with a silver haze. He was surprised to see that the weapon no longer dwarfed him. Instead as he drew closer, he found it the size of a large beach ball. Intrigued, he let go of Emma, placed his hands on either side of it, and began to squeeze.

Pain stabbed at the base of his skull. He shook it off and squeezed again. Emma came forward and added what strength she had, though he could see the toll of the effort in her face.

Suddenly it was done. The milky globe shattered into a spray of shimmering gems that fell in slow motion to form a sparkling mist at their feet—deadly molecules incinerated into harmless atoms.

On to bomb number two.

Time blinked.

Heart muscle this time, the contractions rapid and powerful. The body was terrified, facing death. He knew the pressure waves should be buffeting him without mercy, but he felt none of it. This bomb was anchored to tissue, yanked back and forth with the ferocious currents. He reached out a fist—the harbinger of death disintegrated in a spectacular blossom of flame.

Bomb number three, was in the spinal cord. Swiftly annihilated. But after its destruction Emma's form crumpled with exhaustion. His own head throbbed and lances of fire shot up and down his neck. He clasped her hands, willing some of his strength into her. They made it to number four, in what he took to be the carotid artery—after a long effort, vanquished it, but the world swam sickeningly. With a shock of horror, he realized that Emma's phantom image had begun to fade. She floated listlessly, and didn't respond to his touch.

Emma no! Without her help he couldn't find the last bomb.

He gathered her in his arms and willed them into the ether. Colors, textures, smells and sounds whirled past them. The straight path he began became curved, twisted, knotted, darting aimlessly in one direction and then another. He couldn't find the way alone! He pressed his face to hers and tried frantically to reach her mind. There was no change. Was there?

He drew his face away, and became aware of the bomb, floating silently behind her. A gossamer honeycomb formed the backdrop, glinting at its junctures like the facets of jewels.

Her brain.

Before he could react, he saw a tiny crack begin near the top of the shell, and spread jaggedly downward. Launching himself toward it like a projectile, he clutched the globe fiercely to his chest and pressed with all his remaining strength. Agony ricocheted like shards of glass through his body. His head was ready to explode. The world sizzled with shooting sparks of lightning, impaling him like daggers.

Then nothing. Silence, deafening in its totality.

The bomb was gone.

Slowly, so slowly, he became aware of his physical self again. Random shapes and colors bled into one another until they formed a coherent whole: a world of familiar things. The real world—the normal world, if those terms still had meaning. He could not move, could only lie there gulping fresh air. Then, at last, he crawled toward Emma's still form, wrapped his arms around her, and held onto her like life itself.

Darkness swallowed the world and it was a very, very long time before he felt anything else.

## 70

The submersible was sinking.

That bilious surge in his gut was half-weightlessness, half-fear. He'd begun to surface before the power died—now the weight on the end of the manipulator arm was pulling the craft back to the bottom, pitching the bow downward. How far would it fall?

Christ! The impact with the seabed kicked most of the breath from his lungs. The rest leaked out in a low moan. Helpless... he was totally helpless. He drew his hands to his face. Were his eyes open or not? Open, he thought. There was a blue luminescence at the edge of his vision, so faint that he might be imagining it. Or it might be outside light through the viewports—light only in contrast to deeper blackness inside the pod. As he lowered his arms again, the blue glow made ghostly apparitions out of his fluttering hands and struck a pale gleam from fluorescent gauges: eyes in the night.

Though the vent overhead still gave a sibilant hiss, he felt his chest tighten in anticipation, fearful that the next breath would be thick with poisonous carbon dioxide, and the next after that...empty.

He fought for control. There were things he could do—he'd trained and practiced until he could find his way around the submersible blindfolded.

Sightless, just like now.

A long screech made him jump, his mind filling with primal images of creatures of the deep.

Bullshit! It was only some scrap of wreckage the hull was sliding over—the sub was still on the shallow slope, not at the edge of the precipice. Not yet.

He could manually trim the ballast. The risk was that it would weaken the smooth steel hull's contact with the ocean floor—make it more vulnerable to the downward-flowing current that might carry it to the brink.

The shell of his world cried out again, squeezed in a tightening vice.

Should he increase the inside pressure? Or would it merely steal away his last reserve of life-giving breath, destroying any chance of a last-minute rescue?

Don't lose control. Help will come.

What help? Without ship's power, he couldn't signal, couldn't tell them where he was. The crew topside on the rig knew where he'd been working, but once he'd begun to surface they would have left their scopes to get the crane ready to retrieve him. When the sub lost power it wouldn't have fallen in a straight line. There was a strong current running, especially downward toward the deep. Unpredictable cross currents could have pushed him many meters to the side. Sonar would be confused by the clutter of wreckage scattered over the bottom. The water was black as the Pit.

The craft would someday be retrieved, but its pilot might be long past retrieval.

The sub tipped and returned, tipped, and hung poised in the balance. Would it roll? Down slope lay the mother of all cliffs. The pipelines ran another two thousand feet into the abyss to a place where his steel cocoon would be crushed like a discarded paper cup.

He flung his arms out for a handhold, tried to dig his heels into the floor as the hull tilted farther, and still farther. It passed the point of equilibrium and a forest of toggle switches gouged his scalp as the world somersaulted. Then it stabilized upright for a moment, but he could feel the hull shift, sliding across the ocean floor. It rolled again. Slipped. Twisted.

His air was almost gone. The dim, winking lights that had kept him company like eyes in the night were going out, too. Soon his own spark would join them.

The sub should have surfaced on its own. There was an emergency circuit designed to drop ballast automatically if anything happened to the pilot, or in the event of a serious power loss. It required regular intervention not to jettison the ballast, and it should have been foolproof.

No such thing.

His mind was becoming sluggish. The air that fed it was slowly turning to poison. How long before his mind lost all power? Would his body conserve its energy, to keep the vital brain cells going just a little longer? What if there was an errant organ or greedy muscle that stole away those last sparks of life first?

A short circuit. What if there was a short circuit in a peripheral system of the submersible that was robbing it of power—paralyzing its motive systems, and interfering with the emergency overrides? Just a trickle of current diverted the wrong way. How could he possibly find it?

He couldn't. Not in time.

It was a thief, and it was killing him. He had to kill it instead.

With the last of his strength he began to pound his fists against the instrument panels. It was one of the instruments, he was sure. One of them was hiding the short circuit that was stealing his life. If he could only smash the right one, the drain would end and the fail-safe would trigger. The dead would rise again.

He was like a demon, staggering, punching, kicking... his fists flinging droplets of blood as they shredded on broken glass. One system after another crumpled and shattered beneath his assault. The last few lights went out, but still he continued his rampage, pummeling, battering, his heart hammering with the brutal effort. He slipped on shards of glass, fell hard against sharp metal, raised himself again, leaking more blood, and threw his body around the blackened cabin in a frenzied attack on anything he could reach.

He didn't even know when he succeeded. The rasping of his frantic breaths hid the sound of the ballast being jettisoned, the hull scraping free of the imprisoning rocks. It was only as he pitched forward in exhaustion and defeat, that he felt the capsule lurch and begin to rise. He had no strength to lift himself from the floor. Oxygen-starved blood filled his brain with dark fog.

He couldn't be sure it wasn't a dream when the submersible rose to the surface at last and a forgiving sea cradled it once more. Bright rays sprayed through the thick glass and filled his mind to overflowing. In this new light he saw that he was not insane. He never had been.

#   #   #

"She's out of the woods, that's the main thing."

Truman Bridges was speaking to Devon Kierkegaard. Their faces went in and out of focus as Hunter raised himself in the bed.

"Doc... it is you! I thought I was dreaming when I heard your voice."

Bridges was startled and began to laugh, then quickly stopped himself, putting a hand to his side.

"It's wonderful to hear your voice, too, Mr. Hunter. You've been in a coma. Then, finally last night, you showed signs of coming out into a normal dream state. But don't try to get up too quickly. You've had surgery."

"Surgery?"

"I'll explain later." Bridges winked. "Look who's here." As he pointed, Hunter realized that the doctor was in a wheelchair, dressed in the gown of a hospital patient. What had he missed? He felt like massaging the base of his skull to ease the pain there, but his touch was blocked by a thick dressing. Then his blurry eyes followed the psychologist's extended arm.

It was Emma, and beside her, Lucy Tamiko with her arm in a sling. Emma's wheelchair was pushed by Skylar Tyson. They distributed themselves along the side of Hunter's bed, and Emma shyly took Hunter's hand. A hint of jealousy crossed Tamiko's face, but then a genuine smile returned. An orderly shepherded an intravenous bag and hanger beside Emma, then left the room.

"That equipment hasn't kept this young lady from spending most of the past twenty-four hours in this room," Bridges observed. "As soon as we would let her out of bed herself."

Hunter was stunned to see her looking so well. "How long have I been out?"

"Nearly a week," Kierkegaard answered. "Six-and-a-half days since the attack." He saw the look of puzzlement. "The man who attacked you—Emma's husband—was part of a larger assault."

"Six-and-a-half days!" The submarine pilot shook his head. Then he noticed there were faces missing from the group. "Where's Gage?"

Kierkegaard had to clear his throat. "Kenneth was killed."

"He died trying to protect me," Tamiko said, tears filling her eyes.

"I'm sorry," Hunter said softly. "He was a good man. I wish I'd known that sooner."

"Yes, he was." Kierkegaard nodded. "And there was more to him than any of us knew, including a connection to a certain associate of ours in Washington." He gave Hunter a meaningful look.

"And Lorelei?"

"Dr. Mallory...was the *mole*." Kierkegaard's words clearly caused him pain. "She'd been involved in a scandal years ago... had been the close associate of a researcher who was accused of selling technology secrets to a foreign power. His guilt seemed to be confirmed by his subsequent suicide. Apparent suicide. The charges against her were dropped, and I decided to give her the benefit of the doubt—she was truly brilliant at her work. Now it appears that trust was misplaced." He looked up from his hands. "However, her... partners had no further use for her."

"I can't say I'm sorry I missed all that."

"You weren't the only one," Kierkegaard continued with a sudden smile. "Skylar slept through it all!"

The scientist nodded. "It's true. I was in the small lab, trying to work out how to re-tune our scanning equipment. I was listening to Mozart rather loudly on a set of headphones...."

"And then he passed out from exhaustion and slipped under the desk," Tamiko finished. "After the attack our people searched the whole building, and there he was, sleeping like a baby."

Hunter joined in welcome laughter, then turned to Bridges. "What about you, Doctor? When I came into Emma's room I thought you were dead."

"Not far from the truth. The bullet nicked my left lung on the way through, but I knocked myself out on something as I fell. Poor Vitale, though—clean through the heart." He bit his lip.

"Was it Emma you were talking about, who's out of the woods?"

"Yes, indeed. She's recovering well. Incredibly well, considering all of the trauma her body has undergone."

"The best of tender, loving care," the young woman said, smiling at her doctor.

"And so, the crisis has been defused," Kierkegaard added. "The surviving attackers aren't talking much, but their equipment and other clues speak for them. Our Washington associate says that good progress is being made to round up *all* of those behind this vicious scheme, and bring them to justice."

The submariner understood the reference. "Uncle Frank" would not escape his due.

"But what was it all about?"

Kierkegaard shrugged.

"It's still technically a secret, but...." He smiled. "The president is about to spearhead a world trade agreement that will be finalized at the upcoming G20 summit. It's designed to prevent a repeat of the global economic collapse earlier this century, by blocking the ability of a small number of players to dominate world markets. Which means it will prevent some very powerful people from achieving the nearly supreme power they so desire." He looked into their faces. "The clues investigators have gathered so far implicate some multinational corporate interests. Very big players in Silicon Valley and the energy industry, particularly. It's not the first time potent conservative interests have taken drastic measures."

"I still don't understand," Hunter continued, "Why threaten Emma in such a complicated way. Why not just kidnap her?"

"You can sometimes kill heavily guarded people, but it's not nearly so simple to get them away to a hiding place undetected. On the other hand, someone can be infected with *nano* devices with a surreptitious pin prick, or infected food, or perhaps soon even a handshake. I think it was also intended to send a message that what we've just been through could easily happen again. No-one is safe."

"The bomb technology is still out there. Someone will use it again."

"Yes, but perhaps not soon. The scientist responsible has been taken into custody. We should have recognized his handiwork earlier. A man named Griffon."

"*Griffon?*" Tyson looked startled. "A brilliant man. A brilliant...rival."

"Yes." Kierkegaard looked very uncomfortable. "Nine years ago, when a congressional appropriations committee was deciding whether or not to fund our project, Griffon was the chief competitor. He was working on methods to deliver medicines to precise locations in the body—cures, not poisons—much more efficient than oral or intravenous drugs. He was very outspoken against our project claiming that it was too prone to adaptation as a weapons system."

"That's ironic. Especially since that fact probably worked in your favor with the committee." Hunter said. Kierkegaard gave an awkward shrug.

"After the committee's decision, Griffon went bankrupt. He'd incurred huge debts and may have had a gambling problem. Obviously that made him an easy target for someone with deep pockets but less altruistic motives. Yet Griffon claims he was duped and I believe him."

"Duped into torturing an innocent woman?" Tyson's face showed more anger than Hunter had ever seen there.

"His new funders told him they were pacifists, trying to *stop* the creation of nano-weapon technology. The president himself would be the victim, brought to the brink of death but not killed. The resulting outcry would kill our project and any others like it."

"And he believed a fairy tale like that?"

"I suppose he wanted to believe it, Lucy. The chair of the appropriations committee all those years ago is the man we now call the president."

"And so a great medical discovery was perverted into an instrument of death," Tyson said in a soft voice. It was a sobering prospect.

A pair of nurses appeared in the doorway. The elder of the two said, "I'm not one to stand in the way of a party, but all of these patients need more rest."

"A couple more minutes, please," Hunter asked. "I just woke up. I need some answers."

Tamiko offered, "Skylar and I can go," and ushered him out of the room. The nurse who'd spoken gave a reluctant nod and led her companion a little way down the hall.

Hunter lowered his voice and asked, "What about me, Doctor? You said I had surgery. What for?"

It was Kierkegaard who answered. "That device we implanted in your neck somehow burnt out. It fused into a solid mass. We don't know what happened, but whatever the cause, it also destroyed part of your

thalamus." He raised a hand to forestall Hunter's protest. "I don't think you have to worry. There's plenty left." The thought seemed to amuse him.

Bridges explained. "The thalamus stimulator was easy to implant but required surgery to dig back out, which is when we discovered that your thalamus has become enlarged—permanently, as far as we can tell. Grown, not swollen. We don't know how to explain it, but there's no reason it should pose any problem for you."

"Easy for you to say."

"In any case," the head of the Project resumed in a heavy voice, "you won't need the device anymore. *Primus* appears to have been destroyed, most likely in the explosion of that sodium bomb. All of the instrument readings went dead at that instant. We've scanned for it, but without success. A damn shame, too. She was a fine ship. Her potential for healing was incredible."

Hunter shot a furtive look at Emma. She returned it with a tiny motion of her head. She had told them nothing.

Unless Curtis Heller had been cremated, the ship could probably be recovered and repaired.

He would have to think long and hard about that.

# # #

Mannis sat at his desk, swiveling slowly back and forth in his chair. He held a small pin in his hand, occasionally rolling it between his fingers, watching the way it caught the light. It was one of many pins in his collection. Recording devices, all of them. He had just been going through a series of very special ones that, at great risk, had been planted throughout the wardrobe of White House Chief of Staff, F. Arthur Black. They were voice-activated, with a capacious memory for something so small, and they contained some damning evidence.

He was saddened by that. It had proven Hunter and Kierkegaard correct, but he would much rather they had been wrong.

The man he had once admired, even emulated, had been a betrayer and a thief, first seeking to steal Emma's innocence, and then finally her life. He deserved punishment; she deserved justice. He, exposure; she, release. Yet the world would not let that happen. F. Arthur Black was too powerful and too important. If the full truth were revealed, the scandal could tear the government into splinters. The country was not strong enough for that, not right now.

So the secret must never come out.

He reached for the remote control and aimed it at the television hanging in the corner. CNN was still showing live coverage from a crash scene: a chaotic light show of flashing beacons, red and white and blue, from the dozens of emergency vehicles that filled the view. All to minister to just one dark mass of twisted metal, barely visible amid the swarming shadows. A fatal accident involving one of the country's most influential men, the White House Chief of Staff. The man known secretly to others as *Patruus*, a Latin word for 'Uncle'.

The cause of the brake failure would never be discovered. In that line of work, the Silent Man was the very best.

# # #

Finally, there came a time when the submersible pilot and the president's daughter were left alone. After a few trial steps around the floor, he walked her back to her room. They didn't speak—it felt strange to do so. Scarcely a few dozen words had ever passed between them. They would have to get over that.

He could no longer sense her mind at all. Its absence was a shock, and a sorrow. Whether it was because of the loss of the *Primus* connection, or the *psi* amplifier in his neck, he didn't know.

What of those last few moments in the clinic with Curtis Heller? Had there really been five more bombs? Had he and Emma really found them and destroyed them together, through no more than pure force of will? Or had it all been a hallucination of an oxygen-starved brain? There would never be any proof, one way or the other.

Maybe it was all a dream.

So much of his experience of the past weeks seemed like that. Had the joining of their minds been a dream, too? If real, it existed no longer. They would have to get to know each other the old-fashioned way, through the words and gestures that had served humankind for so many generations, and yet were still so prone to misunderstanding.

As she lay on her hospital bed, he sat beside her, lightly stroking her arm. Her flesh was as soft and cool as satin, her dark eyes warm and liquid, framed by naturally long lashes. He leaned forward and breathed in the clean scent of her skin and the perfume of her hair, caught the moist sweetness of her breath. When they kissed, he tasted the light salt tang of her supple lips. He could still experience her in this way, through his senses. That should be more than enough for any man.

Except it wasn't a sure thing. He was an out-of-work sub-jockey; she the daughter of the world's most powerful man—two different classes of society, for all America pretended otherwise. On the other hand, Emma's carefully selected and approved husband had tried to take her life. Perhaps even a president could learn from that.

As if reading his thoughts in his face, Emma said softly, "Daddy owes you. In more ways than one. He won't forget that. Besides..." She smiled. "It's not like I'm about to give you up!" Her white teeth matched the sparkle of her eyes, and then she pulled him hungrily to her.

The heat of her kiss infused him, filled him, blocking out the world. He surrendered eagerly as it drew him in...

deeply ...

deeply ....

And then she was there, an undeniable presence within his mind (or was he in hers?), a lightly glowing figure enshrouded in a flowing fog. He could sense that she was naked—devoid of disguise. It felt as if she touched his hands, then held them, and her love wrapped around him like an entity all its own. He basked in its warmth, bathed in its bliss.

Then he knew that the fog would slowly lift and that the horizon was already luminous with the first rays of a new dawn. He was a man broken but not crushed, blinded but with eyes that would learn to see once more.

They had much to discover about one another, perhaps more completely than any couple before them.

But it had not been a dream. The dream was just beginning.

Acknowledgments

Writing is a solitary occupation, but a writer who doesn't involve others in the process is probably making a mistake.

I want to thank two Davids, David Goforth and David Robinson for taking on the Goliath of a (then) unpublished novelist's first attempt at full-length science fiction.

My friends of the Sudbury Writers Guild are as talented as they are supportive and encouraging. It's nice to know you always have my back.

The experience of working with Robin Carson as editor of the first short story I ever sold was so positive, it was fated that we would work together again on my first SF novel. Thanks again, Robin, for performing corrective surgery on the manuscript so professionally and yet so gently that it was nearly painless!

Thanks to Juan Padrón for such an eye-catching cover.

I truly appreciate the support of the Ontario Arts Council in the creation of this book.

And my gratitude always to my first reader and foremost supporter, Terry-Lynne, who never fails to believe.

More Great Reading From Scott Overton

BEYOND: Stories Beyond Time, Technology, and the Stars

Ride a bright flame of imagination across time and space with fifteen mind-stretching stories beyond time, beyond technology, and even beyond the stars.

A man who can walk through walls.

Agents who repair the mistakes of the past.

An invasion from beneath our feet.

A man who learns his replacement body was previously owned and died mysteriously.

A disastrous experiment to harness the awesome power of a hurricane.

Don't be afraid to go BEYOND.

"Scott Overton is a storyteller of boundless skill...a writer to watch."
—Mark Leslie, author of *Haunted Hamilton* and *I, Death*

DEAD AIR

It's a hard thing to accept that someone wants you dead. It forces you to decide if you have anything worth living for.

When radio morning man Lee Garrett finds a death threat on his control console, he shrugs it off as a sick prank—until minor harassment turn into undeniable attempts on his life. When the deadliest assault yet claims an innocent victim, Garrett knows he has to force a confrontation.

"A gripping, insightful debut from a veteran radio personality and gifted wordsmith." —Sean Costello, author of *Here After*

Find out how to add these to your own collection at www.scottoverton.ca .

ABOUT THE AUTHOR

A radio broadcaster for more than thirty years, Scott Overton described that world in his first novel, the mystery/thriller *Dead Air*, published by Scrivener Press. *Dead Air* was shortlisted for a Northern Lit Award in Ontario, Canada. But most of his writing is science fiction and fantasy. His short fiction has been published in numerous magazines and anthologies.

Now a freelance author and voice talent, Scott works from his home on a lake in Northern Ontario. His distractions from writing include scuba diving and a couple of collector cars.

You can learn more and read free stories at Scott's website www.scottoverton.ca .